W9-BMR-773

"Pearson excels at writing novels that grip
the imagination." —*People*

"Pearson tells an irresistible tale."
—*The Los Angeles Times Book Review*

"Ridley Pearson has been called 'the best
thriller writer alive,' and... there's no
disagreement here." — *New York Post*

'A killer combination of Patricia
D. Cornwell and John D. MacDonald
with a soupçon of Thomas Harris."
—Stephen King

"Realistic police work, real people,
real suspense. Ridley Pearson always delivers."
—Tami Hoag

PRAISE FOR *PARALLEL LIES*:

"Pearson (*No Witnesses*, etc.) has written another terrific thriller . . ." —*Library Journal*

". . . Pearson remains near the top of the genre." —*Booklist*

". . . a killer combination of Patricia Cornwell and John D. MacDonald with a soupçon of Thomas Harris." —Stephen King

". . . grabs, he twists, he tightens the screws until you're drained by a superior read." —Clive Cussler

"Pearson works this man-on-the-run episode like a pro . . . you'll be rewarded with a bravura display of acceleration."
—*Kirkus Reviews*

PRAISE FOR *MIDDLE OF NOWHERE*:

"Excitement quotient: high; technology details: intriguing."
—*USA Today*

"Master plotter, reliable thrills from a pro." —*Kirkus Reviews*

"Fast-paced read from beginning to end. Pearson is able to effortlessly intertwine several detailed plot lines while still keeping his story firmly robed in reality." —*New York Post*

"Pearson uses clear, forthright prose that perfectly exposes the psychological doubts and fears of his characters and keeps the plot racing from scene to scene. Craftily, Pearson weaves his web." —*Providence Sunday Journal*

PRAISE FOR *THE FIRST VICTIM*:

"Razor-sharp plotting and timing." —*Seattle Times*

"There is no one writing police novels with the precise touch of Pearson. His stories are thoroughly researched, heartbreaking and full of escalating suspense."
—*Rocky Mountain News* (Denver)

"The gadget man is back with a bag of new toys. You don't have to be a techno-nerd to get wired on this scary stuff."
—*New York Times Book Review*

"Pearson weaves psychology and suspense into this tale of high-tech clues and complex motives." —*Playboy*

"Ridley Pearson is an unequivocal success. I'm hooked again."
—*Entertainment Weekly*

PRAISE FOR *NO WITNESS*:

"Tough and intelligent." —Fort Worth *Star-Telegram*

"Up-to-the-nanosecond techno-thriller." —*New York Times*

"Infused with astonishingly effective overtones."
—*Boston Globe*

"Good old-fashioned storytelling."
—*Washington Post Book World*

"A serious, well-researched, complex thriller."
—*Los Angeles Times*

PRAISE FOR *THE ANGEL MAKER*:

"Exceptionally gripping and full of amazing forensic lore: a top-flight offering from an author who has clearly found his groove."
—*Kirkus Reviews*

"A chilling thriller." —Dell Publishing

PRAISE FOR *HARD FALL*:

"Pearson excels at novels that grip the imagination. *Hard Fall* is an adventure with all engines churning."
—*People* magazine

"Mesmerizing urgency."   —*Los Angeles Times Book Review*

"Nifty cat-and-mouse caper. Crisply written tale."
—*Chicago Tribune*

PRAISE FOR *UNDERCURRENTS*:

"Neatly constructed plot. Hair-raising denouement. Remarkable insight and understanding of the motivations of the criminal mind."   —*Publishers Weekly*

"*Undercurrents* is a roller-coaster ride in the dark."
—Book of the Month

PRAISE FOR *PROBABLE CAUSE*:

"Filled with clues, both planted and missed, fancy forensic footwork, and intriguing snares. A whole lot of suspense. A satisfying, gripping police procedural."   —*Booklist*

"A sleek, cleverly plotted part-psychological thriller, part-courtroom drama."   —*Los Angeles Times*

PRAISE FOR *NEVER LOOK BACK*:

"A masterly debut. Powerful yet poignant suspense story."
—*Booklist*

"A breakneck-action first novel."   —*Kirkus Reviews*

The
ART OF
DECEPTION

RIDLEY PEARSON

The ART OF DECEPTION

HYPERION NEW YORK

MASS MARKET ISBN: 0-7868-9000-2

Hyperion books are available for special promotions
and premiums. For details contact Hyperion Special
Markets, 77 West 66th Street, 11th floor, New York,
New York 10023-6298, or call 212-456-0133.

FIRST MASS MARKET EDITION

10 9 8 7 6 5 4 3 2 1

For Bob and Ellen

I wish to acknowledge the following for their help and guidance in the research and editing of *The Art of Deception*. The mistakes are all mine.

Donna Meade, Rachel Farnsworth, David Laycock, Ray York: Idaho State Police Forensics Lab.
Dr. Alyn Duxbury—University of Washington, Oceanographic Sciences, retired.
Andy Hamilton, United States Attorney's Office, Seattle, Washington
Detective Marsha Wilson, Seattle Police Department
David Thompson, Murder by the Book, Houston, Texas
CJ Snow, BookSource, St. Louis, Missouri
JB Dickey & Tammy Domike, Seattle Mystery Bookshop, Seattle, Washington
The Underground Tour, Seattle, Washington
Heidi Mack, ridleypearson.com website design/management
Nancy Litzinger, Louise Marsh, office management
Mary Peterson, Hailey, Idaho
Chris Towle, Towle and Co., St. Louis, Missouri
Gary Shelton, Ketchum, Idaho
Robbie Freund, Creative Edge, Hailey, Idaho

Thanks, too:

Matthew Snyder, CAA, Beverly Hills, California
Albert Zuckerman, Writers House, New York

Editors:

Leigh Haber
Ed Stackler
Leslie Wells
Albert Zuckerman

The
ART OF
DECEPTION

1 The Ride of a Lifetime

Mary-Ann Walker

She lay on her side, her head ringing, her hair damp and sticky. She understood that she should feel pain—one didn't fall onto blacktop from a three-story fire escape without experiencing pain—and yet she felt nothing.

She saw the Space Needle in the distance, regretting that she had gone up it only once, at the age of seven. Perhaps that had been the start of her fear of heights. Images from her childhood played before her eyes like a hurried slide show until she heard a car start and the first trickle of sensation sparked up her broken legs; she knew undeniably that this was only the beginning. When the floodgates opened, when nerve impulses reached their mainline capabilities, the pain would prove too great, and she would surrender to it.

For this reason, and a desire to glimpse the glimmering black mirror surface of Lake Union, she pushed herself off the pavement with her shaky right arm, its elbow finally propping her up.

She could feel her father's locked elbows on either side of her, smell his boozed-up breath, although he'd been dead in his grave for two years now. She shrank from the contact of sweaty skin, nauseated by his sour smell and the repetition of his needs, and sought sight again of the body of water that had been a kind of bedtime prayer for her.

She clawed herself high enough to catch a moonlike curve of shoreline, just to the left of a bent Dumpster, pitched toward its missing wheel, that loomed over her and made her think of a coffin.

The two white eyes that winked and quickly narrowed before her were not headlights, as she first had believed, but taillights meant to keep drivers from striking objects in their rear path.

"Stop!" But her faint voice was not to be heard.

Her head led the way to the pavement this time, and she answered the call of the pain.

Below her she saw the waters she had come to think of as her own, flat black like wet marble. Darkness punctuated by pinpricks of light swirled as he carried her away from the humming car to the bridge's railing. She had no strength to fight, no will. Not even her acrophobia could power her to kick and claw for her life. Tears brimmed in her eyes, blurring any image of him, blurring the lights, blurring the boundary between the living and the dead.

In the next few moments she would be both.

When he threw her over, it felt like the act of someone distancing himself from something undesirable, like hearing a rat in the garbage bag on the way out to the cans. But as she dropped, she thought of a ballerina's majestic beauty; she saw herself as elegant and refined; she found a balance, a weightlessness that was surprisingly pleasant. And she wondered why she had feared heights all these years. This was the ride of a lifetime.

2 Of Mice and Spiders

Daphne Matthews negotiated the aisle between cots occupied by, among others, a spaced-out seventeen-year-old methadone addict, a girl shaking from the DTs, and a street-worn fifteen-year-old seriously pregnant. With the continuing spring rains and cool weather, like mice and spiders, the young women migrated inside as conditions required.

The basement space held an incongruous odor: of mildew and medicine, spaghetti and meatballs. Bare bulbs, strung up like lights at a Christmas tree sale, flickered and dimmed over twenty-some teens, two resident RNs, and two volunteers, including Matthews. This was the Shelter's third home in three years, a cavernlike basement space accessed via the Second Presbyterian Church, one of the five oldest structures still standing in Seattle. A thirty-block fire in 1889 had taken all the rest, just as the streets would take these girls if the Shelter ceased to exist.

For the past five months Matthews had doubled her volunteer time at the Shelter, less out of a sense of civic duty than the result of a combination of guilt and grief over the loss of a despondent teenage girl—a regular at the Shelter—who had taken her life. The girl, also pregnant, had jumped to her death from the I-5 bridge.

Matthews knew the young woman on the cot before her only as Margaret—no surnames were used at the Shelter. She asked if she could join her, and the girl acquiesced, less than enthusiastically. Matthews sat down beside her onto the wool blanket, leaning her back against the cool brick wall.

Sitting this close, Matthews could see a curving yellow moon of an old bruise that lingered on the girl's left cheekbone, an archipelago of knitted scars curving around that same eye. No doubt Margaret told people they were sports injuries or the result of a fall. She was fifteen going on forty.

"We spoke the other night," Matthews said, reminding the girl. The methamphetamine, booze, and pot wreaked havoc on the short-term memories of these kids. Not that they listened to the counselors anyway. They tolerated such intrusions only to serve the greater purpose of a warm meal, a shower, free feminine products, and a chance to wash their clothes.

"You're the cop. The shrink. I remember."

"Right, but here, I'm a counselor, and that's all. You were going to think about calling your grandparents."

"I wasn't thinking about it. You were."

"After five days you have to leave the Shelter for at least one night."

"Believe me, I know the rules."

"I don't like to think of you up there in the weather."

"That's your problem. I live up there." Defiant. An attitude. But behind the eyes, fear.

Matthews rarely lost her temper, though she could pretend to when needed. She debated her next move in what to her was a chess game that could make or break lives. "You can call for free. It doesn't have to be collect."

"I wouldn't mind getting out of here so much," the girl conceded.

Matthews saw an opening and seized it. To hell with the regulations. She pulled a Sharpie—an indelible marker—from her purse, grabbed hold of Margaret's forearm, and wrote out her cell phone number in letters the size of the top row of an eye test. Clothes came and went with these girls. Notes in pockets came and went. Forearms were a little more permanent.

"Day or night," Matthews said. "No questions asked. No police. You call me and it's woman to woman, friend to friend."

Margaret eyed her forearm, angry. "A tattoo would have lasted longer."

"Day or night," Matthews repeated and pulled herself off the cot with reluctance.

"Can I ask you something?" the girl asked.

Matthews nodded.

"You think this place is haunted?"

Matthews bit back a smile. "Old, yes. Creepy, maybe. But not haunted."

"Haven't you felt it?"

It wasn't the first time Matthews had heard this. "Maybe a little," she confessed.

"Like somebody watching."

"There's no such thing as ghosts," she said, aware she was sounding like a schoolmarm. "The imagination is powerful. We don't want to mislabel it."

"But you've felt it, too," Margaret said.

Matthews nodded, stretching the truth. It took a long time to establish anything close to trust with one of these kids.

"I heard this place used to be a storeroom or something. Pirates, or smugglers, or something. Like a hundred years ago."

"I've heard it called lots of things: a slaughterhouse, a jail, a house of ill repute." She delivered this comically, and won the first signs of light in that face. "Smugglers? Why not?" Matthews hesitated, unsure if she should leave it here—the first tendrils of rapport connecting them—or drive home her point once more. "If you do call your grandmother, we have funding for transportation. No one's kicking you out, you understand. But I want you safe, Margaret. The baby, safe."

The girl glanced around the room, uncomfortable. "Yeah," she said. "We'll see."

As Matthews reached the surface and her car, her police radio crackled, and the dispatcher announced a 342—a harbor water emergency—a body had been spotted. The location was the Aurora Bridge. Matthews ran four red lights on the way there.

3 The LaMoia

John LaMoia awoke from a two-hour afternoon nap (he was on night tour for all of March) wondering where his next Oxy-Contin would come from. Then he remembered he'd quit.

The California King contained his feet despite the fact that he liked to sleep with his arm under the pillow and out toward the headboard. At an inch over six feet, he'd been hanging ten off the ends of mattresses for his entire adult life, so he thought of the California King as a "spoiler," a luxury item that, once used, makes you wonder how you ever lived without it.

LaMoia could get around the bedroom blindfolded, as he'd built it himself, hammer and nail, two-by-four and Sheetrock, as the first element of Phase One of his refurbishing the cannery warehouse loft, a stone's throw from Elliott Bay. He was currently in Phase Three—the last of a series of storage closets by the guest bedroom.

At nearly four thousand square feet, the loft gave him plenty of space to play with.

It remained a quirky space with a bachelor's sense of independence, a cop's sense of budget, and a man's sense of decor. There was no long line forming at the door to shoot it for a magazine spread. But for the view alone it was worth the price of admission.

He rolled over and petted his dog, his nagging dry throat

reminding him of his former addiction. He wondered if it would ever fully go away.

The treatment that had begun following a broken jaw suffered in the line of duty had matured from medical necessity to medicinal abuse, an addiction of legendary proportions. LaMoia still couldn't understand how he had allowed it to happen; and even now, three months into rehab, he found himself still in the unforgiving grasp of need.

LaMoia felt warm breath glance his neck, followed by the wet nose of an Australian sheepdog, formerly called "Blue," but renamed "Rehab" when LaMoia found himself using the dog as a sounding board. LaMoia wasn't entirely comfortable with the responsibility the dog's existence perpetrated upon his bachelorhood. But then again, bachelorhood didn't feel so right either; since recovery, his world had turned upside down.

LaMoia did not run his life as a democracy, but as a dictatorship. He sat on the throne, he chaired the board, he dropped the gavel, he made the choices, and to hell with those who misunderstood him. It had always been so—or certainly since puberty and his discovery that women of every age, shape, size, and color could not do without him. This interest on their part had long since gone to his head. Sex was an addiction all its own. He had lost himself to the sport of winning women for the better part of his adult life. Only OxyContin and prescription drugs had finally lifted him into another realm, where indulging himself in new, untested flesh no longer mattered. In the end, only the pills mattered. Time-release pain medication. What kind of geniuses were these guys? When finally he could neither see nor have any desire to see the benefits of sobriety, he had stood his ground, defiant in his right to self-destruct.

During those long months, work had become a tolerated distraction, a necessary evil. That it was police work might have struck him as ironic had he been capable of conceiving of irony.

But such conceptions escaped him, especially objectivity. To the contrary, during this period he had been as self-absorbed as any other time in his thirty-odd years, and entirely blinded to it. Beyond caring. A living illusion. And entirely without hope.

Six months ago, with his lieutenant, Boldt, on leave at the time to assist a capital murder investigation in Wenatchee, Washington, LaMoia had found himself in charge of the Seattle Police Department's Crimes Against Persons Unit. It had been like putting a kid in the cockpit of a 747. He had floundered his way through insignificant homicide investigations that might have meant something to him had the OxyContin not dominated his every thought. A domestic here; a gang bang there. Could do them in his sleep. Morale at Homicide hit at an all-time low under his stewardship. When Boldt returned, he pasted things back together and identified LaMoia's addiction. At that point, things had gone to hell in a handbasket.

LaMoia had wrecked the Camaro, totaling his only one true love, and requiring hospitalization and more painkillers. He took a leave of absence, and that proved his undoing—too much free time. One November night, Lou Boldt and Daphne Matthews had performed an intervention—confronting LaMoia with his drug problem and offering him a chance to save himself or to face the inevitable consequences. The intervention had worked. By Christmas, LaMoia was prescription-free and enjoying turkey at Boldt's house. By New Year's Day, he'd been back on the job.

But a dark, cold March evening in rainy Seattle could own a bite, could drill an ache into formerly broken bones and make it hurt just to walk across the room to the toilet.

Heaven came in all shapes and sizes: whether a 34C, a hot Seattle's Best, or a clear head. With sobriety, solid thinking had returned, but oddly enough, not the overriding need to have every woman who eyed him. LaMoia wanted something different now. More connection, less infatuation. He wasn't sure what love was, but he thought that might be it. As a result, he stayed away from the "badgers" at the cop bars, the coworkers, the waitresses who came on to him, avoiding the urge to slip his hand between the jeans and the soft skin and light them up. God, how he had lived for that power, the ability to reduce a grown woman to outright need. They still called, leaving casual messages on his answering machine, the implications and invitations subtle but not misunderstood. They wanted him. Only months ago, he had let that want of theirs run his life, dictate his arrogance, demand his attention. And now he had to live with that past, and he found it embarrassing.

When the phone rang, he peeked at the caller-ID, dreading to play that role—the flirtation that came packaged with expectation. But the phone number proved familiar to him: the fifth floor. A case. Something to get him outside himself. He answered the phone: It was a jumper, a drowning. As good a way to start a night tour as any.

4 Bridge Over Troubled Waters

The bridge shook with traffic, making her knees dance. Daphne Matthews tucked her rain-dampened hair behind her right ear in a gesture that was more automatic than necessary because of the headband. Her hair fell into her face if she let it because of a haircut she didn't like but could do nothing about. The result was a black velour headband that put a speed bump just behind her forehead and, she feared, made her ears stick out.

The blue emergency strobe lights from patrol cars, the amber lights of Search and Rescue, and the blinding white pulses from an ambulance whose services would not be required hurt her eyes to the point of headache. This, along with the rain and the vibrations coming up her legs, gave her a bout of vertigo. She reached out to steady herself but stopped at the last moment, discovering she had not yet donned the latex gloves required at any crime scene. Her hand locked instead around a forearm, nearly as hard as the steel bridge railing. When she realized this arm belonged to King County Deputy Sheriff Nathan Prair, she let go and stepped back and away.

"It's been awhile, Daphne."

"Deputy Prair." She addressed him like a hostess to an uninvited dinner guest. Nathan Prair had been a client of hers—a patient. Departmental counseling following a shooting. She'd had to pass Prair off to a civilian colleague when he'd attached to her, professing he loved her. It had gotten to the point where thanking him or even speaking to him risked leading him on, sending some unintended signal.

The question was why he was here. This bridge was within city limits, SPD jurisdiction. Why the involvement of the King County Sheriff's Office? Either one of their guys had spotted the body—she hoped it wasn't Prair—or perhaps the lake itself fell into KCSO jurisdiction. The way politicians drew the maps, anything was possible.

"How have you been?" Prair moved to fill the space she'd made between them. He was in that group of patrolmen that spent a couple of hours a day at the gym, though he lacked the jutting jaw and heavy brow that seemed ubiquitous features of the other G.I. Joes. In fact, Prair's overly round face housed narrow-set soft brown eyes that left him a confusing mixture of boyishly handsome and mean-spirited. Even with the Marine cut, Matthews had always thought his blond hair was more that of a surfer than the take-no-prisoners cop he hoped to portray. Prair's biggest problem was that he believed women found his looks irresistible. It had gotten him into all sorts of trouble. It had gotten him dismissed from SPD and later moved over to the Sheriff's Office.

"Deputy Prair, I don't think it appropriate that we have this, or any conversation." She looked around the bridge for John LaMoia, who was supposed to be on the scene already.

Prair shook his head, smile still in place. "That was what . . . over a year ago? I got a little jiggy—it happens. Tell me that's never happened to you before, one of your couch potatoes getting hot for you."

"I'm glad you found reassignment," she said as a concession. "I hope it works out for you on the job."

"You sound like my grandmother, or something. This is me, Daphne!"

"It's Matthews, and it's lieutenant. Your charm is lost on me, Deputy."

He leaned closer and he lowered his voice into a whisper that cut through the damp air. "So it was *you* the *Titanic* hit. Mystery solved."

She stepped back as John LaMoia called out her name and approached in a stiff-legged hurry.

John LaMoia didn't walk, he swaggered, carrying his entire personality in a confident stride, for all to see. Most of all, LaMoia existed to be noticed. His trademark ostrich cowboy boots easily cost him a month's salary, and he was not shy to replace them when they scuffed up. The thick brown hair, cascading in waves and curls, proved the envy of every woman on the job. The deerskin jacket seemed an anachronism, a relic of the flower power generation into which LaMoia barely fit, having been born too late to be certifiably hip and too early to be a yuppie. Equally loved by the brass and the patrol personnel—not an easy feat—as a detective LaMoia got away with behavior that would have won others suspension. He crossed boundaries and even violated ethics, but always with that contrived, shit-eating grin of his, and always in the name of right and good. Like everyone else, she had a bit of a soft spot for him, though she would never admit it.

LaMoia's timing couldn't have been better. She'd have to thank him later.

"The shrink and the shrunk," LaMoia said. No love was lost between most detectives on the force and Nathan Prair, a man who by most accounts had tarnished the SPD shield. "I need to borrow her a minute." He hooked Matthews by the elbow and steered her away, out of earshot, back down the bridge toward a gathering of patrolmen.

"Am I ever glad to see you," she said.

"Listen, you stand too close to garbage, you start to smell like it. Couldn't let that happen to you."

"Oh, sure."

"Truth be known, *Lieutenant*," he emphasized, "I'm surprised to see you here. Night tour, raining, and all."

"I was nearby when I heard the call," she stretched the facts slightly.

"This wouldn't have anything to do with that other teen jumper, and you getting all sideways over your not stopping it?"

"Who's analyzing whom?" she asked.

"I'm just asking."

"You're using an interrogative to make a statement, John."

"I just love it when you talk dirty."

She elbowed him playfully, and he chuckled. This was not their typical rapport, and she found herself enjoying a LaMoia moment.

"You can almost see your place from here, huh?"

"I suppose." She was looking down toward the black water where the scuba divers swam beneath the surface with powerful flashlights, the beams of which looked gray in the depths. The body, believed to be a woman's, had been spotted on the surface less than an hour before but had blown its bloat and sunk during the attempt to recover it. Some people didn't want to be found.

"SID caught it," he said. Scientific Identification Division— the crime lab.

"Caught what?" she asked.

LaMoia was spared an answer as a semi passed too closely— a patrolman shouted at the driver to slow down—causing the hastily erected halogen light stands to shake and nearly fall. Instead he pointed to where a lab technician worked over what looked like a tiny patch of dried blood on the bridge railing.

Sight of the blood took her aback—not for what it was, but

for what it implied. She'd come to the crime scene because of the implication of a jumper. The presence of blood indicated foul play.

"How'd we find that?" Matthews asked.

"Very carefully," the woman lab technician answered without looking up. She added, "Doesn't mean it's hers."

"Of course it's hers," said LaMoia.

"We'll know by morning."

"Could be anything," Matthews said.

"Yeah, sure. All sorts of bleeders choose this section of the bridge for a view."

It was then Matthews saw the drip line. Some of the droplets had been stepped on and smeared, but the line was clear. A second technician was busy delineating the area of sidewalk that contained the blood pattern that led from the roadway. A more scientific study of the blood splatter would determine both direction and approximate speed of that trail, but on first glance it seemed obvious.

"Car parked there," LaMoia said. "Guy hoists her out of the trunk or the backseat, carries her to here—carries, not drags—bumps her against the rail as he gets a better grip and voilà. To bed she goes."

"Whose lead?"

"*Moi*," LaMoia said.

"Try Spanish, John. You don't wear the French very well."

"*Si*," he said.

The Hispanic lab tech winced at his lack of accent, or maybe she was flirting with him. She wasn't the first.

Matthews studied the drip line again, a part of her relieved that maybe it wasn't another jumper. She knew she couldn't voice such a sentiment—others wouldn't understand.

Excited shouting from below alerted them to the diver that

had surfaced and was waving his flashlight toward the nearby dive boat. MARINE UNIT was stenciled on its side. A phone number. A website address. A new world.

A King County Sheriff's special operations section, the marine unit's involvement helped explained Prair's presence.

"They found her," LaMoia said, stating the obvious.

A quiet descended over the four of them. A moment of respect, as the shouting spread up onto the bridge. Two of them were collecting her blood. One of them was assigned to figure this all out and attribute it to someone.

Matthews was there to observe. But as the pale, swollen mass that had once been a woman came to the surface with the three divers, she turned and walked away, very much aware that Nathan Prair watched her every step from his huddle with several other KCSO officers. She crossed her arms a little more tightly.

Happy to be gone from the scene, she realized she might leave, but she could not, and would not, leave this case behind. This one was hers as much as it was LaMoia's.

5 Pretty in Pink

Late afternoon the following day, on the heels of several detectives-in-training poring over the two dozen local missing person reports, as well as the pages of six three-ring binders filled cover to cover with sheets of reported runaways suspected headed to the Northwest (these binders representing only the last two months of flyers sent to SPD), a phone call was taken by the duty sergeant at Public Safety.

"Yo!" LaMoia answered.

"Sergeant, it's Phil at the front desk."

"Yeah, Phil. Whassup?"

"Phone call just now come in. The individual is one Ferrell Walker. Male. Sounded kind of young. Claims the description in the paper fits his sister, and that for all he knows she's gone missing—something about some asshole boyfriend who won't return his calls. Should I kick it upstairs on a memo or what?"

"No. I'll take it. Give me the four-one-one."

The duty sergeant read the particulars to LaMoia and repeated his recollection of the conversation.

"Give me the TOD," LaMoia said, wanting the exact time of day the call had been logged. All incoming calls to the switchboard's main number were recorded digitally. LaMoia could access and listen to the message himself, but his preference was that I.T. lift the message off the master and preserve and protect it so they'd have it available later.

He caught up with Daphne Matthews in her seventh-floor office, a hundred and fifty square feet of femininity in an otherwise grayish male world. It always felt comfortable to him, which he supposed was the point—she did her counseling here—chintz curtains on the window, landscape artwork on the walls. But it was the personal furniture that made such a difference, even if it was from Home Depot as she claimed—dark wood and leather, instead of the gunmetal gray steel that came courtesy of the taxpayers. An electric kettle, a wooden variety box of tea, and packets of Splenda occupied a counter to the right of her desk.

"Here's my problem," he said without a greeting.

Matthews was packing up for the day, filling a narrow black briefcase that looked more like a handbag. "I'm done for the day."

"The Sarge keeps asking me to rewrite the report on the bridge."

"Try English, John."

"Ha-ha. You're really cracking me up, here."

"I'm *not* writing your report for you."

"And in the meantime," he continued, "I got this guy that says his sister's split the scene and that she matches the description we gave to the paper."

She looked up.

"The thing is, I got to make like Shakespeare here for the next couple hours, and when you call the number this guy gave the desk it comes up some grouch who says our boy ain't coming to the phone while he's on the job—and the job turns out to be cleaning fish up at Fisherman's Terminal—and seeing as how that's damn near on your way home . . ."

"That's a stretch," she said.

"But you'll do it."

"I shouldn't. I'm tired, and I want a glass of wine."

"But you *will*." He said, "I swear, if I didn't have this damn report to write—"

"Yeah, yeah," she complained. "And I'll whitewash your fence while I'm at it."

"I don't have a fence," he said, "but I *do* have a couple closets I just built that need a couple coats."

"Rain check," she said, standing at the ready. "Tell me again whom I'm looking for?"

She left the Honda alongside a rusted heap of a pickup truck in a parking lot of cracked and heaving blacktop that oozed a brown mud apparently too toxic to host even the heartiest of weeds. Dickensian in both appearance and smells, the commercial fishing docks of south Ballard had changed little in the last century. A dozen or more small trawlers, battered and destitute in appearance, evacuated their catch to cleaning tables with open drain spouts that ran pink with guts and grime emptied back into the canal water where overfed seagulls and shore birds battled noisily for territory, their cries piercing and sharp, yet apparently unnoticed by all but Matthews.

A few of the men, mostly young and scraggly, overtly inspected her as she followed directions down the line to the third of the cleaning tables. Even in jeans and a work shirt she would have felt self-conscious in this setting, but dressed in tweed wool pants pleated at the waist and crisp in the crease, and a navy blue Burberry microfiber rain jacket with leather trim, she felt about as comfortable as the silver salmon under the knife.

Ferrell Walker looked more seventeen than twenty. LaMoia had pulled two driver's licenses for her: Walker's and his sister's, one Mary-Ann Walker, twenty-six. Matthews knew from the data that his eyes were listed as green, his hair brown, his weight 170 and that he wasn't an organ donor. He wore a black rubber apron smeared with the snotty entrails of his livelihood.

The apron attempted to protect a pair of filthy blue jeans and a tattered sweatshirt equally smeared with resident stains. He pulled off mismatched thick rubber gloves, one black, one yellow, stuffing them into a torn pocket on the apron that hung down like a giant tongue. He rinsed his hands in cold water from a rubber hose that ran constantly above his cutting stand. He dried them on a soiled section of torn towel and thankfully did not offer one to shake. Obliged to display her shield, she made sure he saw it.

Walker's face was pinched, as if he'd been sat on as a baby. She couldn't see the green for the dark, deep eye sockets. Behind him, on the high wooden workbench where the water ran pink, a wood-handled fish knife rested, its curving blade like an ill-fashioned smile. Walker's Adam's apple bobbed like a buoy as he answered her first question. Had he called the police to report his sister as missing?

He looked at her almost as if he knew her—men did this to her all the time, but Walker's variation was pretty convincing, and disquieting.

"Not like Mary-Ann to miss work," Walker said. "And when that asshole said he hadn't seen her either, that didn't sound right, so I called you guys . . . you people . . . whatever."

She asked for and received the sister's pedigree, some of which matched what she'd learned from the driver's license: twenty-six, blond, 135, five foot six, smoker, worked here at dock five. Last seen—and this was the most troubling to her of all—roughly three days earlier. Those in the know put her in the water over forty-eight hours. This timing made Mary-Ann Walker a likely fit. Matthews had a Polaroid of the woman's waterlogged, crab-eaten face in her pocket but couldn't bring herself to deliver it to this kid. Mention of "that asshole" made her think she might have another candidate to ID the body.

"You're making reference to a boyfriend?" she asked.

"Wait, tell me it's not Mary-Ann," he said. "Tell me this didn't happen."

"What's her boyfriend's name?"

"Lanny Neal." He still had hope in his voice. "The description in the paper . . . tell me I'm wrong about it sounding like Mary-Ann."

Matthews looked around for a place to sit, but thought better of it. She didn't like the smell here, the sound of the dead fish slopping wetly down onto the cutting tables. She didn't like the sad look in Walker's tired eyes, or the thought that LaMoia had passed this off to her so that she'd be the one delivering bad news.

"Anna's a cleaner, too," Walker said. "Boss is on me that it's somehow my fault she hasn't showed. So basically, I'm picking up her work, putting in a double." He hesitated. "She wouldn't leave me hanging like this—not without calling or something. This body . . . it looks like her?"

"Unfortunately, the body doesn't look like much, Mr. Walker. Too long in the water. Now, you asked this Lanny Neal about her, and his reaction was what exactly? And I urge you to recollect what was *said*, not what you *felt* about what was said." She interrupted herself again. "I take it your sister is living with this individual, or involved in a way that suggests he might have knowledge of her whereabouts?"

"He's jumping her, if that's what you're asking. And, yeah, she's pretty much shacked up, since we don't have the boat no more. Which is on account of Neal anyway. 'Cause once they started hanging out, she bailed on me—thirty years of our family fishing these waters, down the drain—and that pretty much finished me off with the fucking bankers, thank you very much."

"Mr. Neal's reaction to your call?"

"Lame," Walker answered. Dead fish were piling up, awaiting him. "You mind?" he asked, indicating the table.

She did mind, but she told him she didn't, and so they stepped up to the cleaning table where Walker, gloved once again, worked the curved blade of that knife in such an automatic and efficient way that it bordered on graceful. He tore loose the entrails and tossed them into a white plastic pail.

"Take me through the call, please. You asked to speak with Mary-Ann."

"Listen, lady . . . lieutenant . . . whatever . . . Neal's a scum-sucking piece of shit. I know it, and he knows I know it. He beats her up, and she goes back to him, and I just don't fucking get that, you know? And me? I'm looking out for her, and she blows me off like I'm the pond scum, not that dirtbag she's hanging with, so what I'm saying is, we didn't exactly get into it, Neal and me. He essentially blew me off."

"His exact words were?"

"Just tell me it isn't her." His fingers moved, the blade sliced and another fish was processed.

She waited for his attention. He was sad-eyed by nature, a dog starved for affection. Her job biased her into such snap appraisals, and though loath to admit it, she went with first impressions. "I sincerely hope the Jane Doe is not your sister. The fact remains, your cooperation is essential if we're to clear Mary-Ann's name from our list, and that means answering my questions as they're asked. Do you understand?"

Walker's gaze lifted off the fish he was cutting, the look he gave her so penetrating that she averted her eyes.

"We haven't identified the body." She now wondered whether she had handled this correctly. She observed grief on a regular basis and tried to avoid labeling it. Some screamed, some cried, some went silent, some became violently sick. Some became violent, period.

"Neal said she wasn't there, that he hadn't seen her, and that at this point if he did it would be for the last time."

Matthews scribbled down notes. "Okay . . . ," she said automatically.

"It's *not* okay," he said. "The guy beats her, lady. He's awful with her, and if he's done anything to her . . ." He lifted the fillet knife. "I'll turn him into chum and feed him to the crabs." His eyes reminded her of killers she'd interviewed. Grief could do that—make us do things we never intended.

"It's important we all keep cool heads, Mr. Walker. We're still just collecting the facts, the evidence. There has been no positive ID—identification—of the body we found. It would be a mistake to make assumptions about Mr. Neal's involvement at this point."

"I'm not making an assumption," he said. "I'm just telling you how it is."

"It isn't anything until we know who, and what, we've got." He was more kid than adult, she thought. A lovesick brother with a fishing knife sharp enough to split hairs—she reminded herself to thank LaMoia for this one.

Rain fell, wetting her pad.

"Did she take prescription drugs? Recreational drugs?"

"If she was drinking and drugging, Lanny got her into it."

She wrote that down as affirmative. Booze, drugs, abuse—the father, son, and holy ghost of domestic disturbances.

As the rain increased, she debated pulling up the hood on the jacket but decided she wanted him to know she could take the weather.

"Do you have an address, a phone number for Mr. Neal?"

Walker recited a Wallingford address and Matthews wrote it down. He went back to the fish. This time, he hacked the head off with a single blow, then the tail. Then he minced the body, entrails and all, into pieces and swept it down the drain and the seagulls attacked the surface of the water with a frenzy.

"Remember, Mr. Walker, we have not connected Mr. Neal

to any suspicious act. This is the first I've heard of Mr. Neal. Are we clear on this?" Matthews worried where a younger brother might take this. He'd lost the family boat, the family business. What had she been thinking, implicating Neal? She hoped she might steer her way back out. "Women disappear, Mr. Walker. Tens of thousands every year. Some just up and walk away, from their families, their husbands, their boy-friends—their brothers. That's right. Most show back up, a few days, a few weeks later. I'd like to think we can pretty much put Mary-Ann in that last category."

He dragged a salmon in front of him with the knife's sharp-ened tip. "If it is Mary-Ann," he said matter-of-factly, "then all the more reason you'd better talk to Neal. Anna's afraid of heights."

"Acrophobic?"

"Whatever."

She made note of the phobia on the page of her notepad.

As it rained harder, she again almost pulled up the jacket's hood but decided against it once more. Rain drizzled down both their faces. His eyes hardened, making him seem much older than his twenty years.

"So what do we do next?" he asked.

"You tell us if Mary-Ann shows back up." She passed him a business card that carried the office number and wrote La-Moia's extension on the back. "I'm concerned I may have given you the wrong impression, Mr. Walker. About this being Mary-Ann. I apologize for that. I don't want you doing something stupid—harming Mr. Neal in some way. All for nothing."

"People get what they give in this world. It's no concern of yours."

"Sure it is. It's every concern of mine." She added, "Could you give me a phone number? Residential. Something other than work."

"I told you, after Neal got into her head . . . I don't have a phone."

"An address?"

"I'm kind of between places right now, okay?"

"This is pretty miserable weather, this time of year."

"There's ways around it."

"So this is where I reach you," she said, looking around. "What's your work schedule right now?"

He ignored the question. "I asked what's next, in terms of if I don't happen to call you, if Anna doesn't happen to show back up."

"We're attempting to identify the body."

"And I should be part of that."

She heard herself say, "We could arrange for you to view the body, but there's absolutely no requirement for you to do so at this time. Mr. Neal could do it, if you'd prefer."

Walker read meaning into her statement. "That help you get him? Watching him look at her? Something like that?"

"I'm not going to speculate on where the lead detective might take this. I am not the lead detective."

"You are as far as I'm concerned," he said.

Matthews wished she could start again.

He said, "If Neal looks at that body, then I want to be there. I got any kind of rights like that, me being her brother and all?"

"None whatsoever," she said, unsure herself. "It's all up to the lead detective."

"Yeah? Well, you tell him I want to be there."

"I'll pass it along."

"You do that," he said, hoisting the next fish on the tip of the knife to its place of evisceration. "You help me, I'll help you."

6   Bowing to Buddha

Lou Boldt had an ordinary look that few would expect in a cop. Fewer would expect the traits that accounted for a homicide clearance rate that shattered every SPD record: an enduring patience and an empathy with the victim that had gained such legendary proportions that the man made the law enforcement lecture circuit a second source of income. His heightened sense of hearing not only kindled a love of bebop jazz but also could discern the most subtle nuance in the voice of a suspect or a witness in the throes of a lie. His rise through the ranks had been predictable, though far from supercharged. He got the job done and seemed to enjoy himself in the process. He shunned exposure in the press, and yet notoriety proved inescapable. The only sergeant to decline consideration for a lieutenant's shield five years running, he had remained in that position for more than a decade, succumbing to promotion only when family finances necessitated. He walked with something of an exaggerated stoop—typically lost in thought. A family man, he'd come to fatherhood somewhat late in life. Whenever he attended preschool parent functions, he found himself with little to talk about. Dead bodies, murder, and assault made him a reluctant conversationalist. It was while at one such function that his wife, Liz, had introduced him to Susan Hebringer.

Hebringer, who had last been seen downtown, had now been missing for several weeks, following on the distant heels of one

Patricia Randolf, who'd disappeared nearly two months earlier. Both missing, and now presumed dead. The case was eating a hole in Boldt's stomach to go along with other such scars—his medals were empty bottles of Maalox liquid, discarded like the bodies of victims whose deaths he hoped to solve. Thankless work, but a job he wouldn't trade. The Susan Hebringer case was an exception—it put a voice to the face, a child watching the back door for mommy—it put Boldt on notice, serving up a reminder of the randomness of it all. It could have been Liz. It could have been him and his two children staring at that back door, waiting. The ghost of Susan Hebringer, a woman he'd met only briefly, but a friend of his family, had come to own him.

Boldt's relationship with Mama Lu, on the other hand, had begun with an illegal immigrant scam involving shipping containers, and it had developed over time into a professional association of sorts, in which she acted as an unpaid informer in exchange for later favors. Boldt understood perfectly well that such relationships were two-way, and he believed that his current visit to Mama Lu signaled traffic flow in the reverse direction—she needed a favor, and he was obliged to do his best to deliver. Tonight he knew only that her inquiry involved a death and that like it or not, if he could help, he would. If not, he would do his best to appease her.

Boldt knew from prior visits to the Korean grocery that he needed to clear himself with the first of the two Samoans, a thick-necked, squinting structure of a human being dressed in black. It felt vaguely humiliating for a twenty-odd-year homicide veteran to seek the approval of a bodyguard, but Boldt came to get the job done, not pee on a fire hydrant, so he flashed the man his shield, playing along, and announced—he did not *ask*, his one concession—that he was there to see the venerable Great Lady.

Thick with the smell of pickled ginger and sesame, the grocery's interior made him suddenly hungry. An elderly Korean man with few teeth, a chapped grin, and expectancy in his arched eyebrows welcomed Boldt from behind a deli counter that offered mostly unrecognizable cuts of meat, fish, and poultry. Fish heads and chicken feet quickly killed Boldt's appetite.

Canned goods and sundries reached floor to ceiling, enhancing the narrowness of the aisles—a claustrophobic's nightmare. Two ceiling fans spun lazily, a dusty cobweb trailing from a paddle like a biplane banner at the beach. Boldt climbed the steep stairs, cautious of a trick left knee, the sweet pungency of chai overtaking the ginger. Oddly out-of-tune Chinese string music grated on his musician's ear. Of all the affronts to the senses, this dissonance proved the most difficult to take.

A Buddha of a woman, Mama Lu occupied an ornately inlaid black lacquer chair like a queen on a throne, so wide and vast of flesh as to fill out a muumuu like a sleeping bag in a stuff sack. Her eyes shone like tiny black stones in a balloon of a face accented by generous swipes of rouge, implying cheekbones now submerged in an overindulgence at the soup bowl. Her lips gleamed a sickening fire-engine red, a color echoed in an application to her blunt fingernails, one of which, her index finger, curled to invite Boldt closer.

"Mr. Both," she said, having never gotten his name right in the several years they'd been associated.

"Great Lady."

"You like some soup?"

"Thank you." He had learned long ago not to refuse. A female attendant of seventeen or eighteen, a petite thing with a wasp waist who wore embroidered silk from neck to ankle, delivered a small table before him. She averted her face, avoiding his eyes as he sat.

Mama Lu chewed on a string of Chinese words, and the girl

took off in a flash to points unseen. The place was a rabbit warren.

"You mentioned a death, Great Lady." He tried to push her, knowing she might drag this out for over an hour. He didn't have an hour. Neither did Susan Hebringer. Mama Lu smiled, but said nothing in reply.

There was only the music as they awaited delivery of the steaming bowls, also black lacquer. A wonton dish with streams of egg swirled in a dark broth. The Chinese spoon, flat on the bottom and wide at the mouth, allowed the soup to quickly cool. Mama Lu concealed a burp that she clearly savored.

"Greatest detective ever work this city."

"You must need an awfully big favor," he said.

"Do I exaggerate?"

"Always."

"My heritage." A face-consuming grin. "Please excuse."

"You are a friend to this city, Great Lady. You give much back. Others should follow your example."

"You humor me."

"I honor you," he said. "You are a dear and noble friend."

"Since when you running for office?"

"I'm just trying to stay above water these days."

"Soup make you feel better. You tell Mama Lu what troubles you."

Boldt took a spoonful. The soup defined depth and character. "The two women who've gone missing," he said, feeling no need to fill in the blanks—the whole city knew about Hebringer and Randolf. "My wife and I knew one of the women."

Mama Lu grimaced and after a long moment nodded.

Boldt ate more and requested a second bowl, winning great favor with her. If he could have raised a burp, she might have adopted him. "You should write a cookbook sometime," he said.

She said, "You busy man, Mr. Both. Forgive an old woman her selfishness."

"I am always at your service, Great Lady." Protocol was not to be dismissed. Boldt let her have her self-deprecating moment but waited for her to reveal the true nature of her summons. The second bowl of soup proved even tastier than the first.

"You familiar with water main break, Mr. Both?"

"I might have missed that, Great Lady."

"Yesterday night."

"I caught the rain. We had a couple of assaults overnight. A huge trash spill in the bay. I think I missed the water main."

"Lucky you. Not so lucky for second cousin."

Here it came—the reason for his soup. Her cousin. A euphemism for anyone of Asian descent for whom the Great Lady felt morally or physically responsible. Over the years, Boldt had learned some of the code. Not all, not by any stretch. "Do you mind if I take notes?"

She gestured for him to do so. Boldt pulled out the worn notebook, taller than it was wide. It fit into his hand like a cross to the devout.

She said, "Billy Chen. His mother sister to my cousin's husband." She smiled. All an invention on her part. "Work road crew, here in city. Good boy, Billy Chen."

"And how was Billy unlucky?" Boldt said.

"Billy dead," she said.

"I'm sorry for your loss," he said. "How did it happen?" And then it registered, though too late. The sinkhole on Third Avenue. Interpreting "yesterday night" had left him on the wrong date, and it took him a moment to back up the calendar, to relocate himself. The sinkhole raised a red flag only because of its location. The only two reliable witnesses in the Susan Hebringer disappearance had put her last-seen nearby on Columbia Street, once on First Avenue, and a few minutes later crossing

Second heading east, uphill. Randolf was believed to have been in this same area at the time of her disappearance. Shop owners had been questioned, bus drivers, pamphlets distributed—and to date, not a single other lead had come. Then that immense sinkhole. And now a dead body. He sat up, his pulse quicker, pen ready.

"Billy working broken water main. Your people say he drown fixing it—that he no good at job. Medical examiner office. Mama Lu, not think so, Mr. Both. Billy Chen no good worker? Want better job done. Much grief, Billy brings us all. Mama Lu have no answer. Turn to good friend for answer."

"Where exactly was the body found?" Boldt said.

"Do I ask you to do my cooking for me? Run grocery?"

Boldt grinned. She intended for him to start from the start. This woman didn't run a grocery, she ran Seattle's Asian economy. Who was she kidding?

He said, "The medical examiner, Doc Dixon, is a close friend. He can be trusted. He's very good at his job. If he says Billy Chen drowned, then I'm sure that's right. I don't know the particulars, but if Doc Dixon—"

"You will know particulars, yes, Mr. Both? If not accident, you investigate. Yes? As favor to good friend."

"We—my department—are only authorized to investigate deaths ruled suspicious causes, Great Lady. I can certainly look into this . . . accident, or whatever it was . . . no problem. But unless there is a determination of suspicious causes, my hands are tied."

"But you untie as favor to friend."

"I can work after hours. Maybe take some lost time. I just wanted you to understand it may go a little slowly."

"I no understand."

"I'm very busy right now. The family might prefer a private investigator, someone who can tackle this full-time." He couldn't believe he was recommending they use a PI. He hoped he'd worded this carefully enough. He didn't want to offend the likes of Mama Lu. Not now. Not ever.

"Chen family prefers you, Mr. Both." She set her spoon down and gently pushed at the small table before her. She meant she preferred him. As she dabbed her chin with the generous linen napkin, the wisp of silk swept through the room and the bowl of soup disappeared. A magician at work.

As close to a direct order as he was going to get. The choice was now his. "Let me see what Dixie, the ME, has to say about it." Boldt nudged his table. Same reaction: bowl gone; table dry; table removed from in front of him.

"You like fortune cookie?" she said.

"No, thank you."

"You no like fortune cookie?"

"We make or break our own fortunes. I don't need a cookie interfering."

"But taste so good," she said, crunching down on hers and raining crumbs into folds. She smiled. Thankfully she had her teeth in.

"Billy Chen," Boldt said, making sure he had the name right. "C-h-e-n."

But he was thinking about both Hebringer and Randolf having last been seen in the same general area when Mama Lu said, "Little birdie tell me Cherry and Third part of old underground city. How you know what kill Billy until you look?"

"The Underground extends up there?" Boldt asked, adrenaline warming him. In the late 1800s, Seattle had been rebuilt following a colossal fire. The reconstruction, made in large part because of tidal flooding, developed a city on top of a city— enormous retaining walls built around each of twenty city blocks and streets between them built up with soil and rock sometimes as high as thirty feet. A good deal of the original city now lay underground. He'd done the tour once—it was a world unto itself down there: antique storefronts, stuff wreathed in darkness for more than a century, some of it frozen in time, some intruded upon by shop owners desperate for storage.

Boldt couldn't have been less interested in Billy Chen. It was all Hebringer and Randolf for him at that moment. A paved-over section of the city left undisturbed for a hundred years. *The Phantom of the Opera,* Boldt was thinking.

"Maybe so," she said, but with a twinkle in her eye that told him she knew more.

"Who is this 'little birdie,' Great Lady?"

The wide shoulders shrugged.

Boldt suddenly possessed enough energy to jog back to head-quarters. *The Underground?* She'd handed him a hell of a lead. "I can look into this," he told her, trying to hide his enthusiasm.

"You good man, Mr. Both," she said, reading whatever was on that fortune and finding it extremely amusing. Her body shook like a mountain of jelly.

7 Hide and Peep

Nordstrom and the tourist thing had worn Melissa Dunkin's legs down to a pair of aching calves that would be shinsplints by the following morning. At 7 P.M., practically stumbling into her suite in the Inn, she headed straight for the bath. With dinner scheduled for 8:30, she had no time to waste. A few minutes for a "lie-down" in front of CNBC if she hurried.

Melissa used the brass security hook-and-latch lock to ensure her privacy against a random minibar inspection or turndown service. She started the bathwater and began undressing immediately, the water steaming piping hot and making her think, for no reason at all, of home and her husband and kids, whom she missed. On reconsideration, more honestly, she was happy to have the time alone. Nothing wrong with some self-indulgence once or twice a year.

Her blouse off and hung up, she drew the living room sheers across a large window with a panoramic view of Puget Sound. Slate-green water, densely forested islands, and the Olympic mountain range served as a backdrop. She drew the curtains in the bedroom as well, mildly annoyed that they wouldn't close completely, but as they faced a darkened construction site, a skeleton against the slowly fading evening sky, she didn't worry about it. She undressed fully, off to one side. Nothing mattered much at this point but that bath.

She slipped into the complimentary terry cloth robe, angled

the TV to face the bathroom, angled the bathroom door's full-length mirror, and readjusted her efforts twice so that she could see a reversed image of *Market Wrap* from the tub. Turned the volume way up. Toe in the water. Heaven.

She shed the robe, slipped into the foaming tub, and nearly squealed with delight it felt so damned good. A moment later, she climbed back out, ignored the robe, and sneaked into and across the suite's living room where she snatched a beer from the minibar. She returned to the tub a conquering hero.

Twenty hedonistic minutes later, Melissa Dunkin dried herself off with a towel the size of a rug, slipped back into the robe, and headed straight for bed. Do not pass Go. The covers drawn, she shed the robe and lay back into the crisp sheets, naked, glowing, the bath's heat slowly seeping out of her flushed skin. She zapped the TV's sound and dozed, as relaxed as she'd been in ages. If that dinner hadn't been on her Palm Pilot, she'd have let herself sleep until morning.

She would never have accused herself of woman's intuition. She left that for the touchy-feelies, the Birkenstock set who frequented the whole-food stores and took Chinese supplements they couldn't pronounce. Melissa Dunkin considered herself pedantic but effective and efficient as a businesswoman, adequate as a mother, accomplished as a lover. She pulled the sheet up over her chest as she cooled, luxuriating in the serenity of a self-induced stupor.

It was at that moment she saw the man's reflection in the bathroom mirror, which, at its present angle was trained with a view out the bedroom window. He glowed red, then suddenly green as a traffic light changed. He held something to his face.

Binoculars.

Aimed into her window.

At her.

Naked, until only seconds before.

Oh, my God!

She coiled into a fetal ball, stretching for the phone while clinging to the sheet that hid her from him. She snagged the handset and ended up dragging the phone by its cord across her oversized pillow. She was dreadfully cold all of a sudden, her skin coursed with gooseflesh, her teeth actually chattering. The talking head on the TV looked out at her, so calm and collected. The collision of fear and dread inside her left her nauseated.

She wasn't about to call some minimum-wage hotel receptionist. Not Melissa Dunkin. She dialed 9 for an outside line and punched in 9-1-1.

8 Catch, As Catch Can

The ringing phone demanded to be answered, but John LaMoia hesitated. In Crimes Against Persons the telephone was its own kind of crapshoot, its own lottery. The detective that answered a call automatically accepted whatever case presented itself, sometimes a murder worthy of his time, but mostly domestics. Beatings with baseball bats, stabbings with kitchen knives, gunshot wounds of every variety—it was enough to keep a man like LaMoia single. Enough for him to give it time to let someone else catch this one.

He'd had one bit of good news, and he felt reluctant to spoil it with some worthless case that would demand his time: A truck driver had read a story about Mary-Ann Walker and had called in that he'd seen a car parked on the bridge right before midnight. He hadn't gotten a good look at the driver, but LaMoia had put a detective on a telephone follow-up (the trucker was currently on a run to Boise) to try to get a decent description of events. When the trucker returned to town, they would follow up yet again.

His office cubicle was personalized with a *Sports Illustrated* swimsuit calendar, an audaciously pink rabbit's foot hanging from a thumbtack, a collection of classified newspaper ads, each offering a Chevy Camaro, and a *Life in Hell* comic-strip frame. His home, eight to twelve hours a day, or night, or holiday. Never mind the razzing he took for the pressed blue jeans, the ostrich cowboy boots, the deerskin jacket. He, and only one other CAP detective, carried a sergeant's shield. If he didn't want to answer a cold call, then he wouldn't.

Finally he picked up the phone—duty overcoming reason.

"LaMoia."

"Is this a detective? Am I speaking with a detective? I'd like to report a Peeping Tom."

He immediately had her in his mind as white, thirties, well educated. The caller-ID helped. The Market Inn catered to a certain set, a set that could make trouble for a detective.

He sat up in his chair and grabbed for a pen. Any homicide detective worth his salt would have paid attention to this call. Susan Hebringer, one of the two women missing from downtown, had reported a peeper twenty-four hours prior to her going missing. An alarm sounded in LaMoia's brain—he'd caught a good call.

"Sergeant, ma'am. Crimes Against Persons. It's my squad."

She whispered into the receiver. "He's . . . right . . . across . . . the . . . street. Right now. I can see him over there."

"Let's stay calm, okay?" He checked the clock and wrote down the time: 7:38 P.M. "I'm assuming you're in the Market Inn. What floor?"

"Five."

"Do you happen to know what direction you're facing?"

"No."

"The water? Do you have a water view?" LaMoia spun around to face the map of the city and the clearance board above it that tracked which cases remained active. *Hebringer* and *Randolf* were up there in red marker with Boldt's name in the Lead column. They'd both been up there way too long.

"The living room. If I'm facing the water, this guy's to my right."

"North. Okay. Fifth floor. And you are currently where?"

"In bed."

"Alone?"

"Yes, alone." Indignant. Afraid.

"Clothed, or unclothed?"

"Not clothed, no. There's a robe on the floor."

"I'd rather you not move, if he's still there."

"He has binoculars, I think."

LaMoia's pulse pounded at his ears. A peeper with binocu-lars. *Susan Hebringer.*

"I'm going to ask you to sit tight. I'm going to take your room number and call you back on my cell phone. I'm maybe five minutes away, max. I'll have patrol cars in the area in less than that. The key here is not to give this guy reason to bail. If he thinks you've made him, he's out of there."

"I *want* him out of there."

"I understand that, Ms. . . . Your name please?"

He wrote down the particulars and practically begged her to remain in bed and to act calm. He made the calls on the run for the elevator. For a lousy peeper report, this would be the biggest show of manpower SPD had ever mobilized.

Susan Hebringer. If he had time, he'd get a call to Boldt. If not Boldt, then Matthews: top of the lineup; he needed the heavy hitters.

Assuming his role as commanding officer, LaMoia directed dis-patch to put out an 041 for the Bay Tower construction site. Officers in two patrol cars responded within seconds and were advised to enter the area "cloaked," with a BOL (Be On Look-out) issued for an adult male possibly fleeing the area, possibly in possession of a pair of binoculars or a telescope. Another three foot soldiers called in, all in the general vicinity, and once advised of this fact, LaMoia used them to bracket the area in case the guy slipped the two teams from the patrol cars.

With just five minutes to act, he felt he'd done as much as humanly possible to throw a net around this peeper. The phone call to Boldt's residence put him onto voice mail, and he left a cryptic message to return the call. He asked dispatch to send Boldt a page. A call to Matthews paid off—she was on her way over.

He juggled all this while keeping an open channel and something of a running dialogue with Melissa Dunkin, still curled up under a cotton sheet in suite 514. When Dunkin reported the peeper gone, LaMoia dialed up the urgency to his people on the ground. Ten minutes later, fifteen minutes after receiving the call from Dunkin, a search was on in the construction site with LaMoia fearing they'd lost him. Thirty minutes later, that search included fifteen patrolmen, the foreman of the construction site, and a vice president of the company putting up the building.

By the time the construction site was crawling with law enforcement, LaMoia found himself sipping coffee in the company of a visibly shaken Melissa Dunkin, who had eschewed the go-juice in favor of vodka on the rocks from little minibar bottles with tiny aluminum caps.

Dunkin wore a dark wool suit that she'd thrown on hastily, judging by the wrinkled and incorrectly buttoned blouse. Matthews arrived in blue jeans and a T-shirt, looking great. Introductions were followed by the explanation that the prosecuting attorney's office no longer permitted a male detective to interview a woman without a female officer present. The truth, it was hardly why Matthews was there. A patrol officer would have satisfied regs. LaMoia wanted Matthews "to look under the hood," and she was present to willingly oblige.

"A dot-com in Redmond?" he asked.

"Yes."

"But you did tourist stuff around town here today."

"After lunch. Yes," Dunkin said.

"Shopping mostly?" Matthews asked.

"Not only shopping, but it included shopping. Yes. The aquarium. Pioneer Square. The monorail."

"A busy day," LaMoia said.

"Very."

Matthews asked, "And did you then, at any time, sense that you might be being followed or watched?"

"Not at all. Not in the least. My God, you think this guy was *following me*?"

LaMoia recapped. "You came back to the hotel, locked the door to your room, pulled the drapes—as far as they'd go—and undressed for a bath."

"That's correct."

"You were in a state of undress only twice when outside the bathroom," he repeated from his notes. "The beer, and in bed after the bath."

"I was in the tub," she reminded, going on to describe her arrangement of using the door's full-length mirror to afford her a view of the television.

This was a new one for LaMoia, and so he had her show him. He placed a hotel towel into the damp tub, stepped in, and sat down. She aimed the door until he could see the bedroom's armoire. She asked for him to verify the angle.

"Yeah, there," he said, stopping her. "I got the television, but I'm also looking right out that window at my men over there on the construction site."

"He had a view of me," she mumbled. He didn't know if her slurred tone was a product of the booze or shock. "I think he had binoculars. He was holding something in his hands."

LaMoia believed with certainty that a perv peeping a naked woman would most certainly be holding *something* in his hand, but he didn't comment. Instead, he asked, "A camera?"

"Oh . . . God! You think? What, I'm going to find myself circulating the Internet?"

LaMoia doubted there was a lot of demand for pictures of naked middle-aged execs, even on the "Internet-ional House of Porncake," as he called the Web, but he bit his tongue. "Let me ask you this, Ms. Dunkin, and I apologize in advance for the way this may sound, but is your business with the Redmond dot-com of such a nature that advantage might be gained by . . . influencing you in any way?"

"Blackmail?"

"Influence can take many forms."

"It's an LBO."

"Hostile or favorable?"

"I refuse to think—"

LaMoia interrupted. "Thankfully, you don't have to. That's why you brought me in on this—us—we do the thinking for you." He offered her his well-practiced smile. "We consider everything—every possible scenario—and then go about eliminating them, one by one. The more options we eliminate, and the more quickly we eliminate them, the sooner we're on the most probable set of circumstances, the sooner we're on a suspect and putting that person away for this. It's as simple as that."

"All parties involved support this buyout," she said. "This has nothing to do with that."

LaMoia was inclined to believe likewise but also didn't want to jump to the conclusion that she'd just been peeped by a serial kidnapper responsible for Hebringer and Randolf. He thought about Boldt, wondering why his lieutenant hadn't returned his call.

LaMoia considered bringing SID techs into the room to determine the likely line of sight; that, in turn, might suggest the exact spot the perv had been standing. From the suite he could see his guys scouring the construction site across the street.

Dunkin saw this too, and for the first time it occurred to her that the police were working a little hard for a simple peeper report. "Hey," she said, "what's with all the guys over there anyway?"

"They're looking for evidence."

"I understand that, but why, exactly?"

Matthews said, "Hopefully to help identify the person responsible."

"You do this for a peeper? A sergeant *and* a lieutenant? An evidence team? Am I in some kind of trouble here that I'm not aware of?"

"Maybe you'd better sit down, ma'am." LaMoia indicated the padded bench at the end of the bed.

"This may take a minute to explain," Matthews said.

Dunkin kept looking out the window. Several more officers had arrived to pull yellow tape around an area of the construction site.

"There have been some disappearances," LaMoia said.

"Women," Matthews added.

Melissa Dunkin sank to the edge of the bed and listened in stunned amazement.

It wasn't long before the hotel bedroom hosted an elaborate setup of tripods, measuring sticks, and a portable laser meant to re-create the angle from which the perv would have been able to view the room.

A Japanese-American SID tech wearing a Don Henley World Tour T-shirt called out for LaMoia. He showed him the setup and explained that the laser would "lay a frozen rope" out the window, across the street to the construction site. He switched on the laser, allowed it to warm up, and then sprayed a fine powder into the room. A tiny stream of bright green light hung in the dusty air.

"You do the voodoo very well," LaMoia said.

The radio crackled. "Got it," a deep voice reported. One of the guys across the way had located the beam and was waving back at them as he spoke on the radio.

LaMoia said, "I want the mirror shot out of the bathtub as well. Combine them and have that section of the platform over there dusted for prints, photographed, you name it."

"No problem."

"It *is* a problem," LaMoia corrected. "It's just not your problem."

Less than an hour later, LaMoia, Matthews, and two SID techs stood on the fifth floor of the construction site. The laser work had identified a square yard of floor space where the peeper had stood. On the edge of that area, delineated by crime scene tape, a tiny plastic stand held a two-inch, yellow plastic triangular tag bearing the numeral 7 that indicated several small piles of geometric mud and dirt presumed to be, because of the vague pattern it formed, discharge from a shoe or boot sole.

The construction elevator stopped, clanged open, and a silhouette of a fairly big man emerged. LaMoia identified Lou Boldt by the determined stride of his brisk walk.

"Hey, Sarge." LaMoia continued to address his lieutenant by his former rank, the same rank, the same job that LaMoia now occupied. Even in the relative dark of the construction site, Boldt looked tired and worn. LaMoia put this off to Susan Hebringer's disappearance. Some said he was having trouble at home; others claimed he was sick. But LaMoia knew the true source of

Boldt's physical decline, whether his colleagues understood it or not.

"Good work, John," Boldt said, shaking hands with his sergeant as they met. He nodded cordially at Matthews.

"Shoe treads," said the evidence guy, a little overeager for recognition. Boldt had a Norman Schwarzkopf reputation within the department. Newcomers always sucked up to him.

LaMoia said, "Maybe it's nothing more than some hump working his joystick."

Boldt looked to Matthews for confirmation. "He stayed in here a long time. He had at least a couple of opportunities for full frontals of her. Lots of time with her stretched out on the bed—also naked. If it was masturbatory, as John's implying, it would have been over much sooner."

"Maybe the guy's on Viagra," LaMoia said.

Fighting a grin, she said, "*Another* explanation would be that it wasn't masturbatory at all—but a collection phase, subsequent to trolling and prior to—"

"Abduction," Boldt said, completing her thought.

"A possibility is all," she said, "but yes."

Upon learning, after the fact, that Susan Hebringer had reported a Peeping Tom to police just prior to her disappearance, CAP's homicide squad had worked closely with Special Assaults to chase down each and every reported incident of sexual harassment and voyeurism, focusing a great deal of attention on any such reports in the downtown corridor, or filed by downtown residents. Uniformed patrols had been alerted to pay special attention to vacant buildings, billboards, parking garages, and construction sites—all possible viewing platforms for the peeper. Private security firms directly responsible for these same structures were contacted as well.

"Do we have any idea how long he was up here?"

LaMoia held his flashlight between his teeth while consulting his notes to make sure he had it right. Boldt liked it right the first time. "The vic personally witnessed him out here for twelve minutes. Digital alarm clock on the bedside," he explained. "Could've easily been a lot longer than that, since she was in the tub for over twenty and on the bed snoozing for an undetermined time."

"Any fluids or emissions up here?" Matthews asked the SID technician.

"Nothing to the naked eye so far. We could Luminol and the like, if you want." Under black light, when reacting with the chemical agent Luminol, human blood glowed green. Other tests existed for bodily fluids of so-called secretors—people whose blood contained a set of specific blood proteins.

LaMoia answered, "We want."

Boldt added, "Please. Any tricks you've got to detect saliva or semen. And if we come up with anything, I'd like it DNAed and run against the state and the fed's databases. Whether you get a hit or not, I want everything kept on file, and full written reports."

"Got it."

"Along with every girder up here, I want you to dust for prints on the stairway railing at every landing, both sides of the turn." He answered the technician's curious expression: "It's where people take hold. Just do it."

He signaled LaMoia and Matthews to step away, and the three shared a moment of privacy.

"Anything?" Boldt asked.

LaMoia looked across to Dunkin's hotel room. The Japanese tech was waving at him. LaMoia felt stupid waving back but he did so. These lab guys would never be cops.

"She'd done tourist stuff," LaMoia answered. "Some shopping."

"Anything specific in the shopping? Lingerie, swimsuit, anything that would have had her outside of a changing room partially clothed or at least wearing less than her street clothes?"

"I should've asked that," LaMoia was ashamed to admit. Boldt had been a paper shuffler for a couple years now yet still had better instincts than any two street detectives combined.

"Was it random?" Boldt asked.

"The million-dollar question."

"Your gut check?" Boldt requested.

Matthews shook her head no. LaMoia said, "Not random. Deliberate. But I got serious problems with that: Even if he trolls the tourist spots, even if he follows 'em to their hotels or their condos, how the flock does he know what room she's in?"

"Unless it's the other way around," Boldt suggested.

They'd worked these angles raw back at the Public Safety Building. For the sake of hearing it aloud, LaMoia said, "He spots 'em from up here—wherever—then waits for them to leave the hotel, and knowing what they look like, he stalks them. For whatever reason, at least twice he grabbed them."

Matthews said, "Timing and location—those are your reasons. Nothing more complicated than that, which opens up the possibility—depending on why he took off—that our Ms. Dunkin just made his list."

LaMoia told Boldt, "She leaves town tomorrow. Taxi, straight to the airport. He won't be following her."

"Lucky for her. Too bad for us," Boldt said.

"We could still bait him," LaMoia suggested. "Install some babe on one of our squads to strip in front of windows."

Matthews said, "I wonder who'd be volunteering to oversee that operation."

LaMoia mugged at her.

Boldt was not happy. "The problem is it's *not* a specific hotel, a single building. Hebringer and Randolf both lived here. Ten blocks apart. You can't bait every town house, every hotel."

They'd been around this track enough times back in the situation room. Weeks, even months of it now. Boldt was in rough shape, under fire from the press, the brass, the families of the missing women, and even his own wife.

"So maybe Hebringer getting peeped was nothing but shitty coincidence," LaMoia said, referring to what they knew about the missing woman. "Drawing a look from us when it doesn't deserve it. Maybe it's got us by a nose ring when it's nothing but a black hole. Maybe I walked into that tonight."

"Maybe not, John," Matthews said. "We don't ignore this," she told Boldt. "His sticking around—that counts for something."

"Keep it up," Boldt told them. Pointing to the cordoned-off area, he said, "Make him talk to us, would you, please?" He added with a snarl, "A confession would be nice."

Doc Dixon, a big bear of a man with hooded eyes and a wide face, signaled Matthews and won her attention before pointing toward his receptionist, who manned a sliding glass window looking out onto the medical examiner's waiting room. His sign meant Langford "Lanny" Neal, the possible boyfriend of their Jane Doe, had just arrived and was being kept waiting.

Matthews acknowledged, checked the wall clock, and debated calling LaMoia one more time, resigning herself to the fact that a phone call wouldn't help the traffic situation. Nothing would help Seattle's traffic, not even an act of God.

Feeling obliged to do so, she'd left a message at the fish dock where she'd met with Ferrell Walker, providing the time and location of the identification at the medical examiner's office, hoping the message might not reach the grief-stricken brother in time. But one eye continually tracked to the reception window, wondering if Walker might appear.

Matthews had never liked the medical examiner's office and avoided it whenever possible. Dixon ran the ME's more as a doctor than a bureaucrat, displaying a keen interest in each and every body that passed through his doors and the legal system that claimed control of them in death. Matthews didn't have the same kinship or friendship with Dixon that Boldt shared, but through Boldt she had acquired a profound respect for the man. Where most of the homicide detectives had developed at least an uneasy comfort at the ME's, Matthews, a rare visitor, found the basement setting, the medicinal smell, and the overpowering silence repulsive. Perhaps her feelings stemmed from the doctor-office look of the place: tube lighting, gray carpet, white lateral filing cabinets, the efficient young men and women spanning Seattle's ethnic palate, all dressed in white lab coats, some carrying clipboards, some answering phones. It felt too *normal*. One expected something more dismal and final—sweating rock walls and bars on the window, a doctor with a speech impediment, a nurse with a limp. This felt more like her OB-GYN's office. This setting didn't work for her at all.

LaMoia entered, his sergeant's shield clipped to the pocket of the deerskin jacket. He winked at the receptionist, an African American woman who had to be in her sixties, low-fived one of the young docs who made a point of catching up to him, and took Matthews around the waist, steering her toward the double swinging doors that led into the "meat locker"—the primary receiving room that housed twenty-one refrigerated drawers and sported three stainless-steel autopsy tables with drains, lights, and video cameras. There was at least one other autopsy room that she knew of—more of a private surgery suite where Dixon or his chief assistant occasionally tackled a sensitive or particularly gruesome case. She abruptly put on the brakes, not allowing LaMoia to escort her through those doors before it was necessary, and her effort had the unintended effect of turning LaMoia toward her and briefly making contact with her. They bounced off each other, gently, and for a moment there was only that contact lingering in the nerve endings of her skin.

"That our guy out there?" LaMoia stepped back from her, keeping it business.

"Yes. Langford Neal," she said, giving her jacket a small straightening tug. "Boyfriend, or former boyfriend, if it's Mary-Ann Walker in there."

"And the doc thinks it is."

"The doc got hold of a better driver's license photo than I did. One of her eyes, the left, I think, is still where it belongs, and it's apparently a match for color: blue. Height's about right. Weight could be right, discounting for saturation and bloat. I've got a call in to the brother to try to locate dental records for her."

LaMoia glanced in the direction of the reception area. "Let me tell you something about our little angel, Neal. Two convictions as well as a number of complaints from previous love interests. This guy plays rough. He served thirty days in county for one of the convictions. The second, he was in for six months, out in four."

The news moved Neal up the list in both their minds. She understood the added spring to LaMoia's step now—he loved having the jump on information. "That certainly helps," she said, "but we shouldn't lose sight of the brother, either."

"Ten-to-one she was killed in or near the boyfriend's pad, given the underwear, the bare feet, and the rest of it."

"The brother could have harbored jealousy and anger over his being deserted for Neal. That's powerful stuff."

"Neal has two convictions for knocking women around. You kidding me? Not losing sight of the brother, that's okay. But we focus on Neal. If he does, in fact, ID the body as her, then from what you were saying, your take is to run him straight up to the bull pen and have a go at him. Is that right?"

"That, or use a conference room here."

"You're thinking that this viewing may put him off-balance— her being so ripe and all—and that we pounce while we have the opportunity."

"You're a lot smarter than you look."

He took it in stride. LaMoia had his timing down to an art form. He kept it business—for the time being. This put her on edge, her defenses at the ready.

"You want to sit this one out, I'm okay with that. You're way too . . . sweet . . . for a floater. Especially one that's been in the meat locker for a few extra days."

She knew she could handle it, she'd seen plenty of dead bodies, some in dreadful condition, but it didn't mean she *wanted* to. "I'll take that as a compliment. I think."

"You think too much," he said, meeting her eyes to drive home his point. LaMoia had large brown eyes and knew how to use them to effect.

"Meaning?"

"You gotta teach yourself to *feel*, Matthews." He leaned against one of the two swinging doors. He wasn't going to make her follow inside. "You're all engine. It's the handling that counts." Everything came down to cars for LaMoia. "You get that down, you'll be just about perfect."

"Who said I wanted to be perfect?" But he didn't answer her. He left her there to think about it. The door flapped shut behind him. Timing was everything.

Decades earlier, in municipalities across the country, medical examiner and coroner offices had learned to separate the individual making an identification from the room containing the body, as the smell tended to cause fainting and vomiting. Some used video, some a window—most used both, as did the King County Medical Examiner's Office, where a color TV was mounted to the left of a narrow window that housed a venetian blind controllable from the inside.

Lanny Neal was handsome in a ski bum kind of way, cocksure of himself judging by the rigid shoulders, the smug expression, and his willingness to blatantly check out Matthews, leveling his gaze and drinking her in, head to foot.

She knew she should wait to question him, but he'd fired the first salvo with that rude survey of her topography, and she fell victim to the challenge.

"When did you last see Mary-Ann?" she asked.

The question didn't rattle Neal in the least—although La-Moia looked a little uncomfortable. Neal remained calm and collected, as if he were there applying for a job. This further irritated Matthews.

"Couple nights ago."

"How many nights ago?"

"Saturday, I guess."

"You guess, or you know?" Matthews pressed.

"Saturday night. Late."

"You weren't worried about her?"

"Pissed was more like it."

"You didn't report her missing. Why's that?"

"Why should I? She blew me off. Her tough luck."

Mary-Ann was gone. On to the next. Matthews knew the attitude. She asked him about the last time he'd seen Mary-Ann. Where they were at the time, what Mary-Ann had been wearing, her mood.

LaMoia interrupted. "I think they're ready for us."

A plain white sheet on a stainless-steel gurney filled the video screen. LaMoia knocked on the glass and the blinds came up like a curtain being raised. A hand appeared, on both the video and through the glass, drawing back the sheet and revealing the remains of a woman's head, at once both pathetic and terrifying. The lips were grotesquely distended, as if pumped full of air. An eyelid had been stitched shut, apparently to spare Neal the sight of an empty socket.

Matthews heard herself catch her breath. LaMoia remained intractable. Neal stared at her for a long time, exhaled slowly, shook his head slightly, and looked away with glassy eyes. It was not the reaction she would have expected of a murderer—she and LaMoia met eyes and she knew he felt much the same—leaving her to wonder just how good an actor Lanny Neal might be. This, in turn, prepared her for the Q&A she was already planning in her head.

"Yeah," Neal said, still looking away from the window.

"Mary-Ann Walker?" LaMoia asked.

Neal looked a little green, his skin carrying a light sheen that hadn't been there moments before. "You got a men's room around here?"

LaMoia directed him down the hall, meeting eyes once more with Matthews and communicating his own surprise at Neal's reaction.

The commotion came from the front of the office, where the receptionist stood out of her chair too late to prevent the entrance of a man wearing a torn sweatshirt and filthy blue jeans.

It took Matthews a moment to identify the late arrival as Ferrell Walker.

Walker paused in the middle of the medical examiner's central office looking lost yet determined. Matthews immediately picked up on the kid's frenetic energy. It jumped around the room like sparking electricity. He held the attention of everyone in the office as heads lifted and a silence of apprehension descended. These people had no idea he was a grieving brother. This was the wild man on the subway, the lunatic in the hotel lobby. Of the employees in the room, only the receptionist made any attempt to intervene, and she reconsidered after taking a few steps toward the kid. Lanny Neal didn't yet see him.

Matthews left the small hallway that offered the viewing window and moved across the central room toward Walker, who avoided her by closing in on Neal. The fingers of his right hand danced like a gunslinger's.

"Don't!" Matthews shouted, but her reprimand had the unintended effect of stopping not Walker, but Neal, allowing Walker to close the distance even faster. Matthews *knew,* without knowing, what Walker had in mind; *knew,* without knowing, that for a few precious seconds Walker remained impressionable; *knew,* without knowing, that she was going to have to talk Walker down.

Walker, now to her left, lunged with reptilian speed, pinning Neal, who was a good deal larger than him. Down the small hallway, LaMoia drew his weapon instinctively, but Matthews waved LaMoia off as the curved blade of Walker's fillet knife flashed through the air and came to rest against Neal's throat.

"The question you have to ask yourself," Matthews began, addressing Walker as if she'd rehearsed for the role, "is not whether you believe Mr. Neal harmed your sister, or whether you think yourself capable of doing harm to him; it's not even about the prison time you will serve—you'll get a life sentence for something like this, Ferrell, meaning Mr. Neal will have destroyed both you and Mary-Ann—the question is what Mary-Ann would say to you, were she here at this moment, whether or not she would approve of you destroying your own life in an effort to save hers, a life already beyond saving." She inched closer, now fifteen feet away.

She won his attention, though with no immediate results. The blade remained against Neal's throat.

She said, "Mr. Neal identified Mary-Ann just now. She's here, and you can see her for yourself if you want." She pounced on what she believed would be his greatest desire—to see his sister again—never taking her eyes off Walker as she pointed toward the hallway where LaMoia waited. She had to steer him back into his grief and away from anger and blame. "Do you want to see Mary-Ann again, Ferrell? That would be nice, wouldn't it? Believe me—you keep up like this, you'll never see her again. You'll be in prison when it comes time to bury her, and your actions here, right now, will have delayed any possible prosecution of Mr. Neal, for whatever role he may or may not have had in your sister's death."

Lanny Neal strained through clenched teeth, "This . . . is . . . bullshit."

Walker's eyes danced.

Matthews moved yet another step closer. Twelve feet now. "You're lying to yourself, Ferrell, if you think you're doing Mary-Ann a favor. You think murdering a man in cold blood is going to help her? How? Do you think it's going to help *your* situation in any way? You're making a lot of trouble here." She nodded at LaMoia. She wanted Walker's attention divided. "John! Is this going to save you trouble?"

"Me? I'm looking at writing up reports for the next week if this guy makes the wrong choice. Not doing me any favors."

"No," Matthews agreed. She extended her open hand toward Walker. "Once you pass me that knife, this incident is closed. Do you hear me, Ferrell? Closed. There's only Mr. Neal's word against your own. The sergeant and I, the people in this office: No one saw anything. A grieving brother got a little out of control. Big deal."

LaMoia said, "Where's the foul?"

"He did this to her!" Walker said, his voice raw.

"Bullshit I did," Neal groaned.

"We don't know what happened," Matthews said. "That's still being determined. If you're right, then you're right. But it's a risky assumption on your part. And what if you're wrong, Ferrell? What then? What if you *kill* an innocent man here to-day? Where's that leave you? Mary-Ann's killer at large, and you, in jail, behind bars, where you can't do anything to help us. We need your help here, Ferrell. You're her only surviving kin—that's hugely important to our investigation."

Walker tensed instead of handing over the knife.

A man's thunderous voice boomed from the far side of the room. "Put down the knife, young man!" Doc Dixon, sounding like God himself. Behind Matthews, and to her right.

Walker glanced over in that direction, increasing the pressure on Neal's throat as he did so.

Dixon said, "You don't use a knife as a weapon in the basement of a hospital." It sounded so convincing. "There are a few hundred trained doctors in the floors immediately above us. Emergency rooms. Surgical suites. I'm a doctor. Several of my assistants in this room are also doctors. We're *not* going to let him die. No matter what you try, we're going to save him. The moment you try anything, Sergeant LaMoia over there will either put a bullet in you or break every bone in your body. And another thing to think about: No one here is going to be in any great hurry to help you, believe you me."

LaMoia was maybe ten feet behind her now. "This is one way, do not enter."

Matthews said, "There's a legal process that's meant to handle this. It's a process that works, Ferrell. Knives don't work. Trust me."

"Knives are messy," Dixon said. "You mess up my carpet and I'm going to personally beat the spit out of you."

Dixon moved for the first time, growing ever larger in her peripheral vision, cobra-like, as he approached. Matthews had somehow overlooked Dixon's formidable presence all these years. Suddenly she understood much more clearly the attraction between Dixon and Boldt—birds of a feather.

Walker's pale eyes flipped between Dixon and Matthews. "Stop right there," he warned.

Matthews took a step and said, "Hand me the knife and it

stops. That's the only way it stops. Put Mary-Ann in this room, Ferrell. Take the rest of us out of here. It's only you, Mr. Neal, and Mary-Ann. Put Mary-Ann right here where I'm standing—you can do that, I know you can—and then ask yourself what she'd say. How would she react to your threatening Mr. Neal this way? What would she tell you to do?" She took yet another step toward him. Six feet. "Don't listen to me; don't listen to Doc Dixon; you just listen to her, to Mary-Ann."

Walker stared at her. She said, "Drop the knife, Ferrell."

To her amazement, Walker dropped the knife.

LaMoia rushed him, tackled him, and had him on the floor, Dixon assisting.

Lanny Neal leaned over him. "You worthless piece of shit."

Matthews retrieved the knife from the carpet. It was heavier, sturdier, than she had imagined.

LaMoia cuffed Walker out of routine but then wondered aloud if they should book him, and Matthews put it onto Neal to make the decision to press charges or not. A grief-stricken brother facing a possible viewing of his murdered sister's body. How tough would the legal system be on Walker?

"Murdered?" Neal said, repeating her.

"Well, at least you're listening, Mr. Neal. That's a good place to start."

10 **The Debt**

"Where is he?" Ferrell Walker asked. He occupied one of the two guest chairs in Doc Dixon's spacious office.

Matthews patrolled the area behind Dixon's desk, where, at head level, the room's only window looked out at ankle-height to the sidewalk above.

"You need to convince me, Mr. Walker, that we're making the right decision concerning your release."

"The other guy's got him, right? The guy who tackled me?"

"You're not helping your case any."

"If I was going to do anything to that piece of shit, it would already be done. Okay? You think I'm going to have a chance like that again?" He tracked her constantly as she paced, his deep eye sockets fixed onto her every movement. "You saved me."

"I didn't save anyone. I intervened, and on Mr. Neal's behalf, not yours." *Do not twist this around to your liking.* "If we release you, we need some reassurance that you're capable of controlling your emotions, your anger."

"I lost my head." He grinned at her, cool and collected, like so many of the street kids they dealt with. "Is that what I'm supposed to say?"

"There is no 'supposed to,' " she lied. In fact, that, or something close to it, was what he was supposed to say, but she didn't appreciate the irreverent tone. "And it's not what you say but what you do that matters to us."

"Okay. I get it now. If you let me go, then I owe you," Walker said. "You're saying I owe you something. Like a snitch. That kind of thing. Right? Listen, no problem."

"That's not at all what I'm saying."

"I get it. It's okay. I want to help you nail Lanny."

"It's not okay. You do not owe *me*, you owe it to Mary-Ann to let us do our jobs. You owe Lanny Neal the right for us to bring evidence against him or not. He is not guilty simply because he was her boyfr—"

"He hit her. Did things to her."

"And we'll look into all that. But in point of fact, Mr. Walker, a homicide investigation typically looks at the immediate family first, relationship partners second, and close friends last. *You* are the immediate family, the one we should be looking at first, not Mr. Neal."

"So look at me," he said, opening his arms to her.

"Did you kill your sister, Mr. Walker?" For Matthews it was a question that begged to be asked. She studied his body language carefully.

He stared at her, dumbfounded, cocked his head and said, "Who *are* you people? He *beat* her. He said he'd do this, and now he's done it."

He displayed none of the reactions she might have expected from a guilty party—a pregnant pause, rapid eye movement or breaking eye contact, adjusting himself in the chair. Even so, the idea would not leave her entirely and lingered in the back of her mind. Neal had the more likely motive, Neal the opportunity. And, if what they knew about Neal was true, he had the sordid history as well. Walker's rage, his vengeance, was so prevalent that it filled the room. Assigning guilt was an easy jump for her.

He said, "From what I'm hearing I owe you a favor for helping me out. Stopping me like that. I'm good with that. I didn't want him seeing Anna before I did. I was . . . upset. Okay? I can't thank you enough for what you did."

"It can't happen again," she said.

"I realize that. I'm sorry." The student cowering to the teacher; the little boy who knows better.

She cautioned him, "We will instruct Mr. Neal to file a restraining order against you. It'll be his choice to do that or not. That doesn't bring charges against you, but it serves to put you on notice. It draws a line in the sand that you'd better not cross."

"Anna and I, we repay our debts," he said.

"*There is no debt.* Are you hearing anything I'm saying?"

"I'll be a good boy."

"Don't push me, Mr. Walker."

"Lanny Neal is the one who needs restraining. You see to that, Lieutenant Matthews, and you'll have no problem from me."

"It's not how it works," she said. "You're damned close to threatening a police officer."

"She was murdered. You said so yourself. You have her killer in custody. So do something about it. You need help, I'll help. You helped *me* out. I won't forget that."

"You'd better forget it. That is *not* the point!" She'd lost her patience and her composure. Walker seemed to take this as a victory.

"He broke her legs, didn't he?"

Matthews felt a stab of surprise in her chest.

"You see? I *can* help you, if you'll let me. He said he'd do that . . . said he'd break both her legs if she ever tried to leave him." He watched her reaction, confirmation, and his eyes welled with tears. "He broke her legs, didn't he? Oh, God, poor Anna."

"I'm not at liberty to discuss the particulars."

He sat back. "Look at it this way: I didn't want your help either. Just now, I didn't want you getting in my face, in my *head* like that. But you did and it worked out for the better. Right? See? All I'm saying is . . . sometimes we get help when we don't see it coming. It's a good thing. I can help you like that."

"We're done here," she announced. "We'll want to speak with you again, and when we do we'll find you at your workplace."

"Unless I find you first," he said childishly, meeting eyes with her and straining to communicate something more.

She winced. "Go back to work. Go back to your life. If anything comes up regarding the investigation I'll make sure you're informed."

"You see? Another favor."

"That's *standard procedure,* Mr. Walker. That is *not* a favor. None of my actions should be construed as personal favors. Any such misinterpretation—"

"Save it," he said, rising quickly to close the gap between them. She could smell the overpowering fish odors and his sour perspiration. She nearly retched. "The only question I have is whether or not you give me back my fish knife."

Matthews glanced down at Dixon's desk where the gunsmoke gray blade rested by Dixon's pen stand.

"That knife has history," Walker said. "Family history."

It felt wrong returning that knife to him, but it felt equally wrong to confiscate the one item that was probably all he had left of his family. "Against my better judgment," she said, holding it by the blade and offering the knife back.

"I won't forget this," he said.

She closed her eyes as he left the office, torn between reversing her decision and watching him go. But then he was gone, the decision made for her.

Crossing the ME's to a conference room where LaMoia held

Neal, she put away her thoughts of Ferrell Walker. As she swung open the door that led out of the offices and into the small reception area littered with magazines, Matthews caught sight of a brown sheriff's uniform. The medical examiner's office was a county, not city, department, meaning KCSO had as much or more business here than SPD. Nonetheless, she knew in advance, knew instinctively, who this uniform belonged to.

The wide shoulders turned, the blond head swiveled, and just before the door shut she caught a glimpse of the profile of Deputy Sheriff Nathan Prair.

What business did Nathan Prair have here? Was it Mary-Ann Walker or was it Daphne Matthews? She turned around quickly, hoping he hadn't seen her. She hurried toward the conference room, a part of her wanting escape; she knocked once, turned the handle, and stepped inside, her heart beating a little too quickly.

"Why don't you walk us through the events of the night Mary-Ann went missing," LaMoia said.

Neal's erratic eye movement, constant swallowing to fight dry mouth, and perspiring upper lip warned Matthews to pay strict attention to the lies she felt were certain to follow. Here was more what she'd been expecting of Walker when she'd put the question to him. By prior agreement, she'd let LaMoia kick things off. At an appropriate time, yet to be determined, she would take over and he would be the one to stay quiet. If they sensed they had a live suspect, they would finish up by double-teaming Neal, at which point Matthews would play the hard-ass, and LaMoia the more patient, reasonable cop, turning stereotypes on end and hoping to keep Neal guessing.

"We'd been at my mom's, the two of us. We'd had a couple drinks. Dinner at my mom's. My mom likes rum. We'd had a few rums, I guess."

LaMoia clarified, "This is you, Mary-Ann Walker, and your mother?"

"Right."

"State your mother's name, please."

"Frances. Frances Kelly Neal."

"You had dinner, the three of you. Which night was that?"

"Saturday."

LaMoia took a moment to make a point of counting backward. His favorite line of offense was to play the fool to begin with, slowly migrating to the hard-line cop any suspect learned to fear. "March twenty-second."

Neal said, "We come home after dinner . . . to my hang, you know? And went to bed. I watched the sports while she . . . you know, she was *busy*."

"Busy, how?"

"You know?"

"I'm afraid not."

"Busy." He pumped his cupped hand up and down. "Beneath the sheets."

"Ms. Walker was performing oral sex on you while you watched the sports news."

Neal grinned proudly, but he couldn't keep his eyes still. "That's it."

Lies, she thought, as LaMoia caught her attention and rolled his eyes.

"What time would that have been?" LaMoia asked.

"After dinner, like I said."

"That would be the local news?"

"Q-13."

"That would be Fox."

"That would be correct." He mimicked LaMoia, and the sergeant impressed Matthews with his ability to remain calm and not rise to the bait.

Neal liked to hear himself talk. That played in their favor. "She wanted some of that action for herself—if you know what I'm saying—and I wasn't exactly complaining, but—"

LaMoia interrupted. "We'll skip the play-by-play, if you don't mind. You did, or did not have intercourse with Mary-Ann Walker on Saturday, March twenty-second?"

"That's a 'did.' For sure."

Matthews asked, "Using a condom, or without?"

"That would be without." Neal gave her a tennis pro smile.

LaMoia said, "Following the intercourse, you watched more television, or read, or went to sleep, or what?"

"Slept. At least I did. Mary-Ann might have gone out the window."

"You want to explain that?"

"For a smoke," Neal clarified. "Can't stand that shit. She used the fire escape. Used it all the time. I saw her out there on the fire escape. It was later, a lot later. Probably for a smoke. Right? I saw her out there, yeah. I just said I did." Confusion fanned the edges of his eyes.

"Approximately what time was this?"

"Later."

"Can you be more precise?"

Neal glanced first to Matthews, then to LaMoia, as if hoping one of them might help him out. He pinched his temples between the fingers of his right hand and apparently appealed for divine intervention. She was beginning to put more faith in Walker's suspicions. Lanny Neal was a self-centered egotist who had a record of abusing his girlfriends. He didn't lie very well, despite what must have been a great deal of practice.

"I remember her out there . . . seeing her out there. I didn't like it when she went out there dressed like that. She never seemed to give a shit what she was wearing. Claimed no one could see her, so high up and all. And that's another thing—she don't even like heights, but for a smoke, shit, she'd climb the Space Needle. Anyway, she'd go out there in like a T-shirt and underwear, showing skin and all.

"She was talking," he continued. "At first I wondered who the fuck was out there with her. Then I saw the cordless phone was missing. She was out there on the fire escape on the goddamn phone with someone. Maybe it was the phone ringing that woke me up in the first place. And I *do* remember what time it was." This seemed to dawn upon him, and Matthews thought he was making it up as he went. "All twos flashing at me. Two twenty-two. The clock by the phone on her side of the bed. I remember that. Two, two, two. Flashing away. And I looked out the window, and there she was on the goddamn phone."

"Two twenty-two A.M."

"You ought to be talking to that brother of hers. Always begging her for money, bugging her. Punk-ass kid, blaming her for everything bad happening to him. Probably him on the phone. Probably him who did this to her."

"What exactly do you think happened to Mary-Ann?" LaMoia asked.

"How should I know? All disgusting like that, the way she was. Looked like she drowned or something. Is that right?"

"What exactly was Mary-Ann wearing at the time? Out on your fire escape."

"I just told you! Next to nothing."

"A description of that clothing could prove useful to the investigation."

"Well, she sure as shit wasn't going to go out there bare-ass again, you understand. Not after the last time. I'd caught her again—"

He stopped himself.

LaMoia met eyes with Matthews, communicating that they had their first real look at Langford Neal's inner workings. Interrogators lived for such moments.

LaMoia supplied, "You'd smack her around, let her know who was boss."

"I didn't say that."

"Did you smack her around that night, Lanny? Hit her upside the head, or knock her off the fire escape, or what? She was bleeding, wasn't she? She was bleeding and you didn't know what to do."

"That's bullshit. I seen her out there and I went back to sleep. End of story. She would'a had on butt floss. White butt floss. She always wore the same thing."

Matthews said, "Thong panties. And what about on top? A T-shirt? A blouse? A robe?"

"One of those camel-things."

"A camisole."

"Two humps right where they belong. Nice and tight."

Matthews cringed at his reckless confidence. "A camisole and thong underwear. No sweatshirt, no robe?"

"She's hot-blooded, I'm telling you. Went out there all the time in next to nothing. For a smoke. A sweatshirt—how the hell should I know? Does she own one? Yes. But that night it was a freak show anyway. Warm for a change. You can check that, right?"

LaMoia said, "We'll check all of your statement, Lanny. Every last word."

He looked briefly bewildered, but then regained his confidence and restated that the last time he'd seen her she'd been out on the fire escape. "Woke the next morning and she wasn't there. Not that that was all that unusual. She went to sleep later than me and got up earlier. Probably headed straight for a coffee hit, a Seattle's Best, down a few blocks. You should check with them. Right? They open at six, and she's always one of the first through the door."

"So her clothes were gone," LaMoia stated. "In the morning, I'm talking about—when you woke up, whatever else she'd been wearing—those clothes were gone?"

"What clothes? How the fuck would I know?" Clearly flustered, Neal shook his arms in front of himself as if his hands had gone to sleep. "She wore them to bed, that's all I'm saying."

LaMoia reviewed his notes. "A moment ago you said you fell asleep after having sex with Ms. Walker. That you fell asleep *after* the sex. Now you're saying she wore panties to bed? Can you be more precise?"

"She wore them to bed *before* I took them off her." He added, "And that would have been *after* the sports, *after* the hummer, to be *more precise.*"

"And what clothes if any, did she leave behind at your apartment that morning?"

"She's the one picks up, not me."

LaMoia said irritably, "So you're saying she cleaned house that morning, before she left for the coffee?"

"Listen, she had clothes at my place, okay? How the fuck do I know what was there and what wasn't? She lived there with me, don't forget. Right? Clothes? What? On the floor or something? How the hell would I know?"

Matthews thought the story was getting away from him. The little pauses. The rapid eye movement. She excused herself and left the conference room, returning a few minutes later with autopsy photographs of two different women.

She wasn't hoping to win a confession, to cause some Perry Mason moment in which Langford Neal hung his head, weeping, and detailed the events of that night. She did, however, intend to run Neal through a litmus test. If she came away with anything, she hoped to at least identify his lies and to make sense of his motivations for telling them. Making a legal case was not her responsibility. All that she wanted was the truth. Until the attorneys were invited in—Neal had yet to request one—she could basically say anything she wanted, could match him lie for lie. She knew how to use her looks against guys like Neal. Just before reentering the conference room, she tucked in her blouse and squared her shoulders, emphasizing her chest. Let him look all he wanted to. Let him be distracted.

She placed the photos in front of Neal. LaMoia knew they'd made the handoff—Neal now belonged to her. She said, "We had a similar fatality last year. Also a young, attractive woman. We're investigating possible connections."

"The connections being bridges and water," Neal said.

"And/or the men these women dated."

"You're looking at me for some head case that jumped off a bridge a year ago?"

"No, we're looking at you for Mary-Ann Walker, Mr. Neal." She made a stage show of looking over at LaMoia. "Who said anything about Mary-Ann jumping?"

"Not me," LaMoia answered.

"Nor did I," Matthews said.

"Try the papers, the television," Neal protested.

Matthews said, "Mary-Ann Walker did not jump, Mr. Neal."

"But you just said—"

"She was beaten badly, possibly raped, and subsequently was discovered in water wearing a torn thong underwear and a cotton camisole top—just exactly as you've now described for us. How she arrived into that water remains under investigation."

Neal lost the shit-eating grin.

"You're clearly a smart man," she lied. "A man who under-stands women. You don't have to tell me that some women get themselves into difficult spots. Make promises and change their minds. Get a little too drunk and ask for it and then beg off the sex with the old headache excuse. They cocktease a guy and then refuse to put out."

LaMoia did a double take on Matthews.

Neal looked uncertain.

"Right?" Matthews said.

"Yeah, sure. I'd buy that."

"And sometimes a guy's got to tune her up a little, let her know who's boss. Sober her up. There's a way this works and there's a way this doesn't work, and it doesn't work when she's in some drunken, willing mood one minute, and then an ice maiden the next."

Neal saw the trap then. "I . . . ah . . . I don't know what you're talking about."

"No?"

"No."

"We've got a half dozen prior complaints against you, Lanny. All of them are for taking a heavy hand with your girlfriends. You logged a thirty-day stint at county. You put a girl named Eileen Rimbauer in the emergency room with a broken collarbone. Are you aware that Mary-Ann Walker had five such emergency room visits in the last six months? Did she happen to tell you about those? Her brother knows, I'll tell you that. She claimed to have fallen down the stairs of the boat, said her hand got caught in a winch." She read all this as if it were printed on the page, which it was not. "Pretty lame excuses, you ask me. She also had some woman problems that make a lot more sense if some guy is playing it a little kinky and rough. So what you need to look at, Mr. Neal, is not the door, not my chest, not the detective, as you have been, but what happened that night. You need to look at the underlying circumstances that started whatever argument resulted between you, the conditions that escalated that particular argument into violence. We're cops, yes.

But believe it or not we're human. We've heard it all—there's nothing you can tell us that will surprise us. This being your third strike, with the battered-woman law in effect you're facing a serious uphill battle, if convicted. You want half a chance? Convince us that you and Mary-Ann had a disagreement that night, that things got a little out of hand. A disagreement takes two people, Mr. Neal. That's a whole lot better than some guy pounding on his woman for no reason whatsoever. Can we start there?"

"She was out on the fire escape. Talking on the phone maybe. I'm not sure about that. Smoking a cigarette, 'cause otherwise no way would she have been out there. I'm telling you, she did not like heights."

"Not to get away from you?"

"We had sex is all. Maybe I was rough. I don't remember. I was pretty loaded that night. But I'll tell you one thing: You never heard Mary-Ann complaining about the sex, believe me. She liked it rough. She asked for it rough. That night, out there on the fire escape, that's the last I seen of her."

"Two twenty-two A.M.," Matthews repeated.

"The woman hardly slept."

"You understand that where there are mitigating circumstances in a case—an argument, for instance—the investigating officer is required to take them into consideration. These things come out in trial no matter what. There's no sense for a detective to push for capital murder if there's a domestic case where the girlfriend was complicit—say, acting like a drunken slut one minute and going for a carving knife the next. You need to think about that, because a guy beats up a woman, the sides get drawn long before the jury sits down for the first time. Believe it." Neal wore shock in his eyes, which Matthews took as a small victory. "Am I getting through, Lanny?" she asked rhetorically.

"She was all fucked up in the head. All bent out of shape

over her asshole baby brother. Said she'd let him down, losing the fishing boat and everything. That she owed him big time. But shit, he was just working her. Mooching. Crying in his beer. I wanted her taking care of things around home. For us to get something going. But I'm telling you, she was all fucked up."

"Okay." Matthews took a deep breath and savored the surprise that he'd begun to open up.

"She'd been drinking a lot that night, got herself all dumb and loopy. We had the sex, you know, just like I said. Her on top, all angry like. Fast and furious and, I don't know, mean-spirited, you know? Like she didn't want to be doing it."

Matthews didn't like the next images that filled her head—sweating through the camisole, sticky hair, the slapping of flesh.

"Sometimes it was like that with her," Neal said, quieter for the first time. "A little strange like that. Like she wasn't really there, you know? Tripping out. The more I seen of her like that, the weirder it was, to tell the truth. She'd get *herself* off. It wasn't about me. It was like I wasn't there."

Matthews attempted to wipe those images from her mind, but they wouldn't fade. She spoke over them. "Was there anything that night in particular that the two of you argued about? Anything said that maybe'd come up the other times you'd seen her like this?"

"I'm telling you, she got the most pissed off when I brought up Ferrell, and how it was bugging me the way he never left her alone. Jesus, the guy was always showing up at the weirdest times. Sniveling about money and how she'd fucked everything up. And she didn't like me talking about him. Bitching about him. She'd pretty much taken care of him since their old man bit it. Her mom—I don't know nothing about her mom. Whether she bolted or croaked, or what. She could be dead, too, for all I know."

"So you argued about the brother," Matthews said.

"That night? Not that I remember. I'm telling you: We got back to my place and she went all horny on me. She's half undressed and going down on me practically before I got the tube on."

"According to you, she was out on your fire escape in her panties and a camisole top. Maybe a sweatshirt; you don't know. Can't remember. I'm assuming barefoot. And now, fast-forward, she's in the water." Matthews paused. "There are problems with your story, Mr. Neal. Are you aware of that? We started out with you and Mary-Ann pretty much in the same miserable condition. You watching your sports broadcast while she services you. Now you say she was oversexed and practically raping you. We started out with her getting up in the morning and heading out for coffee. But we know for a fact she ended up in the water the night before. How'd she get there?"

"How'd she get to the water?" Neal asked, as if he was suddenly on their side. "I'm telling you, I saw her out on the fire escape. Heard her talking on the phone."

He appeared less confident now. If there was a part of his story to exploit, it was Mary-Ann out on the fire escape. Matthews tried again. "How about this? Maybe she's still drunk out there on the fire escape. Maybe you've got the time wrong. Maybe she's drunk, tired, a little shaky still from the sex, and she smokes a cigarette and goes a little dizzy and goes right off that fire escape."

"Oh, yeah, I'm with you," LaMoia said.

"It wasn't like that," Neal objected.

"She's trying to help you out here," LaMoia said.

"She goes off the fire escape and she isn't getting up, and you, Mr. Neal, realize with your history this is not going to look right. Not good at all. Your half-naked girlfriend, carrying your sperm, at the bottom of your fire escape? How you gonna explain that one?"

LaMoia said, "But the condition of the body—that fits: going off the fire escape. That's good thinking, Lieutenant."

"It wasn't like that," Neal repeated.

"But to a jury? What you've got to ask yourself is how it'll look to a jury. 'Cause I've got to tell you—it's pretty damn convincing to me."

"To me too," LaMoia chimed in.

Neal wore a full face of sweat now, his eyes jumping between his two interrogators.

Matthews leaned into the suspect where he could smell her, where he couldn't avoid her. "But sadly for you, the truth always plays better. You know what I think? I think you hit Mary-Ann. I think you got angry with her and you struck her, and things went badly for you. You thought she was passed out like the other times, but she never got up. Sometime that night, or the next morning, you discovered she was dead. You'd killed her. And now what? Maybe for whatever reasons, it turned you on. Maybe you're like that. Maybe you did things to her after she was dead." She lowered her voice. This was her ground now. "There's nothing quite like that anger of yours, is there? It gets away from you, that kind of anger. It turns back on you, doesn't it? Bites back. Then comes the moment you don't understand. You're riding a rocket while your little sweetheart's gone all limp. You're all over her with your stuff, because that's how the arguments *always* end—right?—the two of you in the sack, clawing at each other and starting out all ugly before the sex starts to heal things. Only this time it doesn't heal, does it? This time she isn't coming awake."

"Who the fuck *are* you?" he asked, his eyes dilated.

"I'm your way out of this mess. We are—the sergeant and I. You want out of this, don't you, Lanny?"

LaMoia dragged his palms across his pants. The jangle was in the air like the smell before a thunderstorm.

She said, "I want you thinking about the lab tests. When that nasty bruising occurred. When she broke those bones—before or after she died. What? You didn't think we knew that yet? Seventeen broken bones, Lanny. What? You thought we'd think her hitting the water did that? And speaking of water, what about when the water went into her lungs? Before or after death? You've got to consider the jury and how this could turn out for you, because this meeting, right here, right now, this is a good chance for you to help yourself. We don't deal in stories. We process the facts and let them tell the story. And that's the story the jury believes. The one and only story. The more you bend it around, the worse your chances of cutting a deal with us."

Matthews stood up and made a point of smoothing the wrinkles in her shirt, as if she'd picked up some of his filth by sitting a little too closely. Lanny Neal remained fairly composed, maintaining an air of self-importance that he wore on his face along with the good looks he didn't deserve.

Interrogations were as much about timing as the questions asked. She and LaMoia exchanged looks and LaMoia cut Neal loose, asking that he "stay close to home." No travel outside the city without notifying the police.

"Impressive," LaMoia said after Neal was gone, "if a little unorthodox."

"What'd you think of *him*?" Matthews asked.

"Mixed review," LaMoia said.

She felt disappointment seep through her. She wanted so badly for this to be over, to wrap it up and put Mary-Ann Walker to rest. But her review was mixed as well—Neal seemed something of a contradiction. "We wait for the lab results. Both SID's and Dixon's. Maybe that'll clear it up for us."

Wishful thinking, and they both knew it.

A Drowning Is a Drowning, a Fall, a Fall

The signature combination of antibacterials and preservatives never failed to remind Boldt of death, images of bruised and bloated corpses indelibly stamped in his consciousness from the 134 autopsies he had attended. He never lost count.

This was a place where the soles of feet bore identification codes in black marker, where nakedness reigned and was never attractive. Floor-to-ceiling stainless-steel refrigerated drawers with sliding trays capable of supporting four hundred pounds and six-foot-two frames. He hoped beyond measure that it was a place Susan Hebringer would never visit. But he had his doubts.

Although state law required investigators to attend autopsies of any death of questionable or suspicious causes, it was not any such requirement that brought Boldt here. That requirement had already been fulfilled by Detective Chas Milner. Instead, it was because it was here, at the ME's, that the dead whispered their last words through their translator, Doc Dixon. He of the large head, wide eyes, and soft smile.

Boldt said, "I hear things got a little western earlier."

"We all handle grief differently. That kid is wound pretty tight."

"Daphne's not convinced she should have let him go."

"She cooled him off. I think he'll be all right."

"It's the other guy I'm worried about," Boldt said, "this Langford Neal."

Dixon nodded. "Yeah, I know what you mean."

None of this was Dixie's problem. Boldt and Dixon discussed a re-release of a Chet Baker compilation on CD, Boldt describing the man's singing voice as "cream and honey." Dixon leaned toward Baker's horn playing, being a trumpet fan himself.

"Since when are you into vocalists?" Dixon asked.

"Liz is trying to convert me to opera."

"Sounds like she's trying to cure your insomnia."

"Same thing."

The cadaver in question was that of Mama Lu's "cousin," Billy Chen. Dixon double-checked the address, swung open the square stainless-steel refrigerator door, and slid out the tray containing Chen on silent rollers.

"Let me ask you this," Dixon said. "Since when do you show interest in what went down in the books as an accidental drowning?"

"It's a favor to a friend."

Dixon answered by lowering his head and giving Boldt a look over the top of his reading glasses.

Boldt explained, hoping Dixon would see the connection. "This guy was found within a block of where Hebringer was last seen."

"There was a water main break."

"Caused by what?" Boldt asked.

"In other words, you're letting Hebringer get to you."

"Is that from Liz or Matthews?"

"I can understand how a disappearance is harder than a homicide. The lack of closure."

"Two disappearances."

"Even harder."

"Susan Hebringer's husband calls Liz about every other day. She's stopped telling me about it, but I know it's continuing. Their daughter and Sarah are in the same ballet class."

"You're a lieutenant. What the hell are you doing in the field?"

Boldt answered, "The captain cut me some slack. She smelled a task force coming and wanted to avoid that. She untied my leash on this one. So what?"

"It should be your sergeant's case, not yours."

"You've never taken an autopsy away from one of your assistants?" Boldt asked. That seemed to sting Dixon, but Boldt wasn't sorry. He enjoyed the freedom of the past weeks and didn't want it ending just yet. An exception had been made for him and he wasn't about to challenge it.

" 'You lose perspective, you lose focus.' Isn't that a Boldt-ism?"

"There are no Boldtisms," Boldt said. "There are two missing women and an experienced street worker who drowned in a couple feet of water. Add to that an area of unexplored Underground."

"That part of town?"

"That's what I'm told."

"So that makes things more interesting."

"Sure does. But tell me Chen was an accident, and I'm out of here."

"I wish I could." Dixon unzipped the body bag to the neck. Chen's face was the color of an athletic sock that gets washed with the wrong load of laundry, a faint purplish yellow. His lips were circled in a brown blue.

Boldt's chest tightened. Oddly, he needed complications, he needed unexplainables, he needed Billy Chen to point him somewhere. And yet he didn't want it. If Susan Hebringer walked into Sarah's ballet class tomorrow, Billy Chen went back into cold storage. Boldt was feeding off the dead, using Chen's death as a possible stepping-stone, and the thought of this repulsed him.

"His lips?"

"Believe me, I'd rather not admit this office made a mistake."

That word from Dixon's mouth electrified Boldt. "The source of this mistake?"

"My guess is that it resulted from this coming in as an accidental death. Head trauma. 'Suffocation due to immersion of the nostrils and mouth in a liquid.' There are no pathonomic findings for drowning. We put head trauma way up our list. Chen suffered head trauma, ergo, the drowning fit. We sometimes look for what we're told to see. It happens. Someone has a lunch date, he goes through the motions and lets his expectations determine his findings. We see a fine white froth or foam in the air passage, evidence of vomiting—a drowning is a drowning. A fall, a fall."

"His lips," Boldt repeated, wanting Dixon to translate the purple bruise that surrounded Chen's mouth.

"Michael, one of my best assistants, overlooked two items. The lividity is inconsistent with the suspected cause of death." Dixon drew Boldt's attention to the clown's face of discoloration around the man's mouth. Then he unzipped the rest of the body bag, snapped on a pair of disposable gloves, and lifted the corpse at the waist. "Notice the buttocks?"

Boldt observed a purplish, orange-black doughnut of discoloration on the dead man's left buttock. "Lividity."

"Exactly."

"Buttocks *and* lips?" Boldt asked.

"That's the point. One is either sunny-side up or over easy when one dies. We can't be both. This lividity," he said, returning Boldt's attention to the dead man's buttocks, "probably occurred while he lay waiting to be found. Not after he was bagged. Not while he awaited his turn on the slab. Long before all that."

Boldt remained confused, and said so.

Dixon explained, "A head trauma drowning means that Chen took a blunt object to the head—an I-beam, a slab of cement— probably as a result of the huge volume of water down there. He's either dulled or unconscious. The lungs fill with water. He coughs and vomits. At this point he's unconscious for sure. The heart stops pumping, the blood settles to the lowest spots and coagulates. In this case, his heels and buttocks." He hoisted the cadaver's stiff left leg. The bottom of the man's heel showed a similar discolored circle.

Boldt prompted him, "Which brings us to the lips."

"The discoloring around the mouth is not lividity, but more likely a hematoma."

"Asphyxiated?"

"His lungs contained only a few cc's of water. Enough to kill him, to be sure, but not the lungfuls we'd associate with accidental drowning."

"Resuscitation?"

"The EMT report doesn't indicate resuscitation, no. Chen was flat-lined when they found him down that hole. No vital signs. They never got far enough along with him to attempt ventilation. The patient was unresponsive to their initial attempts at CPR."

"Maybe they left something out of the report," Boldt said.

"Any of the various procedures would have showed up in- directly with inventoried equipment charges. We're not seeing that on Mr. Chen. Check, if you want to check."

"I'll check," Boldt agreed.

"Ask them about oxygen at the same time."

"Oxygen?"

"Michael missed this as well. He read the accident report, the EMT report, and he saw what he expected to see. What he missed was an elevated oxygen level in Mr. Chen's venous blood gases. We expect to see levels at right around seventy-five percent. Mr. Chen's venous oxygen level was eighty-eight."

"He's in shape? A runner?"

"No way. Supplemental oxygen is the *only* explanation for levels like that."

"We're going around in circles. So you're saying it was the EMTs. They *did* attempt resuscitation."

"No, not according to their report they didn't. What I'm telling you is we've got inconclusive evidence to support a clear-cut method of death. It's entirely possible that Mr. Chen was caught from behind," Dixon said. "Whoever it is, he's pretty strong. Chen struggles, winning the hematoma surrounding the lips. His assailant manages to drop him. Chen encounters the blunt object. He's unconscious and he's about to drown, and don't ask me how, but the air around him is spiked with O. I'd check to see if anyone was welding down there. Oxyacetylene. Something that might explain it."

"A sloppy EMT report explains it."

"We work closely with these people. I'm not going to mud-sling."

"Help me out here, Dixie. I've got a pair of missing women."

"With that sinkhole raining down around them, the EMTs could have hurried him out of there, and then later covered it up when it came report time, because they realized the guy died in their care. Improper care. You never know."

Boldt wasn't sure that helped him. He had no desire to prosecute a couple EMTs.

Dixon suggested, "A fireman would have supplemental oxygen. Who responded to that cave-in?"

"A fireman killed Chen," Boldt said in total disbelief.

"I know it doesn't make any sense."

"Not unless it was someone who didn't want to be found."

"Then why apply the oxygen?" Dixon asked, as frustrated as Boldt.

"That's what we need to answer."

"We?"

"You'd better write it up, Dixie. I may have to stick it to those EMTs."

12 The Gift

"Lieutenant, we got a delivery at the Third Avenue entrance for you."

Matthews, who wasn't expecting anything, said, "Just sign for it and send it up, would you, Pete?"

"Can't do that anymore, Lieutenant, sorry. New regs."

She'd read that memo at some point. *What a pain in the neck.* "Well, at least sign for it, then. I'll be down to get it."

"Guy says he won't leave it for anyone but you."

"Then he's going to have to wait."

"He's been waiting, Lieutenant. This is my third call up there."

She'd been in meetings and hadn't checked her messages. It seemed possible. "Ask him what it is, who it's from."

She heard the inquiry through the receiver. Then Pete said he was going to put the guy on the line.

"Hey, Lieutenant."

She knew the voice, but it took her a moment to identify it. "Mr. Walker?"

"I told you I could help."

She suffered a chill like a small shudder rippling through her. The image that filled her imagination was that of the family dog leaving a dead squirrel on the doorstep. "We discussed this."

"You *had* to say those things. I understand that . . . I understand the way things work."

"I'm not sure you do. What's in the package, Mr. Walker?" She took a wild guess. What would the adoring student bring the teacher? "Some fish? Fresh fish?"

"Fish? It's *hers*," he said sadly. "Proof that sack of shit is lying if he says he didn't do anything to Mary-Ann."

"Mr. Walker . . . Ferrell, it's illegal to involve yourself in an active investigation. We went over all this." Another chill swept through her. This wasn't the first time a bereaved relative had attached him- or herself to a case, but she'd never personally experienced it. Instead of celebrating the cooperation, she felt boxed in.

"You've got snitches, right? So, I'm a snitch. Don't knock it 'til you check it out."

"If you leave the package for me, Mr. Walker, I'll pick it up later."

"No way. I get to see you, or I take it with me. What's *wrong* with you? You want to get this guy or not?"

"You have to leave the package, Mr. Walker. There's nothing I can do about it. They X-ray them, electronically sniff them—there's all sorts of security now that I can't do anything about. It takes a couple of hours. I'll look at it and I'll call you."

"No way. I'm waiting."

"What happened to your double shift?"

"New arrangements."

"Mr. Walker—"

"I'm waiting, like it or not."

She could hear the phone being passed back to Pete.

"Lieutenant?" the gruff voice inquired.

"Tell him I'm on my way down. Go ahead and start it through security, okay, Pete?" In fact, such security took only a matter of minutes. She wondered if it was stupid to show Walker she'd exaggerated the situation. To hell with it: She'd accept the package, get Walker out of there, and warn him not to try it again.

A few minutes later she passed the lobby coffee stand and approached the busy security checkpoint at the building's main entrance on Third Avenue. Ferrell Walker stood waiting—there were no chairs—just on the other side of the twin metal detectors, to the left of the lumbering X-ray machine. He wore the same sweatshirt and blue jeans that she'd seen him in earlier the same day. She could imagine that smell even at a distance.

Pete, a burly patrolman in his early fifties who'd worked the front entrance for years, indicated a somewhat soggy brown corrugated cardboard box that waited on a folding table. The noise generated at the entrance by all the security questioning and the signing in and the beeping of the metal detectors and the grinding of the X-ray machine's conveyor belt created a jagged tension in the air that Matthews always felt in the center of her chest as a threat of violence. She used the garage entrance on most days, appreciating the calmer approach taken there as a result of an officers-only policy. But here, in the coffee-scented foyer with its high ceiling, standing under the faint light of overhead fixtures with dull bulbs chosen for their low consumption of energy, she felt more like a tourist at the security check of an airport in a foreign country.

The cardboard box seemed to grow in size and significance. She lost sight of Walker, due to the security installation, but could feel him standing over there staring at her.

"Bring him through, please, Pete."

The officer on duty signaled for Walker to step through the metal detector, but Walker refused.

Matthews stepped around to where she could see the kid and said to him, "You can leave it with him. In the plastic tray. They'll give it back to you when you leave."

Walker looked skeptical.

"They'll give it back to you," she repeated.

Walker removed the long fishing knife from a hand-sewn leather sheath tucked inside the waist of his pants and hidden by his sweatshirt. He seemed impressed that she should have anticipated this. He placed it in the dirty plastic tray, and Pete, making a face of open curiosity, moved it aside and out of reach. Walker passed through the metal detector and Pete fanned his hand in front of his face, making light of the man's fish odors.

Matthews and Walker stood in front of the cardboard box and she asked that he open it. Pete drew closer, protective of his lieutenant.

"You open it," Walker said somewhat childishly. But there was a menace to his voice as well.

"It's policy that as long as you're here, you open it yourself, Mr. Walker. I gave you the chance to drop it off." She checked her watch, merely to drive home her next point. "We either do this now, or not, but I haven't the time to stand here discussing it." She wanted to show him a firm hand, dispel any notions that he might have that they had formed a personal friendship. She knew all too well that if she didn't watch it, Walker could attach to her, letting her fill the void left by his dead sister. She didn't want any part of that.

"It was behind the Dumpster, in the alley behind his place," Walker said, digging into the box. He pulled out a navy blue Michigan sweatshirt, with yellow block letters. Matthews tried her best not to react. Neal had mentioned the possible existence of a sweatshirt. This fit with that part of his statement, and she felt elated with the discovery. He tried to pass it to her, but Matthews refused and then called to the security officers, "Gloves!" She directed Walker to hold it at the shoulders, pinched between his fingers, attempting to initiate as little contact with him as possible. She fired off questions at him: "How much contact have you had with this?" "Can you identify it as your sister's?" "Exactly where and when did you find this garment?" He answered her crisply that he'd boxed it for her, that it was his sister's, and that he'd found it behind the Dumpster in a search he'd done that same morning following their encounter at the ME's. Once protected by the gloves, Matthews took possession of the sweatshirt, turning it around to inspect the random pattern of dark brown orbs that speckled its fabric and a similar, but larger stain on the neck of the sweatshirt. Dried blood.

"I'm going to need an evidence bag here," Matthews instructed one of the gate personnel. This person took off at a jog toward the bank of elevators.

"I done good, right?" Ferrell Walker asked, testing her.

"You may have contaminated a vital piece of evidence." Matthews would not acknowledge that Walker had accomplished what she had not, could not, without a court order to search Neal's residence. Without probable cause—hard evidence against Neal—they still lacked that court order. Ironically, the sweatshirt, if found in a public area as Walker claimed, might present the necessary probable cause.

"I'm telling you: He did this."

"You have to leave this to me. Your participation has to stop here. Are we clear on that?"

"You helped me, I helped you," he said, looking a little wounded. "We're helping each other." Only his tentative tone of voice gave away that he was testing the situation, the relationship. "I help you just like you help those girls."

Her breath caught: He knew about her volunteer work at the Shelter. Had he followed her? "We'll take it from here," she said strongly. "I'll be in touch."

"Not if I'm in touch first," he said, voicing the same childish sentiment he had earlier in the day. He stopped at Pete and took his knife back, though Pete required him to reach the other side of the security gear first. Pete said, "It's illegal to conceal that weapon."

"I'm a snitch," Walker said proudly.

With that announcement, Pete spun around to check with Matthews, who just shook her head in disgust. When she looked again, Walker was nowhere to be seen.

13 Now You See Him, Now You Don't

It went against all her training, her substantial education, and certainly the rules set forth for volunteer workers, but upon hearing from an SPD narcotics officer that a street kid—a girl—had invoked her name during a sidewalk shakedown from which the girl had been released, Daphne Matthews found herself personally involved. Her first stop was the Shelter, where she learned that Margaret had been kicked loose after the maximum stay allowed. Where to look next?

A late March storm swept angrily over the city, driving frigid rain behind a nasty wintry wind that made it feel more like December. She pulled up her collar and ran for the Honda. This wasn't a night for a pregnant girl to be out in the elements, and Matthews didn't want Margaret having to negotiate street favors for the bare necessities of warmth and a place to sleep. She knew what these girls did in order to survive. With Margaret putting her name out to an officer—an obvious cry for help—how was Matthews supposed to return for the evening to her houseboat and a glass of wine? She decided to make one loop of downtown looking for the girl. Forty-five minutes, max. It wasn't as if she had a hot date waiting.

Once into the driver's seat she brushed the rain off her and turned toward the backseat in search of her umbrella. Looking out the car's rain-blurred rear window, she thought she saw a figure—a man, for sure—standing behind the railing of the wedge-shaped concrete parking garage. Standing there, and looking across at her.

Turning around in the seat, adjusting her rearview mirrors— both outside and in—she picked him up again: a black silhouette like a cardboard cutout, standing absolutely still on the second level of the triangular parking garage.

After the first spurt of panic iced through her, she thought it was probably Walker, and though disturbed he might be following her, she'd done nothing yet to shatter his regard for her, nothing to turn a fan into a foe, though she knew how fine a line she walked.

As she calmed ever so slightly, not one to shrink and wither, she decided to face up to him. She threw the Honda in gear, bumped it out of the Shelter's parking lot, and drove quickly around the block and into the garage entrance. She resented taking the parking stub, realizing it would cost her a couple bucks to get her message across to Walker, but peace of mind was cheap at twice the price.

She drove up the ramp to level two and parked in the first open space she encountered. She grabbed her purse, locked the car with the remote, and walked quickly toward the area of the garage where she'd just seen the silhouette. No one.

She called out, "Mr. Walker?"

She took hold of the railing and eased her head out for a more panoramic view. The new football stadium loomed to her left, dominating the skyline and obscuring a good deal of "The Safe," as residents called baseball's Safeco Field. To the right, skyscrapers competed for a view of Puget Sound. She looked above her and below her in the same general location, wondering if she'd gotten the level wrong. When she looked straight down at the sidewalk, she took into account all the pedestrians, alert for anyone hurrying, anyone fitting Walker's general build, his sweatshirt and jeans, anyone looking back up at her.

It was during this surveillance that she spotted the rooftop light rack and bold lettering of KCSO patrol car #89. It appeared on the street to her right, immediately adjacent to the parking garage's exit. Prair? she wondered.

A daily runner, Matthews ran, and ran hard. She flew past the rows of parked cars, circled down the oily car ramp she'd driven up, all in an effort to keep her eye on that moving patrol car as it cornered the parking facility. She wanted desperately to get a look at its driver. She wasn't merely running, but sprinting down the echoing confines of the garage, the myriad of colorful lights—neon, traffic lights, headlights, and taillights—spinning like a kaleidoscope.

Focused as she was, she didn't see the group of four street punks until she was nearly upon them. Huddled together under the overhang of the garage's next level, they looked over at her with hollow eyes—hollow heads, was more like it—the pungent odor of pot hanging in the air.

The patrol car sped by on her right. She looked out, but too late.

One of the bigger boys in the group came out toward her from between the parked cars. "What are you looking at?"

She debated displaying her shield but decided against it. Kids like this held a particular dislike for authority. In doing so she experienced what must have been a defenseless civilian's panic. But if high on pot, they didn't represent much threat of violence, no matter what the posturing. It didn't fit the model. If the pot were an attempt at a comedown from an amphetamine high, though, she had problems. Her volunteer work at the Shelter had not gone for naught.

Another of the young toughs, this one with peroxide hair and a face that held enough piercings to set off an airport security check, followed on the heels of his friend. "She's *fine*-looking, eh, Manny?" The kid coughed and spat, the phlegm attaching to the car he passed.

Matthews stood her ground. "There was a man up here. Up there," she said, pointing to level two. "Just now. Maybe six feet tall, looking west. Maybe in a sweatshirt and jeans, maybe a uniform."

"Take it somewhere else," the bigger one said, but his eyes had locked onto her purse.

"She is damn *fine*," the kid with the dye job whispered to his buddy, encouraging him forward, defining his own interest in Matthews.

"Did you see a patrol car? King County Sheriff's?"

"Yeah, right," replied the leader sarcastically.

"Up there on level two," she said.

"There's four of us, lady." He stepped out from between the cars, now only a few feet from her.

Where was that sheriff's car now that she needed it? This south end of town was rough at night—the very reason the Shelter was no more than a block away. Some of these hotheads carried weapons; she didn't want that in the equation. Bribery, on the other hand, had its place. "Twenty bucks answers my question." She tried to put his attention on her purse out of her mind, not wanting to see him as a criminal but instead as a source of information. If the blond kid wanted to try his doped-up luck at groping her, the purse carried a Beretta, a can of Mace, a single pair of handcuffs, a mobile phone, and a Palm Pilot. Connecting that purse to the side of his face would put the kid in the next county. Reaching into the purse, grabbing hold of the weapon, chambering a round—all that would probably take ten seconds that she wouldn't have.

"Didn't see no cruiser," the leader said, "but maybe the uniform, yeah. How 'bout that twenty?"

The option presented itself for her to grab the gun while pretending to retrieve the twenty, though it upped the stakes considerably. She had no intention of shooting some stoned kid, nor of provoking the remaining three to fire on her.

She asked, "What color uniform?" This question would separate fact from fiction. Blue for SPD. Dark brown khaki for KCSO.

"Army maybe." The kid took another step closer.

She found his answer intriguing, for if he'd believed a khaki uniform meant an army officer, it added credibility to why he and his pals hadn't fled, whereas a blue uniform would strike the fear of God into any one of these kids. But khaki was more likely King County Sheriff, not army.

Evaluating her situation came down to mapping an exit route. She felt confident she could outrun any one of these kids. The problem was that this leader stood between her and the exit. The only ramp available to her led up and into the garage. Cars streamed around this parking garage, their lights glinting like those of a carousel. So many people, so incredibly close by, and yet oblivious to her predicament. Her extreme isolation—one against many, alone and yet surrounded—bore down on her.

"What color shirt?" she asked.

"What about that twenty?"

She faced a choice then—her gun or the payoff? She clicked open her purse, and for a moment the sounds of the city surrendered to the intense drumming in her ears. She drew a twenty from her wallet, keeping her hands hidden behind the screen of her purse. There lay her gun. On the bottom of everything was the small can of pepper spray, a far more reasonable means of defense given the threat. She made one stab for it—fingers dart-ing through the contents of the purse—and by an act of divine intervention, she touched the can's cold metal and drew the Mace from her purse, her hand concealing it.

They all heard the car enter from the other side of the building, saw the spread of its headlights as shadows crawled across the stained concrete. During this brief distraction, Matthews placed the twenty at her feet and, cradling the pepper spray, turned and walked toward the ramp that led to level two. She heard the big kid hurry to retrieve the money, the scratching of the soles of his boots on the concrete. She sensed the other kid's bold advance as he tested the possibility of following her, maybe scoring a little payoff of his own—maybe money, maybe something else.

"Dude!" the big one called out as the headlights swung to encompass them all.

Matthews hurried then, not running, not wanting to signal her fear, up the ramp and straight toward her Honda. The lights flashed and the horn beeped behind the signal from her remote button.

She wondered what the message was, as she bumped the Honda out into the busy street, like stepping through a stage curtain and walking into the audience. She searched for significance in every incident, every encounter she experienced, the psychologist seizing upon every opportunity to learn something about herself.

In the process, she nearly forgot about the man in the khaki uniform overlooking the Shelter's parking lot. Nearly, but not quite.

"You want peepers? We got peepers. But I gotta tell you, Johno: Your guys have been through these already, because of Hebringer and Randolf." Marisha Stenolovski slid a file cabinet drawer open. The files went back twelve or fifteen inches.

Stenolovski stuck out a few inches in all the right places herself. He'd been there, done that.

"Last thirty days. I'll know it when I see it."

It had been a year earlier. A cop bar. Both of them flirting a little too openly. She stood a good three inches taller than he. Lanky. Dark Slavic skin, brooding eyes. A screamer—he remembered that as well. It had lasted a week or two. He'd dumped her for someone, no doubt. Couldn't remember for whom just now. The problem with relationships at work, they came back to bite you.

She lowered her voice. "You're an asshole, John. Until you need my help, you don't give me the time of day. What am I, damaged goods? Leftovers? I don't care that you leave me for some singer. Good riddance. But the way you avoid me now. It's disrespectful."

The singer. He remembered now. "I don't avoid you."

"Have we said two words in the last six months?"

"A woman got peeped over at the Inn. I'm looking for similar complaints."

She slapped the steel file drawer. "There. All the peepers a guy could ask for. Look hard, Johnny. Maybe you're in there too."

She walked off. He remembered that walk. Strong. Alluring. Legs to the moon. One foot placed exactly in front of the other, like a runway model, so her butt shifted back and forth like a pair of puppies in a paper sack. She'd donned a pair of his boxer shorts one morning. Topless, just the boxer shorts, nothing else. They ate bagels together at the kitchen table, her, dressed that way. He remembered more about her than he might have thought.

It shouldn't have surprised him that the one case file that interested him turned out to have Stenolovski's name listed as the investigator. Life was like that. He should have known, because there were only a couple full-eights in Special Assaults— SA. The rest worked it part-time.

He caught up to her as she sat atop a metal stool in an office cubicle covered with magazine tear sheets of barefoot water skiers. A photo of a nephew. Another of Prague or Moscow, someplace gray, bleak with billboard ads he didn't recognize. Definitely Eastern European. In the photo she had her arm around a very old lady with hair the color of winter clouds.

He cleared his throat. "With me, you get what you get. Sometimes that's a good thing. Sometimes not. If you're pissed, you're pissed. But if I apologized, it would be wrong because it would be insincere. I'm not sorry for any of it, anything we had, except that since then maybe I've treated you wrong."

She smiled, "So pull up a chair, asshole."

He smiled back. "Yeah. Thanks."

"Ms. Tina Oblitz?" The phone cradled between his shoulder and ear, LaMoia was guessing that the Oblitz file had been passed over during the Hebringer/Randolf race for lack of what his department called "connective tissue" because Oblitz herself had tried to withdraw the complaint. That sticky note in the file would have tainted it—why further investigate something that "didn't happen"?—but it was just this Post-it that intrigued John LaMoia.

"This is she."

LaMoia introduced himself by rank and awaited the mandatory pause of shock value. Telephones weren't the greatest.

His beeper chirped and he yanked it off his belt, wondering if Rehab was bugging the neighbors. The dog had attached himself to LaMoia and reportedly would wail hours on end when LaMoia was off on night duty. No such problem during the day shifts. The dog needed a shrink. Maybe Matthews would give it a spin.

He recognized the phone number on the pager as the ME's—Dixon must have completed the autopsy on Mary-Ann Walker.

"Yes, Sergeant?" Tentative. Cautious.

"You recently filed a voyeurism complaint with us. Then you called back to attempt to retract the complaint."

"It was nothing. I was mistaken."

"And we," he continued, as if uninterrupted, "Detective Stenolovski, actually, informed you that once filed, a complaint cannot be retracted."

"It's fine. It's nothing."

"It's not fine with me, Ms. Oblitz. I've got a case I'm working, a stalking, voyeurism. I've just been reviewing a similar case file. From your initial complaint, I'm thinking our current case might be the same guy who was watching you."

"No one was watching me, Sergeant. I was mistaken."

"If there's blackmail involved, extortion, then I can help with that, Ms. Oblitz."

"It's nothing like that."

"Then what is it like?"

"I beg your pardon?"

"Stenolovski says the initial complaint was quite convincing. You saw this guy out your hotel window. That's important to me, Ms. Oblitz. Then you call to distance yourself. Suddenly you don't want anything to do with it. I've got to ask myself: Is it because you're afraid? Have you been threatened? Extorted? I need to know about that."

"It's not that . . . it's just that I was mistaken."

"Okay, so I'm wrong. I still got to talk to you, Ms. Oblitz, about that original complaint. A woman's gone through something awful—two others have gone missing—and I think you may be able to help me with this. I think you know what she's going through."

A long pause. He could hear her breathing. "Not now. Not over the phone."

LaMoia experienced a great sense of victory. He closed his eyes, drew in a deep breath, and combed his free hand through his hair. "Okay. Thank you. So when? Where?" He added, "You're in . . . the Bay Area. It's going to have to be by phone, I'm afraid."

"I'm traveling up there on business, Monday. I'm in the W."

"Name a time," he said.

She asked him to wait a minute. "I have an opening at four. Four to five. Will that suit you?"

"Four o'clock. Fine."

"Whatever you do, don't announce yourself at the desk, would you not, Sergeant? Just call up to the room, please."

"Done." He hung up the phone with a smile. He owned Ms. Tina Oblitz. She just didn't know it yet.

15 The Discovery Process

"Bernie Lofgrin typed the blood on that sweatshirt your boyfriend delivered," LaMoia explained to Matthews. "It matches Mary-Ann Walker's. They're running DNA now. Meanwhile we're here for a little chat."

"SID?" she asked. "We're going to search his apartment, right?"

"If he lets us in, we get a plain-sight search," LaMoia answered. "But for anything more than that, we'll need a court order, and for that Mahoney wants a print or prints developed on the sweatshirt, some hairs other than Mary-Ann's, a second blood type, semen . . . something to bring Neal into the picture with physical evidence."

"And the lab?"

"Is working on it." He added, "Call me reckless—I don't feel like waiting another twenty-four hours on this."

"And I'm along because?" she asked.

"Because I like you, Matthews. Why else?"

She felt herself blush and tried to cover it by saying, "Gee, John, you've got me all feverish."

"That's the idea," he said. "We'll cool off with a drink later."

"Don't count on it," she said, though it didn't sound so bad. *LaMoia?* she asked herself. Who was she kidding?

"Because you see things the rest of us don't," he said, answering her original question. "And because someone has to keep an eye on him while I inspect his car." He allowed this to sink in. "She was sitting up facing a car when she was hit, not standing, not running away. Dixie can prove that. If not the sweatshirt, maybe Neal's car. The point being *something* is going to win SID a ticket into Neal's apartment, and I'll take it however we can get it."

He gave her one of his high-voltage smiles as he used a credit card to trick open the lock on the apartment house's street-side door.

The dark stairwell smelled sour, of spilled beer and wine, tobacco and other things in various states of organic decomposition that she didn't want to think about—street sex and intravenous drug use, and always that tinge of the sea. These combined with an odor that she took to be poisoned mice or water rats entombed in the walls in various stages of silent decay.

"Should we have maybe called for backup?" she asked in a forced whisper.

"We're fine," LaMoia said, climbing the stairs two at a time and reaching inside his jacket for his handgun as he got to the landing.

It didn't feel all that "fine" to her, and she nearly said so.

"You didn't have to come," he said.

"Then why'd you ask me along? What the hell, John: These aren't even my hours."

"Because I knew if I didn't you'd be all moody about being left out." This irritated her—not the comment, but the fact that he had her dead to rights. "I asked you because I knew you had nothing better to do tonight, and I thought you might enjoy seeing me take this guy down."

"Seeing *you* take him down," she restated. "So I'm what, your audience?"

"It's not like that and you know it."

"What is it like, John?" she whispered. They stood outside the apartment number listed on LaMoia's slip of paper. She was angry now. Angrier still that she allowed it to show.

He met eyes with her and whispered back, "I like your company, Matthews. You're smart, you're clever, and like I said, you see things in shit-balls like Neal that the rest of us miss. A case like this . . . maybe we find evidence, maybe we don't. And if we don't, the evidence may boil down to this guy's behavior. His reactions. Am I right? And who better than you to sit up on that witness stand and charm the shorts off a jury to where they buy a collection of circumstantial evidence that pins him as capable of anything, including lying."

LaMoia reached up and rapped his knuckles on the door. He indicated for her to step back, and he readied the weapon before him.

She understood then that the pistol was nothing more than posturing on LaMoia's part—he wanted to scare Neal with this entrance, to establish a degree of distrust that would set the tone for the interview to come. She admired him for this gut instinct of his; sometimes she wondered who, of the two of them, understood human behavior better.

"Who is it?" Neal asked through the door.

"Sergeant LaMoia and Lieutenant Matthews, Mr. Neal."

The man opened the apartment door with none of the reluctance or hesitation that Matthews might have expected of the guilty, and she took note of this. Such cocksure confidence could be its own telltale, its own undoing for a rare breed of suspect.

The door opened into a room dominated by a large worn couch covered in an unpleasant green cotton that looked more like a bedspread, a wooden chair facing it, and a coffee table with badly scratched veneer that clearly doubled as a footrest. A shabby, aluminum card table that belonged in an Airstream trailer held two empty beer bottles and a pair of disposable pic-

nic containers of salt and pepper. The table was situated in front
of a large double-hung window. Its jamb and sill pockmarked
by a dozen coats of poorly applied paint, it looked out onto a
black metal fire escape and beyond, an unexpectedly impressive
view of Lake Union. Finding the one-man kitchen neat and clean
surprised her. She would have expected Neal incapable of house-
keeping. A plain-sight search of the small bedroom revealed the
television he'd mentioned previously as well as a second window access out onto the fire escape, also part of his earlier statement. At least in his description of the place, his earlier
statement held up.

The artwork, if it could be called that, amounted to travel
posters of beach resorts showing scantily clad bronzed women
enjoying bright sunshine while surrounded by palm trees and
umbrellas.

He caught her staring. "I was an Internet travel agent until
the meltdown happened. Put most of us out of business."

"And now?" LaMoia asked. "I don't think we established
your employment, Mr. Neal."

"A little of this, a little of that. Between jobs right now."

"Between women, too," LaMoia muttered.

"Mary-Ann was helping with the rent?" Matthews said.

Neal shrugged. "A little. You'll hear it from the maggot anyway, if you haven't already."

"The brother," LaMoia clarified.

"He's a parasite, and don't look at me like I'm the pot calling
the kettle black because it's my apartment in the first place, my
car, my things. I'm between jobs is all, and Mary-Ann helped
out. So what?"

LaMoia said, "Sit down, Mr. Neal," an order, not a request.

Neal displayed his disgust as he slouched into the grasp of
the green monster, outwardly reluctant in this act of obedience.
Matthews purposefully stood over by the table, out of Neal's

peripheral vision but with a clear view of him, temporarily pushing away the continuing concern for Margaret's whereabouts and
the confusion over both Ferrell Walker and Nathan Prair that
had robbed her of sleep. She focused on the suspect, alert for
every twitch, every nuance as he reacted to LaMoia's line of
questioning.

With his detective's notebook lying on his pressed blue jeans,
LaMoia said, "You mentioned your car. What kind of a car is
it, please?"

"Ninety-two Corolla."

"Color?"

"Kind of gold."

"Champagne?"

"Right, champagne."

"You said the car was yours?"

"Yeah."

"Only yours?"

"Yeah."

"You have the only set of keys, or did Mary-Ann have a
set?"

"Listen, we weren't married."

LaMoia said, "So she did *not* have a key."

"People who spend a lot of time in boats, they don't make
the best drivers. Mary-Ann . . . she was a danger in that car."

He repeated, "She did not have her own key."

"You're real quick, Sergeant." Neal craned his neck then to
locate Matthews. "I figured you were probably snooping around
while the sergeant here held me riveted with his line of questioning."

"You figured wrong," she said. "We're trying to show some
respect by coming to your home, rather than dragging you downtown. We're trying to get to the truth of what happened to Mary-
Ann."

LaMoia said, "I didn't see a champagne Corolla out on the street on our way in."

Neal shook his head and grinned at the same time. "So you knew about my car before you asked me. Is that supposed to scare me or something, Sergeant?"

LaMoia responded, "I know a lot of things before I ask you, Lanny. That's why your answers count so much."

"I know what you guys are thinking." He wormed his hands together and wouldn't look at LaMoia, interpreting the spill patterns in his worn brown rug instead. "But that's bullshit, and we both know it."

"What are we thinking?" LaMoia asked.

"Don't hand me that. You know, and I know. So that's that."

"Yeah," LaMoia agreed, "that's pretty much that."

"It doesn't make me good for this."

"A person's history is an inescapable thing, Lanny. Think about it. We got it down in black and white that you like to backhand your women."

"That stuff's not admissible."

"So you're a lawyer now. What happened to travel agent?"

LaMoia's comment won another spark of eye contact between the two, and Matthews saw a conflicted personality working hard to contain himself. Lanny Neal wanted to release some of the pent-up anger he was feeling but was smart enough to know that would work against him.

LaMoia said, "Let's get back to the location of that Corolla."

"Parked in a space out back."

"Has it been to the shop recently?"

"No."

"Been to the car wash?"

"Oh, yeah, I spend a lot of time at the car wash with the soccer moms in the minivans. You got me nailed, I can see that. Reading me loud and clear."

"I need a straight answer on this one, *Langford*. You have or have not cleaned the car in the past six days?"

The directness of LaMoia's question sobered Neal. He sat up straight—the kid in the classroom caught doodling—suddenly understanding the severity of LaMoia's questions.

"What's with that?"

"An answer is all."

"Have not. What? You think in killing her I drove her to the Ballard Bridge and tossed her? You want to search the car? Is that it?"

She'd gone off the Aurora Bridge. Matthews made mental note of the mistake.

"If you wouldn't mind," LaMoia glanced over at Matthews, "it might help to clear this up all the more quickly if I took a look at it, yes."

"Have at it."

Another look between Matthews and LaMoia. LaMoia said, "The lieutenant'll stay here while I go down and check it out."

Neal clearly didn't like the idea. He appeared to weigh the value of dissenting but indicated a hook by the apartment door where a set of keys hung.

"I won't be going into the vehicle," LaMoia corrected. "I won't even be touching it. A cursory, external examination is all."

"Because you don't have a warrant. Are you guys *charging* me with something?"

"Should we be?"

"Fuck no! I'm just asking what's going on here."

"What's going on," LaMoia replied flatly, "is that I'm going to go out and look at your car while Lieutenant Matthews asks you a few questions." He added, "Do you have any problem with that?"

"No . . . problem," he confirmed, reluctantly.

LaMoia left the apartment and Matthews moved around to the same chair in front of the green couch and faced Neal. The man's demeanor changed noticeably, which came as no great surprise to her. Accustomed to controlling women, Neal would believe he could gain the upper hand over Matthews. It occurred to her that she couldn't rule him out as the man watching her from the parking garage. If those kids had lied about the khaki clothing, then *anyone* could have been up there watching her.

"When was the last time Mary-Ann was in your car, Mr. Neal?"

"What is all this with the car? Why do you have to hassle me? I didn't do anything to Mary-Ann."

"When you say you didn't do anything, exactly what do you mean? Anything of a violent nature, is that it? Because we know you had sexual relations with Mary-Ann—you've already told us about that. You cohabitated here in this apartment," she reminded. "You argued, at least you implied as much. I need to advise you, Mr. Neal, that we take your answers seriously. They're being written down, and we're assuming you're making every effort to aid us in our investigation. Are you going to tell me now that you never struck Mary-Ann, never threatened her, never abused her in any way or fashion—because when you make a sweeping statement like the one you just made, you force me to reconsider every other answer you've given us."

"I didn't kill her," he said, though he sounded much less convinced, and Matthews made note of the last minute of their exchange. As she was writing he said, "She was in the car all the time. Okay? Maybe not every day, but all the time."

"Did you ever strike her when she was in the car?"

"I'm not saying I *ever* hit her."

"Do you need for me to repeat the question?" She found herself interested in his ability to pay attention to the questions and identify some of the traps she was trying to lay. Neal was no stranger to such interrogations, if she had to guess. Her colleagues in Special Assaults didn't keep track of the number of times a person was brought in for questioning—but had they, she believed Neal's jacket would be littered with such interviews.

"I never hit her when she was in the car. Never hit her, period."

"Was Mary-Ann ever in an accident in the vehicle?"

"Damn near, the way she drives."

Matthews noted the present-tense answer, wondering at the same time if Neal had yet to fully accept Mary-Ann's death, or if it was merely a slip of the tongue. Guilt and remorse could play tricks on the brain. "Should I repeat the question?"

"No accidents, okay?"

She let the tension in the air settle, like waiting for smoke to clear. "Then you could see no reason, no explanation, for any of Mary-Ann's spilled blood being found in or on your vehicle—this nineteen ninety-two champagne Corolla?"

"Blood?" His eyes went wide and she could feel his chest knot with panic. He was wondering how she'd jumped to this, thinking what he'd overlooked, what she'd led him into.

"It's a simple enough question," she said, "or would you like me to repeat it as well?"

"What's all this about?"

"The question concerns possible explanations for blood found in your—"

"I heard the goddamn question. I asked what it's about."

Neal gave the impression of genuine surprise at her implication they might connect Mary-Ann's blood to his car. She didn't trust this impression, but she took note of it nonetheless. If he could play his girlfriends, then why couldn't he play investigators? Guys like Lanny Neal grew accustomed to playing everyone around them to get what they wanted. It made him difficult to read, and she found it even more difficult to trust her own assessments. Domestics—and this had every indication of being just that—usually cleared on a confession or a statement by the guilty party. Some eighty percent of domestic homicides were cleared through confessions to the first officer to arrive on the scene. Lanny Neal was bucking the odds, but it didn't let him off the hook.

LaMoia stepped through the door without knocking. "Hands in plain view, Mr. Neal," he said strongly, approaching the couch. "Keep them on your knees."

Matthews understood immediately where this was headed—Neal did, too, for that matter. She stood out of her chair, wishing LaMoia had consulted her first. She'd softened up Neal with her questioning, might have gotten to a confession if LaMoia had given her some time. He then asked Neal to stand and carefully patted him down, searching for weapons. This completed, he delved into the cushions and cracks of the green monster—she didn't envy him that job—brushed his hands off, and set the suspect back down into the couch.

"Are you familiar with court-ordered search warrants?" LaMoia asked Neal.

Matthews wondered if the pat-down had been motivated by real evidence or LaMoia's desire to imply the discovery of real evidence. With LaMoia, one could never tell. She continued to believe she knew where this was headed, though for the first time she began to question from what it had come.

"Yeah."

"I've applied by phone for permission to search and seize your property, Mr. Neal. Specifically, your car. I'm well aware that we already had your verbal permission to inspect the vehicle, but this more formal step is necessary to protect what we call the chain of custody, in terms of evidence collection. Do you understand?"

"Not really. The warrant stuff, sure. But why?"

"I thought you might tell me," LaMoia said. "It could save us all a lot of time."

Matthews told the suspect, "What we were just discussing is of relevance here."

His face reflected a mixture of annoyance, anger, and uncertainty. "If there's blood in that car, I've got *no idea* how it got there. *None*."

Matthews informed LaMoia that they'd just been exploring various possibilities for any such evidence. She dropped the hammer with, ". . . since we know that Mr. Neal has the only key to the vehicle."

"It's not the only key," he spoke up. His eyes pleaded for understanding. "You asked if Mary-Ann had a key. She didn't. But it wasn't the only key. I've got one of those spare key things inside under the driver-side rear wheel."

This news hit her like a bomb, and she could see it had with LaMoia as well, though he hid it cleverly from Neal, disguising it as a yawn that he covered with his hand. He wanted Neal thinking he was bored. Anything but.

"A second key," LaMoia said.

"Rear wheel, up on the axle. One of those magnetic boxes."

Matthews asked, "And you would expect that key to be in place at the moment?"

"Last time I used that was a good two months ago. It's gotta be there."

"Locked yourself out?" LaMoia asked.

"Over on Forty-fifth. We'd gone to that Thai place . . . Vietnamese . . . whatever it is. Mary-Ann's birthday."

"I'm going to check it out," LaMoia informed Matthews. "You okay here?"

"Fine," Matthews said.

"I hit a bird last week," Neal volunteered. "Right side of the car, right?" he called out after a retreating LaMoia.

LaMoia stopped. "With your permission, Mr. Neal, I'm going to check for that key." He waited for a response.

Neal looked back and forth between the two, clearly weighing cooperation versus objection. He looked as if he might ask a question of Matthews, but she made no effort to encourage this. If LaMoia was operating on a bluff, the wrong answer now could sway Neal to start protecting himself—the last thing she and LaMoia wanted.

Neal said, "What the hell?" LaMoia opened the door but did not leave. He turned to Neal and nodded faintly, sending the man a signal. "You have my permission," Neal conceded.

If a randomly placed key existed somewhere on the car, any decent first-year defense attorney could shred their attempts to lay blame on Neal for any damaging evidence collected. Confusing Matthews further was Neal's willingness to cooperate with the search. His earlier conviction and brief prison time, when combined with what was obviously an above-average intelligence, should have prevented him from making any such agreements. *Guilty or not,* she thought.

"I hit a bird," he repeated for her benefit.

"Sure you did," she said, trying her best to sound utterly unconvinced.

"No key, Mr. Neal," LaMoia announced when he returned less than five minutes later. "I checked the same location behind all four tires."

"Yeah?" His bravado seem to crumble. Matthews had seen

this dozens of times before: that point when the lies collapse under the weight of truth. "Then it fell off somewhere. . . . Or maybe . . . I never put it back after the last time."

"Sure."

"I'm telling you . . ." But he couldn't think how to complete the thought.

LaMoia was just getting warmed up. "Crawling around under the car just now, you want to know what I found?" He asked this to Matthews, as if Neal weren't in the room.

"What's that?" she answered.

"Some hair. A nice little smudge of blonde hair and blood. Bottom of the rear bumper, and more on the bottom of the gas tank. Rear of the vehicle," he said, for Neal's sake. "You ever hit a blonde bird, you scumbag? Backing up? Maybe you'd like to start doing some talking, on account SID is going to collect all that physical evidence—including, I want to bet, some blue cotton fibers from the sweatshirt that you, yourself, put Mary-Ann in that night—and you're going to lose any chance you had to put us, or the court, on your side of this. You understand how that works, don't you? You're no stranger to the process."

"An argument," Matthews said, seizing on LaMoia's discovery of this evidence. She felt energized, gripped by adrenaline. "Maybe she shoved you. Hit you. Swore at you. All that affects the way the lawyers look at a domestic."

"But if that evidence piles up ahead of time," LaMoia said, "then what the hell do we need you for? How the hell you going to get anyone to listen if we've already got you in the bag?"

"We're listening right now, Mr. Neal," Matthews said. But Neal looked as paralyzed by LaMoia's announcement as she felt. Every time they had a leg up on this guy, he threw her into doubt with an unexpected reaction. She cautioned herself to work the Boldt method—listen to the victim, follow the evidence, discount witnesses, and ignore the suspect completely until all the facts were in. She tended to react emotionally to suspects, at least on a surface level, and to trust that reaction. It was this opposite approach of theirs that made their combination such an effective team. With LaMoia, things were a little different. He tended to cut to the chase, go for the heart and then leave it to her to show the suspect the error of his ways. She added, "We won't be around forever, Lanny. This thing will be out of our hands soon," she said, wondering if they could be so lucky, "and into the hands of the attorneys. At that time, your chance of gaining any points for cooperation pretty much disappear."

"I don't know anything about any blood being under that car."

"That's the wrong answer," LaMoia said. His cell phone rang. "And you know what that is?" he asked the suspect, viewing caller-ID. "That would be my court order coming through to search this dump." He silenced the ringing of the phone with the push of a button and held the device to his ear. "LaMoia," he announced into the phone. "Talk to me, darlin'. Tell me what I want to hear."

16 Voice Male

A blinking message light was no great surprise to Matthews as she returned to her office that evening. In what had become an automatic gesture, she dialed in to retrieve her voice mail, which announced that she had six messages. She cringed as she intuitively anticipated that at least one of these could be from Deputy Sheriff Nathan Prair. He'd attached himself to her once before, and now, with their renewed acquaintance, with the description of the brown uniform in the parking garage, she felt nearly certain she would need to deal with him again.

The first message on the system was an earlier one from LaMoia asking for her company when he went to interview a possible peeper victim, Tina Oblitz. He explained Oblitz's prior attempts to "cancel the order," as LaMoia put it, and how he hoped he might gain insight into Hebringer's and Randolf's "vanishing act."

She felt closer to John—his teasing bordered on flirting. His earlier struggle with the OxyContin had revealed a more human LaMoia. Some people were helped by such challenges, and LaMoia had the makings. She scribbled down his initials—this was how she took note of all such phone messages—a reminder to return his call.

The second message caught her by surprise, and because of her premonition, she mistakenly assigned the voice initially to Prair, though her brain quickly straightened her out. "Lieutenant

Matthews?" It was Ferrell Walker. "I wondered if my gift helped you out? I don't have a phone, so . . . listen . . . I'll call you back."

Her image was not of Walker at the ME's half out of his mind with grief, nor was it the boyish man delivering his sister's soiled sweatshirt as a gift; it was, instead, an image of Walker in his bloodied apron standing in the falling rain, his eyes bloodshot with fatigue but looking up and down her body, his wet, matted hair. One black rubber glove, one yellow—she remembered so many details of that interview.

"Pass," she said aloud, deleting the message.

At the start of the third message, the first vestiges of concern warmed her, spreading through her like a shot of alcohol. "Me again." She was mad at herself for being distracted by Prair, only to be blindsided by the much more obvious, emotionally unstable Ferrell Walker. Trouble came in threes—she'd heard detectives talk of this for years, though dismissed such superstitions—and yet, it seemed she'd been served up a pair. Walker said, "I forgot to mention that I love what you're wearing—especially the orange blouse." It was peach, not orange, she thought as she looked down past the phone and took in her clothing. "Listen . . . we could have a beer, or coffee, or something. Talk about the case. Do you even drink coffee? So much to learn about you."

How had he managed to see the color of her blouse? she wondered. She'd worn her gray rain jacket all day because of the persistent drizzle. She'd taken it off only when inside. The thoughts connected like a magnet picking up filings. She glanced over at her office window. The blinds were twisted open. *Not possible!* She pressed the keypad to save Walker's message, then crossed the room, peered curiously out her seventh-floor window, and twisted the blinds shut. It wasn't as if she wore her rain jacket zipped to her neck—he could have seen her anywhere away from the office. But to do so, he would have to have been watching her, and watching her closely.

The fourth message played automatically from the speakerphone as she stood across the room. Walker's voice yet again: "Me again. Sorry. But we could take a walk or something. It doesn't have to be a drink. Later."

She took a deep breath to clear her thoughts. She'd worked with dozens upon dozens of disturbed men, some across an interrogation table, some in a corrections facility: sex offenders, drug addicts—homicidal, suicidal—social misfits. Ferrell Walker was still grieving, no doubt, and had clearly transferred some of his feelings for his unavailable sister onto her. Such transference was more typically directed at people considered close to the individual, not a virtual stranger, but there were no rules to such things, no commandments to follow.

Walker's final message ran goose bumps up her arms then down her spine and into a nauseated stomach. "I hope I'm not scaring you with these messages. I know women—especially attractive women—must be scared in this city right now. I'm not going to hurt you or something. I want to help you get Lanny Neal is all. The sooner, the better, as far as I'm concerned." The unspoken message there was that in fact he might be planning to hurt her if Neal was not brought in.

She sat down heavily into her chair, her hands steepled before her lips. One more thing to deal with. She struggled to evaluate him as she might a patient. With the death of his sister he had preexisting emotional conditions that allowed the possibility of a fantasy stage where Matthews was seen as his solution to all ills and injustices. She'd made a mess of it by not laying down strict guidelines at his first offer to help her. Worse yet, such a fine line existed between love and hate that she now faced a very difficult job of distancing herself without repercussions.

The sixth message was from Boldt—just the sound of his voice came as a great relief. Something about Mama Lu, an autopsy, and a possible connection to Hebringer and Randolf, though she didn't focus on it clearly, Walker's bloody apron still foremost in her mind. Without the mounting evidence against Neal, without Walker's initial call-in and his attempt to assist in Neal's prosecution by turning over that evidence, she might have believed Walker capable of having killed his only sister himself. She couldn't rule it out entirely, even so.

"End of messages," the voice mail announced. A pleasant, automated voice that had no idea of the worry those messages instilled in her. She stabbed the speakerphone button and disconnected, Walker's messages and his unflinching tone echoing in her head. First things first: She would start a file, detailing the passing of the sweatshirt, making notes about the silhouette in the parking garage, transcribing the various phone messages. If he continued to harass her, the existence of that file would help her make a case. She would not allow him to rattle her. She'd seen much worse than Ferrell Walker, although in her patients the conflict, the violence, the obsession or fixation was always directed at others, not her. Always someone else's problem. She was the facilitator, not the target. The cop. Not the victim.

She packed up and headed home, but found herself checking her rearview mirror a little more often, glancing around while stopped at red lights, and triple-checking the car's automatic door lock. Walker had put the bug in her, and it wasn't going away.

Her houseboat on Lake Union had been bought well before the city's techno renaissance, when the floating one-and-a-half-story homes—actual houses on pilings and accessed by a wooden dock down the middle—had been a latent-hippie community, nonconformists who wanted a home in the city but not the cost of the land beneath. The houses had been dirt cheap back then, an awkward phrase given their setting. Now those same homes went for high six figures, and Matthews had long since realized she was living in her 401(k); at the very least, she had quadrupled her investment.

Her houseboat, last on the left of dock 7c, was constructed of gray shiplap. Thirty-gallon terra-cotta flower tubs sat to either side of the hemp rope railing that surrounded her deck. No green thumb, she'd tried annuals in the tubs for a while but kept killing them off. They currently housed a variety of Korean boxwood that required no attention.

She walked briskly down the dock, her Cole Haan flats clapping like gunshots, her heart rate elevated as she wondered if she'd been followed. Her houseboat's front door was African mahogany and bore a carving of a dove she could do without. She entered, locked the door, and threw its deadbolt. Removing and hanging up the rain jacket reminded her of the color of her blouse and reintroduced a wave of brief panic at the thought that Walker not only had managed to see her with her jacket off but was brazen enough to mention it.

The downstairs was finished cedar, the furnishings spare—a foldout couch, a wood-burning stove, a hand-carved cherry rocker. An eight-by-eight post in the center of the small living room supported the roof. The galley kitchen was separated from the living area by a small island countertop that hosted three stools, a walk-around phone, a cutting board, and a suspended wooden rack that was home to wineglasses. The killer home stereo had taken her three years to acquire. She fired up Sarah McLachlan's *Surfacing* and cranked the volume. If anything eventually sank this place it would be the high count of books and professional journals that overflowed the bookshelves and rose to towering stacks on the floor. A narrow, padded window seat offered her favorite reading nest. Snuggled in there, a fire going, a throw pulled across her legs, she had consumed many hours of pure bliss—at least those hours that weren't tied down. They'd been increasingly few in the last several months. Something drove her to not just fill her schedule but pack it full of work, volunteering at the Shelter, running, and the gym—it didn't matter as long as she filled 6 A.M. to exhaustion without time to think. For thinking was the real enemy: thinking about herself, the lack of romance in her life, the isolation, the poverty of public service, the missed opportunities.

After a dinner of broiled chicken breast and a green salad with rice vinegar, she changed into flannel PJs, built a fire, and tucked herself into the window seat, a glass of Archery Summit Pinot in hand. She felt a bit guilty about not stopping by the Shelter to inquire about Margaret, but Walker's phone messages had unsettled her, and the comfort of home proved just what the doctor ordered, she being the doctor. Chapter by chapter, she lost herself to Barbara Kingsolver's *Prodigal Summer*—a book she found unexpectedly titillating—a rare and much-needed escape from psychology reviews. She caught herself dozing off. Luxury came cheaply these days.

At 11:32—she noticed the firm, bright green display of the kitchen's digital clock—she heard what her mind registered as an unfamiliar sound. The houseboat had a life of its own, never perfectly at rest, battered by water and weather, always shifting, settling, creaking, and groaning. These pops and grunts, the wooden cries and long, eerie sighs helped to form a personality uniquely its own. Matthews knew that personality well. These same sounds lulled her to sleep. They woke her up. On some occasions they frightened her, as they did on this night.

She suddenly felt more awake. Her brain sorted through the database of familiarity with what she now heard, filtering out the noises that accompanied any night on Lake Union: the seaplanes landing and taking off, motor craft, highway traffic, distant ferry horns, sirens, and the noises of her neighbors going about everyday life. She lay there, ears ringing slightly, as she "stretched" to hear beyond the walls. She couldn't be sure what she heard, or whether or not it was just a bad case of nerves. Those phone messages had rattled her. So had her experience at the parking garage. More than she had thought. She promised herself that she wouldn't let this get the better of her, yet she glanced across the room to her purse, which hung by its strap from one of the three ladder-back stools—her handgun, cell phone, the small can of pepper spray, and a mini Maglite. Barbara Kingsolver drew her eyes back to the novel as she told herself that noise carried well and did funny things across water. No reason to get all worked up.

But she'd momentarily lost the chance at sleep. Another few minutes passed behind the efforts of the delicious pages, the melodious singing, and the sumptuous wine. Going on midnight. Feeling tired again at a chapter break, she inserted the bookmark, spun her legs off the window seat, and mechanically folded the throw. She hand-washed the wineglass in the kitchen sink, its glass squeaking, and placed it carefully down into the drying rack. She watched a seaplane land—the last of the night—as it taxied across the lake's black water. As the groan of the propellers faded, she heard yet another unfamiliar creak from the bones of her houseboat.

This time she grabbed her gun and moved to the front door, intent on escorting Walker off the dock. Never mind that the residential phone numbers and addresses of police officers went unpublished, never mind that she'd carefully watched her car's rearview mirrors and had assured herself she hadn't been followed; she remained convinced it was Ferrell Walker creeping around out there, and it was beginning to get to her.

Thumbing aside the curtain on the narrow window to the left of the front door, she peered out toward Bob and Blair's place.

Their downstairs lights were off, the blue glow of a television emanated from the window of the loft. She saw that Robert and Lynn were still awake next door. Lynn's nephew, Gin, visiting from Japan was currently prowling the refrigerator. She'd been pulling the blinds extra carefully on that side of the houseboat, as Gin had a teenager's voyeuristic tendencies. With all the sounds, she knew she wouldn't sleep well if she didn't take a security lap around the house. It wouldn't be the first time she'd lapped the house. More typically, such trips were made to ensure structural integrity in the middle of a raging storm. Heading out now, on a relatively calm night with only a slight drizzle, while pushing her chest into a knot, hardly compared with challenging a forty-knot wind and sideways rain.

She grabbed the halogen penlight from her purse, pulled the Gore-Tex jacket over her pajamas, and let herself out while throwing the night latch to ensure no one sneaked in behind her. Precautions. Any practicing forensic psychologist learned to live with them—ex-cons who blamed you for their incarceration returned to pay their respects; ex-cops who'd been tossed from the force for drug abuse or continued spousal abuse decided you were the instigation behind their removal; prosecutors and detectives arrived at all hours believing they had every right to free advice.

Barefoot on the redwood decking, she headed counterclockwise around the corner, increasingly cautious with each turn. Her toes curled from the cold, wet wood, she tiptoed in bare feet, moving in a trained, controlled fashion, and snagged a splinter in her foot. Hopping on one foot to avoid the shooting pain, she balanced against the house and lifted her foot to the light. The thing was the size of a toothpick and sunk in pretty deep. Her focus shifted beyond her foot to the deck, where a thin film of rainwater left a silvery patina. Offset from that sheen were two muddy boot prints that led in succession from where she stood to her mudroom window. The window was beneath an overhang, dark in shadow. Suddenly it felt much colder out. There had been boot prints found at the construction site overlooking the hotel and Melissa Dunkin's room. She envisioned a man—hands cupped to that window, peeping her. Her orbit of the house completed, her nerves tingling, she hurried around to the back door and the hidden house key. LaMoia needed to hear about this. A moment later she was locked and bolted inside, the splinter and the pain it caused a forgotten footnote.

She wanted to tell LaMoia immediately, given that he was currently working a similar case. His tour over, he'd likely be home by now.

She hurried through the house, pulling blinds and double-checking locks, feeling both exposed and vulnerable. She shed the raincoat but wrapped herself tightly in a thick robe, poured herself another wine, and sat down by the phone, staring at it. What to do? A pair of possible boot prints? Was that *any* kind of evidence? A couple of noises heard outside? As it was, she walked a delicate line in the department, part professional head-shrinker, part cop. This duality, a full lieutenant who had been through the academy, yet a card-carrying Ph.D. in psychology, left most of the department thinking of her as a shrink, not a cop. An outsider. To raise a red flag over a pair of boot prints would make her look green, to say the least.

She picked up the phone and dialed. When LaMoia's recorded voice spoke, she nearly talked over it. "You said it, I didn't. So leave it, and don't sweat it . . . I'll get back to you." *Beep.*

She spoke his name, reconsidered, and hung up.

A minute later her phone rang. The caller-ID returned: OUT OF AREA. Her hand hesitated over the cradle, and she caught herself terrified to answer. Then her brain engaged—she would *not* allow anyone to do this to her.

She answered.

"You rang?" LaMoia, cool, calm, collected. She resented that tone of his.

"I got your machine," she said.

"I screen," he said. "Caller-ID caught your name and number. You ought to be blocked, you know?"

She scribbled out a note to herself. "Got that right."

"What's up?"

She hesitated, his calm making her not want to sound like a schoolgirl.

He said, "Not to be rude, but I'm not exactly on your speed dialer. It's going on one o'clock in the morning. The late late news is rolling around in a couple minutes. The weekend coming up or not, I picture you as an early-to-bed, early-to-rise kind of person, beauty sleep and all that, not that you need it; and so then I get to thinking that maybe you're checking up on me, making sure I haven't succumbed to the great temptation, and I want you to know—"

"I wouldn't do that, John," she interrupted. "Not ever. You know that. What we did—Lou and I—we did out of . . . friend-ship. It started and stopped in your kitchen that night. I'm not the Percodan police. Don't think like that."

"What am I supposed to think? Help me out here, Doc. Why'd you call, if not to check up on me?"

She stuttered and said, "To . . . to . . . check up on the lab work of Neal's."

"At twelve-thirty?"

"At twelve-thirty, yes."

A skeptical hesitation on his part. "Okay."

"What do we know?" she asked.

"Nothing yet," he suggested, clearly intrigued. "It's a little soon, don't you think?"

She couldn't bring herself to sound like a whiner. She overheard detectives mocking such women all the time, women on and off the force. She told herself that if she'd actually seen someone out there with her own eyes, if she could have supplied a description, *anything* at all worth investigating, then yes, she would have included him.

He asked, "You wouldn't happen to be lonely, would you?" Back to his old self.

"I beg your pardon?" If she told him now, this far into their conversation, he'd either overreact or laugh out loud. She couldn't handle either reaction right now.

"You sound . . . I don't know . . . a little off," he said.

"I'm fine." She wanted to keep him talking, to hear his voice.

"You sure? I could rent a video, something like that. There's a twenty-four-hour Blockbuster over on Denny. You got any popcorn?"

LaMoia offering friendship? Maybe she was the one on drugs. "It wasn't a social call."

"We could make it one."

"No thanks," she said, though surprisingly reluctantly. The offer didn't sound bad at all. "You're right about my hours. How about a rain check?" She felt touched that the usually selfish LaMoia could be so giving of himself. Ulterior motives? How badly did he want her at the hotel interview?

"Whatever," he said.

"Thanks, John." She felt an obligation to hang up, but at the same time, didn't want to. She left a pregnant pause on the line.

"So, are we done here, or you got a minute?" LaMoia tested.

She liked the sound of his voice. "I've got a minute," she said casually, trying to sound nonchalant and wondering if she'd pulled it off.

He said, "A businesswoman, name of Oblitz. The one that filed a complaint and then tried to withdraw it, the one I left a message about."

"Who tries to withdraw a complaint?"

"Yeah, I know. I tried to explain that to her. Stenolovski before me. I thought you might tell me why a woman reports a peeper and then tries to back out of it."

"That's a no-brainer: She had a guest."

"Or she's being extorted."

"Maybe, but more likely her friend pressured her to withdraw the complaint or they got there together."

"Yeah? Well, it's set up for four on Monday. The W— the suspender set, the new one across from the Olympic." He said sarcastically, "She made an opening for me in her busy schedule."

"Good of her."

"We'll crack Hebringer and Randolf wide open with this. You and me. I can feel it. Whadda you think Hill would make of that?" Sheila Hill, their captain, Boldt's immediate superior, had been LaMoia's former lover, a fact that Matthews was not supposed to be aware of. But there wasn't much she and Boldt hid from each other. They had once been lovers themselves— something no one was supposed to know, and no one did.

"No one would believe it." She and LaMoia were known to tangle.

"Fuck 'em if they can't take a joke."

Hearing his voice brought her a long way out of herself. She wanted to thank him for that but held her tongue.

He asked, "You sure you're okay? Offer of the video still stands."

A LaMoia she didn't know, and frankly didn't trust. Had he run out of women in the department to conquer? Had someone in the locker room put him up to this, challenged him to go after her, because she had steadfastly refused to date anyone on the job? (She didn't count Boldt as a date and never would.) Nearly one in the morning, and LaMoia making like it was early evening. Night tour did that to people.

"I'll do the interview with you," she agreed.

"Well, that's a start."

By the time she hung up, she had almost forgotten about the pair of boot prints.

17 Two Peas in a Pod

The W's split-level lobby featured twin stairways that led around an island bearing a flower vase and up to the black lacquer reception desk where young people in black clothing and wearing wireless headsets greeted guests with white teeth and tones of way-too-cool-to-get-excited. The halogen lights were set so low that these receptionists seemed to emerge from the haze. Hip-hop pounded from speakers in the ceiling.

LaMoia territory, to be sure. He had the appropriate sarcasm and cynicism down pat.

"Yo, yuppie puppy," he said to the male receptionist, flashing his badge against the request of his interviewee. "April Fools is tomorrow. This is the real thing." He drew a blank expression from the kid with the wet-look hair and the silver stud in his left ear. The kid wanted him to think he saw such shields all the time. But clearly, he did not.

"Hotel guest, Oblitz. She's expecting us."

The black arm—40 percent cashmere—pointed. "There's a house phone to your—"

"Did I ask for a house phone? That headset must do *something*, right? Hotel guest, Oblitz." He barely hesitated, "Now." Crisp. His voice echoing off the stone. A few heads in the lobby lifted and turned.

The kid moved his mouth like a beached fish.

Matthews spoke into LaMoia's ear. "Such bedside manner."

"Don't criticize what you haven't sampled."

"You really *are* shameless. Is the whole world a fire hydrant to you, John?"

He flashed her a look that ended it. "A guy's gotta make his mark."

From a distance, she saw the figure of a man enter the hotel, look up toward the registration desk, and then leave as quickly as he'd come. The wrong address, the wrong hotel? she wondered. Or had that been the man in the boots outside her mudroom window the night before? Had those boots even *been* outside her window the night before? She wore her paranoia tightly around the neck.

"Room nine-eleven," the rigid receptionist said in his best I-want-to-sound-older voice.

Matthews returned to the job at hand.

"Room nine-one-one," LaMoia repeated. Cocking his head to Matthews, he said, "How perfect is that?"

She said, "The word you're looking for is ironic."

"Elevators to your right." The man-child wanted them gone.

"Chill," LaMoia barked, keeping the kid attentive.

Matthews explained, "First, we'd like a look at your registration log for the past three months."

LaMoia added, "And the corresponding billing charges."

Tina Oblitz had the gray power suit going, a shimmering metallic silver blouse, string of freshwater pearls, silver Tourneau, black pumps. Narrow dark eyes that preoccupied themselves with Matthews. To the left of the desk phone lay a sweet little 9mm semiautomatic clipped into a black leather holster designed to be worn in the small of the back. The holster was weathered and sweat-stained, indicating years of wear. The obligatory laptop, mobile phone, and pocket PC sat atop the black enamel desk.

"Plain sight," she said, noticing LaMoia's attention on the handgun. "I didn't want any surprises. Permit's in my purse, if you want to see it."

"Glock?"

"Glock seventeen," she answered.

He'd heard of the model but never seen one. "Weight?"

"Light as a feather. Polymer grip. Magazine holds ten. Used to be seventeen but it was heavier, of course."

"This is not a recent addition to your wardrobe," he said.

"Did I panic when this Peeping Tom showed up and then run out and buy a gun? I don't think so, Detective. I believe in a woman's right to defend herself. In seven years, no shots fired, but it has served its purpose a couple times. It's never more than a few feet away from me."

"Lucky it," he snapped.

"I'm at the firing range once a week. You both know what I'm talking about."

"It's sergeant, not detective. And it's Lieutenant Matthews," he corrected.

"My mistake."

"No," he corrected, his contempt for the executive set obvious, "your mistake was trying to cancel this harassment complaint you filed. Why the back-pedal?"

"You want a seat?" she asked.

"I'd like an answer," he said. LaMoia turned to Matthews. "You want a seat?"

Matthews shook her head, declining.

He looked back at Oblitz. "No, we'll stand."

Tina Oblitz took a corner of the small couch, withdrew a cigarette from a fancy holder that lay on the glass table, lit up, and hogged down that smoke like an addict who'd been away from it for years. Her body consumed it. When she exhaled, hardly anything came out. She looked satisfied, like a boozer after a stiff drink.

She said, "The other detective and I . . . we discussed this."

"The complaint is still on file, Ms. Oblitz, and seeing as how we've got an active case that could use a lift, your cooperation would be appreciated." He said, "I explained this over the phone. I believe you know that's why we're here."

"I never agreed to two of you."

Matthews said, "The department requires a woman officer be present in any interview or interrogation involving a female." As she said this, as she looked at this woman, something nagged at her and then danced out of her thoughts as Oblitz spoke.

"You're the chaperone?" Oblitz asked sarcastically. "Hope you don't mind my saying so, but you don't look the part."

"I don't mind," Matthews said, unflinchingly. It took a lot to intimidate the gray-suit set. She asked, "Have we met before?"

"Are you sure you won't sit down?" The ember of the cigarette went nearly white with the next inhale.

Whatever it was, it nagged at Matthews again, as elusive and annoying as a mosquito in the dark.

LaMoia said, "We believe your attempt to withdraw the complaint may have arisen out of your being compromised," LaMoia said, "or that an attempt was made to compromise you."

Oblitz wore a lot of makeup, but where her real skin showed, it turned paler. "Is that so?" she said.

Matthews said, "Voyeurism escalates to rape. Rape can escalate to homicide. We've lost two women already—they went missing from downtown. How many more until you decide to cooperate?"

"Shit."

LaMoia reminded, "I mentioned that over the phone . . . that we had ourselves a situation."

"We're not the tabloids," Matthews said. "Contrary to what you might believe, not every piece of information leaks from a police department."

LaMoia said, "It's only the big stuff, and believe it or not, your sex life doesn't register anywhere on that Richter scale."

"Shit. Shit. Shit."

LaMoia asked, "Do you remember anything about it? What he looked like? Where he was at the time? How he might have singled you out?"

"No, it completely slipped my mind."

They both took the sarcasm as the first step toward open communication.

"You're married." Matthews had noticed the showy rings, but Oblitz apparently felt obliged to display them for her anyway. "You were with a partner other than your husband."

"You know," Oblitz snapped, "you're going places, Lieutenant. Sharp as a tack, you are."

Matthews contained her anger well. "Mr. George Ramirez paid the hotel incidentals, including three room-service charges and an all-day adult film pass."

LaMoia answered her puzzled and pained expression. "You know what they say? The titles don't show on your bill? Don't believe it. An order number does: *Sweet Valley Thigh,* Ms. Oblitz. Your man-friend talked you into attempting to withdraw the complaint you filed with us. For all we know he talked you into all sorts of things, including the warm chocolate and the whipped cream—room-service order number three, at four-seventeen P.M. Your business. We could care less. But that peeper is our business and we'll *ride* you, Ms. Oblitz, until we come away with whatever you can tell us about it."

"Two peas in a pod." Oblitz picked up her cigarette lighter and flicked it so that the flame burned. She held it out between her and LaMoia, peering through its yellow glare. She placed

the lighter back down. Somewhere in the process another cigarette lit. Smoked spiraled.

"We're not looking to indict you for your sexual preferences
or practices," Matthews said. "We're here because we believe
you can aid our investigation, that your experience may be directly connected to at least one of the women who've gone missing." Sometimes it took voicing the words, airing her thoughts.
Her spine tingled and the hair on the nape of her neck stood on
end. Change the hair color, and Tina Oblitz looked a lot like
Susan Hebringer. Too much like her to be coincidence, Boldt
would have said.

Matthews told the woman, "You wear a scarf on your head,
or a hat, when you go out." She clarified, "A dark scarf."

A sideways glance of disbelief. "Now just how the hell
would you know that?"

"May I see you with it on?"

LaMoia gave Matthews this leeway, though he clearly didn't
understand the request.

Oblitz grunted a complaint, retrieved the scarf, and tied it
over her head. "My hair doesn't hold up under your *constant*
rain," she complained. "Not without spray, and I hate that look."

"Do you see it?" Matthews asked LaMoia, who continued to
look confused. "The resemblance," she completed.

"Hebringer," he whispered. More of a gasp. "How could we
have missed that?"

"We didn't miss it," Matthews said. "It just took us awhile
to see it."

Oblitz looked on, her head tracking them comically like a
spectator at a tennis match. She stood by the couch, cigarette
flaring, focused on Matthews. "What do I do?" she asked. "To
help?"

"Tell us about your day," LaMoia said. "The run-up to your
spotting the peeper."

"It's been awhile," Oblitz said.

"Whatever you remember," Matthews suggested, a newfound kindness in her voice.

Oblitz settled back into the couch, still wearing the scarf. "I had a few extra hours," she recalled. "I hit the museum. The Annie Leibovitz show. Some of your tourist stuff."

LaMoia shot a glance toward Matthews. His normally dull, chocolate eyes were alive with excitement.

They hurried down the dimly lit hotel corridor toward the elevators, when Matthews steered them to the fire door and the stairs. LaMoia had just been notified that the preliminary lab report on Lanny Neal's car had come through, and both were eager to learn the results.

"It doesn't make our job any easier, nor does it make me feel adequate in predicting him." She held the door for LaMoia.

"*Our* job?" LaMoia said, stopping only inches from her. "I like the sound of that."

"Don't get all mushy about it." She held her ground, not allowing him to intimidate her with this closeness, her back to the cold metal door, the two of them nearly chest to chest. She said, "Construction sites, tourist traps. I don't see Hebringer and Randolf fitting into that, both being locals, both living downtown. But I suppose we start there, because it was handed to us."

"We work well together," he said.

"Leave it alone, would you?"

"No."

He headed through the door then and down the first flight of stairs. Matthews hesitated for a second, regaining her composure, controlling herself.

His voice echoed up the concrete stairway. "Chocolate and whipped cream—ever tried it?"

"In your dreams."

"You got that right," he said, his shoes slapping faster and more loudly as he continued his hurried descent.

18 Chumming

Matthews stood in the parking lot by her Honda, awaiting Walker as he punched out at a small shack at the foot of one of the fishing docks. The air pungent with saltwater, the wind heavy with a cold mist, she squinted against the blow, taking in the damp and the beauty of the shipping canal and the greenish gray hill rising toward the blinking radio towers. American flags hung everywhere, even in the rain. A boy rode his bike, a mangy dog running to keep up. The sound of rubber tires running on wet roadway had become so familiar to her that the scenery did not exist without it, the same way downtown demanded the low cry of the ferry horns bellowing out into Elliott Bay. This great city was fungal smells and mystical sounds, dreary skies and paper cups of steaming coffee. It was rubber boots and rain slickers, a place pedestrians waited at cross lights. The trawlers had serviced these same docks for more than a hundred years. Matthews could hear the clip-clop of horses' hooves on cobblestone. She could hear the fishmongers shouting out prices as little blond-haired boys carried fillets wrapped in newsprint over to well-dressed house servants and cooks.

"You need my help again, don't you?" Walker called out to her across the blacktop.

"Some questions is all," she said loudly, as he was still some distance away.

He wore an old pair of running shoes, not waffle-soled boots as she'd expected. This discovery bothered her, for it still left the person responsible for the prints outside her mudroom window in doubt.

"How 'bout that drink?" he said, catching up to her. He wore the same clothes she'd seen him in before. Wet at the knees, caked with mud on the lower leg, they did not appear to have been washed.

"I don't want you calling me anymore, Mr. Walker." She added, "Any further attempts to make contact on your part will be considered harassment. Do you understand?"

"That's the thanks I get?" He cocked his head, "What? You're teasing, right? You want more stuff, is that it? Something you need done?"

"I'm sorry for your loss," she said. She saw confusion register on his face. "If you find it difficult to get over the grief, there are programs, counselors I can—"

"What the fuck? Counselors? You want me off your case, then you—"

"We're closer to an arrest in this case," she said, cutting him off.

This hit him like a slap in the face. Some spittle bubbled at the corner of his lips. "You need me," he whispered. "I can help you."

"I need you . . . to stay out of this. Your involvement could compromise our efforts, Mr. Walker."

"That sweatshirt? That *compromised* your efforts, I suppose?"

He'd caught her, and the slight hesitation on her part cost her, though she salvaged the moment by turning it to her advantage. "Okay, I'll admit it, there is something you can do to help us out."

"I knew it," he said deliberately, a quiz show contestant confident his answer had been right all along.

"I need to see your driver's license, and I need to confirm your residence. Next-of-kin paperwork," she explained, although this wasn't the real reason behind her query.

"I don't own a car, and I don't have a license because I let it expire. But you probably know that already, right? I mean, what's the point?" He indicated the docks behind him. "I bus up here. I bus back into the city. Home's a hole in the ground, a place out of the rain. I've got a tarp, a box of some stuff. That's home. That's what fucking Lanny Neal left me with when he took Mary-Ann off the boat." He stepped toward her, another wave of anger gripping his eyes, another pulse of nausea seeping into her. "Why ask questions you already know the answer to? Are you toying with me?"

"I was under the impression you'd driven Lanny Neal's Toyota Corolla," she lied. She went fishing with the fisherman. It wasn't an impression, but a suspicion that resulted from the lab work on the car. "Your sister's birthday dinner a couple months back."

"That's bullshit. Neal drove." This was her first confirmation that Neal had been telling the truth about that particular night. It was also the first she'd learned that Walker had been along for the celebration—his sister's idea, no doubt. She couldn't see Neal inviting him.

"He got locked out of the car. Is that correct?"

"The guy's a numb nuts. I've been telling you that."

"Did Mary-Ann hurt herself that night?"

"Hurt herself how?"

"I was hoping you could tell me."

"He beat on her all the time, if that's what you're asking."

"I'm asking if you witnessed any violence between the two in Neal's car that night."

Again, Walker cocked his head. "I get it," he said, nodding slowly. "Sure he did. Damn right he did."

"Mr. Walker, it does no one any good—least of all Mary-Ann—if you fabricate your responses. If you lie to me."

"Sure, I can see that," he said, still with an almost whimsical, beguiling expression. "But I'm not lying, am I, Lieutenant? I *did* see him. He *did* hit her that night. Knocked her around."

"You risk invalidating everything we've ever gotten or will get from you if you're caught in a lie. You understand that, Mr. Walker? That includes the sweatshirt."

"What do you *want* from me, Daphne? Am I allowed to call you that?"

This was a device she used on suspects—establishing rapport through use of a given name. Having this reversed on her ran chills up her arms—the sleight-of-hand magician who's caught in the act.

"I want the truth. I want some answers. That's all."

"I'll tell you anything you want me to tell you. You've just got to let me know."

"It doesn't work like that."

"Lanny Neal's still walking the streets, so don't tell me about it working. *It's not working*. I can help with that, Daphne. Me and you . . . we can team up here . . . we can get stuff done. You know what I'm saying."

"It *does not* work like that."

"It works however we make it work."

"I have a kit in my car," she announced. "It's a fingerprint kit. Real simple. Takes about five minutes. You don't even have to clean up. There are forms to fill out—consent forms."

"What's this about?"

"It takes us another step closer to Neal. That's what you want, right?" she asked.

"Of course that's what I want."

"So we'll roll out some prints and help move this forward, if it's all right with you." She hadn't wanted LaMoia along for this reason—two cops wanting prints would have put even an eager beaver like Walker on notice.

He stared at her until she finally met eyes with him—a concession of sorts. "There's so much I can do for you."

She struggled with a response. "We'll start with the prints and take it from there, if that's okay with you."

Five minutes later Walker was rolling his right index finger into a box on a WSDOJ card. He sat in the front seat of her car, out of the mist and the rain, her cell phone and Starbucks tea between them. NPR played from the radio. She turned it down and then cracked a window to vent the smell coming off him.

"How'd you know he locked himself out of the car?" Walker asked. "He tell you he was that stupid? He tell you I could'a had him in that car and the engine running in about three minutes flat? Let me tell you something—you work on boats long enough, you can do anything, any kind of mechanical, electrical repair, whatever kind of problem there is. Numb nuts didn't have a clue. All stressed out over losing his keys. Fuck me. Guys like that ought to be taken out back and shot."

She set him up to roll prints from his left hand. The ink pad was colorless, though he left a fingerprint on the card.

"This is all about the car, isn't it?" Walker asked, fidgeting. "You started by asking about the car. Mary-Ann drove his car. I can help you with this stuff. We're solid on this, right, you and me?"

"There is no you and me," Matthews said. "I meant what I said about no more contact."

"Sure you did."

"No drink, no coffee, no contact."

"Right."

"Mr. Walker?"

He directed himself to Matthews then, turning to face her in a deliberate, overly dramatic way. "I . . . can . . . help . . . you," he declared, popping open the door and slipping outside. A chill, damp wind took his place beside her. As he leaned back inside the car, a darkness overcame his face and she thought that this was a side of the man she had not yet seen. "Do your job," he said, "or I'll do it for you."

19 Nothing Ventured, Nothing Gained

Matthews attempted to keep up with John LaMoia, whose long strides carried him quickly across the sky bridge leading from the King County Corrections Facility, where Lanny Neal had been held for the weekend. Traffic ran some fifty feet below them, the vibrations of the sky bridge reminding her why she never liked taking this route. She preferred a good old sidewalk.

"I'm just saying there may be inconsistencies worth taking a look at," she told him.

"It's an arraignment, that's all. We're up against the time limit. It has to be now. He pleads not guilty. On with the show. The inconsistencies can wait until the probable cause hearing."

"I don't think they can."

"Well, keep that thought to yourself, if you don't mind."

"I'd like to review it all with Lou."

"He's not interested."

"I think he will be."

"Riddle me this," LaMoia said. "If not the boyfriend, then who, the brother?" He didn't allow her to answer, cutting her off. "You're the one saying the brother failed to give you the signals you'd expect. You're the one saying Neal had motive, opportunity, and a predisposition toward abuse. Pardon me if I'm stepping on your psychological toes here, but we *saw* the brother bust his bubble and vent his steam: The guy went after Neal with a knife. A knife is a weapon of passion. A brother doing a sister is most likely a crime of passion, so why didn't he fillet her if he blew his stack? Why'd he toss her off Lanny Neal's fire escape and run her over using Lanny Neal's car and leave her sweatshirt behind Lanny Neal's garbage bin? Does that kind of planning fit with what we know about Ferrell Walker's personality?"

"I'm not against the idea of Neal," she said calmly and yet determined to have her point heard. "I would just like to see the proper paperwork, the proper order to things. This is rushed."

"It's an *arraignment*. We're fine. Trust me."

They dodged a couple of young lawyers who worked for the state. LaMoia took Matthews by the elbow and guided her to the wall. "Don't do this, okay? Don't muddy the water. You want to turn in your psych evaluation? Fine. Evaluate and write it up. You and I are on to better things with Oblitz. Her and Hebringer looking alike. I can taste it." He leaned into her now, so closely that she couldn't hold focus on his face. "I've got guys watching construction sites, guys patrolling the tourist traps. We're running backgrounds on all hotel employees, from maintenance to the bellhops. Something, somewhere, is going to break. The Sarge is all over this water main break and some Chinaman who cashed it in down there, but I'm thinking we beat him to it and deliver him the prize, and I don't need fucking Lanny Neal on my plate right now. Okay? The shit heap backed his car over his girlfriend. He stuffed her into the backseat and then launched her from the Aurora Bridge. SID can prove most of that. Does it bother me that SID didn't do as well in his apartment? There's nothing that can hurt us. Were either of us expecting a smoking gun? Not me. Maybe I was holding out a little hope for blood evidence, but that's all right. He's our guy," LaMoia held up a manila envelope, "and I have it on the authority of the UW's Oceanography Department that he's a lying sack of shit when it comes to seeing her out on that fire escape with two twenty-two flashing on his clock. According to this, Mary-Ann did her swan dive *before* midnight, otherwise the tide carries her toward the locks. They back it up with tidal charts, computer printouts—the works. He's caught in a lie, and that makes him good for it as far as I'm concerned."

This latest information was news to Matthews. Her impression had come from the gut—from watching Neal's reactions as they had questioned him. He wasn't what she expected of a guilty party, and though she knew she couldn't take that to the bank, arraignment would start a countdown to a probable cause hearing. They'd have anywhere from one to ten days to make their case—and for her sake as well as LaMoia's, she wanted to be sure that case stuck. If Neal skipped on a technicality, she worried where that would send Ferrell Walker.

In the courtroom thirty minutes later, Matthews and LaMoia sat among the pimps, prostitutes, and drug addicts awaiting Neal's three-minute arraignment. Spanish and Asian translators stood just behind the appointed public defenders doing their best to keep the suspect apprised of the rapid exchange and instant negotiations between the bench and the bar. After a half hour of this, it seemed more like assembly-line justice than the real thing. As an expert in her field, Matthews had spent a good deal of time in the witness chair, but attending a district court arraignment soured her mood.

Just prior to Neal's entrance into the courtroom, Matthews felt the hair on the nape of her neck stand rigid, and she intuitively turned around to examine the myriad faces in the crowded courtroom. LaMoia turned as well and, so typically of him, spotted Walker first. "There," he said, without pointing. "Back row. Far left."

As Matthews met eyes with the forlorn brother, he hoisted a brown paper sack into view and gestured that he'd brought it for her.

"This is not good," she said to LaMoia.

"You want me to handle it for you? Happy to do it."

"He has every right to be here. I warned him I wanted no more contact with him. If you don't mind, I think you're handling it might make it seem more official to him."

"What are you not telling me?" he asked, perceptive as always.

"I held off because I didn't know the best way to handle it. At this point, I'd like to talk to you and Lou about it. What I should do."

"The late-night call?" LaMoia asked.

She answered him with a saddened expression.

"You're shitting me!"

"Some phone calls. He may have followed me to my place, I don't know." She explained finding the boot prints outside her window.

"Matthews!"

"Don't, okay?"

"I'll rip him up and use him for chum."

LaMoia stood. But at this same instant, Neal's name was announced by the bailiff, and the man was led into the courtroom by a uniformed officer. Matthews tugged LaMoia back down into his seat.

Lanny Neal pleaded not guilty, expressed remorse for the loss of Mary-Ann, and was offered bail of fifty thousand dollars, an astonishingly low amount, given the charges. With a bail bondsman, he'd walk for five thousand, putting his car up for collateral. The wheels of justice rotated, and less than five minutes after he first appeared in the courtroom, Lanny Neal left under escort, essentially a free man. There would be a probable cause hearing set, and much later, a court date. All the while, Lanny Neal was likely to remain free on bail.

Matthews knew the importance of cooling down Ferrell Walker in order to avoid a Jack Ruby moment.

Touching LaMoia's arm, she said, "Let's talk to him together."

LaMoia glanced down at her fingers resting on his forearm, and she jerked them quickly away.

They pushed past the waiting suspects and the exhausted defenders, finally reaching the aisle.

LaMoia called out to Walker and stopped him at the door to the courtroom. The three moved as a group out and into the wide hallway outside the courtroom where wooden benches offered family and friends rest for weary legs. Heads hung. Desperate voices exchanged overworked clichés in worried whispers—"it isn't fair," "he didn't do it." The uniformed guards, bored with hearing such claims, looked straight ahead in a stony silence. LaMoia moved them over to the water fountain, where a noisy compressor would help cover their conversation.

"He walked," Ferrell Walker said with some heat in his voice.

"It's only an arraignment."

"They let him go."

LaMoia said, "They let him make bail. That surprised us, too, but it's not unheard of. Believe me, Neal is going away for your sister."

Walker made no indication he'd heard LaMoia, his full concentration was on Matthews. She experienced his attention as nothing short of worship, an intense adoration that felt invasive and a little sickening.

"I told you we'd handle it from here," she said.

"I told you you needed my help," he contradicted, holding up the same paper sack he had indicated earlier.

"Lunch?" LaMoia said.

Matthews and Walker locked into a stare that excluded all else. She understood then that this was the moment Walker would cross the line from love to hate, and that she would be the one who pushed him over that line, and that she had no choice in the matter. This inevitability frustrated her, tightened her voice, and shortened her breath. Walker was, in fact, doing this to himself; she was nothing but a proxy, required to deliver the crushing blow to separate them.

She said, "I don't want or need your help. Not now. Not in the future. We're all done here."

His dark eyes flared behind his resentment. He dropped the sack at her feet, though it seemed to float in its descent. "We'll see about that," Walker said.

He glanced up at LaMoia, for the first time acknowledging him, though in a roundabout way. "You should have stayed out of this."

He turned and walked away, quickly lost in the crush of the county's judicial process.

"Shit," LaMoia said.

Matthews picked up the paper sack. She opened it, looked in, and asked for a pen from LaMoia. She then stirred through the contents: a wristwatch, a pack of cigarettes, a butane lighter, a woman's wallet with what appeared to be a speeding ticket clapped in its leather jaws.

"What do you want to bet he broke into Neal's apartment and confiscated this stuff?" she said.

"If he did, he just screwed us."

"He thought he was helping. That's the sad part."

"If it's from Neal's apartment, it'll invalidate it as evidence."

"If it's evidence. I'm aware of that, John."

"This shit won't do. We gotta do something."

"I think I just did it," she said, regretting the tone she'd taken with Walker, and wondering at the consequences.

A Wallet and a Watch

"Knock, knock."

"Come in," Boldt said. When he saw it was Matthews, he said, "Hello there. It's been awhile. Have a seat."

Matthews wondered where his compliments had gone. Boldt had always had something nice to say to her, little observations that had always made her day. They weren't there anymore, and she missed them.

He said, "John told me about the guy outside your window."

"He shouldn't have. It was shoe prints is all."

"I've asked SID to take a look. Better late than never." Before she could protest, he explained, "On the off chance it's related to our hotel peeper."

"It's not."

"They're over there now."

"Does anyone ever ask around here?"

"We have a photo of a waffle pattern from the construction site—the voyeur watching the hotel. Maybe we can match them."

"You won't. I have two candidates of my own," she said.

"Suspects?"

She shook her head. "Listen, it could have been a handyman. I had my screens put on a couple weeks ago."

"That was optimistic of you. Still feels like winter to me."

"The prints are not connected to Hebringer and Randolf, Lou."

"I'd rather an educated decision on that be made, a group decision. Okay with you?"

"You're not yourself."

He pushed back the office chair and studied her. "You know, after about a hundred people telling me that, I'm tired of hearing it. Yes, even from you."

"I'd suggest you hand off Hebringer, but I know you better."

"Yes, you do. So drop it." He apologized, "I'm sorry. You didn't deserve that. Something else is bugging me."

"The city worker drowning?"

"The EMTs tell me there's a section of the Underground there, still intact. The city won't let me down the sinkhole because it's too dangerous. Can you believe that? Someone tell that to Susan Hebringer. So I'm exploring the possibility of an alternate access. There's a woman at the U, a Dr. Babcock, looking into it." He added, "So are you going to tell me who your suspects are, or is your plan to try to distract me?"

She never got much past him. She wasn't even sure why she tried. "The floater, Mary-Ann Walker?"

"Right." He knew the case.

"She has a younger brother that's number one. There may be a little transference going on. He seems to think he's Watson to my Holmes."

"Lovely."

"The other possibility is Nathan Prair."

"Again?"

"He was on the bridge the night we investigated. Sheriff's Office is involved—don't ask me how. He's his same old creepy self, and I think there's a chance he was watching me, or at least keeping an eye out for me, over at the Shelter."

"You want me to talk to him? Bring him in?"

"A personality like his? No. Thanks, but no thanks. Guys like Prair, they live with expectation. Bringing him in, we'd add fuel to the fire, and at that point he'd have to prove to himself, to me, to everyone involved how right he was about the perfect match he and I would make. I've been through this before with him. The best approach is to give it distance."

"And that's it? A list of two? We can handle that."

"That's the short list," she said. "The long list includes every con I've ever helped put away who's now out on parole. It might have to include Langford Neal as well—the boyfriend we've charged with running over Mary-Ann and then tossing her off that bridge. He's a controlling personality, has a history of abuse. I'm a woman who's making decisions about his future, and that's bound to sit wrong. I can see him getting curious about me, and that can lead to some ugly behavior."

"I'm not liking where this is headed," he said.

"That makes two of us."

"So let's do something about it."

"It's a passive crime, Lou. That complicates matters. Walker leaves me phone messages that turn my stomach. Prair shows up in parking garages and then disappears. I've got some mud and dirt outside a window. What charges do we file? And how much do I want to discourage Walker, given that he just supplied us with evidence we otherwise might not have found?"

"What evidence?"

"Some of his sister's personal effects, her wallet, a watch, and a pack of cigarettes. There's some paperwork in the wallet, including what appears to be a traffic citation. We left it all off with Bernie before we dug into it. He'll process it for latents and hairs and fibers, and then give us a look."

"If the brother is compromising evidence, then that's obstruction. You want him locked up, we'll lock him up."

"John wants to question him, sure. But I may have scared him off earlier. I was pretty tough on him. I had him roll some prints. My guess: He won't be showing up at work for a couple days. The other thing is, we don't know where he got this evidence. At first, John was furious, and rightly so. But then we thought it through: If Neal had this stuff hidden, if Walker found this stuff hidden rather than in plain sight—it actually could help us build a case."

"That's playing with fire, and we both know it, Daffy. You don't want to get in the middle of this."

"I'm already in the middle. What I'd like is to get to one side, to let John be the center of this guy's attention. That takes a little manipulation with personalities like this. It can't be done all at once."

Boldt put down the pen and removed his reading glasses. A depth to his eyes drew her in. So much going on in there. "So how can I help?" he asked.

"Mersi-do and Mersi-don't," LaMoia said, entering Boldt's office without knocking. He hooked a chair with his boot, spun it around to face them and plopped down into it.

"We're discussing Daphne's being harassed, possibly stalked," Boldt said.

Hands in the air, LaMoia quipped, "It wasn't me," and flashed another trademark smile. "My recommendation is that Heiman and I kneecap Walker, and that's the end of it. He slides around the sidewalks on one of those little dollies for the next ten years. Teach him to mess with our family."

Matthews chuckled nervously.

"I'd prefer we play a little more in-bounds than that."

"Suit yourself. Save the taxpayers a wad." Looking at Matthews he said, "And I gotta tell you, it's one job I'd put my heart and soul into." He was openly flirting with her, and she wondered why that surfaced in front of Boldt, of all people.

She wasn't sure if she should share this or not, but if Boldt found out later that she'd withheld it, there would be hell to pay. "He made an indirect reference to Hebringer and Randolf."

Boldt stiffened. "Such as?"

"It was one of the phone messages. He said it was dangerous out there. That I didn't have to worry about that with him."

"Then I want you out of your houseboat. You'll take a hotel room courtesy of the department until we've had a chance to follow up."

"That's unnecessary." She had feared an overreaction.

Boldt reminded, "You found boot prints outside your window. Whatever the situation, I want you off of that houseboat." To LaMoia: "With Walker mentioning the disappearances, I want him brought in for questioning."

"You're reaching, Lou, and we *both* know that. Listen, phoners rarely stalk; stalkers rarely phone. Two different patterns, two different personalities, and I'm thinking two different people."

"Walker and Prair," Boldt repeated. "But you don't know that!"

"Whoa, there," said LaMoia. "When did Prair get into this?"

Matthews explained most of her encounter at the parking garage—that "a witness" had seen a man in a khaki or brown uniform. She added, "An infatuation like Prair's is harmless, it's just annoying. Honestly, I'm more concerned about Walker's overeagerness to please. But connecting him to the disappearances? That's unworthy of you."

"He made that connection for us," Boldt said.

"It's a daily news item, Lou. The whole city's talking about Hebringer and Randolf. Come on!"

LaMoia attempted to break the tension between them. "Nathan Prair is not harmless," he said. "Just ask that motorist he iced."

Boldt spoke up quickly. "He was acquitted of that, John. It was found to be a good shooting."

"It was never a good shooting and the three of us damn well know it," LaMoia said.

An uncomfortable silence overtook them. LaMoia moved restlessly in the chair. "I'm with Sarge," he said. "The houseboat is too dangerous for you right now. I'll clean out my guest room. You'll stay with me until we make sense of this."

Matthews barked out her reaction, glancing at Boldt, who grinned.

"Talk about the wolf in sheep's clothing!"

LaMoia was not beyond laughing at himself. "I'm not going to hit on you. You—both of you—did me a favor awhile back. I'm returning it, that's all."

"Yeah, right," Matthews said. Her beeper sounded from inside her purse, silencing all three. Hesitation and expectation hung in the air: If LaMoia's or Boldt's pager went off within the next few seconds, then typically it meant a major crime. All three held their breath as Matthews inspected the device, the possibility of another Hebringer or Randolf on everyone's minds. Her shoulders relaxed. "The Shelter," she said. "Don't worry: I know what it's about."

"Consider the offer," LaMoia said.

She looked up at Boldt, anticipating another moment of shared amusement. Instead, Boldt said in all seriousness, "Consider the offer, or pick a hotel. You are *not* going back to that houseboat."

21 | Silhouettes

A sense of relief washed through Matthews as she spotted Margaret across the cavernous basement room. The pregnant girl had returned to the same cot. These cots were as close as it got to something they could call home. She wanted to thank Sheila for paging her, but it would have to wait.

Margaret's eyes had sunk deeper into their sockets, as if the skin on her face were shrinking. Her hair was both tangled and flattened and oily. She caught Matthews studying her.

"Rough day at the office," the girl said, reacting to that stare.

"May I?" Matthews indicated the opposing bed.

"You're wasting your time."

"It's mine to waste," Matthews said.

Closing her eyes appeared difficult for Margaret, as if she might be in pain.

"Are you feeling okay?"

"Have you ever been pregnant?"

"No," Matthews said. "But I'd like to be sometime."

"Don't be so sure. It sucks. I feel sick most of the time. Unless I'm high. When I'm high, it's not so bad."

"When you're high," Matthews said, "your baby's high, too."

"Lucky her, him, whatever. You going to preach to me? 'Cause if you are, maybe we could do this another time."

Sobriety was a requirement at the Shelter, but its definition remained unclear. Most of the girls arrived high. Anyone caught using while in residence was first counseled and consulted—usually involving Matthews—but was kicked out on the second offense. Repeated violation of the rules won a girl a thirty-day ban from the premises. As a rule the staff tried to limit the proselytizing. Some of the Christian centers suffered for their evangelizing—the girls didn't want to hear that Jesus or anything else could save them. Nothing had saved them so far.

"No. Not going to preach," Matthews said. She tried to sound relaxed as she thought about health problems for the mother and neurological and other damage to the fetus.

"I didn't ask for this baby."

"It's beyond that now, like it or not."

"I knew you were the preachy type. You got that look, you know? Sister Teresa." She rolled her head, facing away on the pillow. "Please go away. I got a headache."

"And I've got a hole in my stomach, Margaret. This isn't about just you anymore. You can't ignore that baby. What about your grandparents?"

"Forget them, would you? There's a place south of Safeco. Once I've got a place . . . it's gonna work out."

"I'd think twice about staying here in the city. You're underage. There are people who prey on girls like you, Margaret. They'll have you dealing for them. You'll get arrested. Call your grandparents—they're your chance out of here."

"You know them real good, do you?"

"The baby will be born addicted. How fair is that?"

"Fair?" She placed a hand on her swollen belly.

"Are you getting enough food? The baby needs nutrition."

"Pizza crust. You might say I'm eating Italian."

"What if we called them together? I'd be willing to do that."

"You don't get it, do you?"

"Maybe not."

"They'll tell her—my mother. She's their daughter, after all.

They're gonna tell her. And she'll tell *him* because she's a pathetic, weak woman, and that's just what she does. And it's *his* baby—you understand that, right? His baby, her boyfriend's baby. And he'll either kill me, or keep sleeping with me. Making me do things . . . you understand that, right? I am *not* going back there. Forget it."

"So, we'll think of something else."

"Will *we* really?"

Matthews saw a possible solution—jail time. A women's juvie facility would offer health care for mother and baby. The irony didn't escape her; as a cop she couldn't recommend to Margaret that she get herself arrested. "You're good here for another few nights. It gives us time to think about this."

"Just forget it, would you? I'm here for the food, the shower, and the bed. Not for you, not for counseling. I like it up there. I have friends up there. They're like family."

"If you use, your baby ends up addicted."

"I got that the first time."

Matthews took the girl's arm and turned it to make sure her own phone number was still inked there. She reminded the girl that cop or not, she would never be a cop if Margaret called.

Margaret said, "Yeah, yeah."

Matthews crossed the room discouraged. She thanked Sheila for the heads-up, but didn't get into particulars. For all her problems, Margaret was in relatively good shape by Shelter standards.

She fixed a weak cup of tea and sat alone in the corner trying to sort out options. The tea bag leaked onto the table once she removed it. She drew patterns with the discharge, stretching it like a river across the plastic veneer. She finished the tea still stuck on talking Margaret into getting herself arrested.

The rain had started and stopped again by the time she left. She crossed the church's fairly well lit parking lot, arrived at the Honda, key in hand, and climbed in. She couldn't help reminding herself of her most recent visit, and her spotting the man up in the parking garage, and though she fought the urge to do so, she took a moment to check the garage again.

Seeing no one up there, she told herself to forget about it, but found it easier said than done. Rush-hour traffic jammed the downtown streets, and understanding that at best it was the lesser of two evils, she elected to try Aurora, willing to suffer the five o'clock creep for the lack of lights and the ability to circumvent downtown.

She left the church parking lot. Traffic flow was indeed like blood in a clogged artery. It took her ten minutes to make three lights. When she finally managed a left, she checked her side mirror for any cyclists or other yahoos trying to cut the corner on her, and she spotted a light rack that was at once both familiar and unfamiliar. It wasn't an SPD patrol car; she knew that much. It might have been SFD, except the fire guys used red, not blue, lights in their rooftop racks. The blue lights indicated police or *Sheriff's* Office.

She blamed her reaction on the fact that they'd just been talking about Prair, less than an hour earlier, putting the man solidly in her thoughts. Sight of that light rack spiked both fear and anger in her. Was Nathan Prair following her around town? Following her home? Watching her from parking garages? Had it been Prair outside of her mudroom window, and if so, how much of her had he seen?

It added up, now that it seemed so obvious to her: As a law enforcement officer, her home phone and address went unpublished, but it was well within the pale that a King County deputy sheriff could obtain that information. Walker was unlikely to know the location of her houseboat; Prair could get it with a phone call.

She waited at the intersection behind a flurry of angry horns and, as the light turned yellow, quickly took the left turn, trapping those behind her with the red light.

Asking LaMoia to come out into this mess of traffic at first seemed unthinkable, yet that's just what she did. She would execute some evasive tactics and eventually find her way home—hopefully with LaMoia close behind, looking for anyone following her.

"Yo," he answered.

"It's me."

"Hey, you."

"Listen, it may be nothing, and I'm keeping my eyes peeled, but I have half a notion that Prair is with me in traffic, and I wondered if you could use your connections over there to see if he happens to be on duty at the moment, and if so, if they know his ten-twenty. Traffic's bad. And it's getting dark. I'm heading down toward Safeco. I thought I'd loop it once—give it four right turns in a row. You know."

"Do it, and then put yourself in a holding pattern—make it a couple laps—I can be there in a matter of minutes."

"Sweet of you, but it's a mess out here. I'm going to go get some of my things at my place and then take Lou up on the offer of a hotel. He suggested the Paramount. If you want to meet me there, I wouldn't complain."

"I'd rather catch up to you now, catch Prair in the act."

"There's no law about driving around the city."

"Listen, I can make these calls from the car. Keep orbiting Safeco. I'll be there in five minutes." He hung up.

She felt incredible relief. He'd done as she hoped, but not as she asked, proving that he was predictable in an unpredictable way.

A half mile later, the relief gave way to panic as she reached Safeco Field and the Honda unexpectedly sputtered and died.

22 Knock, Knock. Who's There?

As her car drifted to the side of the road, Matthews cursed herself for choosing such a remote part of town. In all of Seattle you couldn't buy yourself an empty street at this time of day, except around a sports stadium that wasn't in use.

A curtain of rain fell all of a sudden, its impact deafening. She reached for the handle, but then locked her door, reminding herself to stay inside.

"It's me," she said, when LaMoia answered her call less than a minute later.

"What's your ten-twenty? I'm jammed, traffic is a bitch, and just for your information, Mr. I-haven't-got-a-Prair came on duty with the night shift. He's believed to be on bus duty downtown. My guy's checking all that. But here's the humdinger—" He paused. "You ready for the humdinger?"

She didn't think she was. She wanted to explain her car had died and get some help on the way. But before she could tell him, he continued right on.

"The citation, the speeding ticket Walker slipped you at the courthouse? His sister's speeding ticket—Mary-Ann Walker? That citation was written up by none other than Deputy Sheriff Nathan Prair."

Her world folded in on her, like the legs of a card table collapsing. She felt trapped, pinned down. She blurted out, "The Honda died. I'm dead in the water over by Safeco Field."

"Died how?"

"Sputtered and quit. I coasted to the side of the road."

"Gas," he said. "I don't like it."

"Well, it isn't my dream vacation either," she said, a little testy.

"You could have been sandbagged, Matthews. You sit tight."

"Do I have a choice?"

The phone went silent and she dropped it into her lap. She had hoped he wouldn't disconnect the call, the sound of his voice so reassuring, but she hadn't been about to ask him to stay on the line. Prair had known Mary-Ann Walker ahead of her death. That made her feel terribly vulnerable.

At that moment of realization, a car pulled up behind her, headlights shining in her rearview mirrors like spotlights. Her eyes burning, she strained to identify it as LaMoia, then quickly realized it wasn't.

Her purse lay on the floor to her right. It contained her defense arsenal. She stretched for it, and as she did, she turned the key, the engine grinding along with the rush of blood at her ears. She caught the strap and sat back up. In her outside mirror she saw a man's dark silhouette approaching, and was reminded once again of the parking garage. She warned herself not to overreact, spotting her own sudden weaknesses.

She dragged the purse across her lap and was reaching inside when she jerked her hand out with a start as bare knuckles rapped loudly on the window glass.

"Help you?" Male. Deep voice. The rain obscured a decent view of him.

Swish, swoosh, the rubber blades did the only dance they knew. Rain coming down hard now, like pebbles cast into a pond.

Knock, knock. Again. "Can I give you a hand?"

Strong—his voice told her that much. She didn't want to look at him because she knew that eye contact empowered the attacker. She silently begged for John to hurry up. Her fingers crept back into the purse, though nervously this time, as if she might get caught.

"No, thank you." Too soft-spoken, she raised her voice. "NO, THANK YOU! ALL SET." She thought to add: "SOMEONE'S ON THE WAY!"

"I'm good with cars."

Fixing them, or breaking them? she wondered. "I'm all set."

"Put it in neutral," the deep voice instructed. "Let me at least get you out of this lane."

It was, in fact, a lousy place to have come to a stop, halfway across two lanes. Small tendrils of terror began in her crotch and rushed up through her. "NO, THANK YOU." How many times did she have to say that?

His rapping on the window bothered her. She wanted him to go away. "Stop it!" she bellowed. She didn't mean to say that, didn't mean to sound scared. Predators fed on such fear.

"I'm trying to help," came the male voice. "You're gonna get hit sticking out like this!"

She cracked the window less than an inch, just enough so there would be no mistaking her words or her tone. "I'd like you to leave now, please."

"Lady, I'm trying to help here."

"Go away now!" She used too urgent a tone, too frantic. She didn't want to give him that. She rolled up the window and looked straight ahead.

"Lady!" Shaking the car, he pulled on the driver's door handle. "Put the damn car in neutral and let me get you out of the road."

Her right hand, now inside her purse, touched the butt end of the handgun. Her left hand joined her right and she chambered a round, still out of sight.

He shouted, "You're going to get yourself hit sticking out like this!"

A huge sound erupted all at once, and she jumped. She thought she'd been rear-ended. The Good Samaritan's belt buckle pressed up to the window glass, the fly to his pants at eye level. She briefly considered firing her weapon at that target.

"Leave the lady alone, asshole."

Although she couldn't see her rescuer, she recognized the voice as that of Nathan Prair, and a trickle of dread ran through her. Which was the spider and which was the fly?

"Do not pass Go! Do not collect two hundred dollars." This time, it was LaMoia's wisecracking voice she heard, unmistakable and welcome. It must have been to Prair he said, "You're a long way from home, sailor. You wait over there."

In her lap, the mobile phone's timer continued to count the seconds: 3:07, 3:08 . . . She had never disconnected the call. LaMoia had heard the entire exchange with the man who'd stopped to help her. Words were traded out there. Tempers were flaring.

A metal clicking of handcuffs so familiar to any police officer. LaMoia informed the stranger, "The woman asked you to back off and leave her alone. You refused, which means you're under arrest for harassing a police officer."

The stranger's astonished voice said, "A police officer?"

"You have the right to remain . . ."

Matthews threw her head back. The dull off-white of the ceiling fabric formed the sky above her. The gun's knurled grip warmed in her hand. A throbbing pushed at her temples, a membrane ready to explode.

Prair's arriving on the scene had triggered a whole series of thoughts. She caught sight of his flashing roof lights in her rearview mirror, wondering when he'd turned them on and why she hadn't seen them until then.

The sound of the rain and the three men arguing filled her ringing ears. The rain shook the car. Prair had hidden that he'd known—or at least had met—Mary-Ann Walker prior to her murder. Why? And what impact did it have on the case? On Daphne Matthews?

Unable to take the isolation, she climbed out into the rain and glanced toward the side of the road, from where Nathan Prair looked back at her, out the side window of his cruiser. The rivulets of rain cascaded down the gray glass, looking like rows and rows of tears on his face. Prair stared at her, as cold a look as she could recall. Had he read her thoughts? Her fear? Did he sense that they knew his dirty little secret? She wanted the truth—such a simple thing to ask, so difficult to attain.

Prair rolled down the window. The tears disappeared. "I was trying to help," he called out.

She nodded. Some rain came off her hair, sparkling in the glare of LaMoia's headlights. She said back to him, "I've been getting a lot of that lately."

"Is this waiting really necessary?" an uncharacteristically impatient Daphne Matthews asked LaMoia, the two of them watching the detainee through the interrogation room's one-way glass.

LaMoia said, "You know the drill."

Yes she did: The waiting allowed the suspect time to comprehend the severity of the situation, and police the time to collect as much information on the individual as possible, but she'd never waited out that time as a victim before, and the resulting anxiety owned her.

"What about Prair?" she asked.

"What about him?"

"You let him go."

"Let him go?" LaMoia asked. "He's a cop who responded to a situation. Under normal circumstances, he'd be considered something of a hero for helping you."

"Hardly. Are we going to talk to him?"

"Not formally," he answered.

"But the ticket . . . his having known Mary-Ann . . ." She felt exasperated, everything turned on its head.

"We don't show that card until we can back it up with something. It'll send him so deeply underground we'll need to dig through five layers of lawyers to know what clothes he's wearing."

"He *lied* to us."

"Not on the record, he didn't. He's a cop, Matthews. However he's involved in this, he knows exactly how we're going to play it. We do the dance or we lose him—it's as simple as that."

"I want to pressure him," she said. "Tonight, tomorrow, as soon as we can. I know the way this one thinks, John. If we squeeze him we stand the most to gain."

"You going to pull rank on me?"

"Is it going to come to that?" she asked.

The two studied each other.

LaMoia said, "Okay . . . But he'll talk his way out of it, and we won't have squat."

"I'm being impetuous?"

"You're reacting to a tough situation . . . that wasn't easy out there. You're lashing out at all available parties."

"Who's the psychologist and who's the detective?" she asked.

He nodded okay. "You want the detective? Your fuel line was crimped, probably with a pair of pliers."

"And maybe it was a rock that one of the tires kicked up." She'd overheard this preliminary report from the police garage; she didn't want LaMoia making it worse than it was.

His annoyance manifested itself as flaring nostrils and a worried brow. LaMoia's level temper was one of his most valuable qualities—she'd heard that when he lost that temper things could "get a little wild," as a patrolman had once put it. She had no desire to be the object of that display.

"The guy we arrested wears clodhoppers with monster soles. It's entirely within the realm of possibility that this asshole frequents empty construction sites. I can detain him on harassment charges at least until the T1 is back on-line and we know for sure whether he has a record or not."

"Where are we?" Boldt asked from behind them. She could

read Boldt by his tone of voice; she heard concern. They met eyes, tenderly and with feeling. She wanted to hug him. Studying her face he said, "Knowing you, you already think we're wasting our time."

LaMoia quipped, "Andy Sipowicz's got nothing on you, Sarge."

"He was offering help," she said. "Now he's cooling off in the Box like a street thug. I wonder if that's the right way to handle it."

LaMoia told Boldt about the gas line.

Boldt said to Matthews, "Well, there you go." Adding, "Listen, you're not the first stalking victim to think we've got the wrong guy. That's victim response one-oh-one." He asked LaMoia, "What's his pedigree?"

"Gary Hollie. West Seattle. An accountant with something called Cross Ship LLC." LaMoia held himself back a moment before saying, "I hate accountants."

A young patrolwoman approached at a brisk walk and delivered a coy grin to LaMoia as well as the awaited computer printout. Matthews tried to ignore the woman's open flirting.

"Never met her." LaMoia defended himself without looking up from the printout. It was his prescience that disturbed her the most. She didn't want him reading her thoughts.

LaMoia said, "Seems our Mr. Hollie went down for illegal trespass in Maryland less than two years ago."

"That could be anything," Matthews said.

"Including a peeping charge dealt down," LaMoia said.

"He's yours," Boldt told LaMoia, strategizing a game plan. "I'm a presence, that's all. You take the chair. I want to pace."

"Got it," LaMoia said. Already at the interrogation room door, he looked back at Matthews. "You see something you don't like, give us a knock or a buzz." A gracious offer, but also a little patronizing.

"What if I don't like *any* of it?" she called out.

LaMoia motioned Boldt through first. "Age before beauty," he said.

Gary Hollie's oversized head was reminiscent of a jack-o'-lantern, and had nearly as much hair. He wore a neatly trimmed black mustache above pursed lips that struggled to contain a simmering anger. Forest green chinos, a white button-down shirt, and the thick-soled office shoes completed the look. If they ended up pressing charges they would have a good look at the waffle pattern of those shoes.

LaMoia introduced Boldt as "the guy who runs the show around here." He then took a seat in an uncomfortable chair across the war-pocked table from the suspect. Everything about the Box was austere and drab, from the vinyl flooring to the acoustic-tiled ceiling punctuated with randomly lanced pencil holes. Boldt wandered the perimeter, studying the familiar walls like a building inspector. A mirror of one-way glass occupied most of the west wall, a window through which Daphne Matthews would observe the interview.

Hollie complained in a tight nasal whine of a man held hostage by stress and tension. "This is what I get for trying to help the lady? Who are you people?"

LaMoia played the game, allowing a drawn-out silence to settle into the room beneath the steady presence of forced air. "We appreciate your taking a few minutes to help us sort this out."

"I have a right to an attorney."

"Yes, you do, and you may exercise that right at any time. No one here has denied you that right. You'll recall that I offered you the chance to place that call if you so desired."

"You also threatened to charge me."

"I *informed* you that the involvement of attorneys would necessitate I book you. Those are the facts, Mr. Hollie. Currently, I can still change my mind. Right now, we're just two guys talking about an incident that's as likely to go away as it is to stick. If you want to walk out of here, then I've got to make your arrest go away. That's what we're doing here, me and you: We're making like magicians. We're working out the disappearing act."

"So what's *he* doing?" Hollie indicated Boldt.

Distracting you. Worrying you. "The boss is here to make sure I don't knock you sideways and use you to mop the floor, because I'm known to have a little bit of a temper when it comes to defending my family. The woman you threatened is a police officer I work with—we work with. Highly respected and loved by all. You picked a hell of a target, Hollie."

"I did not target her."

"She asked you to back off, several times. Her phone was on. I heard it."

"Her car was blocking two lanes."

"She told you to go away. You chose to ignore her request."

"She was being unreasonable."

"Whereas banging on a window, wrestling with a door handle, and shouting at a driver is the epitome of reasonable behavior."

"The . . . car . . . was . . . blocking . . . the road," Hollie said, his attention alternating between Boldt and LaMoia. "I was trying to help. The car was stalled in traffic. Would you have just driven by? The headlights were on. It was raining. A woman inside. Alone."

"You see? Now we're getting somewhere," LaMoia said. "Like, for instance, how did you know there was a woman inside that car? How did you know she was alone?"

He stammered, looked a little dazed, and then recovered. "Because I went up to the window and looked inside."

"You get off on looking in windows, do you?" LaMoia asked, turning to make eye contact with Boldt.

"What the hell does that mean?"

"Maryland, two years ago. You want to tell us about the trespass charge?"

Hollie blanched, chewing nervously on his lower lip like something was stuck in his teeth. His fingers drummed rapidly on the edge of the table as a sheen appeared below his eyes and above his thin eyebrows. A criminal record was like a pole marker on a racetrack—no matter how fast you ran, it kept reappearing in front of you.

"We're calling Maryland right now," LaMoia informed him. "You don't want to work a story on me because I do not like stories. I respect a man who owns up to what he did. The past is the past, eh, Mr. Hollie?"

"You're single, or you wouldn't say that," Hollie said with authority. "There's no such thing as the past when you're divorced. It stays right there with you every day: the alimony, the anger, the memories. You never get past it. Not completely."

"So enlighten me about these charges."

"My ex got it in her head I was going to steal our son from her. I'm talking kidnap. She made up a bunch of crap about me harassing her—*none* of it true—and got a restraining order in place. The woman is psycho. And of course they believe the woman, not the guy, right? You show me one time they believe the guy. The restraining order wouldn't let me within a hundred feet of a house that I was paying the mortgage on. Try that out."

"So you ignored the order." LaMoia realized he sounded less confident, and regretted the letdown.

"I entered the house—*my* house, and when no one was home I might add—and got a bunch of my clothes, a couple CDs, and a picture of my son. For *that* I got arrested, and charged, and convicted." He huffed and shook his head. "I'll tell you something: I drew a line on a map as far away from Maryland as I could get—excluding southern California, because that place makes me sick—and I ended up here in Seattle. Away from her and, I might add, away from my son, which is killing me. If you were a father, you'd understand that." Gesturing to take in Boldt and the room, he said, "But take a look around. I'm still not far enough away from her."

Boldt spoke for the first time, asking calmly, "Mr. Hollie, would you have any objection to our lab guys making a quick impression of your shoe soles, maybe looking over your car?"

"What are you talking about?" Hollie seemed caught between a laugh and a cry.

"Agreeing to the search will expedite the process," Boldt advised, "however you're under no obligation to cooperate, and there are no guarantees of the outcome."

Hollie squinted his eyes shut like a man kneeling before the altar asking for forgiveness. "All I wanted to do was help the woman out."

"Out of the car, or out of the road?" LaMoia questioned, turning his words.

"The opportunity still exists to help," Boldt advised. "By clearing you, our lab guys can move on." It was a bit of a stretch, but sounded convincing enough.

LaMoia and Boldt awaited his answer expectantly, a pair of gamblers waiting for the roulette ball to drop.

"I've got to call a lawyer first."

LaMoia's head bounced in defeat. "We brought you in for answers. Now we get lawyers?"

"If the lawyer says it's okay, I've got no problem with you looking at *anything* of mine. Shoes, car, what do I care?"

Hollie made it sound as if he were cooperating, or intended

to cooperate, but it was all a ruse: Not even the stupidest PD would advise him to submit to such a search without evidence and charges in place.

The suspect reminded them, "I'm starting all over out here. Though I've got to tell you I'm reconsidering that decision as well." He met eyes with Boldt, who wore his disappointment openly. "Is there any place left in this world where anyone— and I mean anyone at all—is still sane?"

Boldt signaled LaMoia. He wanted a chat in the hallway. They had the wrong guy, and both cops knew it.

24 Of Bridges and Badges

"Thank you for meeting me."

"You didn't say anything about him being here." Deputy Sheriff Nathan Prair pointed to LaMoia like a man ready to pick a fight. Prair lived coiled like a snake, ready to strike.

"I'm the translator," LaMoia explained. "You feed her the bullshit, and I'll sort it out later."

"Real cute."

Prair's round face and surfer-blond hair normally took ten years off his forty, but on this day fatigue painted his eyes a sickly gray. It wasn't his workouts holding his shoulders square and high, but a steely determination not to appear intimidated in the company of a police sergeant and lieutenant bent on questioning him. He fought off that fatigue like a driver too long behind the wheel, blinking continually and overexposing his eyes so they looked, at times, wide with fear.

The three stood outside the Nordstrom's Rack store on Pine, an unattractive street corner only yards from a bus tunnel station entrance. Matthews had let Prair name the spot, and it intrigued her that he'd chosen this place. He was on duty, but taking a few minutes of lost time to meet with her. A warm wind ripped off Puget Sound and carried a seagull at blazing speeds overhead. LaMoia tracked it like a hunter. His eyes fell onto Prair, and the deputy stiffened.

Against LaMoia's wishes, Matthews handed Prair a photocopy of the moving violation that Prair had written up on Mary-Ann Walker. She said, "We could probably give you a dozen false reasons why we're here, Nathan. But the thing is, we're all cops. We all know better. We could put you in the Box and talk around the edges of this and see if we couldn't get something to spill out of you. But you've been through enough of that to know better. Don't you think? I do. So I'm just going to put it to you straight: We've got the ticket that you wrote up for Mary-Ann Walker a week prior to her going off that bridge. We're asking ourselves why in the world you would withhold that information from the investigating officer, seeing as how it could come back to bite you, as now it has."

Cars and trucks rumbled by. Some yahoo across the street had a blaster playing rap music at the decibel level of a jet taking off.

"And here I was thinking you were going to thank me for getting you out of a jam yesterday."

"I guess I'm just lucky you showed up," she said.

"Life is just chock-full of happy coincidences."

"Like you knowing Mary-Ann," LaMoia said.

"Just like that," Prair agreed. He radiated a smile. "What? You two think I actually had any way of knowing, standing up on that bridge, that the woman below was one of probably sixty or more violations I'd written up that week? Are you kidding me?" He addressed LaMoia, "You ever work traffic? You know what I'm talking about."

Three kids in clothes too big for them went by on skateboards timed perfectly to catch the pedestrian crossing light.

"Never had the pleasure," LaMoia said. "I came up gumming sidewalks."

"The night Mary-Ann was killed you took forty minutes of personal time—"

"Killed? She was a jumper last I heard."

"No way," LaMoia said. "You were on that bridge. You

knew we'd found the blood trail, knew what we were thinking. You were there, Prair. We were all there together. Skip the theatrics. You're ripping yourself a new one."

"McD's," he said. "I went off the clock—eleven, eleven-thirty—for a quarter-pounder and fries." Right or wrong, she read his face as truthful.

Whether Prair knew it or not, he'd just supplied the window of time suggested by the university's oceanography department. Neal's claim of seeing 2:22 A.M. on the clock had proved far too late to account for the physical sciences of the ocean. Mary-Ann Walker had gone off that bridge before midnight. Matthews caught LaMoia's eye and knew he was thinking the same thing.

LaMoia had his detective's notebook out and in hand. "Which McDonald's?"

Prair buried his face in a large hand. "Shit." He cleared his expression and supplied LaMoia with the address: Marginal Way at the turn for SEATAC.

Matthews asked, "Are we going to find you had a history with Mary-Ann Walker beyond this moving violation?"

"Excuse us a moment, would you?" Prair seized Matthews by the arm and led her out of earshot from LaMoia, who craned toward them as if hoping to hear. Seeing this, Prair moved her a little farther.

A couple of big, hefty women came out of The Rack carrying too many bulging plastic bags—they looked like elephants with saddlebags. Both talked at once, going on about the deals they'd just made and all the money they'd saved. Matthews thought: You've got to spend it to save it, does anyone see the irony?

He said, "Lieutenant, forgive me for saying so, but whatever was said in sessions with you was privileged and said in confidence, and is supposed to stay that way."

"You have fantasies about having sexual relations with the

women you pull over, Deputy. On several occasions those fantasies have had a direct influence on your behavior. Was that the case with Mary-Ann Walker?" *Is that the case with me?*

"That's got nothing to do with this."

"Prove it." She was wondering if that *was* the case with her as well. Had Prair crimped her gas line in order to play the hero and save her? Had he hoped to win a roll in bed as her thank-you?

"I don't have to. There's nothing to prove. You're coloring your opinion based on privileged information, Lieutenant. Never mind that there's nothing to it—it wouldn't hold up if there was."

She broke his grip and stepped back. LaMoia moved in, ever the protector.

She said to Prair, "You should have come forward when the body was identified last week."

"Would'a . . . should'a . . . could'a . . . let me ask you this: Would you have come forward if you'd been me? My history?"

She probably wouldn't have, but she didn't say so.

"That shooting colors every impression there ever is of me, never mind that it was ruled a good shooting. No one remembers that part. If I'd have come forward on Walker I'd have distracted the investigation—exactly what's happening now—and that helps no one."

"Especially you," LaMoia said.

Matthews glanced over at the patrol car Prair was driving. Registration plate: KCSO-89. She'd looked down at the rooftop of that same patrol car from the parking garage across from the Shelter. There was no room for coincidence in such matters. She felt the blood drain from her face.

"You just happened across me, broken down like that yesterday," she said.

"What if I did?"

"I'm asking: Do you make a habit out of following women around in their cars?"

"It's not like that."

"Then write it up the way it is, the way it was," LaMoia ordered. "Do it voluntarily, do it by tonight, or we'll pass an official request through channels that'll have you hoisted up a flagpole by your short hairs. Every meeting with Mary-Ann—chance encounter or not—every phone call, the four-one-one on your whereabouts every waking second the night she died. If so much as one comma is out of place, this thing is going to rain down on you, Nathan. We're going to want your time sheets for the past month, we want copies of every moving violation you issued. If there are holes in your time sheet, we're going to want detailed explanations of every missing minute. Witnesses to your whereabouts, you name it. You carried the gold shield once—you fill in the blanks."

Prair's eyes went icy. Knots formed like hard nuts at his jaw. "That'll be it for me. You two know that. My record? Time sheets? Ticket carbons? Are you shitting me? That puts me square in the crosshairs."

"That's where you *are*," LaMoia informed the man. "Deal with it. Ten tonight, on my desk, or the shit starts raining down on you."

With that, the skies opened up, as if on command, and dumped buckets. LaMoia and Matthews ran for the bus tunnel entrance. Prair headed for his patrol car. The seagull reappeared overhead, caught in the rain, barely able to fly. Matthews saw it struggling, and then it was gone, lost in the gray, along with hundreds of pedestrians scurrying for shelter from the storm.

Boldt awoke to the sounds of Liz showering and the fish-eye distortion of his son's peaceful sleeping face, nose to nose with him. He didn't remember Miles having snuck into bed with them. For one blissful moment, he lay there staring at the little man, realizing this would likely be the best part of his day—then, like tiny sprouts ripping open the seed husk, thought began to penetrate that peace.

He had an appointment later in the day that might supply answers about both Chen's death and possibly—he allowed himself to believe—the disappearance of Susan Hebringer. He had at least two administrative budget meetings on the schedule that he dreaded. Liz's minivan needed to find its way from the bank's underground parking to a body shop on Broadway. Sarah had after-school ballet, and if Liz's car wasn't out of the shop by then Boldt would need to arrange pickup by five.

"What's your day look like?" Liz stood naked in the doorway, toweling off. She'd added back some of the weight the lymphoma had claimed, finally covering her skeleton again in delicious womanly flesh.

"Not too bad," he said. "Looking up at the moment."

"You want to lock the door a minute?" she asked.

"Yes, I do." Along with her weight, some appetites had returned as well. Boldt slipped out of the covers so as not to wake Miles, crossed the room, and pulled the bathroom door shut behind himself. As he brushed his teeth, she undressed him, pulling down his pajama pants and helping his feet out the same way she did with the kids. He considered teasing her about this, but didn't want to ruin the moment. He left the sink water running to cover their sounds.

Liz dropped the towel, pulled herself up onto the countertop, and turned to face him. "This okay with you?" she asked.

He stepped up to her, gently eased her legs apart, and they embraced. "Do you hear me complaining?"

Responding to his kissing, she eased her head back against the mirror. Drops of water raced down its smooth surface. Her fingers wormed into what remained of Boldt's hair as he dropped to one knee. "Good morning," she said in a husky, appreciative voice.

Starting out that way, Boldt was thinking.

Dr. Sandra Babcock could have modeled in a blue jean ad, and proved to be much younger than what Boldt had expected of a tenured professor of archaeology. Mid-thirties at best, she had a clear complexion, soft green eyes, and a slurry, southern way of speaking. She had a playful sparkle to her eyes and the distracting habit of rolling a mechanical pencil between the fingers of her right hand like a majorette with a baton.

If her office reflected her thought patterns, then they'd get along fine. Neat and tidy, not a paper clip out of place. Two discarded yogurt containers in the trash—nonfat strawberry. He noted that she'd saved the plastic spoon, as it stood out amid a group of pens and pencils in a *Weekend Edition* coffee mug. But for all the organization, the pretension that accompanied the director of any university department, Dr. Sandra Babcock churned inside, as her fingernails were gnawed to the quick. He appreciated knowing that in advance. *Birds of a feather,* he thought.

They killed a few minutes in social discourse. Boldt lectured regularly for the criminology courses at the U and Babcock had done her homework. They got through the do-you-knows and have-you-mets without too many overlaps. After a few tentative silences between them, Boldt saw clear to open up the conversation to the purpose of his visit.

He said, "Day before last I interviewed a pair of EMTs. Either they lied to me, or there's an explanation for events that I'm missing. As I explained over the phone, Dr. Babcock, I need the Cliffs Notes on this city's Underground and, if possible, access—I need to get under that section of Third Avenue, and the city won't let me down in."

"EMTs?"

"They claimed they had not attempted resuscitation on a man who I believe died later than what they put down in their report. It's not them I'm after. I just want the right answers."

"Where exactly on Third?"

"Between Cherry and Columbia."

She glanced up to a large wall map of downtown Seattle that was nothing like what he'd ever seen—instead of city blocks, a good deal of downtown was represented as excavated walls and floor plans.

Boldt said, "I have only a vague notion of the city's Underground. A couple of blocks around Pioneer Square. The fire in the late 1800s, the tidal floods, and the decision to elevate the shoreline of the city. But according to these EMTs, they encountered what they believe was Underground clear up on Cherry and Third."

A few strands of hair broke loose from behind her ear and cascaded into her eyes. She brushed them aside. "Twenty-two city blocks were buried when they filled in the flats a hundred years ago. Retaining walls were built surrounding the old ground level, and then the streets backfilled to elevate them some twenty feet higher. It took over a decade to complete. The Underground tour accounts for only three city blocks. Plenty of other sections of the Underground still exist, most sealed off and awaiting us like time capsules. For the most part, they're on private property, they're dangerous, and though we're constantly trying to gain access in order to inventory and photograph, fears of lawsuits and insurance coverage discourage cooperation. From the early 1920s on, city utilities were run along the old underground sidewalks, the perimeter area between these retaining walls and the brick walls of the old buildings down there. When I read about the sinkhole, I'd hoped the city engineers would allow us access. But the needs of archaeology took a backseat to getting traffic running again and the complication of much of this being private property. On the other hand, if you could get me—this department—access, you'd be doing the history books a favor. I'd be happy to tell you what you're looking at."

"I was hoping this might work out the other way around."

"I'm afraid not. The city flat-out turned down my request. But a police lieutenant? Can't you gain access, even to private property, if you want?"

She'd clearly granted him the interview because she saw Boldt as her ticket into the Underground.

"It doesn't work like that." He said this, but his mind ground through the possibilities. Dixon's confused autopsy might provide enough unknowns to win Boldt the necessary paperwork.

Babcock teased him into wanting this with her explanation. "As the city streets were filled in, to lift them above the flood levels, people moved block to block by climbing ladders, crossing the new streets still under construction, and then back down a ladder to another block. It went on this way for *years*.

Eventually, the retail stores moved up to the new street level, but the old storefronts still existed.

"They're still down there," she continued. "What used to be Main Street is now underground. I imagine that's what your EMTs found themselves in: stores and shops and sidewalks that haven't been touched for over a hundred years. You're the one with the ruby slippers, Lieutenant."

Giving in to her urging, he said, "I'll need the name of the owners."

"I can get that for you. No problem."

"It's to be treated as a crime scene first, an archaeology dig second, if at all."

"I can live with that." She extended her hand for him to shake. "I'll leave the decision to you."

Boldt accepted her handshake, though somewhat reluctantly. He had the feeling he'd walked into a trap.

Babcock had the callused hands of a farmer or field-worker. She said, "Okay, you've got yourself a deal."

26

The Hearing

Matthews considered the evidentiary hearing—a probable cause, or preliminary hearing—a formality. She'd attended only two such hearings in her decade of service, and then solely because she'd been called as a witness. When LaMoia informed her that he'd included "some of her paperwork" in his report to the prosecuting attorney's office, and that because of this she was advised to attend the hearing, she lost her temper, admonishing him for submitting a report that was little more than "notes on a napkin."

She arrived at courtroom 3D like a plane coming in too fast for a landing, tires smoking and wing lights flashing.

"What the hell were you thinking?" she said to LaMoia, where they sat three rows behind the prosecutor's table.

LaMoia held his finger to his lips, requesting she lower her voice. The hearing was not yet in session, but the prosecutor, a stump-faced woman named Mahoney, sat within earshot.

He said, "We do what we do." His only explanation.

"I scribbled out a memo to you, John. That was not a psych evaluation."

"It is now."

"No, it isn't. That's just the point."

"We both want Neal for this, Matthews. I included the memo because it supports his frame of mind at the time of his statement, which was when he lied about the window of time. It's that false statement that Mahoney's hanging our case on for the time being. Let's not forget that. The blood on the sweatshirt came back Mary-Ann Walker's, yes. But hell if Mahoney is going to put Ferrell Walker up on the stand to tell us all where he got that sweatshirt—"

"From behind a Dumpster in the back alley," she said. "Within a few yards of the same vehicle we know ran her over. That works, John."

"But it brings Walker onto the stand for possible questioning. It opens up the threat on Neal's life at Dixie's and a personal thing between them. That'll not only invalidate the sweatshirt but confuse the judge and leave room for reasonable doubt. We gotta trust Mahoney on this. She knows what she's doing. She wanted the psych report."

"It *wasn't* a psych report. You think the PD won't know that?"

"It's a *hearing,* not a trial. There's all sorts of leeway here, Matthews. Calm down."

"You or Mahoney should have asked me for a psych report."

"With all the time we had," LaMoia said sarcastically, annoyed with her now. "Mahoney's going on vacation next week, and I wanted her to handle it. Besides, defense agreed to the scheduling, and that means they had as little time to prepare as we did. 'When the shoe fits . . .' I'm not saying it's perfect, but you play the hand that's dealt you."

"Do *not* start quoting country music clichés, or I'm out of here." She sat back and stared at the ceiling, wondering how LaMoia could take the wind out of her so effortlessly. When he got a few too many beers in him or, on rare occasion, submitted to the pressures of the job and lost his cool, he had a tendency to start spouting sidesplitting one-liners like, "I've got tears in my ears from lying on my back and crying over you"—a personal favorite of hers. She heard a little Kenny Rogers heading her way and ducked to avoid it.

"So I'm here," she said, "to support a psych evaluation that isn't a psych evaluation."

"But the point is, you're here," LaMoia said, realizing the worst was over. "See? There's a bright side to everything."

The hearing ran like a scaled-down trial; it was Mahoney's job to make a case against Neal, and she went about the task in workmanlike fashion, offering Neal's vehicle as the murder weapon—hairs, blood, and tissue had been collected from the undercarriage of the Corolla. A small amount of this organic evidence had been subjected to DNA testing and had been matched to Mary-Ann Walker. There was more to come, the lab tech announced from the witness stand. Mahoney hurried her presentation, apparently knowing that the court, too, regarded such hearings as pro forma and did not want to belabor her points, thereby annoying an overtaxed judge prior to the actual trial.

Matthews's evaluation was regarded as icing on the evidentiary cake—a way to incorporate possible motives for the crime and to subtly bias the judge against the defendant at the earliest possible moment.

The public defender, a slightly overweight second-generation Indonesian man in his late twenties named Norman Seppamosa, with thick glasses and a pug nose, seemed outgunned and overwhelmed until he surprised everyone in the courtroom by requesting to cross-examine Matthews, a request immediately granted. He stood from his chair at the defendant's table—an act of grandstanding normally not seen in such a hearing, as there was no jury to impress, and ran through a litany of questions that established Matthews's credentials.

Daphne Matthews saw Ferrell Walker directly behind Mahoney, occupying a seat in the last row. He nodded hello to her.

As Seppamosa got started, Mahoney said, "Your Honor, I think we're aware of Ms. Matthews's credentials and qualifications."

The judge, an African American woman in her mid-forties and an outspoken liberal, clicked her tongue disapprovingly at Mahoney.

Matthews found herself distracted by Walker's presence.

"The reason I ask these questions, Your Honor," Seppamosa explained, "is merely to establish that we, and the court, should certainly accept the credibility of such an experienced and well-established expert witness."

Matthews felt her internal early-warning radar flash an alert and saw a similar concern sweep the patronizing smirk from Mahoney's face as well.

With an unwanted heat swarming up her spine and across the flesh of her back, Matthews had but a few precious seconds to prepare herself for a round of aggressive questioning. Having sat through nearly half an hour of unchallenged testimony, she had arrived in the witness chair believing Seppamosa would merely take furious notes, lifting his head occasionally as he had been doing all along, and await the calling of the next witness. With the man standing at the end of the table glaring at her, with him sweating so profusely as to stain the underarms of his suit jacket, with him addressing the court and lauding her expertise and reliability, she knew she had trouble. He had been lying in wait, nothing less.

The judge sternly reminded Mahoney that if she had an objection, she would be well advised to address the court formally, not in unannounced outbursts. "This is not a revival meeting,

Ms. Mahoney." This reprimand indicated an erosion of support that clearly wounded Mahoney and drove her back to her yellow notepad to where Matthews couldn't tell if she was listening or not. If Seppamosa was coming after Matthews, then she believed it was to get some, or all, of her testimony tossed. Exactly what testimony remained to be seen.

"I see in the investigating officer's report that you were present at Mr. Neal's apartment on March twenty-eighth of this year."

"That's correct," Matthews said, checking a calendar offered by the bailiff.

"In your *expert opinion,* Dr. Matthews, at that time did Langford Neal display any hesitation or reluctance in granting his permission for police to search his nineteen ninety-two Toyota Corolla?"

"He did not."

"And in your *expert opinion,* Dr. Matthews, given that the state has made a case that evidence collected from that vehicle suggests the vehicle's possible involvement in the crime, is this behavior—this willingness to share such evidence with police—consistent with what you'd expect in your vast and well-documented experience of a guilty party? Yes, or no?"

"No."

"Is it consistent with what you'd expect of an innocent party?"

Matthews hesitated, but realized her hesitation hurt their case more than quick, efficient answers. "Surrendering such evidence would be more typical of an innocent party, yes, but not reserved to—"

He interrupted her. "Because basically Mr. Neal was handing over the smoking gun," Seppamosa said. "Was he not?"

Mahoney reminded the court there was no pistol or firearm

associated with the Mary-Ann Walker homicide. The bench reminded Mahoney to object formally or face a court fine.

Matthews was instructed that she did not need to answer the question.

"Ms. Matthews," Seppamosa said, suddenly dropping her title, an omission she took seriously, "because the state has failed to produce any witnesses, other than oceanographers, as concerns the timing of this event, and seeing as how counsel is basing a good deal of their suspicions of my client on what they call this 'inaccurate window of time,' I'd like to question you about the Q&A session—should I call it an interrogation?—of my client, Mr. Langford Neal. You were in attendance, were you not?"

"I believe copies of the investigating officer's report of that interview have already been put into evidence by Ms. Mahoney," Matthews said.

She was directed to answer the question.

"Yes, I was in attendance."

"So it says here," Seppamosa said.

"Then maybe you don't need my help," Matthews said, winning a suppressed grin from Mahoney, "or shall I read it for you?" Seppamosa clearly intended to play hardball. The psychologist understood the importance of staking out her own territory and showing her willingness to engage. She sent the message that she would not roll over for him, and the attorney looked over at her with a renewed appreciation following the comment.

"Not the *entire* document," he said, a smug expression winning his face. "I would, however, appreciate if you read for the court page seven of the transcript, lines eleven through eighteen. I've taken the liberty of highlighting the section. This would be the defendant, Langford Neal, speaking to you and to Sergeant

John LaMoia, Crimes Against Persons, the lead investigator on the case."

Point, counterpoint—he'd turned her small joke around to sting her. She was now to read some part of the Neal interview into the court record, while simultaneously indelibly searing it in the judge's mind. Mahoney thumbed a document with the dexterity of a chief librarian. Seppamosa handed Matthews a copy. She read the lines and had no idea where he was going with this: Seppamosa seemed to have missed the point of the expert testimony; reading this line would only support the strength of Mahoney's case against Neal. Matthews cleared her throat away from the microphone and then read:

> *NEAL: Maybe it was the phone ringing that woke me up in the first place. And I do remember what time it was. All twos flashing at me. Two twenty-two. The clock by the phone on her side of the bed. I remember that. Two, two, two. Flashing away.*

"And to your recollection, Ms. Matthews, is that verbatim?"

"To my recollection, yes it is."

"This then is the contradiction to which Ms. Mahoney referred in her questioning of the oceanography expert, a Dr. Bryon Rutledge."

"It would be inappropriate of me to answer for either Dr. Rutledge or Ms. Mahoney."

"This is your understanding of the conflict, is it not?"

"It is. The body had to have gone off the bridge *before* midnight. Therefore Mr. Neal could *not* have seen her on a fire escape two hours *past* midnight. That's the kind of inconsistency that wins an investigator's attention."

"Indeed."

Seppamosa returned to the defense table, foraged inside his salesman-sized briefcase, and came out with a bedside digital clock in hand. He then had Matthews read from a police inventory that accounted for all items in plain sight as documented. This, based on a court-ordered search of Neal's apartment. She read the make and model of Neal's bedside clock, and the court confirmed that Seppamosa now showed Matthews the exact same model of clock.

Matthews did not see what was coming, but knew without a doubt that she'd been led into an ambush. She searched her thoughts in order to attempt to anticipate the attorney's take on the bedside clock but still had no idea where it was leading. She glanced out into the gallery, only to see that both Mahoney and LaMoia looked equally puzzled and on guard. To anticipate the question was to be prepared for a clever response. Failing this, she felt set up and ready to play the scapegoat.

Seppamosa plugged the clock into a floor receptacle alongside the stenographer, and it occurred to Matthews that he'd practiced this at least once—he knew where the power was; he knew what he was doing. He fiddled with the clock and turned it to face her.

"For the benefit of the court," he said, making sure both the judge and Mahoney were shown the face of the digital clock, "would you please read the time of day represented on the clock?"

"Two twenty-two," Matthews said. "I can't tell if it's A.M. or P.M."

Seppamosa said cheerfully, "It's A.M. There's a little light that glows indicating P.M. If the court wishes—"

The judge cut him off, insisting the court did not wish.

Seppamosa noted for the sake of the record that Matthews had correctly identified the time of day as represented on the clock. He then dropped the bomb that Matthews felt in the center of her chest as a current of electricity. "And is the number represented on the clock steady or flashing, Ms. Matthews?"

"It's steady," she reported, not only reading on the page in front of her but hearing aloud in her memory Neal's statement of "all twos flashing at me . . . flashing away."

"For the benefit of the court, I am now unplugging the clock." Seppamosa quickly replugged the clock, then aimed its face at Matthews. "And now? The time and the quality of the numerals?"

"Twelve o'clock—one, two, zero, zero."

"And are the numerals steady or flashing?"

LaMoia came out of his seat and headed for the courtroom's back door, practically at a run.

"Flashing." Her heart sank, for now she knew exactly where he was heading.

"Flashing, as in Mr. Neal's statement to you and Sergeant LaMoia."

"Flashing, yes."

"What time does the clock say now?" He showed her the face again.

"Twelve-oh-one."

"One minute past twelve, if it please the court."

The judge bid him to continue, not quite following the line of presentation.

"Dr. Matthews, do you recall the window of time that Mary-Ann Walker's body had to have gone off the bridge, this, according to testimony provided by the state's expert witness, Dr. Rutledge?"

Matthews hesitated. She'd just stated this herself.

Seppamosa said, "Your Honor, I'm happy to have the court stenographer reread the—"

"Between eleven-fifteen P.M. and twelve A.M.," Matthews

said, seeing no point to stretching this out even longer. Rule number one in court: Keep it quick when you're losing.

"And to simplify that testimony, this was determined by the direction of tidal flow, was it not, and the distance the body had reached prior to retrieval?"

"Something like that."

"Your Honor, if it please the court, I could reread—"

But the judge was not in a pleasing mood. "The significance of this presentation, Mr. Seppamosa?"

"Is in the nature of the numerals, Your Honor. Flashing. Which is exactly as the defendant, Mr. Neal, reported initially to police. The numbers of such clocks flash only when there's been a loss of power and the battery backup is insufficient. The clock resets to twelve midnight, and then begins to keep time again."

Retrieving a sheet of paper from his table, Seppamosa crossed the room toward the witness chair. "Ms. Matthews, I'm going to ask you to read one more item for the benefit of the court."

Mahoney stood up and properly objected this time, suggesting that Seppamosa was badgering the witness in asking her to read documents that did not pertain to her expertise in any regard.

Seppamosa defended his choice of Matthews because she was a respected member of the police community and could be trusted to tell the truth. He then offered to subpoena a variety of expert witnesses, if the court would prefer. "Clock manufacturers, power utility representatives . . ."

The judge heatedly declined the offer, clearly rebuffing the man in the process, but Seppamosa was not to be deterred—he was a man with a mission, more alive and cheerful than any PD Matthews had seen stand before the court.

Matthews was directed by the judge to read the letterhead

off the sheet of paper supplied to her. "The letterhead is for Puget Sound Energy. It appears to be a Web page printed or faxed to Mr. Seppamosa."

"The highlighted text, please," Seppamosa said, practically crowing by this point.

She read, ". . . an area that included all of Ballard, Wallingford, Greenlake, and Phinney Ridge experienced a power interruption at eight fifty-nine P.M. on March twenty-second. This interruption lasted an average of three minutes, with the maximum lost time in Phinney Ridge estimated at seven minutes, twenty-seven seconds."

Seppamosa spoke loudly, luxuriating in his Perry Mason moment. "I submit to the court, Your Honor, that this power outage switched off Mr. Neal's bedside clock at exactly eight fifty-nine. Subsequent to that, the power remained off an additional three to five minutes. Somewhere around nine-oh-four the power came back on—while Mr. Neal and Ms. Walker were still at Mr. Neal's mother's house having dinner—returning power to, and resetting the clock, which now began to track time as if nine-oh-four were actually midnight. Mr. Neal *did* hear Ms. Walker on the phone. He *did* witness Ms. Walker out on the balcony. Mr. Neal *did* see the clock *flashing*—flashing, as it is reported in the statement he signed for the police, the very same statement they are claiming condemns him by invalidating his reporting the correct time of night—flashing the numbers two-two-two. Two hours and twenty-two minutes *after* the reinstatement of power by PSE at nine-oh-four, or, *eleven twenty-six* P.M., Your Honor. The very discrepancy the state is attempting to use to suggest guilt on the part of my client is in fact the discrepancy that proves *beyond a reasonable doubt* that Mr. Neal's original statement to the police was factual, entirely factual, and does nothing whatsoever to suggest my client in any way lied at any time to authorities. Nor has he at any time contradicted the window of time for this crime put forth by the state's very own expert witnesses."

The judge took this all in and directed her attention to the prosecutor's table. "Ms. Mahoney?"

"The state requests a continuance to review the material that has come to light."

"Continuance nothing, Ms. Mahoney," an annoyed judge declared. "You've insufficient evidence, Ms. Mahoney. If the state wishes to try Mr. Neal, you'll need to start again."

She lowered the gavel lightly and released Neal on his own recognizance.

Matthews heard a commotion at the back of the room. She looked up to see Ferrell Walker leaving as fast as he could.

27

Three Blocks North of Safety

With Tom Petty's "I Won't Back Down" running in her head, Matthews abandoned the idea of a hotel room for a second night and returned to her houseboat, angry over losing ground at the probable cause hearing, angry at LaMoia for not anticipating the contradictory evidence put into play with the flashing clock, angry at herself for allowing Seppamosa to manipulate her and the facts to his client's advantage. She wanted a drink. She deserved the comfort of her own home—she was sick and tired of being told what to do.

She climbed the ladderlike stairs to her tiny bedroom, weary from a long afternoon of meetings.

Meetings begot meetings—a tried and true axiom of police work. She wasn't looking forward to the following day. She poured herself an expensive glass of a near-perfect wine—again the Archery Summit Pinot—drew a hot bath, and settled into the idea of spending a mindless, somewhat inebriated night in front of the television. But as preparations for the bath continued, she thought about Margaret out on the streets and found it impossible to enjoy herself. She thought about Nathan Prair and the fact that he had yet to submit the report LaMoia had demanded be delivered—a report Matthews hoped would clear up whatever relationship had existed prior to the young woman's murder.

As she undressed in her bedroom, paranoia crept in, despite

the fact that she'd covered every inch of glass in the house, whether by window blind or thumbtacked towel. Down to her bra, she couldn't bring herself to disrobe any further. Still partly clothed, she wrapped herself up in a robe and headed back down to the houseboat's tiny bathroom, where, with the door locked, she undressed. She caught herself folding clothes she knew were headed for the laundry and recognized the action as a warning sign—hairline fractures in her sanity. To make matters worse, she overreacted, knocking the stack of dirty clothes into the sink and stirring them up into a tangled ball.

Having forgotten her glass of wine, she donned the robe again and headed out to retrieve it, but found herself walking extremely slowly, attentive to every errant sound. Part of the problem for her came from the look of the place, the fact that covering all the windows had shrunk the space to a claustrophobic size. She resented the intrusion, her feeling forced to defend herself this way, the depressing darkness of the room with the lights along the lake removed from view.

Wine in hand, she relocked the bathroom door, intent on soaking away both the day's tensions and her increasing fear. Some sounds, some dirt found outside a window, a few strange phone calls from a disturbed kid—when she quantified the events of the past week they seemed nothing to get worked up about. Had she been on the receiving end of this list as a psychologist, she'd have wondered at the fuss. But being on the receiving end as a potential victim heightened the urgency in a way she had never fully understood before.

The piping hot water helped the wine go to her head, but the wine failed to quiet her imagination as she'd hoped. What should have been a few luxurious moments of peace found her swapping places with Melissa Dunkin bathing in the hotel room. Despite her being locked in a windowless room, she could feel a stranger's eyes feasting on her. Anything, anyone, could be out there at any time. There was no place that could be considered completely safe. She mentally reviewed locking both doors and all the windows, but she didn't trust herself. The bath itself seemed like a failed idea—it would lull her into a stupor, she'd come out of the bathroom a half hour later, dazed and dull, the perfect victim. Catching herself slipping back into paranoia, she reached for her wineglass—her medication—and missed, knocking it to the tile floor where it smashed at a volume twice as loud as it should have. Shards of jagged glass wall-to-wall awaited her bare feet. The spilled red wine looked like a pool of blood.

"Goddamn it!" Her voice rang out equally loudly, bouncing off the mirror, the tile, and the tub.

She felt foolish. Idiotic. The bath was a bust. The whole evening felt like a bust.

Where a certain personality might have left the mess to enjoy the bath while the water remained hot, Matthews felt obligated to clean it up immediately, martyring herself in the process.

Using the toilet seat as a stepping-stone, she climbed out of the tub, forgoing a towel for the robe and the sense of privacy, and inched her bottom along the countertop and finally leapt out the door and into the hall. She slipped her feet into a pair of rubber boots at the back door, grabbed a broom and dustpan, and went about cleaning up.

As she accounted for the last of it, she felt another wave of anxiety steal into her chest. Stewing in self-pity, she saw her life as her stalker must see it: jam-packed and yet empty. She thought it too bad she couldn't clean up the pieces of her recent past the way she had this shattered wineglass. Two broken engagements, still partly reserving herself for an unavailable married man who showed less interest now than ever before. She'd made a career of repairing other lives but had proved unable to mend her own.

She looked around to see a virtual cocoon, the windows covered, the doors locked and dead-bolted. Afraid of her own shadow, she was the person to whom others turned to be rescued from their fears.

She decided against the wine—it was only making things worse—and tried some Mahler instead. Nice and loud, like sitting in the second row of Benaroya Hall. She sought refuge in a mindless television show but found it unsatisfying, unable to shake the feeling that someone was watching her. Back to the wine, and another deep glass; she now felt warm to the core but still worried.

Feeling pathetic and childish, Matthews nonetheless took the commercial breaks to patrol the houseboat. On one such foray, she grabbed a pair of flannel pajamas and returned to the bathroom and changed into them, electing to continue to wear the robe. In the process she missed a crucial part of the television show and turned off the set on the verge of tears. Another glass of wine, and she was feeling drunk.

Unable to lose the feeling of being watched, a few too many glasses of wine in her, she determined that Walker or Prair or *someone* had hidden cameras in the house, and she made it her mission to find them. What was so unreasonable about that? There were "spy stores" in town that sold fiber-optic cameras that fit into smoke detectors, electric switch plates, bathroom fans, and heating ducts.

She started out methodically, but within minutes found herself frantically pulling books from shelves, yanking artwork off the walls, and uprooting potted plants. Had she looked behind herself she would have seen a path littered in destruction and might have stopped herself. But it wasn't until she'd come full circle that she saw her downstairs in ruins—books scattered, plants and lamps tipped over, the walls bare and crawling with unfamiliar shadows from lamps on their sides.

Hurricane Daphne.

Actions did in fact speak louder than words. She saw her rampage as a sustained scream, a cry for help of epic proportions.

Her mobile phone chirped from somewhere on the kitchen counter. She searched for it contemptuously, as if it, too, might be watching her.

"Matthews."

"Daphne? It's Ferrell."

Her breath caught. He'd called again. With impeccable timing. And on her *cell phone,* a number he simply could not possess.

"You let me down, Daphne."

She felt as if he'd poured ice water down her back. "I asked you not to contact me." Could he sense her terror? Did she dare hang up on him?

"You said it was a process, a system. That it worked. I don't see it working, Daphne, and I don't see you doing anything to fix it."

"It's a process that takes time, Mr. Walker. Believe me, we're doing everything—"

"Don't hand me that crap! If you were doing everything you could, he'd be locked up, not free to do what he wants."

"You and I talking about it is not going to help. I'm going to hang up now."

"I brought you her sweatshirt!"

"Get this straight: The more you try to help, the more you hurt our chances of putting away your sister's killer. Tampered evidence is inadmissible."

"Since when can't an informant supply evidence?"

"Since the informant held a knife to the suspect's neck. Since the informant is related to the victim. Since the informant has repeatedly been asked to stay out of it. Since the informant is not an informant in the first place! Police informants are recruited and managed, and records are kept of their activities. You are *not* a police informant, Mr. Walker. You are not helping things."

"Okay, okay. Cards on the table?" Walker asked.

"Mr. Walker, you are not listening."

"I can help you, Daphne."

"Mr.—"

"The two missing women."

The sudden silence in the room and over the phone was replaced by a pounding in her ears as a slide show of recent events flashed through her consciousness. Hebringer and Randolf had stolen away Boldt and his CAP team for months. She had personally worked up profiles, interviewed family members, and torn open the lives of these two women to where secrets no longer existed—sex toys, family turmoil, medications, and past lives included. As a resident of the city, Ferrell Walker certainly knew of the department's dedication to the investigations—so was this tease of his an act of desperation or a legitimate offer? If the latter, did she dare refuse him?

"I'm listening," she said, her heart continuing to race as adrenaline coursed through her. She reached for the wine bottle and upended it.

"I'll help you find those women if you'll get Lanny Neal behind bars for good."

"We've been looking for those two women for a long time, Mr. Walker. What makes you think—?"

"Because I know things you don't."

"And how am I to believe that?"

"Let's just say I've had a vision. The two of them strung up like marlins. Maybe you've been looking in the wrong place."

She didn't consider herself easily rattled—*"strung up like marlins"*—and yet this homeless, bereaved street person had her shrinking and shaking as she took yet another swig of wine in an attempt to settle herself. "A dream, or something more concrete?"

"Wouldn't you like to know?" Childish. Toying with her.

"Yes, I would, Mr. Walker."

"You're scared because I know more than you," he said. "I can understand that. But there's no reason to be. We're friends, the two of us. I wouldn't hurt you. You wouldn't hurt me. I can *help* you; you can help me. Tell me you'll help me."

The psychologist pushed aside the frightened woman in what she considered a moment of personal triumph. "The arrest and conviction of Lanny Neal isn't about you, Mr. Walker. It's about us doing our jobs. As for your contributing to our ongoing investigation into the disappearances—"

"Then do your job," he complained.

"We are. We're doing just that."

"By letting him go? By buying a bottle of red wine and taking the night off?"

Oh God: He'd followed her, watched her. He knew her *cell number*. She fought to hold herself together, to place the psychologist ahead of the victim.

"How'd you get this phone number?" She blurted it out without thinking, her internal wiring a mess from the unwanted cocktail of wine and adrenaline. She realized that the phone would reveal to her the caller-ID information once she disconnected. She had to know where he was calling from, and she had to hang up on him to get the information. But with Walker dangling information about Hebringer and Randolf, she knew she couldn't hang up. Not yet.

"Why cover the windows like that? It spoils the view."

Her entire body twitched as her nerves seized. She never let these guys win, yet the temptation was to hang up. She could stare across any interrogation table faking self-confidence and leveling intimidating looks that made even the most heartless think twice about going up against her. So why couldn't she face Ferrell Walker over the airwaves?

She disconnected the call.

Her fingers fumbled through the phone's menu choices in search of caller-ID.

PAY PHONE #945

She lunged for her home phone and dialed 911 as her mobile began chirping again. The caller-ID blinked on the screen:

PAY PHONE #945

Walker, calling back.

"Emergency operator," a controlled voice answered.

Matthews introduced herself, recited her shield number, and requested the street address for pay phone number 945.

She was placed on hold as her mobile continued to ring. Then the mobile went silent as the voice mail engaged. Two transfers later, she reached a supervisor. Nearly five minutes after that, minutes consumed by the supervisor establishing her legitimacy, she was finally supplied the address of pay phone 945. An address just two blocks south of her.

Hanging up the phone, she sensed the walls of the room closing in on her—physically moving—and though she'd heard such anxiety attacks described in sessions from the other side of the couch, only now did she experience the terror associated with the physical environment shrinking. Suddenly the houseboat was but a cage from which to be plucked. Walker was two blocks away and watching her.

Already on the run, she snatched up car keys, purse, and cell phone, giving little thought to stepping outside the safety of her home. Clomping down the dock in a pair of rubber Wellingtons, her robe slipping open to expose her flannel pajamas, Matthews fished her handgun from her purse and chambered a round.

She lumbered past a well-dressed couple, neighbors returning from dinner. They made way for her, the woman calling out and offering help.

A blur of white terry cloth, Matthews clomped her way up a set of wooden steps that led from the dock to street level beneath an overhang of limbs, maple trees and a sycamore reaching down with their long bony fingers, an area where even she had to duck and maneuver in order to avoid having an eye poked out. Her head averted, she ran smack into a person. The unexpected contact took her breath away—part solid physical contact, part shock. In such close quarters, amid the jumble of lacelike mottled light from a streetlamp, she saw only the brown uniform at first, the resulting wave of terror filling her head like a rush of blood from standing up too quickly. She'd struck a man's chest. A tall man. She looked up into the eyes of Nathan Prair.

"Daphne?" His surprise sounded genuine, though hers won the moment. He took her by the shoulders. "I . . . ," he stuttered, "was just coming to see you . . . I wanted to apologize for—"

There was no rational thought or logic guiding her at that moment, only a primal instinct to flee. No calculation, no clever excuse for the bathrobe and Wellingtons. What came out of her mouth was half scream, half alarm, like a martial arts grunt while delivering a blow. She shoved Prair, connecting in the center of his chest, and to her great surprise, sent him backward and off-balance.

She crossed the street to the parking lot and stood a fraction of a second too long looking for the Honda that wasn't there, only to realize it was in the SPD repair shop. Behind her, Prair had regained himself and had turned toward her.

"Daphne! Wait up!"

A moment later she had the departmental pool car unlocked and started.

Prair ran across the street toward her.

Gravel and mud flew as the car skidded out onto pavement in a lazy fishtail that nearly decapitated a row of mailboxes. She raced past a standing pay phone that she assumed to be number 945, craning her neck to take it in. It stood empty, forcing her to wonder where Walker had gone. To her houseboat? The Chevy blew through a red light into traffic. Car horns sang protest behind her as she fishtailed yet again, careening into the opposing lane before jerking the wheel to correct and recrossing the double yellow line. The car's speedometer needle twitched as she rattled over potholes, doubling the speed limit. In a perfect world she would have had the time and presence of mind to make a call and ask dispatch to electronically clear traffic lights, affording her a straight shot into Public Safety. She would have, at the very least, announced herself to Traffic Patrol.

The wet roads shone like polished stone. As she took a sharp left, she lost the back half of the Chevy and, like crack the whip on ice skates, found herself floating at unbearable speeds. The Chevy connected solidly with the front grill of a Mazda coupe, the sounds of shattering glass bigger and bolder yet somehow less significant than her shattering wineglass of only minutes earlier.

She realized that Walker had won the game, and the resulting anger caused her to lay on the accelerator and drive the car on a steady course. In her mind there was no stopping for an insurance swap; she was three blocks north of safety. Two more red lights slipped behind her before it registered that she had just hit-and-run a motor vehicle. There would be hell to pay if anyone had caught her plate.

She skidded the tires to a stop in the police garage, threw

the shift into PARK, and ran from the car like it was on fire. Two grease monkeys on night duty looked up in unison. The building's heavy steel door came open awkwardly, Matthews struggling to find the strength that normally required little effort. With her back pressed up against the concrete block wall, she fought to catch her breath, the first sensation of security melting through her. The red glare of the EXIT sign caught her eye, the color suiting her for some reason. This hallway smelled of old tires, gasoline, and human sweat.

From inside the building, a pair of uniformed officers, young kids assigned night duty, approached her while clearly trying not to stare. The woman officer turned and asked, "May I help you?"

"Lieutenant Matthews," she identified herself.

Fighting off a grin, the young woman asked, "You're kinda in the wrong place, ma'am. Do you have an appointment?"

"I *am* Lieutenant Matthews, Officer." She badged her.

"My mistake, Lieutenant." The woman officer sobered and straightened, a poster girl for good posture.

"There's a situation," Matthews said, attempting to explain the robe and rubber boots that had clearly won their attention.

Saved, as the door to the garage jerked open and one of the grease monkeys, a civilian named Roy who'd worked the garage for years, said, "Hey, listen, Lieutenant—a Chevy or not, this here's a pool vehicle, and it went outta here looking good, and you brung it back with half the rear quarter panel tore off. We got us some paperwork that's got to get done."

"Send the paperwork up to my office, Roy," Matthews said, striving for dignity. Realizing the futility of that effort, she turned her back on all three and stomped her green rubber boots toward the waiting elevator.

Safety had come at the price of humiliation.

28 Throwing the Net

When the phone rang at 10:15 P.M., there was no doubt in the Boldt home who should answer. He received fewer of these calls since the promotion to lieutenant—paper pushers weren't in demand as much as squad sergeants—but he still kept his finger in the pot. Boldt's team rarely made major decisions without his input. He'd been hoping for word from Sandra Babcock, hoping to gain access to the Underground given that the city had refused him entrance through the sinkhole due to safety concerns.

He answered the living room phone, listened to LaMoia on the other end, and agreeing with everything his sergeant suggested, grunted out "Yes," five or six times in a row. As he hung up, it suddenly felt more like 7 A.M. inside his head—wide awake.

By this time Liz had appeared in their bedroom door wearing a sky blue pajama top of a synthetic that had all the qualities of satin, hanging on her like a coat of paint down to mid-thigh. He knew she wore only that top and nothing else, for that particular choice was her signal for what she had in mind, and he felt sorry to disappoint them both. As he cradled the receiver, he also hung his head.

"Too bad," she said. "You would have liked it."

"Yes."

"Me, too, for that matter."

"Nice to hear."

"Can you be twenty minutes late?"

"Wish I could."

"Yes, you do," she said, offering an understanding face and sympathetic eyes. Being a policeman's wife couldn't be easy. He knew this and tried to cushion the blows whenever possible. They'd made it through the most dangerous years, the most stressful years, both of them straying from the marriage, but only once as far as he knew, though Liz for a much longer period. He'd never learned the identity of her lover and wondered if he ever would. As a lieutenant, the demands were on his time, the pressures more political in nature, the internal problems of his people leaving him feeling like a camp counselor. This call proved a little bit of all three. She wouldn't want to hear about it. They both worked hard to leave their jobs at the office—an unattainable ideal, but one worth striving for.

"How long?" she asked.

"An hour if I'm lucky," he said. "All night, if I'm really lucky."

He won a grin from her, a small but important concession. "Good for you." Had they not been personally tied to the disappearances, it would have been out of bounds for her to ask if it involved Susan Hebringer, and Boldt might have felt uncomfortable about including her. But the rules had changed since the mother of their daughter's classmate had gone missing, and Boldt thought maybe it was for the better—Liz deserved to know more about what took him away at 10:15 at night.

He told her that LaMoia had called, that Daphne Matthews had jammed herself up, and that it needed untangling, but that yes, there seemed to be an unexpected connection to Hebringer and Randolf.

"Then go," she said, knowing this made no difference to his decision, and yet it did. "I'll stay up and do some prayer work."

They came at life's solutions from two different angles, but Boldt had finally settled into feeling right and good about it, believing that maybe one couldn't exist without the other, that the material and spiritual were far more interconnected and yet entirely separate at the same time. He was still learning about her world; she'd given up on his the day she walked out of medical treatment for the lymphoma. And yet there was a meeting of the minds more often than not. "I could use that," he said, wanting to support her efforts.

She had something to say to him but kept it to herself, a coy grin taking the place of the words. He wanted to hear it but knew better than to ask. The secret to the success of their marriage these days was as much about knowing what not to say as it was knowing what to say. He admired her for her restraint. They shared a kiss. She smelled softly of the lotion that he knew her to spread all over her body prior to bed.

This was a night of great sacrifice indeed.

"Where is she now?"

"Back at her place," LaMoia answered, the two of them at a near run as they approached Homicide's situation room. When Boldt shot him a disapproving look, LaMoia explained that they had a patrol guarding her dock.

"Everyone else is here?"

"Heiman, Gaynes, DeLuca, and Morse. Brandon's home sick, Marsha's still on pregnancy leave."

"Listen up!" Boldt shouted, addressing the gathering, as he and LaMoia entered the bland conference room that served as a staging area for major investigations. The four detectives were strewn around the room, Heiman in a chair, Gaynes propped against a file cabinet, DeLuca towering over a stack of equipment trying to get the room's video projector switched off before Boldt realized they'd been watching a movie on TBS. The room smelled of coffee and old socks. The video went to a solid blue panel, though the sound of the action flick lingered for another few seconds until DeLuca found the right switch.

"Research," Morse said, winning a round of nervous laughter from his colleagues.

Boldt managed to suppress a smile—the trick to effective leadership was to keep people guessing.

"Here's where we stand," Boldt explained in a military-like tone. "Matthews had a call suggesting a possible lead in the disappearances. Name of the contact is Ferrell Walker, brother of the jumper—the case that LaMoia caught a little over a week ago. We have a sheet, including a Department of Licensing photo," he said, indicating for LaMoia to pass out the flyers. "Note that the photo is a couple years old now. He was just a kid at the time. This guy's gone seriously downhill. He's wearing the street, looking about twenty years older. Last seen in dirty jeans and a ratty sweatshirt that zips up the front. Navy blue, or black maybe. Works day labor cutting up fish down at the fishing docks on the canal. Might have friends around there. Made a reference to Matthews that he was basically homeless, so that's what we're assuming. We've got to keep the patrol units on the construction sites and the hotels. We've got another on Matthews's residence, so we're a little short-handed in terms of uniforms available to us. You all clock out in an hour, but I want you to stay on this at least until two—until we find him, if we're lucky. LaMoia has assigned each of you a section of the city. I want you to toss every homeless person you encounter until we find Walker, or where he might be holed up. Bring him in for loitering, vagrancy, public nuisance—I don't give a damn, just get him in here."

LaMoia added, "Consider him dangerous. He carries a blade—a serious knife—like a goddamned sword." He indicated his right side. "Over here, in a scabbard."

"Sounds like a fucking pirate," DeLuca said. A couple of the others chuckled.

Boldt addressed DeLuca. "Brian, you'll work the bars around the canal." He and LaMoia had worked out the assignments that went with the sheets. "But listen, I want all of you to get the word out on the street that there's a Hamilton for information that proves good."

"Each of you grab a radio," LaMoia said. "Along with cell phones, we've got no excuses for losing touch. No lost time: no doughnuts or burgers or fried chicken," this to Morse, "no video games or talking up the waitresses a few minutes longer than necessary. Okay, guys?"

"This is Hebringer and Randolf Walker's talking about," Boldt reminded. "Let's not forget that."

If anyone had been thinking of throwing a wisecrack into the mix, Boldt's comment stole the oxygen from the room.

"Go," LaMoia said, watching the four hurry and feeling a sense of power that his word counted for so much.

Gaynes paused by her bosses. "You need a woman to hang with Matthews, I'm good for that. Whatever the hour, I don't care." She moved on, knowing better than to wait for a reply.

"You?" Boldt asked his sergeant.

"Something you said just now . . ." LaMoia tapped his temple with his index finger, ". . . you got the juices going, Sarge."

"Are you going to share this kernel of wisdom?"

"I'm gonna skate by Matthews's crib and roast a few marshmallows with her. Anything comes of it, you'll be the first to hear."

"Why do I doubt that?" Boldt asked.

LaMoia flashed him the trademark smile, a Tony Randall smile complete with the animated sparkle coming off the front tooth.

"Get gone," Boldt said.

"Hi, Mommy, I'm home," LaMoia called loudly to the house-boat's front door. He held up an Einstein's Bagel bag, displaying it, knowing it was her favorite. "Trick or treat?" Matthews had yet to make a sound, but he knew she was in there, knew she wouldn't want him waking the neighbors.

The front door opened slowly, the living room dark, Matthews looming as a gray figure in sweatpants and thin white T-shirt. She looked good despite herself—with no makeup and uncombed hair this was a Daphne Matthews he'd not seen before. But he liked it.

He attempted to pass the bagel bag through as an offering, saying, "You look like that kid in the *Exorcist*." Standing at the door, he smelled the stale and closeted air from inside. But she wouldn't accept the bag.

She said, "I've got all the Girl Scout cookies I need. How about a rain check, John?"

"I need your help," he said. When a woman was locked up, he could nearly always find the key. He lived for such challenges.

He said, "I've got a riddle for you."

"Pass."

"Ah, come on."

"I don't want to play, *Johnny*."

"Sure you do. And I'll tell you why: Because you can't stand anybody having the answers ahead of you, of being out of the loop, and *I've got the answers,* Matthews, answers you need. Believe it. You shut that door and I go to Boldt with what I've got."

Sad eyes searched his face. The door opened a few more inches. LaMoia could taste victory. He said, "Little Joe knew you volunteer at the Shelter—do you remember that? Tonight he called your cell phone, a number he couldn't possibly have turned up without a direct connection to you. Am I getting your attention?"

She swung open the door and LaMoia stepped inside.

"Love what you've done to the place. The Martha Stewart bomb shelter thing is fetching."

"Fetching?" she said, as if he'd spoken a foreign language. She locked the door's dead bolt and latching hardware. LaMoia noticed the police bar to the left of the door, realizing she'd had it barricaded.

"Towels on the windows? Nice."

"Lighten up."

"Can I turn on a light?"

She said, "I like it this way."

"That worries me."

She snatched the paper sack and peered inside. "Sesame."

"Toasted, with light cream cheese."

"But how—?"

"Matthews, I know more about you than you even want to consider. Believe me."

She looked askance at him. The bagel pleased her and he felt good about it. She lathered it up with cream cheese and took a ferocious bite. An appetite was a good sign. She spoke through a mouthful of food, uncharacteristic of her. "It's a mandatory leave until they review it. I failed the Breathalyzer, did you know that?"

"I heard, yes."

"A couple glasses of wine and I failed it. I was *not* drunk, John. I was scared," she said. "But there you go."

"Boldt's on it. He'll ramrod it through. It's paperwork mostly. You'll be back in the saddle in a day or two."

"Four or five's more like it. Meanwhile, I'm without my shield and my piece."

He heard it coming then, realizing he'd been invited inside not for his offer of a bagel and shoptalk, but because she needed something from him. This wounded his pride.

"So, what is it?" he asked.

"A drop gun," she said.

Her request hit him like a slap in the face. "You, of all people?" Matthews was the most vocal opponent of handguns on the department.

"Times change."

"Not that much they don't."

"Funny what a good dose of reality will do for you."

He said, "The Sarge asked me what I had to do with it."

"You?"

"I got this feeling he thought we were . . . getting personal. Like that."

"Us?" she asked.

"Not that it's entirely unthinkable," he said, in a tone meant to test her reaction. "I suppose it's within the realm of possibility. You and me. I mean, stranger things have happened."

"Name one," Matthews said. She put on a pot of hot water. Her movements seemed lighter all of a sudden, like she'd ditched a heavy coat. "You're coffee, right?"

He said, "Eight . . . no, nine years we've worked together, and you have to ask what I drink?"

"It's polite to ask."

"Well it's rude when two people have known each other as long as we have."

"It's espresso," she stated. "See?" She was right, of course. "I have an espresso machine someone gave me for Christmas."

"It was for your engagement," he said. "It was Gaynes."

"You remember that?"

He shrugged. He felt his face warm. "Regular's fine," he said, "if you've got it, if it's not a problem."

"A soufflé would be a problem. Black coffee, I think I can handle."

LaMoia asked to use the head, revealing a perceptive understanding that this was a houseboat. She pointed around the corner of the galley, asking aloud if he hadn't been here before. He answered obliquely, as if maybe he didn't remember.

As LaMoia urinated, his eye wandered into her medicine cabinet, left slightly ajar. An orange-brown prescription bottle presented itself. A white cap that was childproof, but not LaMoia-proof. He zipped himself up, flushed, and used the resulting noise of washing his hands to cover his reaching in there and spinning that bottle around. The script was a year old.

His eyes danced nervously to the door, ensuring the lock was in place. Amitriptyline. Ten or more in there. He liberated two of them and slipped them into the coin pocket of his jeans. Safekeeping. A voice in him cried out, *What the hell are you doing?* But the answer came instantly. *Insurance. Relax. It doesn't mean I'm going to take them.* He shut the medicine cabinet door to the exact position he'd found it—ever the good detective. He looked himself in the mirror, astonished that the reflection came back absolutely normal. As he unlocked the door and joined back up with her, guilt spiked through his system like a series of tiny fevers.

"How 'bout I get you out of here and buy you breakfast at my favorite diner?" he asked.

"How 'bout you get me a drop gun?"

"Peepers are nonviolent. You've said so yourself when we've

dealt with them in the past. Walker's got this notion he's part of the investigation. Grief does that, right?"

"Suddenly you're the psychologist?"

"Tell me I'm wrong."

"You're never wrong, John." Sarcasm from Matthews would normally drive him from a room. When she got really pissed off she let her intelligence loose, uncaged like some zoo animal just waiting for the chance, and he knew better than to try to stand up to it. But this time he found himself unwilling to let her drive him out, for that would be a double win.

"Him having your cell phone number," LaMoia said. "That's what our focus ought to be. That's gonna be what connects the dots here, Matthews, because that is the one thing impossible to explain. We solve that, we'll know where to find him."

"We'll find him at the canal," she said, "cleaning fish. Tomorrow morning."

"No we won't. He's blown off work. You know that. My guess is he's in the wind. He knows he went too far with his offer to help with the two disappearances. He's gotta be hooked up to that somehow if he's making that kind of offer. Mentioning it to you was a mistake."

"He is not hooked up to the disappearances," she protested. "He's a grief-stricken, sad excuse of a human being who's lost and emotionally fragile and is trying to bait me into including him with information he doesn't possess just so he can be a part of something. Right now, he's a part of nothing. His sister's murder is all he has left."

"So explain him having your cell phone number."

"He got it off the phone while in the car—it's all I can think of."

"For me, it adds up differently."

"Surprise," she said, again resorting to sarcasm.

Only then did LaMoia notice a massive tangle of wires and a tape recorder by the home phone.

"You know Danielson in tech services?" she asked.

"What's the deal?"

"If I'm to get a restraining order against him, I need at least one of my refusals on tape. Welcome to the woman's side of the new-and-improved stalking law. Same old, same old, you ask me." She made herself tea and poured hot water through a funnel loaded with too much coffee. He didn't tell her. She said calmly, "I need a weapon, and in case I have to use it, I don't want it traceable."

LaMoia churned inside to hear this. "You're making me worried," he said.

"I'm making you coffee," she corrected.

He sampled her effort. It tasted bitter and burned. He told her otherwise. Tea drinkers. What did they know? "Are you going to ask?" he said.

"About your version of the cell phone number?"

"What else?"

"Okay, I'm asking."

"He's been inside the Shelter," LaMoia said confidently. "Your name, your address, your cell phone, they're tacked up on a bulletin board somewhere. Am I right? It talks like a street person, it walks like a street person . . . Who's to question his being down there?"

"Nice theory, but it's women only, John."

"Guys *must* wander down into there now and then, whether it's looking for some girl or thinking it's coed."

"Sure they do, you're right."

"So, one of them was Walker. Maybe on purpose, even. Very intentionally when you weren't there. And he lifted your—"

She interrupted, stuck back on the earlier part of his suggestion. "It would explain his watching the Shelter." She was thinking about the figure in the parking garage. What if those street kids had merely told her what they thought she'd wanted to hear? What if it had been Walker up there looking down on her? More to the point, why did she feel so uncertain about sharing that Nathan Prair had been lurking at the end of her dock? She answered that question immediately, knowing that she hadn't been completely innocent with Prair, had not remained 100 percent objective with him during counseling. Not that she'd ever done anything that could be remotely construed as a come-on, *not even close,* but something about him had made her tack a few more minutes onto a session, had given him the benefit of the doubt when evaluating an answer. Later, she had wondered if she'd allowed herself to be charmed—an egregious error, an unforgivable sin, for any psychologist. She knew Prair's presence on her dock had to be mentioned, *but not now. Not LaMoia.* She feared the CAP sergeant might resolve the situation with a baseball bat, and no one needed that.

"It's open this time of night, right?" he asked.

She answered with a don't-ask-me-to-do-this look.

"The Sarge wants him in for questioning. I want answers how he got your cell number. Call whoever it is you gotta call down there, and let's get the flock out of here. It smells funky in here, you know that?"

"Boy, you really know how to flatter a girl."

"Yeah," he fired back at her. "That's what they say."

It came together for Matthews slowly, like learning the steps to a dance. Not something she could jump into, this idea of Walker in the Shelter. Like so many times before in other investigations, she found the early information too much to process as a whole, a stew stirred up that had to settle before being tasted, its ingredients properly understood. For LaMoia, it wasn't stew but spaghetti, and he was throwing it at the wall as he always did, waiting to see what stuck. For him, she was part of the mix— he'd thrown her up there, too, by including her in his theory. LaMoia didn't develop theories so much as test them. He didn't put his work on paper, he put it in the field, and that pretty much explained to her why she found herself strapped into the passenger seat of his Jetta shortly before midnight. Another of LaMoia's wild hairs, and she along for the ride, as much for the company as anything else.

"You feeling better?" he asked. LaMoia drove fearlessly— his approach to so much of life. She envied him that, while at the same time hated being his passenger.

"I resent you dragging me along, John."

God, he loved women.

She fought against the silence that followed. She said, "Your mind goes to strange places when you feel yourself under attack."

"You're safe with me," he said in the most serious voice she'd ever heard him use. "Always, and forever. No one will ever get to you with me around, Matthews."

She didn't want to cry in front of him. She glanced out her side window only to have her focus shift and the mirror image of her glassy eyes superimpose itself. LaMoia gallant? Who would have thought?

She said, "Making statements like that can get you in trouble."

"I'm always in trouble," he said.

He won a private smile from her.

"From here on out you'll stay at my loft. End of discussion."

She laughed into the car. "That'll be the day."

"No, that'll be tonight. That'll be until we clear this thing."

She searched his profile for any indication he was kidding. The car drifted through yet another greasy turn, and she made no attempt to steady herself. Instead, she settled into the seat, wondering how and why everything suddenly felt a whole lot better.

"Pack a bag." He reached across and took up her left hand— an impossibly caring gesture for John LaMoia. She did not recoil, did not tease him. For an instant they met eyes. He squeezed her hand gently, ran his thumb down her palm. She felt it to her toes. "I know you think I'm crazy. That's all right, Matthews. You, and everyone else." He flew through traffic, colored lights reflected in the black shine of the wet street. "This too shall pass."

They started with LaMoia entering the Shelter alone, just as he assumed Walker would have done. Matthews entered a moment behind him, waved hello to the attendant, checked the guest book, and then walked past a screen to roam the aisles between the cots.

With the midnight curfew a half hour off, a fairly steady stream of desolate young women trickled in as LaMoia stood before a gunmetal gray steel desk listening to a woman who had more chins than a shar-pei as she explained the Shelter's women-only policy to him. The arriving girls read a page of rules and disclaimers before signing in. As the hefty woman in charge oversaw this procedure, a neglected LaMoia looked quickly for where Walker might have picked up Matthews's cell phone number, his eyes combing several bulletin boards, paperwork on top of the desk, and a handful of flyers offered to arrivals. To his discouragement, the only phone number he could find on any of the literature was the Shelter's toll-free hotline.

"Matthews," he called out loudly, finding himself on the verge of being thrown out, cop or not.

Matthews found herself entering the dormitory and reliving the day she'd sat down with Margaret trying to convince the girl to contact her family—she recalled the conversation nearly word for word, her own frustration at Margaret's impertinence. She remembered taking the Sharpie from her purse and using the indelible ink to make a point about her determination to help. She remembered so well inking her cell phone number down the girl's forearm. This recollection hit her like a slap in the face. She spun on her heels and ran, coming around the privacy screen and meeting back up with LaMoia. She stopped abruptly, unable to get a word out.

He tested, "You okay?" and stepped closer. "You look like you've seen a ghost."

Mention of this raised the head of the attendant. He had spoken a Shelter watchword without knowing it. Expectancy hung in the air like static before a storm as this woman and LaMoia awaited her response. The smell of hot chocolate permeated, as did the distant nasal whine of a girl's earphones as she listened to rap music on a portable CD player.

"Other way around," Matthews said hoarsely, her voice belying her stoic exterior. "I think the ghost saw me."

"For once, Matthews, you lost me, not the other way around."

"Her forearm," Matthews said. "I wrote my cell number on her forearm with a Sharpie." She hollered out the general alarm, "Man on the floor!" As LaMoia was led around the privacy screen, he saw several dozen teens—most all wearing surgical scrubs as pajamas. They sat on the edges of their cots aiming their hollow faces in open curiosity. Some girls came down a hall with wet hair. The announcement of a man had cleared the showers.

"Walk me through this," LaMoia said quietly, aware of their audience. "I'm not sure what you're getting at."

"There are two possibilities," Matthews said. "Either Walker met up with Margaret sometime later and she told him what that number on her arm was—"

"I have serious reservations about that."

She nodded her agreement, surprising him. "Second possibility: He overheard my conversation with Margaret and saw me write my cell number on her arm . . . in real time . . . right as I did it. Right here."

LaMoia mulled this over, his brown eyes shifting and lighting on various focal points: her face, the wall, her face again. He asked, "That's the best you've got?"

"John, you know when you know something, and you really know it, no matter how much you can talk yourself out of it? You've been there, right? We've all been there before. This is one of those times. I'm right about this. One hundred percent."

He glanced around the room, saw the girls watching them like some kind of freak show.

"And there's something else," Matthews said, her voice returning to that warm, dark, husky complaint she'd fallen into only moments earlier. Her tone suggested conspiracy, so he leaned even closer to her, to where her breath ran warm on his neck. "For months, the girls have been complaining about this place being haunted." She caught his condescending expression. "No, no. Hear me out! Not creaky-noises-kind-of-haunted, but being *watched*—the feeling they were being watched. Especially in . . . the . . . showers." Was it her imagination, she wondered, or had the whole room gone quiet? LaMoia looked in the general direction of the showers. For her, the hallway suddenly seemed to stretch much longer. "John?" she asked.

"You trust this?" he questioned.

"Completely and absolutely."

He whispered back at her, "Then we'll start in the showers so the girls can't see what we're doing."

"Agreed," Matthews said.

"And Matthews, just for the record: If we strike out, you never talked me into doing this. If I get tagged as a ghostbuster, I'll never live it down."

"I was told this room was probably a salting room at one point," Matthews said, explaining the large drain in the shower room's brick floor at which LaMoia was staring intently.

"Or a stable or carriage house," LaMoia suggested. "You put a drain in a basement, Matthews, especially one close to water, as we are here, and you're going to have water in your basement. Fact of life."

"Meaning?"

"If the Sarge wasn't all hot and heavy about these EMTs mentioning the Underground, then maybe I wouldn't go there. But a drain in a basement? I don't think so. I think this thing was at ground level at some point."

She looked around, studying the shower room's old stone walls. Gray mortar, added sloppily in the not-too-distant past, lay frozen where it seeped from the seams. "You're saying it isn't dirt on the other side of these walls?"

"I'm saying the Sarge is trying to make a connection between a possible underground section of the old city and Hebringer and Randolf. He's the one who put a bug in my ear. Now you raise the possibility of a peeper down here, and I gotta go with that, with you, because you've got this thing—you know what I mean?—and I've gotta take this wherever I can take it, as stupid as it may seem."

"I'm not saying it's stupid, John."

"I am, Matthews. It *is* stupid. But to overlook it? That's even stupider."

"There's no such word."

"Yeah? Well, at the end of this there may be," he said. "Stay tuned."

The cast-iron drain, twelve inches across, was positioned directly in the center of the large room. Some white PVC plastic pipe had been suspended from the stone ceiling as temporary plumbing to supply the shower water. The space smelled of young women, shampoo, and soap, nothing like a men's locker room, and this made LaMoia uneasy. In all his vast experience with women, he had never entered a girls' locker room.

"Turn out the lights," he instructed.

Matthews obeyed without comment, without interrupting his train of thought, ushering the room into total darkness—the only sounds the steady, rhythmic splash of water dripping from the showerheads. That, and LaMoia's shallow breathing.

"How 'bout a flashlight?" she whispered expectantly, even a little anxiously.

Instead, LaMoia struck a match, shadows jumping and bending across the crumbling brick walls. The room was set into motion as he moved carefully along the far wall, the match held close to the bricks and mortar. The flame burned brightly at first, then shrank, the shadows fading, and LaMoia tossed it to the floor. He lit another. The dripping water mimicked a heart beating. LaMoia worked the flame high to low, left to right, his own pagan ritual. The fire flickered, danced, and then blew out, enveloping them in darkness once again.

"Bingo," LaMoia said softly.

With another lit match, he tested the same spot again—a slice of mortar about shoulder height. Again, long shadows raked the walls as the small flame first flickered and then was extinguished.

Matthews asked, "Why keep putting the match out? What's the point?"

"It's not me," LaMoia answered. "It's wind." He held another match between them so they could see each other, but the effect was disorienting. Now the shadows waved and commingled on the floor. "There's a hole poked through the mortar here," he said, pointing, "and here. *Peepholes*, Matthews. Not ghosts. Not goblins. Dirty old men, I'm guessing. And maybe one much younger. One with a thing for a very pretty cop."

She crossed her arms against the chill. "Oh, God," she moaned. "We'd better call SID."

"Let's wait on that. It may be nothing," LaMoia suggested, much to her obvious consternation. He stepped forward and whispered into her ear, "He may be watching."

Twenty minutes later LaMoia had marked with chalk another four such rents in the mortar, all with unobstructed views of the shower stalls where the young women had bathed themselves. He made one last test alongside the brick wall that faced the cot where Matthews and Margaret had spoken. The match's flame blew out.

He and Matthews met eyes, hers filled with alarm. "Sometimes I hate being right," she said.

One of the girls asked what was going on, and LaMoia vamped, saying he was a city engineer checking "structural consistencies of the chemical compounds used in the mortar mixture." This seemed to satisfy the girl and confuse her as well. "You're working a little late, aren't you?" He answered, "I'm volunteering my time, young lady. I haven't been home for dinner yet." "You're pretty buff for an engineer," she said. This, from a seventeen-year-old with a tattoo. LaMoia mugged for Matthews, shutting her up before she leveled him with another sarcastic remark. They reconvened outside the Shelter's main door, in a musty basement hallway that was part of the church.

"I feel sick to my stomach," she said, arms crossed tightly. "That is *so* disgusting . . . so invasive . . . so awful!"

"So common," he said. "Guys start poking holes in walls when they're about eight, Matthews."

"You?"

"Don't ask. The point now is to find these bastards—because these aren't prepubescent kids who don't know any better. These are pervs, cave-dwelling troglodytes that deserve to have their equipment surgically removed." He looked around somewhat frantically. "Give me the dime tour, would you? These guys are on the outside of these walls, and we gotta find out how the hell they got there." He added, "Now, while we can still rain on their parade."

31 Ancient Doors

The Second Presbyterian Church that hosted the Shelter in its basement labyrinth remained open from 6 A.M. to midnight seven days a week, hours the Shelter kept as well. Matthews led LaMoia back to the bottom of an extremely old stone staircase that they'd descended on their way in. A few thousand runaways had traveled this same route over the last year.

"After this we're gonna want to take a lap around the block," he said, "looking for jimmied doors, storm drains, basement windows—something with access to whatever's on the other side of these walls." The walls had been constructed of large stone and whitewashed. "But even though we gotta do that, my money's on the Blessed Virgin—or whatever the flock this particular set of bells is called—because with them leaving the doors open all hours, the bums have got all sorts of access. One door somewhere down here, a few loose stones is all it would take."

"You're a real poet, you know that?"

"Do we know where either of these doors lead?" They were heavy doors, old and of dark wood and cast-iron hardware. Medieval, like something from a castle dungeon. One sat at the end of a small dead-end hallway; the other was set into what appeared to be an exterior basement wall. Both doors were locked.

"*We* do not," she answered, emphasizing their partnership. "There's a lot of history down here. A lot of mystery, too."

He pointed out that both doors had locks that would likely open with skeleton keys.

She said, "Which speaks to the age of this place."

"I was thinking more like how tough they'd be to pick," he snapped sarcastically. He turned to face her. "We've got two choices here: We can talk to the holy roller, whoever's in charge, or, it being midnight, I can do my thing and we can be through either of these doors in about three minutes." He produced a Leatherman utility knife. "Don't leave home without it."

"As long as I'm involved, I'd appreciate it if we did things legally, as unsettling to you as that may be."

"So now you're going to reform me?"

She looked around at the rock walls, the Gothic arches overhead. "Seems as good a place to start as any."

Fifteen minutes later, both doors hung open. The minister was a bald man with an oily complexion, a slight frame, and cantilevered eyebrows that looked sewn onto his forehead. He had a quiet but sunny disposition, as if being rousted at midnight was part and parcel of his job. Perhaps it was.

One of the doors led to storage, a massive masonry cave nearly rectangular in shape, lit by bare bulbs and strewn with cobwebs and layers of dust. Wooden chairs were stacked haphazardly; red velvet seat cushions, the fabric torn open by homesteading mice, leaned as unstable towers; a leather chair had its covering peeled back from the arms like skin from a bad burn. There were candlesticks and file cabinets, steamer trunks and even an abandoned pulpit canted to one side so that its cup runneth over. Old rust-covered chains were bolted to the far wall. Matthews commented on the enormity of the space—it looked to be sixty feet deep or more. LaMoia strategically wormed his way inside, discovering a tunnel with a low ceiling that led to a former wine cellar, also long since abandoned. The dust alone announced that no bums had trodden here.

Matthews picked her way through the rubble, following him.

Together they faced a bricked-over stone arch. In a soft voice LaMoia said, "We want to be wherever that once led."

The minister overheard his comment and informed them that to his knowledge any doorways and windows that had once communicated with what had then been a sidewalk, a hundred years earlier, had all been brick-and-mortared closed. "Permanently sealed" was how he put it.

A storyteller by nature, he held them captive with a tale about an old rum-running smugglers' tunnel said to have run up Skid Row—now Yesler Way—leading from the waterfront and connecting to several churches and speakeasies that predated the Great Depression and Prohibition. "They connected the old smuggling tunnel to these underground sidewalks, where they had quite the black market going for themselves."

LaMoia gave the man only half an ear, impatient to open the second door. When it was finally opened, the other door led to a long underground hallway, off of which was a music room, a small library with dehumidifiers running, a vestments closet, and several more stone-walled rooms dedicated to church administration and service utilities. They took their time to study each in turn, searching for hidden access to the Underground, which from the discovery of the peepholes, and the minister's stories, seemed likely to exist.

While inside what amounted to an oversized custodial closet, a room filled with steel pipe and electric water heaters, LaMoia silenced Matthews and the minister—who, once started talking, proved hard to quiet—and pressed his ear to the cold, sweating stone. Leaning away from the wall, he motioned for Matthews to listen.

"Tell me what you hear," he whispered.

Matthews pressed up against the damp chill, her face then approaching the color of the whitewashed stone. "Voices," she muttered. "Men's voices."

32 Voices in the Dark

The beat-up red door, caked and cracked with generations of paint, hid behind a Dumpster down a dead-end alley a half block from the church's west wall. LaMoia might have missed seeing it had a street person not materialized out of thin air. But with this man's appearance in the alley where a moment before there had been no one, the detective sought an explanation. He and Matthews rolled the Dumpster aside, and LaMoia turned the rust-encrusted doorknob.

The door opened behind the complaint of its hinges. The smell of human piss wafted up, stinging his eyes. He covered his face and turned away.

"Let's call for backup," he said. "This could get ugly."

Thirty minutes later, shortly after one in the morning, LaMoia led the way down a set of steep, rickety, wooden stairs into ripe, musty air, guided only by the narrow beam of a penlight. Matthews followed closely on his heels, and behind her, four uniformed patrolmen, two with nightsticks in hand, two brandishing handguns. Cobwebs, pipes, wires, and valves. "Lions and tigers and bears," LaMoia whispered over his shoulder through the pitch-black. The comforting sounds of the city faded, lost overhead, suddenly translated into a deep, penetrating rumble that rattled one's chest.

Matthews reached out and took hold of his deerskin jacket, a child with mommy's apron. She let go then, LaMoia pretending not to have noticed.

His penlight shone barely five feet ahead, illuminating broken wooden planks that had once been a sidewalk. Together they sidestepped the debris, following along the wall of a perfectly preserved brick building, the windows with much of the glass still in place. LaMoia directed the beam through one of these windows: piles of broken furniture and junk, untouched for years. A time warp. They passed a barber shop and a millinery, the hat racks still in place.

Twenty yards later the wall changed from brick to stone, and LaMoia used sign language—forming his index fingers into a cross—to indicate that he believed this was the church wall. Matthews concurred with a nod, then pointed out the narrow arrows of white light that crossed the sidewalk ahead.

As they slowed, the dust from behind them carried forward and illuminated those shafts of light even brighter. Five white beams in all.

Cupping his hand to her ear he said that someone had to look inside and that it shouldn't be him. Matthews agreed and stepped forward, placing her eye to the breaks in the wall.

Pulling her eye away, she confirmed, "It's the showers," her heartache obvious even through a whisper.

The smell in the air was of peppermint, sour and all too human. The voyeurs had ejaculated onto the walls and the sidewalk.

Matthews covered her mouth, suddenly nauseated. A hundred crime scenes or more, and this was the first time she'd felt ready to vomit.

Suddenly the four uniformed patrolmen pushed past them, a flurry of hand signals and quick preparation of their weapons. LaMoia returned hand signals, taking charge, a silent orchestration of the minutes yet to come.

She understood the urgency then: From up ahead and around the corner she heard the distinct and unmistakable sound of laughter.

They walked inside what amounted to a tall tunnel, the church's basement wall, once at street level, to their right, the mortar-and-stone retaining wall, built to enclose the city block and elevate the street a century earlier, to the left. Overhead, dust-covered wires, encrusted conduits, rusted water pipes, and gas lines had been added haphazardly over the years, tangled like veins in a limb. A halo of purple light fanned out from what had once been a skylight in the overhead sidewalk, back during the decades of reconstruction, when the two sidewalks, the two different street levels, had been forced to coexist, one of the old Seattle, the other representing improvement and change. The din of drunken male voices grew more present, a pack of wild dogs encountered in the forest.

LaMoia, the hunter, cut ahead of the uniforms and peered around the corner. He held up four fingers. To Matthews, it sounded more like ten. Adrenaline cocktails for all, charging her system with a menthol-like chill and drying her throat. LaMoia articulated a series of hand signals to the patrolmen and she envied him his cool. She felt lucky: He was the cop you wanted at your side in situations like this. He thrived on adversity. She recalled his telling her that she was safe while under his care, and though loath to admit it, she knew this was true, accepted it as fact.

In military-like precision the six of them rounded the corner, moving swiftly but silently, her courage returning quickly as she thought of Margaret and the other girls in those showers, the jaundiced eyes of the drunk and the desperate peering in on them. She fed on these guys, her bread and butter. She opened up their heads like cracking nuts.

The patrolmen reached them first, knocking away the beer cans, taking them completely by surprise. But then there was a burst of activity to their right—not four guys, but more like ten, the other six scattering like seeds in the wind.

"Walker!" she called out, believing in the dim light she'd recognized the back of a head. Confusion, as two of the patrolmen took off after them. A flurry of cursing and yelling. One of the homeless guys vomited.

A patrolman who had run off in pursuit returned empty-handed.

"Yo! Listen up! You, too, turd breath," LaMoia addressed the one who'd puked, a bearded guy wearing an old ratty jacket to what had once been a nice suit. "Po-lice," LaMoia said, like a southern cracker. "Me and her, too. We've got a couple simple questions for you. This is *not* the ringtoss: You don't get three chances. You talk, you walk. You lie, and it's straight downtown to central booking—a night in the can courtesy of your city government. We'll check for priors, warrants, parole status, and we'll cash in our miles, all at your expense. So, for the next five minutes, try your level best to do something smart like listen, 'cause me and her, we know the way it is, and if you go all squirrelly on us, we're gonna know that too, and trust me, you don't want to see what happens next. Any questions?" No hesitation on his part whatsoever. "Okay, good. Then let's keep our hands where we can see them, ladies. Sit your butts down on the ground, and we'll do some business."

A moment later, all six sat on the wooden planks of the ancient sidewalk like kids in kindergarten.

LaMoia asked about peeping the showers and got six heads all shaking no at him.

"Don't know what I'm talking about?" LaMoia picked two out of the group, "Him and him," instructing one of the patrolmen to cuff them and "get them downtown." One of these two immediately spoke up, confessing the peeping, insisting, "Didn't do nothing wrong." LaMoia allowed this one to stay behind. He nodded, and the patrolman headed off down the tunnel with the other.

"Any other takers?"

They raised their hands sheepishly, all avoiding eye contact with Matthews.

"Let's hear about it," LaMoia said. "First to speak up gets a gold star."

Matthews felt sick to her stomach as she learned that they'd treated the peeping like a drive-up window. It was guys like this that supported the stripper joints on First Avenue, the adult bookstores and video booths. Diluted beer and sticky floors.

LaMoia seethed beneath the veneer of comic impatience.

"Who here's good with faces?" he asked. "It buys you a trip downtown tonight, but a hall pass the next time there's trouble. Community Chest time, people! Anyone interested?" No one volunteered. He selected the least drunk of the group, a guy probably in his late twenties who looked about fifty. Cheap booze did that. So did the street drugs. Or maybe he had the virus.

LaMoia and the other cops slipped on disposable gloves, indicating an end to discussions.

Matthews slipped on a pair as well, thinking *disposable lives*.

The final patrolman emerged from the dark with two more of the escapees. No sign of Walker.

Had she imagined that? Wishful thinking?

"Time to peep mug shots instead of naked teenagers, you perv." LaMoia grabbed hold of the street person's red handkerchief, knotted around the man's neck, and led him like a dog back down the tunnel.

At Public Safety, LaMoia's attempts to win the man's cooperation ended with the detective providing him hot coffee and buying him a carton of Marlboro cigarettes. At two in the morning, he then worked him through a few dozen mug shots until confident of the man's sobriety and his ability to make identification. The man picked out the faces of three vagrants he'd seen in the Underground. With an anxious Daphne Matthews monitoring the event from the corner of the small interrogation room, LaMoia arranged yet another array—six faces in small windows on a single card—and slid it in front of the homeless man.

Dirty fingers with jagged nails took hold of the card like a nervous gambler toying with his cards. The guy studied the faces in the cutout windows. The cracked skin of his dirty hands flexed as he stabbed a face—bottom left. "This guy's been there a bunch."

LaMoia turned the card around for Matthews to see as she stepped closer.

"He ever use the gallery? The peepholes?" LaMoia asked.

"Sure. All the time."

His finger rested on the photo that was not a mug shot but a driver's license ID. The face belonged to Ferrell Walker.

"We call him the fisherman," the homeless man said, " 'cause he stinks like shit."

Matthews had been to one or two parties in LaMoia's loft apartment, huge affairs, teeming masses, noisy, with music blaring. Empty, it looked less like a bachelor's pad than she'd expected. The collection of modest, mostly mismatched furniture was complemented by the dramatic lighting—nothing but funnel lights on brightly colored wires. The focus of the area was the large, well-equipped kitchen and what was obviously a stunning view of Elliott Bay, for it looked so even at night.

"Wow," she said.

"Yeah, I know." Ever the modest one. He shut and locked the metal door with three locks. Like her and the houseboat, he'd bought his place for a song. He, at a time when the neighborhood had been a needle park and the mayor had been offering tax incentives. Riding the wave of "Californication" and the SoDo neighborhood's gentrification (back when there had been a Kingdome), he now found himself with a piece of a trendy location rejuvenated by the construction of the Safe and the new football stadium. Like her own houseboat, the loft was now worth a small ransom, and like her, LaMoia would one day cash in on his good fortune and ride into the sunset in one of his trademark Camaros.

Blue sighed from the couch and thumped his tail on the cushion. LaMoia scolded the dog for being on the furniture but then greeted him warmly when the dog bothered to say hello. A weekend architect, LaMoia had constructed a few walls into the enormous space, dividing it nicely, but leaving much of it open. Off the central living/dining area and kitchen was a master bedroom and a bath to the south that he showed her with pride, pointing out several details like high-speed Internet connection. To the north of the kitchen was an office with a single twin bed as a couch and a guest bath across a wide hallway. He placed her bag in the office, left her for a minute or more, and returned with a red beach towel, making apologies for his linen.

The towel proved heavier than expected, and before she unfolded it he said, "Don't ask, don't tell."

"Understood."

"The registration comes back expired. Previously owned by a man who smoked too much and died behind the wheel of a Ford Pinto."

"I'll return it the minute they lift my leave."

"Just so we're clear: I was *not* the officer who responded to that wreck. I'm clean. You can't harm me with that, no matter what happens."

"Got it."

"The other thing in there," he said, without naming the Taser stun gun she would later find, "is the same kinda story. Consider it a gift. No strings attached."

"It's all a gift, John. I appreciate everything you're doing for me."

"Yeah . . . well . . ." LaMoia at a lack for words? No quick quip? "We could watch some TV," he suggested.

"It's past two in the morning."

"Wind down."

The dog nuzzled him, wanting bed as badly as she did.

"Listen," he said, "there's wine, beer, pop. Food. Help yourself to whatever you want. *Mi casa, su casa.*"

"I figured you for an empty fridge."

"You figured wrong."

"Meals out at diners."

"I can see I've got an image problem."

"You are not telling me you're a cook."

"Chef," he said. "When it's a guy, it's a chef."

"And you're a chef?" she asked, disbelieving.

"Hell, no. A grill meister and a take-out king. Any food you want, any country, any flavor, and I can have it here in a half hour."

"That's a real talent, a culinary art form."

"Exactly. Me and the kitchen phone. It's all technique."

"Good night, John," she said, thanking him again.

"Happy to have you."

The dog moved in with her sometime before sunrise, warming her feet and taking up too much of the small bed. She woke with four hours of sleep, ravenously hungry, staring out at the beauty of Elliott Bay and the lush green islands beyond, a world unaware of her problems—the exact perspective she needed at that moment. She popped open the window and drank in the sea air. It had a taste to it that she associated with this city.

LaMoia snored loudly from the far room, his Don Juan image unraveling with each breath. She smiled privately and shook off the fatigue, scratched Blue behind the ears where he liked it, and prepared herself for a shower, thinking that on this morning things were okay, going on good, and that a cup of tea and a bagel wouldn't hurt anything at all.

34 Hitting the Wall

Although the Underground access discovered by LaMoia and Matthews had at first interested Boldt as a way to gain access uptown, this interest lessened when it was explained that each block of Underground stood isolated behind a retaining wall and did not, to anyone's knowledge, connect one to the next. More than six city blocks, one hundred thousand square feet each, separated the site of Chen's death and the Shelter. Boldt held out hope that with the help of his university contact, he would be able to gain access.

He began his day by talking a grease monkey in the police garage into taking a look at Liz's minivan since he'd missed the appointment yesterday. He then fired off a vitriolic e-mail to Captain Sheila Hill complaining about Matthews being placed on administrative leave and suggesting that "the situation be rectified by the end of the day" if CAP was "to effectively continue its work into the investigation of Hebringer and Randolf." He reread it twice, spell-checked it, and sent it, convinced Hill would see the error of her ways. A political beast, Hill would not want the possible tarnish of having slowed down an active investigation that carried so much press exposure and baggage. Boldt knew it was prosecutorial suicide to have Matthews sit down with Walker ahead of her suspension being lifted, and he now believed Walker's mention of Hebringer and Randolf key to the investigation. He had, in fact, left Matthews a voice mail encouraging her to "set up a meet" as soon as Walker next contacted her. He'd alerted Special Ops and Technical Services, wanting them ready to move at a moment's notice. He wanted Matthews wearing a wire around the clock and he'd asked a detective, Heiman, to write up a request for a court order to trap-and-trace incoming calls to both her office phone and cell phone. The U.S. Attorney's office could facilitate this request. Ferrell Walker was complicating things. Boldt wanted a rendezvous. He wanted answers.

Less than an hour later, Sandra Babcock finally came through, providing a list of property ownership of eight businesses and stores that she believed might offer access into the section of Underground where Billy Chen had lost his life. This access would circumvent the city's refusal to allow Boldt down inside the sinkhole. Boldt gumshoed for ninety minutes, business to business, store to store, eventually gaining an audience with the vice president of SeaTel Bank, a balding man who smelled of cologne. The VP confirmed the bank sat atop an old basement and summoned a maintenance man to escort Boldt downstairs.

Boldt knew that both Randolf's and Hebringer's finances had been checked and double-checked. Certainly if both had been customers of this or any bank, it would have been red-flagged, but he didn't recall that information off the top of his head, and this left him wondering if his team hadn't made a mistake. Did the abductor troll bank lobbies looking for women cashing large checks? Looking for brunettes who wore their hair to their shoulders? He grew irritable through the waiting, wondering what the hell took a maintenance man eight minutes to reach the lobby. There were times eight minutes meant nothing, and then there were times like this when thirty seconds could set his teeth to grinding.

"That's him," the VP said, pointing across the lobby. Boldt

saw a gaunt man with sleepy eyes, a bad set of teeth, and tight, sinewy arms bearing a tattoo of a red rose on his left forearm. Boldt hurried across the lobby and introduced himself. Struggling against allergies or asthma, the man wheezed, "Basement's over here," forgoing his name. The plastic tag on his coveralls read Per Vanderhorst. He seemed nervous, as did most people when meeting a cop for the first time. Boldt doubted he was the first cop a guy like Vanderhorst had met, but at the same time, if the guy had felony priors he wouldn't be working for a bank like SeaTel.

"I wanted to ask if you saw any flooding in your basement when that water main broke," Boldt said, as Vanderhorst led the way.

"Not a drop." He forced his reply dryly from his throat, sounding like someone was choking him.

Vanderhorst used one of about twenty keys on a ring to open a door marked PRIVATE, then led Boldt down an unattractive corridor past an EXIT sign on the right and another PRIVATE door to the left. At the end of this hall they entered one marked AUTHORIZED PERSONNEL ONLY and descended two short flights of concrete-and-steel stairs, at the bottom of which Vanderhorst hit a second light switch and motioned into a sterile, immaculately kept basement area that provided storage.

"My daughter has a friend Vanderhurst," Boldt leaned on the "u" in the name. He wanted to get Vanderhorst talking, open him up about the water main break, rumors of the Underground's existence, anything he could get from the man, but he'd been given a guy who could hardly breathe, much less make conversation.

"I heard it was the Underground that flooded in this block," Boldt tried.

Vanderhorst wheezed. "This is dry storage mostly." It was stone and concrete walls, steel beams supporting the low ceiling, tube lighting bouncing off white and gray paint. Rows of industrial shelving aligned north to south stretched like library stacks floor to ceiling. Cardboard boxes bearing codes in thick black marker occupied every available inch of space.

"How about below this floor?" Boldt asked. "Anything?"

"Not that I'm aware of." The thin man stood there like a statue. Boldt asked if he'd ever found people down here who didn't belong.

"I'm not going to say it has never happened, because I haven't been here all that long. But this is a *bank*. They don't like the idea of strangers cruising around." They moved on. "Couple more rooms down here you might want to see."

He showed Boldt three other rooms, one jammed with heating/ventilation ducts and equipment; another tangled with electric, phone, and communication wires; a third, larger and much older, that housed plumbing and steam heaters no longer in use. The walls of this third room were brick covered in thick layers of paint. Generations earlier, some window openings had been bricked closed and painted over. Those window holes suggested an outside wall. Boldt rubbed his hand on the cool brick. "I'm looking to get on the other side of this."

Vanderhorst remained disinterested, a maintenance guy going through the motions. "Wouldn't that be dirt?"

Boldt repeated his earlier question about flooding, somewhat astonished that the quantity of water so close wouldn't have resulted in any flooding.

"Listen, what do I know? You could check with my boss." He asked irritably, "You seen enough?"

Still touching the wall, Boldt asked, "Have you ever come across any doors, holes in the wall, the floor . . . anything that might lead somewhere outside this basement?"

"The bus tunnel . . . they had problems with that water main thing, I think."

This comment stirred Boldt's interest—a light went off inside him. "Which wall is that?"

Vanderhorst pointed to the nearest wall of the rectangular room. With some checking, Boldt determined it was the same wall as the one in the utility room with the bricked-up windows.

"We're done here," an excited Boldt announced.

Vanderhorst led the way back upstairs, letting Boldt go ahead as he lagged behind to shut off the lights.

Boldt reached the EXIT door down the hall, which was alarmed with a red panic bar.

"You'll get me fired, you push that." Vanderhorst stood a few yards behind Boldt, watching him. He'd crept up on Boldt, and that bothered him.

"Where's it lead?"

"Onto Columbia. It's a fire exit. You want to see the security people, they're the first door to the right, upstairs, in Admin."

Boldt thanked Vanderhorst and walked through the lobby back out onto the street, debating his next move. He had other businesses yet to explore within this city block, all with potential access to the Underground, according to Babcock.

Frustrated by his lack of discovery at the bank, Boldt called into the office and assigned two of his detectives to do that door-to-door footwork for him.

To his right, he saw the entrance to the bus tunnel station that fronted Public Safety. He made up his mind, choosing the tunnel for himself.

When Washington State builds a transportation project, 1 percent of the contracted cost is budgeted to the arts, for aesthetics. The result is an eclectic mix of sculpture, writing, music, and painting, little gems that catch the public unaware. In the case of the pedestrian entrances to the bus tunnel, it included poetry engraved into the kick plates of the stairs, as well as colorful sculpture attached to the walls.

At the Pioneer Square station, escalators, stairs, and elevators lead down first to a vast tier, an open plaza that spans the tunnel traffic below, providing passengers access to any of several additional stairs and escalators for northbound or southbound bus routes. The incandescent lighting is bright; sounds echo off the concrete and tile, and because the buses run electrically once into the tunnel, there are virtually no odors other than a faint trace of burning rubber, a condition that put Boldt ill at ease. The underground bus tunnel stations had not proven popular enough to account for the enormity of such a facility. It swallowed up the two dozen passengers down on the platforms awaiting the arrival of a bus, and Boldt along with them.

The director of bus tunnel maintenance, a man named Chuck Iberson, was a big man with florid cheeks and thinning white hair. Iberson's military background showed in his attentiveness and respect for Boldt. He had treated Boldt's summons with the utmost seriousness, arriving to meet him in less than fifteen minutes. By nature Boldt couldn't help looking at people as possible suspects. Iberson's overzealous willingness to respond so quickly, like Per Vanderhorst's mealy and vaguely sleazy sniveling persona, made the detective think twice about the personalities that lurked beneath. A bank janitor might have a shot at an unsuspecting woman, as might a man in a position of authority like Iberson. Boldt knew from his years of experience that suspects often surfaced in the most unlikely places.

"I'm interested in the water main break, back on the twentieth and twenty-first of March." He felt impatient. He'd come down here on nothing but a hunch. Nine out of ten times, such spontaneity proved a mistake.

"What a mess." Iberson appeared suddenly uneasy, and Boldt wondered why.

"The possibility, if any, that a person could gain access to the Underground from inside the tunnels," Boldt continued.

Iberson look confused by that suggestion. For impact, Boldt returned to his original question. "I'm investigating the drowning of a city worker. Pinpointing the source of the flooding may help us out some."

Iberson appeared somewhat relieved.

Boldt explained, "The EMTs and Fire Rescue who hauled him out reported being inside an area that sounds to us like a part of the old Underground. Access to that area might solve some of the questions surrounding the worker's death."

"I got no problem with that whatsoever. You want to look at my tunnel, it's yours. But I don't know nothing about no underground city, and if you want to see where we flooded, we'll have to walk it, and it's tight in those tunnels." He pointed to where the station's expanse condensed to the mouths of two concrete tunnels that each carried one-way bus traffic.

"So we'll walk it," Boldt answered.

"Okay, but I gotta put you in an orange vest and hard hat."

"I can live with that."

Ten minutes later, Iberson led Boldt up the left tunnel, walking against the direction of bus traffic. They both wore Day-Glo orange vests and yellow hard hats. The transportation department used a good number of double buses joined in the center by an accordion. Nicknamed dragons—because the second of the two sections was "dragging" behind the first—they stretched some fifty feet stem to stern and were hated by all motorists.

"If I tell you it's a dragon coming," Iberson warned, "you put your back against the wall and keep your toes behind the white line. Them tail sections tend to wander a little, so don't trust what you see."

Passing a gray door marked EMERGENCY EXIT—ALARM WILL SOUND, Boldt asked about the exits.

Iberson explained, "EERs," pronouncing it "Ears." "Emergency Evacuation Routes. Two per block, in both tunnels."

"Where do they come out up top?" Boldt asked.

"Most are spiral staircases leading up to trapdoors in the sidewalks."

Boldt had walked Third Avenue for years and never paid attention to the existence of the trapdoors. "What trapdoors?"

"They look like metal plates up there. Granted, a couple of the EERs connect through to adjacent buildings, but most head straight to the surface, swear to God."

"Talk to me about the ones that connect through buildings." It occurred to Boldt these buildings might be candidates on Babcock's list.

"Listen, with all due respect, I keep the tunnels lit and drained and the ventilation system working. I don't know all that much about the EERs."

There wasn't much of anything to see. A bus approached, and Boldt pressed his back to the curved concrete. It swept past, sucking his tie from under the vest. Iberson never broke stride.

"I'd like a complete copy of the original construction plans," Boldt said, "including the ventilation and drainage systems."

Iberson stopped walking and waited for Boldt to catch up. "I didn't build them, Detective, but I can see what I can do for you." It was lieutenant, not detective, but Boldt didn't correct the man. Iberson pointed out two drains in the roadbed. "This is where we first saw problems. Normal drainage is no problem, and we have pumps that kick in at a certain volume, but once that water main broke, we couldn't keep up. We had two feet down here before we knew it. Enough for the buses to hydroplane, so we closed down. It was a bitch. The overflow had breached the ventilation ducting. It wasn't the drains backing up, which is what we first thought—that our pumps had failed." He pointed to a massive grill installed high on the cement wall. "Don't ask me how, because we still haven't figured it out, but this baby was basically a waterfall."

Boldt said, "That other emergency door we passed. That would be more like the middle of the block?"

"A little north of center."

"I'd like a look at it." Boldt clarified, "Inside it."

Iberson motioned Boldt back well before a dragon rushed past, wind and dust kicking up behind it. He said, "Sure thing."

They walked a distance in silence. By this time Boldt's thoughts were sparking as he assembled a possible explanation for both the missing women and what Iberson had been telling him. He explained as if he absolutely knew this to be fact, "Your ventilation duct penetrates the original retaining wall, constructed to enclose what once were street-level storefronts. When the water main broke, it flooded that area deep enough that your vent went underwater, creating your waterfall and flooding your tunnel."

They reached the door. It was marked 19.

Boldt asked, "This is which kind, spiral stairs and trapdoor, or building access?"

Iberson shrugged. He didn't have a clue. "You want a look?"

"Yes."

Iberson disarmed the door with a key and led Boldt through, saying immediately, "It's *not* the trapdoor variety."

Boldt hadn't thought so, but he said nothing, preoccupied with trying to put himself in Chen's shoes or even those of Hebringer and Randolf.

The floor was textured steel plate, the walls a gray metal paneling. The lights flickered on with the opening of the door.

It was a man-made hallway leading twenty feet straight ahead to another door.

"Detective?"

"Lead on."

They walked twenty or thirty feet before climbing a short flight of steel "fire escape" steps, at the top of which yet another sign on a steel door warned of alarms. Iberson keyed this door as well and pushed it open. It accessed a basement room bearing large EXIT signs directing pedestrians up a flight of stairs to reach the surface. The room itself felt eerily similar to the bank basement Vanderhorst had shown Boldt. If Iberson had his directions correct, then it even seemed possible this room shared a wall with the bank. The basement smelled of fresh paint and mildew. Boldt could hear the rumble of the overhead street traffic for the first time, a sound absent in the bus tunnel.

Iberson said, "Most all of the basement accesses I've seen look about like this. Basically nothing in them but a few signs directing traffic."

Boldt turned and studied the wall the door had led through. It, too, showed evidence of former windows having been bricked up. The hallway they had passed through connected this wall to the bus tunnel.

Boldt stood there for a few seconds, all else tuned out. He put Hebringer and Randolf into this space—a transcendental moment when he experienced an actual image of a man dragging an unconscious woman by the arms. It was a dreamy, jagged image, not born of anything that had happened here, but his own creation. He knew this perfectly well, and yet he went with it, allowing himself the luxury of a vivid imagination. The man had the woman by both wrists. Her hair cascaded to the floor. Her blouse ripped, her bra pulled down exposing her right breast, her head hung to the side, lifeless. The killer pulled the gray door open, only to have Boldt find his own left hand on the cool steel metal. The killer looked back at him, but before Boldt could see the face, it melted, along with the man himself. Susan Hebringer lay on the floor of the man-made hallway connecting the basement to the tunnel. Her eyes popped open, and she looked directly at Boldt. Her face and body changed to that of Chen, the city street worker. Chen had been clubbed on the back of the head and was bleeding. Then he, too, was gone.

"Did you hear anything I just said?" Iberson asked.

Boldt lifted a finger for silence. He studied the door as would any SID tech, running his fingers along its edge, reaching overhead, fingering the crack at the hinges. In a voice he did not recognize as his own, he asked, "How often are the alarms checked? The door alarms," he clarified.

"I . . . ah . . ."

Boldt motioned for Iberson to step through the fire door with him, and the two stood in the steel hallway, and Boldt pulled the door shut behind them. "Arm the door," Boldt instructed.

Iberson's hand shook slightly as he keyed the panic bar.

"Okay?" Boldt asked.

"Okay," Iberson answered.

Boldt pushed against the door's panic bar and swung the door open. No alarm sounded. Boldt shot Iberson a knowing look.

"No fucking way," Iberson said, astonished. "Pardon the French," he said, covering himself.

Boldt examined the doorjamb and located a wire intended for the panic bar. The wire's insulating sheath had been cut open, a thin blue jumper wire twisted to connect two of the four multicolored wires. The main part of the wire had been cut, no longer connected to the panic bar. Boldt pointed out the modification to Iberson.

"Fuck me," Iberson said, no longer apologetic for his language.

"Check the other one," Boldt said, pointing back toward the

tunnel. Iberson took off at a run. The hallway was like a jetway at an airport. It thundered as Iberson ran.

Boldt turned and studied the hallway as Iberson stepped through the far emergency door and back into the bus tunnel. The man pulled the door shut behind him. A moment later when he pushed through, it was to silence. No alarm.

"I'll be goddamned. How'd you know that?" Iberson's surprise seemed authentic. If he'd had anything to do with the tampering of these doors, he was a damn good actor.

Boldt reasoned it through—the disarmed doors gave the perpetrator access from both the tunnel and from wherever the basement exit led. He reconsidered: Was it access, or an escape route? Was it both? His chest tight with anticipation, he knew this was a solid discovery—the tampering all but confirmed it. He thought it through again: *an exit or entrance from the bus tunnel, an exit or entrance from the basement of some building up on Third Avenue.* "It doesn't help him," he muttered.

"What's that?" Iberson asked, studying the sabotaged wiring on the tunnel door as Boldt had on the interior door. "Same story here."

Boldt moved panel to panel along the hallway wall. He pushed, thumped a fist against the steel, then jammed his fingers into the cracks and pulled hard as if trying to open a cabinet that had lost its handle. One after the next, he proceeded down the length of the hallway, crossed over, and started up the north side of the hall. The third panel away from the bus tunnel rattled loudly when he thumped it with his closed fist. He signaled Iberson to join him, and the two of them ran their fingers into the cracks, attempting to pry. All at once, the panel jumped off its frame several inches. It was held by a wire—a section of the same colored wire used to bypass the alarm systems—twisted on the far side of the panel. In the dark.

A damp, heavy air surged through the open crack. It smelled like a swamp in there.

Reaching for a pair of latex gloves, Boldt said, "You're going to have to close the southbound tunnel. Make an excuse."

"Like hell!"

"In about ten minutes, this place is going to be crawling with lab personnel." Boldt checked his cell phone service. No signal. "I've got to get to the surface," he said anxiously. "In the meantime, we lock this up. You and I go out together. No one touches anything. And if anyone asks, you tell them it flooded again. Whatever you want, I don't care. But I want no mention of police, no mention of my visit, no mention of the lab guys. You screw it up, I'll not only have your job, I'll have you in for obstruction. Are we clear on that?"

"I got it," Iberson said. He glanced back at the partially open wall panel and shook his head. "If I hadn't seen it with—"

"You didn't see it," Boldt said.

"Yeah, yeah."

"You didn't see it," Boldt repeated sternly.

"The hell I didn't," Iberson said. "I gotta put my boss into the loop. You want, I can put you two in touch directly. Closing down a tunnel, that's serious business."

More serious than you think, Boldt nearly said. "I saw pay phones on that upper level."

Iberson checked his pants pockets as he shut the EER behind them. "You got any quarters?" he asked.

35 Running Blind

Four out of the six available patrol cars were stationed around the section of downtown defined by Second and Third Avenues and Columbia and James, respectively. The officers on duty in these cars had been issued a Be On Lookout for any individual, most likely male, fleeing any door or trapdoor that could be construed to be a part of any building in that block or adjacent to that block. Basically, if anyone or anything looked or moved suspiciously, he was to be taken into custody immediately and brought to Public Safety's central booking.

The remaining two cars cruised the immediate area. These two "rovers" also monitored the city bus dispatch radio channel on handheld walkie-talkies, in case a bus driver reported anything unusual.

The pieces in place, and with Boldt turning over the underground hallway to SID, he and Detective Second Class Bobbie Gaynes, a member of LaMoia's CAP squad and the department's first female homicide detective, lowered themselves through the space created by the removal of the steel panel in EER 19 and slipped into the darkness of a section of Underground that had likely seen few living people in well over a hundred years.

Boldt might have preferred three or four specially trained urban warriors from the Emergency Response Team—ERT—as backup, but such a request would have required a formal appeal to Special Ops and would have wasted too much time. Boldt's impatience had worn thin as it was, it having taken nearly an hour to do what he'd been ready to do the moment he'd pulled that panel off.

The air, extremely cool and smelling dank and musty, hit Boldt in the lungs and he nearly coughed. He and the detective both carried flashlights with theatrical red gel taped over the light, casting a dull, reddish purple light that carried only about eight feet, helping to protect their approach.

They ducked and crawled through infrastructure—gas pipe and a tangle of wires. Boldt shone his light behind them, illuminating an imposing stone and mortar wall that rose beyond the abilities of his flashlight. They climbed over a small mound of chipped and broken brick. Boldt thought he heard rats scurrying but didn't want to think about it. Not his favorite household pet.

He and Gaynes emerged onto what had once been a city sidewalk on what had once been a different level of Third Avenue or whatever they'd called the street in the late 1800s. The sidewalk consisted of short, heavy redwood planking, some of it now rotten, most amazingly strong and intact. To Boldt's right, he saw the old storefronts, ghostly and disturbing. Overhead, more of the clumsy network of pipes and cables braided into an unforgiving mess. LaMoia had described some of this in his report on the arrest made at the church. There really was another city down here, Boldt realized, and the student in him found it somewhat fascinating.

Overhead, steel I-beams shouldered a huge pipe that he assumed to be the water main. After another ten or fifteen yards, the sidewalk gave way to several inches of imposing mud—an area that proved to be the edge of the flood wash from the broken main. He trained his flashlight's red glare down onto the mud, where he saw a series of tracks—shoe or boot prints. A disadvantage of the red light was that it blurred edges. With his heart fluttering in his chest, Boldt leaned closer. *Recent tracks,* without a doubt. *Chen?* he wondered. *The EMTs?* Or did these belong to someone else, the very person Boldt now pursued?

As they waded into the ankle-high muck, the sucking sound proved noisy and concerned him. Boldt led the way, careful not to disturb the existing prints that he wanted preserved for collection by SID. He was not one to believe in prescience or supernatural gifts; it was true that he, at times, possessed an uncanny ability to place himself inside the head of the victim, to experience the crime from this point of view in a visceral, almost tangible way, but he attributed this to the database of experience he had collected in his head, not to an otherworldly spell. It was also to this experience that he attributed his and others' ability to sense when the trail was hot, a skin-prickling rush of adrenaline that forewarned the hunter of the proximity of the prey. He had this feeling now—a keen sense of foreboding, as if a hand might strike from the shadows at any moment.

Ahead of them, the narrow tongue of mud-covered sidewalk opened up, where, to their right, a section of the hundred-year-old brick wall had collapsed. Here they could see through and into the subterranean complex, viewing a cross-section of its history. Over the course of decades past, walls had been torn down, concrete poured, steel beams installed. Sandra Babcock and her archaeology team would celebrate a find like this for years to come. But for now Boldt signaled Gaynes ahead, leaving the deep mud behind as they continued to follow the busy path of shoe prints. He stopped and listened every few yards, his hearing more sensitive than most. He heard a hissing that he couldn't put a direction onto. Overhead? Behind them in the bus tunnel?

The dull red glow from his flashlight caught the delicate lacework of cobwebs both to his left and right, and he realized there were no such obstacles in his path—someone had been through here recently enough to clear out the spiderwebs. With no more shoe prints to follow, the mud now well behind him, Boldt followed scratch marks on the concrete, directing Gaynes with hand signals through an open door to the left, down a hall, and then through another door to the right. Without a doubt the hissing sound grew louder. Closer. Boldt touched his ear and Gaynes nodded agreement—she heard it, too.

He caught himself not breathing, the tension in the air suddenly palpable. He took a long controlled breath, and Gaynes followed suit. She reached for, and armed herself with, her Beretta, though she did not chamber a round for the noise it would cause. Every hair, every nerve ending, told Boldt that something, or someone, lurked nearby.

Having paused long enough for his eyes to fully adjust, Boldt experimented by turning off his flashlight. Gaynes did the same. His instinct had been correct: Enough ambient light existed for him to vaguely see a gray patchwork of the door and wall beyond. This patchwork was barely anything more than absolute darkness, and yet it was *not* absolute darkness, and this held considerable significance for Boldt, for it implied the existence of a source of light, and that, in turn, suggested something, someone, human.

At that moment, the hissing made sense to him: a Coleman lantern. He leaned forward, peering around the corner of the rotten doorjamb and down a long corridor, several doors to either side. The charcoal gray progressed to an elephant gray and, by the far end of the hallway, a pigeon gray—these were the colors that Sarah would name, and he thought of his children and family as he rounded the corner and stepped into the hallway, Gaynes close behind. Neither he nor Gaynes wore a vest, and he thought it a foolish oversight. He'd long ago promised Liz and himself to avoid harm's way whenever possible, understanding the importance of keeping their family whole. Susan

Hebringer had drawn him down into the Underground. Had clearer thinking prevailed, he might have sent LaMoia or Heiman or someone else.

The hallway seemed to dim, though so faint was any light that he couldn't tell. Gaynes tapped him on his shoulder, switched on her gel-covered flashlight, and holding it in her left hand, quickly formed a fist around it. Boldt stopped, as the hand signal directed. She touched her ear. For a moment Boldt could hear only the rhythmic pulsing at his temples and the high-pitched whine of blood pressure. Then, he understood why: The hissing had stopped. He heard a hinge creak, and this, he thought, was what Gaynes had wanted him to hear.

At the same instant, their two-way radios crackled and screeched—a broken signal of code calls from the patrol cars overhead. Neither Boldt nor Gaynes had thought to turn their volumes down. They might as well have shouted out a warning to whatever, or whoever, lay up ahead.

That door creaked again, followed by the unmistakable sound of a person running.

Boldt, and Gaynes as well, took off, dodging fallen objects, ducking out of the way of hanging pipes, his head a knot of pain, his throat dry. Those promises made to Liz raced to the forefront of his thought—he was a father, a husband, he owed people his safety. But at the same instant, Susan Hebringer was being dragged down the hallway that he now ran, and there was nothing to stop him. He rushed through an open doorway and turned left, throwing his right hand out in front of him to send Gaynes straight into another huge room.

They split apart.

The sound of the person running came from farther away, not closer.

He felt he was in some central hallway shared by the back

of what had once been stores. Huge sections of plaster and lathe walls were missing, exposing rooms of all sizes, shelving, overturned furniture, and piles of junk. He made a wrong turn and found himself in a small room, instead of another hallway. He turned around and tried another door, trapped yet again. A maze. Retraced his steps, pushed on a door—a hallway, at last. He charged forward at a run.

"Lieu?" Gaynes, her voice muffled by walls.

"Here!"

"Lost him!"

His radio carried her voice then, as she attempted to alert the patrols up top to keep an eye out. Boldt's radio picked up her signal with ease, but the lack of acknowledgment from above indicated the signal was blocked and had not reached anyone else.

Boldt hurried ahead, making a series of wrong choices, landing in dead ends, in rooms cluttered with dusty junk. The enormity of an entire city block underground registered in him. He'd lost his way entirely, suddenly facing a series of windows, the dirty glass still intact, finding himself looking out onto yet another section of sidewalk. He used the radio, whispering to try not to give away his position. "Gaynes. I'm facing a section of sidewalk. Looking south, I think. Your ten-twenty?"

"Right here, Lieu. Center of the building, I think. A big room. A bar, or drugstore maybe."

"Anything?"

"Nothing."

He waited, straining his ears to hear, well aware the person who had fled could easily still be down here, crouching, hiding, waiting for a chance to slip away.

"I'm going to work west and then north, circling back toward you," he told the radio. "You hold, all eyes."

"Copy."

"Lights on," he said, ensuring they could discern one another from the person they pursued.

"Copy."

Boldt carefully negotiated his way around the perimeter of the enormous underground city block, backtracking and retracing his steps where necessary. He crawled under fallen timbers, stepped through vacant window holes, and eased his way through doorways, alert for rotten beams or other debris raining down onto him unannounced, alert for his suspect to spring up from behind, unexpectedly, and take a swing at him. He found himself in a full sweat, damp and burning up from head to toe, the toxin of fear escaping.

All at once there was more mud, Boldt wondering if he'd gone full circle. He stepped through the goop, reaching a doorway, and scrambled over a hill of metal that had once been a fire escape. His flashlight found Gaynes looking back at him bewildered.

"Gone," she said. "He vanished."

"But who? A homeless person? Susan Hebringer's abductor? Chen's killer?" He tried the walkie-talkie again, to nothing but static. He said, "Maybe they got him up top."

"You can't see five feet with these things." She tore off the flashlight's colored gel. Boldt did the same. They made their way back, Gaynes in the lead.

"That hissing we heard," Boldt said, announcing what they were after.

"Yes," she agreed.

It took them twenty more minutes of false turns and opening doors, of hallways and storage closets and more discarded junk and litter than seemed possible, before Boldt carefully pushed open a door, revealing a cluttered, lived-in room, twelve by fifteen feet. The former storage room had red brick walls and no windows, a mattress with blankets, plastic milk crates containing cardboard boxes of food. Boldt's gloved fingers triggered a battery-powered fluorescent and the room came to life. This hideaway was an investigator's treasure chest.

Its conversion into a living space included a door on cinder blocks that held a camper stove, several white plastic tubs filled with water, and a box of books. Boldt picked up immediately on the cleanliness to the air, the musky stink of the basement barely discernible. Only then did it dawn on him that the light in this room was battery-powered, not Coleman gas, and his eyes drifted slowly behind him as he spun around to see a half dozen four-foot-tall pressurized tanks. Green tanks. Oxygen tanks. One of them with its valve cracked open and hissing.

"Lieu?" Gaynes asked. She knew that perplexed look of his meant he had thought of something she had not.

Boldt said, "Suddenly, the elevated oxygen level in the late Mr. Chen's blood gas makes a hell of a lot more sense." Boldt reached down into one of the milk crates and came up with a New Year's Eve party favor, the kind that uncurls when you blow into it. "I think our Mr. Chen might have spoiled some-one's party."

With little or nothing to do without her suspension first being lifted, Matthews made Margaret her top priority once again, unable and unwilling to take the downtime for herself. She knew this obsession with filling her time went beyond accepted limits, knew she had real problems when it came to allowing herself to relax, knew that at some point such obsessions came to a head and stung you, usually when you could least afford it. Most of all she secretly knew that downtime would allow her the opportunity to take stock of herself, to examine her goals and aspirations, to come to grips with the fact that she had none beyond getting through the day. She had no idea what she wanted for herself—a man, a family, a career, time off, independence, a hobby, a cause? If she took time to stop and think of it, she feared the emptiness of her current existence might prove too overwhelming. Currently, she lived to solve other people's problems, whether at Public Safety or the Shelter. Facing her own was nowhere on her radar, and this, in turn, led her back to finding Margaret and doing something to help her.

A call to the Shelter confirmed what she already knew, because even if Margaret had been thinking of staying there, by mid-morning the place was virtually deserted, the girls back on the street. There were any number of haunts where she could look for her: Pioneer Square, the Market, the area in front of the Westlake Center, several of the malls. Sometimes these girls just rode the bus routes, back and forth, sitting in the last row, talking, hours at a time. As pregnant as she was, Margaret wasn't stripping, wasn't hooking, but she might be drugging, and this Matthews wanted to prevent at all costs. The girl had mentioned eating pizza crusts—"I'm eating Italian"—but Matthews couldn't remember a particular pizzeria. She walked a few more blocks until locating a pay phone that actually had the phone book intact. She was flipping through the Yellow Pages under Italian restaurants, hoping to jog her memory, when her cell phone rang. She turned the face of the phone so that she could read it: BLOCKED CALL. A sharp shudder passed through her.

"Matthews," she answered.

"I thought we had a deal." Walker.

"We do," Matthews said, gripped briefly in a moment of panic, the result of surprise. She tried not to be too obvious about her looking around for him, but felt her senses winning out as she rotated a little too quickly, inspecting every corner, every shop window, every vehicle. *Where the hell are you?* The temperature felt like it had dropped about thirty degrees. Then, a calm overcame her as she reminded herself that she need not allow him any authority over her. *The eye of the beholder,* she thought. She warmed. She had a job to do—Boldt wanted her to bring him in by accepting his earlier offer. This, while allowing him to believe he still maintained the upper hand.

Walker said, "Sure doesn't seem like it to me. Let's see . . . I offer to help you, and you agree . . . then all of a sudden you take off from your place, half dressed, like some ghost is chasing you . . . then you hook up with Dirty Harry. What is *wrong* with you?"

"I think we should get together and talk about it," she said calmly, her experience and training finally able to separate out her personal stake in this. Their discovery of the peepholes at the Shelter had profoundly affected her, forcing her concern away from herself and onto the girls. Her determination now was to bring Walker in for questioning, as Boldt wanted.

"I'm disappointed in you, Daphne."

"I need your help, Ferrell. I want your help."

"Believe me, you don't want to disappoint me. Life's little lessons come so hard sometimes." Like something his mother might have said to him.

"No." It was all she managed to say.

"You lied to me . . . about helping each other."

"No. We can work this out, Ferrell. It's not what you think. Let's get together and discuss it." She racked her mind for some carrot to hold out as an offering to him. "There's a possible witness to Mary-Ann's murder." She let that sit there a moment. "A truck driver passing over the bridge at the time. We may be able to put Neal in a lineup. Let's talk about that—you and I." She continued to search every crack and cranny for sign of him. She didn't believe he had a cell phone—to her knowledge he'd never used one in calling her—so where was the land line he was using? She heard the unmistakable sound of spitting steam, and she immediately spun in a circle. Through a window of a coffee shop on the next corner of the same block, she spotted a figure on a pay phone.

"Hello," he said. He'd seen her turn around.

She lost her breath for a moment. "Hello," she answered. One-handed, she worked her purse open, and her fingers frantically searched its contents for her wallet, wanting the thirty-five cents necessary to operate the pay phone. If she could call through to LaMoia, if she could allow him to overhear this conversation, he might make the connection and send a surveillance unit. She hoped in the next few minutes to trick Walker into sitting down with her to discuss Hebringer and Randolf. If successful, she wanted backup.

She said, "My colleagues don't think you could possibly have information about the two missing women."

"They're wrong," he said, his voice a hoarse whisper.

She allowed that change in tone to get to her, and again reminded herself not to yield to him. She said, "You need to know that we're still determined to build a case against Neal that will stick."

"Just because he lied about the time doesn't mean he didn't do it."

"I understand that," she said, "but our legal case was fashioned around that lie, and we lost ground in the hearing because of that. We haven't given up, believe me." In fact, she didn't think anyone had done anything on the Mary-Ann Walker case since the probable cause hearing—although the lab work continued. "The forensics will be convincing. It takes awhile."

"You're bullshitting me," he said. "You're waiting for me to give you what I've got before you actually do anything."

"That's not how it works." She placed a quarter onto the small stainless-steel shelf. She dug for a dime.

"If you start lying to me, Daphne, then what's left?"

"We have a witness," she repeated. "A truck driver who saw him on the bridge."

She heard only his excited breathing, and realized the seductive role that hope played in his small existence.

Walker said, "You would have used him already."

"No . . . It was night, don't forget. That bridge is dark." Her mind reeled with how to make this sound convincing. Her fingers pinched a dime. She adjusted her position so he couldn't see her lift the receiver and let it hang. She placed her thumb over the cell phone's tiny microphone hole and slipped the two coins into the guts of the pay phone. They rolled noisily inside. She punched out LaMoia's direct line, brought the receiver to her ear, and heard him answer. "Don't talk! Listen!" she said into the pay phone. She awkwardly joined the two phones, inverting the pay phone's receiver, wondering if LaMoia could hear any of this.

She said, "Eyewitnesses are notoriously unreliable, *Ferrell*. We always thought of this guy as a last resort, but we're ready to play that hand now—we could arrange a lineup—and we just might do that if you agree to share what you know about these missing women." God how she hoped LaMoia was getting this.

"You're going to suggest we meet, no doubt."

"Yes, I was."

"Are you lying to me again, Daphne? Would you risk something as *stupid* as that? Playing your little games. Teasing me, like walking around that houseboat in that tight T-shirt and underwear, but never getting naked? What's with that, anyway?"

Her throat went dry. *He could be making that up,* she said, unable to recall walking around her place dressed like that. How could she turn this around back on to him? Why wouldn't her mind get off that image of him looking in on her half-naked?

"Is that how it was with Mary-Ann, Ferrell? You've got us confused, don't you? Was it out on the boat? Did you watch her? You've got us confused, don't you? Did you watch *your own sister*? By herself? With Lanny Neal? What?"

"Shut . . . up."

His tone told her she had scored a hit, and this actually surprised her, for she'd brought it up only as a distraction, something to fill his head with a different image. But that tone of his . . .

Children saw, or overheard, their parents making love and were never quite the same for the experience. With no parents left, had Ferrell Walker spied on his own sister, peeped his own sister? Even with someone else killing her, the guilt over having done that would torment him.

"Where was it, Ferrell?"

"You—"

"At Lanny's apartment? You saw her, didn't you? Saw them, however that happened. Accident or not. Saw what he was doing to her."

He spoke, barely above a whisper, but just enough to be heard. "How could you know that?"

Her arms prickled in gooseflesh. She had him going now— her dentist's pick probing the cavity and striking the nerve. She thought of LaMoia and how he unexpectedly put the accelerator down in the turns in order to avoid skidding. She, too, put down the accelerator. "He was getting things you never got from her and she liked him in a way that she didn't like you, and that hurt, didn't it?"

"You don't know as much as you think." Again, barely discernible, indicating she'd thrown him deep into thought or recollection. These were the moments she lived for—she'd cracked open his conscience and was climbing inside.

The process allowed her to intentionally refocus Walker onto Neal and off of her—also a deliberate act on her part. They had Neal under surveillance as it was. At the very least, this effort of hers might provide them the opportunity to apprehend Walker as he made another attempt on Neal. She asked, "Is that where that anger at the medical examiner's came from? It wasn't just her death, was it, Ferrell? It was more than that. It was that she liked him, loved him, even. And you were left out in the cold in the process. Isn't that right?" She thought of LaMoia listening in. "Here I am on one corner of Marion, and there you are in that coffee shop—how much sense does this make, Ferrell? We can sit down—the two of us, together—and discuss this, our case against Neal, what you know about the two missing women. Mary-Ann's gone, but I'm here for you, Ferrell."

"Here for me? I don't think so. Tell that to Dirty Harry. He's bad for you, Daphne. I warned Anna, and she ignored me. Look where it got her."

Her brain froze, and she saw the events of the past few days in a whole different light, immediately regretting where she'd just now, so carefully, led him. Walker, or Prair, or whoever had driven her out of her houseboat in a state of panic, had also pushed her into LaMoia's care. Walker somehow knew this, resented it, and drew parallels to the loss of his own sister. The massive psychological knot this would cause—first the transference on his part, then her own mimicking of Mary-Ann's shacking up with Neal—might never come untangled, even in the most cooperative patient. Walker found himself watching instant replay, and she now began to see the complications of events that had changed his tone with her, had pushed him across the fine line between adoration and hate.

"It's complicated," she said, suddenly bone-tired, twinges of fear creeping back up her spine.

"I'll show you mine, if you show me yours," he said, suddenly childish again.

His 180-degree reverse was both too quick and too convincing. He was suffering the psychological equivalent of the bends. He'd surfaced too quickly.

"I won't lie to you, Ferrell. I want whatever help you can give me with the missing women." She imagined that by now at least one car was rolling toward their location. Perhaps, even, LaMoia had gotten the switchboard to forward the call to his cell phone, and he was currently listening in while on the way himself.

"Why don't you get us a table?" she said. "I'll come over to the Seattle's Best with you and we'll sit down and discuss this." How many more crumbs did she need to leave LaMoia? She'd both given him the address and named the establishment. At this point, she felt certain it was safe to leave the pay phone and approach Walker. "Ferrell?"

"Ten o'clock tonight. You be at the door to the Shelter. If I see you're alone, we'll talk. If not . . ." Again, she heard his shallow, rapid breathing. She could picture him sweating yet cold, excited yet scared. "Don't be stupid, Daphne."

She heard the steamer again, but a large truck rounded the corner and double-parked, and the sunshine bouncing off it blinded the coffee shop's window.

"Ferrell?" she said, already dropping the pay phone and moving up the sidewalk toward the coffee shop. At first she walked, but then, as the hum of the room grew louder in her cell phone, she began to jog, and finally to run. The blind spot on the window shrank with her angle as she approached, from a blinding silver, to black, and finally to transparent again.

The pay phone's receiver dangled on the end of its cord.

LaMoia's Jetta turned and rounded the corner, swerving out of the way of the double-parked truck. He'd been careful not to show himself on foot—was trying to let her know that he was nearby and available as backup.

But it was too late. Ferrell Walker was gone.

At 9:48 P.M., a matter of hours after Matthews had spoken to Ferrell Walker, she calmly drove her repaired Honda south on First Avenue, the black leather wallet containing her lieutenant's police shield sticking out of the top of her Coach purse. Boldt had obviously pressured Captain Sheila Hill into reinstating her, because there had been no review board or formal review. She'd gotten the call that the meet with Walker had been approved, and that meant reinstatement.

The last few hours at SPD and Public Safety had been the mobilization of a surveillance team that included several plain-clothes detectives from Narco and CAP as well as a three-man, black-clad ERT unit from Special Ops and even a rooftop sharpshooter. Boldt had suspended the search of the Third Avenue Underground while SID combed the lair, and the surveillance of construction sites continued, meaning his manpower was stretched.

As she'd prepared for the meet, Matthews had asked La-Moia to wire her up, an invitation usually assigned a fellow member of the same sex. The idea was for him to clip and tape the transmitter to her pants to avoid ripping hairs off her skin. Although not exactly an intimate moment, it felt that way to both of them, what with him running his fingers inside the waistband of her pants, brushing the elastic of her underwear. True, she wore less clothing, showed far more skin, at a pool or the gym, but men didn't run their hands down your pants at either. He couldn't manage to get the tape to stick very well, so he ran his fingers even deeper. He stepped back suddenly, as if she'd bitten him.

"Listen, I'm not doing such a great job. Maybe we should get a skirt in here."

"Finish it," she said, unbuttoning her blouse at the navel. She fished for the wire he was attempting to pass her.

She asked, "Would it help if I unbuttoned my pants?"

"Not unless you have twenty minutes to spare," he teased.

"Ha, ha," she said, trying to sound like that hadn't fazed her.

He tested the tape, and it held. "I'm fine."

"You don't sound fine," she said.

"Mind your own business."

"When a man has his hand down my pants, it most certainly *is* my business."

"You're playing with me."

"Oh, yes," she said. "Absolutely. I love to see you squirm."

"I'm not squirming."

"Of course you are."

He grunted.

Again she teased him. "Finish the job and get your hands out of my underwear."

"You're nervous. That's what this is about, right? Your nerves?"

"You really know how to woo a girl."

"Woo?"

The tape finally held. Her fingers caught the wire he passed and she drew the small mike up inside her blouse. She unbuttoned yet another button of her blouse and clipped the lavaliere to the elastic bridge connecting the cups, turning to face him as she buttoned herself. For a moment she allowed herself to believe he blushed with the sight of her.

"You have a real way with the women," she said.

"That's what they say."

She brushed herself off, smoothing the blouse.

He looked a little too closely and pursed his lips, bunching his mustache. She'd never liked mustaches much.

"A cry for help," he said, repeating a possible explanation of Walker's behavior that she had raised at an earlier meeting.

"If I have it right—and remember, I may not—then there's a psychological progression Walker's going through, a decline that has everything to do with what is more than likely confusion over his relationship with his sister; Neal's stealing Mary-Ann from him; Neal's abuse of Mary-Ann; the subsequent murder; and then Walker's transference of his need to protect Mary-Ann over to me. Transference comes in all flavors, John, from lite to extra-strength. He latches on to me. He follows me. For reasons known only to him, he has chosen me to represent Mary-Ann in his life. Maybe he's just trying to gather the courage to tell me something. I don't know. Maybe he saw more of the murder than he's shared with us. That wouldn't surprise me—his guilt over watching them in the first place preventing him from telling us exactly what went down. It would also explain his conviction to see Neal put away for this crime."

"But Hebringer and Randolf?"

"I'm not pretending I have the answers," she said, unbuttoning her pants and tucking in her shirt, the act itself implying an immodesty that clearly surprised him. "I could be way off base with any of this. My original thinking was that he didn't know anything more about Hebringer and Randolf than what he'd read in the papers, but that he recognized a way to bait me into meeting him."

"I'm still camping on that side of the river," LaMoia said.

"But the way he made this meet—preempting what was to be an attempt on my part to arrange something inside, something contained, something that worked better for us . . . and the fact that Lou likes Walker being positively IDed for having been in the Underground, and then this guy getting away from Lou and Bobbie down there . . . and Lou never liking coincidences and suddenly thinking Walker could either have something on Hebringer and Randolf, or might even be a part of it himself . . . and here we are."

"Here we are," LaMoia echoed.

She felt his objection to her playing this role and appreciated his restraint in not verbalizing it. Doing her damnedest to appear collected and composed, she said calmly, "Listen, John . . . I think we pushed him over the edge with Neal walking away from the probable cause hearing and with my subsequent attempt to distance myself from him. It was a bad judgment call on my part. If he misses Mary-Ann as much as I think he does, then at some point he will come after me. This level of obsession leads to abduction. It's my turf. I know what I'm talking about," she said, answering his head shaking no. "It could be for something as innocent as a confession—confiding his guilt about knowing more than he's told us—or something . . . more serious. And if he should get me—"

"He will *not* get you."

"—you need to think unconventionally, something you're good at. Neal's apartment is a possibility. The family home— this place he lost when the business went bad. A trawler is entirely possible." She met eyes with LaMoia and lowered her voice. "These places hold significance for him. He'll take me to someplace that holds significance."

"He will not—"

"If you guys lose me," she interrupted, "I'd check those places I just mentioned first. The Aurora Bridge after that."

"Jesus . . . you're as sick as he is."

She continued in her businesslike tone, "If I go missing,

John, don't do it by the book. Promise me that. Time's the enemy, okay? He's an organized personality. He knows what he's doing. He lives to control the situation. When he senses he's lost control, as he did earlier, he takes action. That alone separates him from what you guys think of as 'loonies.' Trust me, if he should get me and then lose control of the situation . . ." She couldn't complete that thought, even in her own head. "Just find me, John. And fast. However you have to do it, just find me."

"Cross my heart," said the all-time rule breaker.

LaMoia opened his arms, an improbable invitation from a guy like him. She stepped forward cautiously, afraid he might make a joke of it. But he didn't, and so she held herself close to his chest, the thumping of his heart like timpani. She tried to think of something amusing to say, to cushion the moment for them both, but the feeling of his arms around her, of that absolute sense of safety, lodged a walnut in her throat and she couldn't get a word out. She squeezed, and he squeezed her back, and for a fleeting moment there was absolute peace in her world.

Driving now past the ALL NUDE storefronts, a wino walking unsteadily behind a grocery cart filled to overflowing, the tourists intermingled with the city's subculture, neither acknowledging the other, she marveled at the tolerance, at the coexistence of two such diverse cultural strata. She felt herself being injected into this, like a vaccine into tainted blood, down through Pioneer Square where groups clustered around street musicians, where gray-haired hippies sold trinket jewelry from the tops of cardboard boxes and college kids waited in lines outside the music clubs.

"Test, one, two," she said into the empty car.

Her dash-mounted Motorola squawked and called back, "Copy that, Decoy."

She hadn't liked the moniker assigned her for this operation, but it wasn't her place to comment on it.

A few turns later, she pulled into the church lot marked PRIVATE PARKING STRICTLY ENFORCED—VEHICLES WILL BE TOWED, and slipped the cardboard permit onto her dash before locking up. She wore her hair over her ears in order to cover the tiny ear bud that carried the network of radio traffic surrounding her surveillance. She tested the gear once more as she dumped her keys into her purse. "Okay, boys, I'm all yours."

"Copy that, Decoy," the calm voice returned softly in her ear. No jokes from dispatch. No humor. These radio operators were the grumpy librarians of police work.

She reached the overhang and the door in the side of the church that led down to the Shelter at five minutes before ten, five minutes ahead of schedule. The sky opened up with a drizzle that felt like the misters over vegetable stands in supermarkets. She thought sarcastically how perfect it was to further complicate things with the added hassle of the rain—traffic would slow, long-distance surveillance would be more obscured, and any right-thinking person would seek some kind of shelter from it, making the undercover roles harder to play effectively without standing out.

She listened in her one ear to the radio reports from the observation points outside her houseboat, for Boldt didn't put it past Walker to use the meet to buy himself a chance to get inside her houseboat, either souvenir-seeking or in order to await her return there. The rain was apparently stronger over Lake Union, and one of those keeping surveillance reported a red-and-black umbrella on the dock, unable to identify the person holding it. "That's a neighbor," Matthews said, barely moving her mouth in case she was being watched by Walker. The red-and-black umbrella belonged to Robert, a man who could have played stunt double to Ernest Hemingway. If they hassled Robert, she'd hear about it for months to come.

Location by location, the four undercover detectives and the leader of the ERT squad reported into dispatch, confirming their positions, reporting sightings considered "possibles" for Walker, filling the radio with activity where no such activity existed in the real world. She knew that LaMoia had parked the Jetta on the second floor of the car park, engine out, and was sitting in the car's backseat (making it more difficult for others to spot him), keeping an eye on her through the car's back window. She felt the attention of all those eyes and ears, both onstage and exposed for all to see. If and when her moment came with Walker, it would be recorded, videoed, and analyzed, as would any subsequent interrogation. She felt uncomfortable in the spotlight, even a little sick to her stomach, as it didn't feel much different to her than walking around her houseboat certain someone was watching. Someone *was* watching—many someones—and for a person accustomed to doing the watching, she found the reversal of roles unpleasant, going on vulgar. Walker himself was no doubt watching as well, and she could only hope he couldn't see or sense the swarm of protection that had been created around her, for she felt certain it would put him off and prevent him from approaching her.

When she needed to speak to dispatch, she would fake a small cough, fist to mouth, and quickly talk. "Nothing so far," she reported, immediately identifying it as an amateurish comment, tagging herself a desk jockey for all in the communications truck to laugh at and make fun of her. She felt tempted to just stomp off and forget about this whole thing—let them find some other way to collar Walker. But a bigger part of her wanted this resolved, both for her own sake—to get Walker off her case—and for Boldt's, because she thought he was putting too much faith in Walker's connection to Hebringer and Randolf.

Standing there in the light rain, the object of so much attention, she felt an added pressure to reassemble the various parts into something that made sense, something that explained Hebringer and Randolf, and felt maddeningly frustrated when she failed after repeated tries. What could Walker tell her that they didn't already know? Did Prair's lurking about—his possible stalking of her—have to do with his infatuation with her or his involvement in Mary-Ann Walker's life prior to her going off that bridge? How could anyone consider a man with Lanny Neal's past an innocent in all this? Round and round she went, the minutes ticking by. Walker was late, or out there studying her along with the others—the reports in her earpiece identifying first a homeless man on the street corner behind the church and then, finally, "possible solid heading for Decoy from southeast corner of lot."

Matthews saw the figure coming, still at a considerable distance—he was the approximate height of Walker, blue jeans, a dark sweatshirt with a hood covering his head. He walked with purpose, either to reach Matthews in a hurry, or to get out of the rain. She tensed and warmed with his approach. She found the radio traffic in her left ear distracting, as dispatch calmly assigned new positions to two of the undercover detectives in the field, placed ERT on alert to the suspect's current location, and asked the sharpshooters to stand down their rifles until further notice. Matthews knew this meant nothing more than that they were ordered to keep their fingers off the trigger—no sharpshooter took his eye off the sight, orders or not.

She resolved to do as little talking as possible—Walker had wanted the clandestine meeting . . . let *him* do the talking.

The closer that figure drew, the less Matthews thought he looked right for Walker, and the greater her sense of dread. His hips moved a little too fluidly, the gait of this person's walk didn't feel like Walker at all. He'd sent a surrogate, someone to deliver a message.

Her muscles had frozen; she wished like hell that rattle in her ear would stop—couldn't they just *shut up*? The approaching person's right arm lifted, and both she and that voice in her ear had the same thought at the same moment: a knife. The sharp-shooters were readied, ERT was assigned a "red alert." But nothing glittered in the pale cast of the overhead bulb; no metal sparkled. The hand grabbed hold of the hood and stripped it off the head. Short hair, but spiked. Smooth skin. A nose stud. It was a young woman heading for the Shelter, nothing more.

"You on a break?" the girl asked Matthews, who held out faint hope she still might be a messenger.

"Something like that. Waiting for someone." Matthews vaguely recognized the face—Carmine? Caroline? Carley?

"In this piss?" the girl asked.

"Is it Carley?"

"Yeah. You're Matthews, right? The cop."

Word got around quickly. Her reputation as a cop could distance her from these girls forever. Or—it occurred to her a beat too late—was Carley testing that she had the right person for the message?

"That's right."

"Is it full?" she asked, pointing to the door. Sometimes the Shelter posted a volunteer out here at the entrance to notify late arrivals of the lack of occupancy. There was a sign that served the same purpose, but the girls rarely paid it much attention.

For the first time in the last fifteen minutes, her earpiece mercifully went silent. The Com Officer had switched it off, both to allow her to think clearly and to ensure the suspect didn't hear any ambient high-pitch chatter coming from it. Matthews hadn't bothered to check inside, but she told the girl there were still beds available, her nerves on edge that Walker's message was yet to come.

"I didn't know you smoked," Carley said, mistaking Matthews's electing to stand barely protected from the rain. "You're okay, Miss Matthews."

Carley reached for the door handle—a large wrought-iron ring. Matthews stepped out of the way, asking, "Is there something you want to tell me?" Carley looked at her strangely. "A message from someone, maybe?" Matthews pressed.

Carley paused, and Matthews could feel it coming. The girl hesitated, the door open now, and said, "Margaret got herself that place south of the Safe. Her and this other girl. Is that what you mean?"

Margaret. Again, that same pang hit her in the chest. "Oh," was all she managed to say. Carley stepped through the door, her footfalls on the stone receding into the basement enclave.

The earpiece popped and Matthews heard dispatch stand down a number of the participants in the surveillance operation. These commands were nearly immediately followed by a male voice interrupting and identifying itself only as "Gray." (With police radio codes a combination of numerals, operatives were given a variety of different "handles," from animal names like Wolf and Dumbo, to nicknames like Sparky and Hooter, to colors of every kind.)

"We got ourselves a cross-dresser, people. Heads-up. KCSO-eighty-nine is incoming from Yesler."

"Eighty-nine?" Matthews clarified, forgetting to try to cover her speaking for the sake of the mike.

"Eight, nine, affirm," Gray replied.

CO dispatch: "Let's run a check on that, South." The instruction was back to Public Safety—the south precinct—and the SPD radio dispatcher monitoring the radio traffic. Normally the Commanding Officer would monitor from there as well, but she knew Boldt was more than likely in the command van.

"Unnecessary," Matthews said. She glanced toward the second level of the parking garage and the area where she knew LaMoia was sequestered, longing all of a sudden for some kind of contact with him, a sardonic turn of phrase, a comforting look, something to make this okay, because this did not feel okay. She allowed herself to believe she saw movement up there, at the back of one of the cars. Her imagination? She wondered.

LaMoia's voice came urgently from a handheld radio, through the dispatch communications and into her left ear. She allowed herself to believe he'd somehow sensed that longing she'd felt. "Listen, Decoy, he's on bus detail over at SO. We *know* this for fact, right? So he could have made your ten-twenty in the course of the job. Do *not* jump to conclusions. You got it? Hang in there. Treat it as a right thing. Let the fish come to you. Acknowledge."

"Copy that," she said, her fist to her mouth once again, slipping back into her role effortlessly. Why just the sound of his voice should calm her, she had no idea, but it had and she wasn't asking any questions.

Gray: "He's pulling over. One block north on Yesler."

This struck her as odd, if this was the normal course of duty as LaMoia had suggested, but she endeavored to stay calm.

CO dispatch: "Officer on foot, heading south. Decoy, he's yours in five . . . four . . . three . . . two . . ."

She picked up Prair's large silhouette as he passed a hedgerow and walked into the parking lot on foot. He walked with his usual confidence, stiff spine, and military demeanor.

"Lieutenant," he said, avoiding use of her first name—a first.

"Deputy Prair," she said, for the sake of the tape recorders out there.

An uneasy silence settled between them as he stepped up to her, only a few feet away. "What is it you want?" he asked.

"What are you talking about?" she said.

"The message."

"What message?"

"The message said you'd be waiting here at ten P.M., that you wanted to see me."

"You want to try again?"

"I got the message, Lieutenant."

She said, "I don't know what you mean, but you could start by explaining your presence at the end of my dock last night."

A gust of wind tossed her hair. Prair's face tightened, and for the first time he glanced around, as if sensing the surveillance. The wind blew again, a mixture of rain and cold air this time, and as he reached out and moved her hair off her neck, a move that briefly terrified her, she realized he hadn't sensed anything: He'd spotted the wire from the earpiece.

"What the hell's going on here? You got a thing going here?"

"You stepped into that thing," she said. "You squirreled it."

"I was told to meet you here."

"What is it with you, Deputy?

"I . . . got . . . a . . . message, said you wanted to see me."

"A written message?" she asked.

"Central took it while I was on patrol."

"I bet they did."

"Listen, Lieutenant—"

"Save it," Matthews said. "We'll have a chat over at Public Safety, sort this all out." Such were the instructions she received from dispatch through the earpiece.

"I'm on ten minutes lost time," he complained.

"Well, we'll make it an hour," Matthews said.

"I got a message. Check it out. Central will have a record of it coming in."

She stepped up to him, her anger rising. "You've got all the bases covered, don't you?"

He held up his hands like he wanted no part of it. "I don't know what's going down here, Lieutenant. But if I squirreled things, I was set up."

"Blue!" Boldt's voice hollered over her earpiece. "Blue: Crash the nest. On my authority, you crash the nest right now!"

Her houseboat.

She understood then that Boldt believed Walker had used the meet as a distraction, had used Prair to cement that distraction, and that the ultimate goal of that distraction had been to penetrate the houseboat.

Prair backed up, out into the rain.

"Don't go anywhere, Deputy."

"You got this wrong, Lieutenant."

He appeared intent on breaking into a run.

"Stay where you are, Deputy."

"This is not my thing, Matthews. You got that wrong. I'm going back to my car, my route. I don't need no trouble."

"Too late," she informed him. "You stepped into it. Now we've got to clean it up."

"To apologize," he barked out, winning her full attention. She tugged the noisy earpiece from her ear. He was beginning to get wet in the rain. "I was there . . . at your place . . . the dock, to apologize. Swear to God. For the way I've been, the stuff I've done. I fucked up not telling you about ticketing the Walker woman. That was wrong. I wanted to come clean for that. Try to set things straight."

"My car," she said, stepping closer and driving him back a like amount. "This parking lot. That parking garage," she said, pointing to where she knew LaMoia was watching. "That was *you*."

"I should have told you about the moving violation. That

was stupid." He wouldn't admit to any role in the sabotage of her Honda.

"*All* of it, Nathan, or none of it. You can't put filters on this."

He moved another step back, wearing frightened eyes. "I was there to apologize," he repeated. "Nothing more."

A pair of plainclothes detectives entered the parking lot at a jog. "You're off-Com, Lieutenant," one of them called out. "We're all done here, thanks to Roy Rogers," he said, addressing Prair. "You won yourself a backstage pass to the fifth floor, and we're your personal escorts, *sir*." They stood to either side of the deputy.

"You got this wrong," he said to Matthews.

"We'll see about that," she said back to him. But she felt half-convinced that he was right, and that left her all the more confused.

38 Alone Again

Nathan Prair invoked his right to a guild representative, a lawyer, ahead of his interview, effectively nullifying that any such interview would take place and, through the process, casting additional suspicion onto himself. He was released, pending a board hearing, though it seemed unclear any such hearing would ever take place, as SPD had little authority to remand a deputy sheriff. It would take the attorneys some time to sort this all out.

Boldt threw a fit in the Situation Room, angry at his team for the failed surveillance operation, the bungled intelligence, furious with Walker for having stung them. He ordered LaMoia to orchestrate a sweep of all known locations for Walker in a bid to bring him in for questioning. LaMoia broke a key off his key ring and handed it to Matthews, asking if she'd mind feeding Rehab when she returned to his loft.

"There's no reason to go back to your loft, John, although I appreciate the offer."

"The hell there isn't."

"We've had the houseboat under surveillance all night long. Twice it has been searched and swept top to bottom. It's probably the safest place in the city right now."

"It's on our hot-spot list, Matthews. Don't give me shit about this. We're going to roust every homeless haunt in this city in the next couple hours. I need all hands on deck for that. We will *not* be watching your crib. We will *not* be sweeping your crib.

You'll stay at my place at least one more night, maybe longer. It's that or a hotel. You know the Sarge. You know the drill. This is not me, darlin'. You want to complain, you go over my head."

"I will."

"Be my guest."

Her bluff having failed, she winced and tried to charm her way out of this requirement. "How 'bout I feed Blue and *then* go over to my place?" She wasn't sure why she'd attached so fiercely to the idea of independence—she didn't actually relish the idea of being alone in the houseboat. Yet something compelled her not to accept his offer. She felt it showed weakness to accept. "Leave just one guy to watch my dock."

"Walker's a *fisherman*, Matthews. He's probably just as likely to try a water approach. I don't have the manpower. Even if I did, I couldn't justify it to a lieutenant who doesn't want you staying there. Do me a favor, don't make me take another meeting with the Sarge. He's in a stink. I don't need it, not tonight. If we turn up Walker, I'll promise to call and let you in on it, okay?" It hadn't occurred to her that they might not include her in on this interrogation, but with her as the "victim," it suddenly made sense. "The number I'm going to call is my own loft, not your cell. You copy that?" He added, "In the meantime, I'm going to advise dispatch that you'll continue to wear the wire, right up until you undress for bed. Okay?" She gave him a look. He said, "Don't give me that. This is not kinky. It's just on the off chance this guy's holding another ace." He wouldn't let her get a word in edgewise. "Don't forget, Matthews, it was you who put this notion into my head that this bozo might be cozying up to nabbing you, not the other way around. You got any peeves, you take it up with the lady in the mirror, not me, okay?"

She resolved herself to the notion that attending Walker's

interrogation was far more important to her than where she laid her head for a night. Besides, secretly, with all his gab, LaMoia had convinced her she didn't want to spend the night alone anyway. Having a dog and a cop down the hall was just fine with her.

The wind gusted as if someone had switched on a fan. Elliott Bay whipped up into a white-capped froth that rocked the lumbering ferries side to side. Upon reaching LaMoia's loft, Matthews had initially misunderstood Blue's incessant whining, believing the dog missed its master, as did she, only to realize he needed a trip around the block to relieve himself. Donning one of LaMoia's slickers and an old felt hat, Matthews set out for a quick trip around the block, bringing the Beretta along in the right-hand pocket as a security blanket. The formerly industrialized neighborhood was a hubbub of commerce by day—a coffee shop, a rug store, a gourmet market, a magazine and newspaper specialist, a smoke shop—but by night little more than a rolled-up sidewalk in a loft neighborhood, the curb lined with Range Rovers and Troopers, the black-leather-jacket set strolling in pairs during good weather, renting DVDs and staying home when it rained.

Blue left his mark on a few dozen vertical surfaces, from the corners of buildings to NO PARKING signposts. He staked his territory out like a surveyor, marking a street corner and actually waiting for her to lead him across the street.

When the slanting rain hit, she thought of her partially open bedroom window—of many of the loft's windows—and picked up the pace of her return. A drizzle was one thing, but this kind of sideways storm could soak the place.

Perhaps it was nothing more than the anxiety of wanting to

seal the loft from the storm and the accompanying adrenaline that pumped into her system, but a few minutes after she picked up her pace, a few minutes into realizing that she and Blue were inauspiciously alone out on this street—where had everyone gone?—an agitation overtook her, like the feeling when a limb aches and itches from the inside out. That awful feeling begged her to check ahead of her and behind, left to right, in an increasingly frantic effort to see if anyone was following her. Paranoia swept over her as quickly as had the wind.

When Blue's pace quickened, the nails of his paws scratching the sidewalk's concrete in a flurry of sharp strokes, it drove her heart rate faster, pushed her legs first into a jog and finally an outright run, the two of them in competition now, Blue heeling to her side, his wet tongue dangling, Matthews lifting her knees, rocking her ankles, controlling her breathing to where they closed the last two blocks back to the building in a full-on sprint.

Winded, and yet laughing as she told Blue what a good dog he was, she let them back into the building and took the stairs, eschewing the assistance of the elevator. It felt much warmer than when they'd left. She reached the apartment door, slipped the key into three of the five locks available, and unlocked it. She unclipped the leash, patted Blue on the head, and was hanging the slicker back onto the coat tree when Blue's slobbering turned her around.

The dog was licking the floor. He glanced up toward Matthews as he did so—as if he knew better—put his nose to the plank flooring, and then advanced several feet and licked again.

For a moment Matthews thought how cute a sight it was, but that moment passed quickly, followed by an inaudible sucking for air in a room that suddenly offered none: Blue was licking water off the floor—water, in the form of wet boot prints.

39 Blurred Vision

A moment earlier, while out on the street, Matthews had been feeling sorry for herself for being alone. Now she wondered if she *were* alone, and wished more than ever that she was. She wondered if she'd tracked those prints into the apartment a half hour earlier herself. Had they already been there then, and she'd simply missed them because of Blue's pestering?

"John?" She called his name three times, each louder than the previous attempt.

She backed up and blindly reached behind herself, never averting her eyes from the expanse of the loft and its long wall of rain-streaked windows, water tangled on the surface like silver thread. With her right hand she unlocked each of the three door locks that she had relocked only moments before—she wanted a quick exit if needed. Her left hand searched the slicker, located the Beretta, and slipped it quietly out of the pocket. She switched off its safety, chambered a round, and took it in both hands, barrel pointing down and slightly to her side.

She cleared her throat. As she spoke, Blue lifted his head attentively. "I am armed!" she called out loudly into the room. "I will shoot on sight! *Go away now*, or announce yourself! I repeat: *I am armed!*" . . . and dangerous, she thought. She squatted, an act that Blue took as an invitation to be petted, friskily trotting his way over to her. She pushed the dog out of the way—an act he took to mean she wanted to play. She pushed him again. Blue nuzzled her, nearly tipping her over.

One set of prints, the beaded water thicker to her right, lessened to her left, the soles of the shoes having shed most of the rainwater after only a few steps. The angle of the track suggested an origin in the guest room—her bedroom.

"Go away now!" she hollered again. To Blue she whispered, "Find him," motioning out into the room. The dog looked at her curiously, nearly obeying, but holding by her side uncertain of the game. "Find him!" she repeated, the dog thumping its tail, a mixture of excitement and confusion. She stepped deeper into the room, her head light, her arms heavy. She considered turning around and running, but only briefly. She was done running, tired of playing the victim. Sometimes the role of victim was a product of one's situation; sometimes it came down to a matter of attitude, a series of choices. She was the one with the training, the one with the pistol, the one with the determination. It was Walker's turn to fear her; Prair's turn to fear her.

She reconsidered those shoe prints, slowly convincing herself that they were hers, as the mind is wont to do under such pressure. She wasn't about to squat and spend more time inspecting the floor, wasn't going to be caught off guard by the intruder.

"Walker?" she called out loudly, moving cautiously through the loft, Blue panting at her side.

She swung the weapon, still aimed at the floor in front of her, right to left, left to right, a slowly tracking metronome. Sweat trickled down her jaw as she flashed with heat, her eyes dry and stinging. The windows rattled in unison behind a gust of wind. The air smelled of seawater and fresh rain, a combination that on any other night she would have found pleasant, even intoxicating.

Just get me through this, she pleaded internally.

Given the loft's open floor plan and vastness of space, she felt like a bug in a terrarium—some unseen, monstrous eyeball tracking her as she moved. Her mind raced, a restless impatience nagging at her to clear the room as quickly as possible, secure the door and windows, and then call LaMoia. Blue followed on her heels, a worried whine escaping him like a leaking balloon.

LaMoia would return home at some point, she reminded herself. One option was to get her back against a wall with a good view of the entire room and simply wait for his return. She could call—get someone down here, regardless of the hour. Lou would come to her aid in a matter of minutes if asked.

The possibility of coincidence existed, as remote as it seemed to her at that moment. Some street skel, some addict, could have broken into the apartment looking to heist what wasn't nailed down.

Blue's whining irritated her. She wished he'd make like a dog and go flush the intruder instead of skulking behind her like a frightened child.

She cleared LaMoia's bedroom, bath, and closet first, moving around and through the doorjambs nervously, in the jerky fashion to which she was trained. She'd not been in this part of the loft yet, and she tried not to pay any attention to the neatness of the room, the stack of self-help books by the bed, the perfectly folded towels on the chair that sat next to the ironing board that was no stranger to where it stood. This suite of rooms told her more about the man than five dinners out would.

She left the master, opened and inspected two oversized coat closets, again marveling at the level of organization in each, and moved through the kitchen/dining/living space (glancing toward the front door and making sure it remained shut). With only two more hallway closets (one of them a narrow linen closet, and an unlikely hiding place), the guest bath, and the guest bedroom to go, she picked up the pace, less nervous, less anxious than only minutes earlier. Blue had stopped whining, leaving her side in the kitchen to go lap at a bowl of water. His tongue slapped at the surface, his collar chimed on the bowl's edge.

She moved closer to this, the final room, to inspect and clear.

"I'm armed," she repeated for the benefit of hearing herself speak, her voice carrying little of the urgency or authority it had only minutes before. A part of her felt as if she were playacting, that the role of tough cop was ill suited for her. She understood and lived with the fact that she was far more feminine than most women on the force. Being one of "the girls" required a toughness of attitude that she'd never acquired. She was more woman than cop, more psychologist than cop, regardless of title, rank, or training. Hovering at the door to LaMoia's guest bedroom, the Beretta beginning to weigh a hundred pounds at the end of her quivering arms, she thought herself a poor example of the woman cop. These seeds of self-doubt sprouted within her, and she found herself distracted rather than pitch-perfect; taut-nerved rather than ready for combat.

A movement or a sound—she wasn't sure which—tripped an internal alarm. Someone was just outside the loft. She jumped into the guest room, leveled her weapon, and saw no one. She quickly locked the window, checked under the bed, under the desk, and then hurried to the front door, grabbing her keys.

A moment later, she and Blue were descending the apartment building's stairs in a flurry of footwork, Matthews suddenly *wanting* a confrontation, wanting closure.

She had taken a flashlight of LaMoia's from its plastic wall bracket on the way out, but found it clunky and awkward to hold in an over/under fashion with the handgun as she descended to ground level. She eased open the building's stairwell back door, buffeted by the wind. The water's edge was a couple of steel warehouses away. They'd be gone soon enough, condos in their place. She didn't want Blue getting loose, so she sneaked out the door without him, immediately winning a complaint of incessant barking from the other side. The fire door clicked shut behind her. To reenter the building, she'd need to reach the front door.

Her back pressed to the wet wall, her nerves jumpy in the rain and dark, she swung the light and weapon around in what to others might have appeared to be a random, haphazard motion, but to her was a methodical sweep of the area. She walked up and over a low stack of shipping pallets, the wood creaking beneath her. She knew that the fire escape outside her west-facing window would terminate around the corner, on the west wall. A part of her didn't want to confirm that its ladder was down, but that was how she found it a moment later, and the discovery pumped enough adrenaline into her to run a marathon.

Her vision blurred by the wind and rain, she cast the light about, looking for him, searching for him, prying the light into dark shadow in hopes of revealing him. She caught her finger on the trigger, and an eagerness in her heart. This was blood lust, something she'd read about, something others had told her about in sessions, but unlike anything she'd experienced. She wanted the excuse. She was ready to use the excuse—a bad shooting or not, she found herself preparing to do the unthinkable.

That thought made her recall Prair, and suddenly in the midst of the wind and rain, and the provocative urge to eliminate Ferrell Walker from the face of God's earth, a pinprick of light formed at the end of what seemed a very long tunnel. She pushed these thoughts aside where they belonged, but the thought process had begun; it churned away inside her, running in her subconscious like a computer virus, just waiting to spring up when least expected.

The overhead lights down by the warehouses flickered once, a warning of a faulty wire. The water level reached through her clothes and undergarments to her skin, invoking a chill. Wet or not, she continued around the perimeter of the enormous building, aiming the flashlight as much overhead—directly into the rain—as anywhere else, hoping to catch movement on the fire escape.

Fear proved itself as insidious as ever, infiltrating her steely resolve. Suddenly she wanted nothing more than to be back in the loft, locked up safe and sound. The idea of shooting Walker seemed far less urgent than that of finding dry shelter and warmth. If anything, she felt bare and exposed, the penetrating cold, wet rainwater making her feel far more vulnerable than she had only minutes before.

"You motherfucker!" she shouted up toward the sky, not knowing who had said that, nor where it had come from. Her arms shook. The flashlight dimmed, smothered by the curtain of water. She'd been dragged out here against her better judgment, against her true will, manipulated in a way that felt both invasive and repugnant. In an effort to end it she'd resorted to his rules, his game, and this proved the most offensive of all.

Far away, she heard Blue's hysterical barking. Beyond that, the dull grind of a jet's turbines and the low grumble of a ship's engine or thunder.

Again, she debated calling for backup, but she knew damn well that those who cried wolf quickly found themselves out of the pack.

She reentered the apartment building lacking confidence. One circling of the building carried with it a lingering doubt about who she was and what she was after.

She retrieved Blue from the stairwell and climbed the stairs, a sodden, dispirited shell of her former self. Whoever had entered the apartment had beaten her, and she resented the hell out of it. If they'd taken anything, they'd stolen a part of her as well.

• • •

The lights in LaMoia's apartment flickered, and she cursed under her breath. She didn't need any more drama at the moment; she wanted nothing more than to be locked up nice and tight, warm, dry, safe and sound.

Soaking wet, she patrolled the loft yet another time, inspecting every corner, every closet. Resolved that she was indeed alone and protected behind a series of deadbolt locks, she double-checked the window in her guest room, worked a chain to lower a bamboo shade, closed the door, placing a ladder-back chair against the knob, and undressed quickly, getting out of the wet clothes. She pulled on a T-shirt and a pair of underwear and the familiar sweatpants and ran a brush through her hair before crossing the kitchen and boiling water for tea.

Reinforced with the hot chamomile, she talked to Blue about nothing at all, found him a dog biscuit, and fed it to him from a stool at the kitchen bar. After that, he sat at attention by that stool unflinchingly devoted to her. She hated herself for wishing LaMoia would return home sooner than later. She didn't want to go to bed without him being in the apartment, without relating her harrowing story of finding wet shoe prints down the center of his living room, without garnering some tiny amount of sympathy for what she'd been through, never mind that it was her fault in the first place.

Staring over the brim of her teacup at the apartment and its appointments, she immediately saw what was wrong then: nothing. Nothing was out of place. *Not one thing,* at least that she could see. If a common thief, one would expect a drawer or two left hanging open, a TV or DVD player gone missing.

Her hand hovered over the phone. She could call LaMoia and ask how long he thought he'd be. Better yet, she could find some clever way to determine his schedule *and* let him know someone had prowled his apartment—that was certain to bring him home in a matter of minutes. But if Lou Boldt had put him on an assignment and she subsequently pulled him off that assignment, there would be hell to pay. Lou was clearly jealous of their closeness as it was—misplaced jealousy as far as she was concerned. Aggravating that wound hardly made sense. Furthermore, Boldt's efforts were aimed at bringing Walker in for questioning. She had no desire to hinder those efforts.

She glanced toward the guest bedroom and thought better of it. She didn't want to fall asleep. There was a TV in LaMoia's bedroom the size of Texas. She thought she might invite herself to surf for a movie—anything to fill the time. Anything but sleep.

40 Working the Room

LaMoia got himself into more jams than a jar of peanut butter. He had a penchant for it, and why they always, *always,* seemed to involve women—*attractive women*—was beyond him, except to say that some guys were just lucky.

Cindy Martin would have immediately won LaMoia's attention even if she hadn't been identified in phone company Local Usage Details, or LUDs, as the person Mary-Ann Walker had called at 11:03 P.M. on the night of her death, the last call placed that day from Lanny Neal's apartment. LaMoia had read and reread the interview sheet on her. A CAP detective name Louis Gilgau had spent nearly an hour interviewing her, one of about ten such interviews. LaMoia now had the job to reinterview because Boldt had ordered him to do so—still convinced that Walker's offer to "help" with Hebringer and Randolf made him of prime importance to that investigation as well as to his sister's murder.

LaMoia would have noticed her not because of her chest, a substantial example of high breasts on a long waist, not because of the farm-girl innocence of her face, nor the faraway stare across the relatively empty barroom, but instead because of her fashion sense. Martin was one of those women who continues to dress the same and wear her hair the same as she had in high school. She still looked the same age as a result. If LaMoia were to pick a pinup girl from a catalog, he'd be hard pressed to do better than Cindy Martin—a buxom farm-girl blonde, with hands like a man and eyes with the intensity of an assassin.

"Hey there," LaMoia said, pulling himself up onto a bar stool and checking out the deerskin jacket in the bar's mirror to make sure it hung right.

"Hi."

"You're Cindy?"

"You're the cop that called," she said.

"About Ferrell Walker," he reminded.

"Like I told the other guy, I only dated him a couple of times."

"Dated?" LaMoia asked. He didn't remember reading a thing about that. How could Gilgau leave that out? "I thought the connection was Mary-Ann."

"Was, yeah, sure."

"But you dated Ferrell."

"Not for long. Nothing serious."

"I'm trying to find him."

"So you said." She met eyes with him, hers a cool gray-blue that he was sure could look frightening if she were mad at you. They could make you feel other things, too.

"You dated him recently?"

"Two years ago."

He understood then why Gilgau would have discounted the importance. That was Ferrell Walker the fisherman, the Ferrell Walker before the fall brought on by his father's death and his sister's deserting the family business. He asked, "A week, a month, a couple months, or what?" He couldn't see this girl with someone so unworthy. Sympathy fucks were one thing—he'd had a few himself—but sympathy relationships?

"Or what," she answered.

"Cute," he said, not meaning it.

She left him, tending to a bearded customer in need of another pilsner.

LaMoia thought about a drink, but it was seriously off-limits. So were pills, though he'd transferred the two he'd stolen from Matthews into his clean pair of jeans, and there they remained, in a coin pocket, only the thickness of denim from his enjoyment.

When she returned, she said, "Off and on. He was fishing then, so it wasn't exactly steady between us. It was fun because we did things with Mary-Ann, that's all. But it kind of lacked chemistry, you know?" She leaned into him with that twin pair of headlights—her eyes and the ones in the sweater—and induced enough electricity to fry a pacemaker. He understood the sign behind the bar then that warned of the health risks associated with the use of microwaves. Probably guys dropping like flies around there before the sign went up.

"Well, if it was a lack of chemistry," he heard himself say, "it wasn't any fault of yours." Mikey liked it. He wasn't sure what drove him to say such things, but there you are. He wasn't sure about a lot of things. He didn't lose any sleep over it.

"That other cop called. You guys are better in person."

"Off-duty we get even better." Where the hell had *that* come from?

"Don't doubt it for a minute." She glanced over at the clock. "I'm off at twelve." Less than twenty minutes.

"I was on night duty for all of March. These past few days it has been pretty much twenty-four/seven. It's hell on your social life."

"I doubt you suffer too much," she said, turning to the bottles after a signal for a vodka on the rocks and overexaggerating the effort as she stretched to reach it. She caught him looking at her assets in the bar's mirror.

"Write me a ticket," he called out to her, not missing a beat. "You busted me on that one."

She grinned. Bit her bottom lip. "Free country," she said.

"And me," he said, "I'm supposed to keep it that way."

She poured the vodka, returned the bottle with a lot less effort, and delivered the drink. Looked like maybe a two-dollar tip for a four-dollar drink—maybe the gymnastics hadn't been for his sake after all. Woman knew her trade.

"Walker claimed to a colleague that Lanny Neal had gotten Mary-Ann jammed up with drugs. That he did stuff to her a guy shouldn't do. Not the good stuff," he added.

"Sounds like Ferrell. Listen, Mary-Ann was a big girl. With Lanny Neal—you got the reputation, if you know what I'm saying. He could be hell on a woman, sure. But he was hell *with* the women, too."

"Got it."

"She knew what to expect. She could have walked."

"You think?"

" 'Course she could have. Except he got under her skin, I suppose." She leaned forward on the bar again. "Some guys do that."

"Women don't tolerate abuse because they're addicted to the sex," he said. "It's because they fear where it'll go if they ditch out."

"You believe that shit?"

"It's in the manual that way," he said, trying to win back some lost ground. He didn't know if he wanted that ground for himself, or so he could continue to work her. That confusion disturbed him. Uncharted territory this, since his recovery. Dangerous ground even. Part of his distraction were the two pills in the coin pocket. The other part was looking him in the eye.

She laughed a good laugh, from the gut with her shoulders raked forward. "You're a piece of work."

"That's what they say."

She could hardly believe he'd said that. Neither could he. Ten minutes to twelve. He had some decisions to make.

He said, "Bad luck, what happened to her."

"Is it true Lanny did it?"

"We're still working that out. What do you think?"

"Me?" That seemed to floor her. "Under different circumstances, no. From what I've read about it . . . if she'd been wearing more clothes . . . something like this . . . I'd say it was just plain bad luck. Wrong place, wrong time. It's a different town than it was ten years ago, right? You've got to see more of that than the rest of us. Whole different place. But I don't know— underwear and a T-shirt. That makes sense for her going to bed like that, and if she was going to bed, that's Lanny, so I'd say you've got the right guy."

"We don't have him," LaMoia said.

This confused her. "But I thought there was just a hearing."

"There was." He realized that people close to Mary-Ann like Cindy Martin had stayed up on events, once again amazed at the connection the media supplied.

"So? There's gonna be another one, the paper said."

"Maybe not."

"No shit?"

"No shit," he said. "Depends on what we turn up."

"Where's Ferrell fit in?"

"Top secret," he teased, making light of it. He lied: "Walker's a character witness in all this. We've got to make sure we got someone we can trust."

"Ferrell's okay."

"Just okay? Maybe that's not good enough."

"In ballet . . . you ever been to ballet? . . . they say you've lost your point. The arch of the foot just can't take it anymore and you lose your point, and you're basically finished dancing.

After the accident . . . Mary-Ann's dad, I'm talking about, not her . . . Ferrell lost his point. Lost me, too. Lost Mary-Ann to Neal. Within a year he'd lost everything else. Their daddy held those kids together. Fucked up the boat most all the time . . . the fishing . . . pissed them both off. Drank too much, sure. But he held them together. Him drowning like that. Probably should have seen it coming, but it fucked Ferrell up worse than Mary-Ann. Father, son, I suppose. Go figure."

"Never heard that 'point' expression." He hadn't heard a great deal of this, but he didn't want her necessarily knowing that.

"Yeah, you don't strike me as the ballet type."

"I'm adaptable," he said, winning another smile from her.

"Why do I doubt that?"

"He says . . . Ferrell, this is . . . that Neal was pretty brutal on Mary-Ann. Put her in the emergency room a couple times."

"I don't know about that. The way she told it, that stuff happened out on the boat. Her and Ferrell out there trying to keep it going without their dad. I wouldn't be so sure about that."

"It wouldn't be the first we've heard about Lanny Neal and his women," he said.

"Listen, he's no prince. Lanny has a wicked temper, no question about it. If Lanny was on meth . . . no, thank you. Makes him goddamn crazy, that stuff. He and Mary-Ann were practically married. Did I notice when she walked funny, or couldn't use a bum arm? Sure I did. But I'm telling you, she said it happened out fishing, and I believed her. Not many girls work those boats, and those that do don't do it for very long."

"I'd take a Sam Adams if you had one." He thought about those pills again, how easily they'd go down.

She drew him a draught beer. He paid with a five and left a couple bucks on the bar. He nursed the beer, not really in the mood to drink but wanting to be a paying customer. She said, "Let me get Stan to fill in behind the bar. I'll catch up with you over in one of the booths." The look she offered him took the darkness out of the dim room.

Ten minutes passed before she joined him. She brought him a fish and chips, telling him he looked like he could use it. She suggested vinegar on the fish, ketchup on the fries.

"Tell me about this accident," LaMoia said.

"What's to tell? Mr. Walker was a drunk. In this business," she said, glancing around the dark barroom, "you get so you can spot them, believe me. Growing up, I didn't know it, but trust me, the guy was a fool for peppermint schnapps." She shook like a wet dog to show her disdain. "The stuff makes me want to puke."

"And he died how?"

"Fell overboard into his own net. Shit happens, what can I tell you?"

"And Ferrell gets the boat?"

"It damn near destroyed him, the old man's death. Him and me . . . we were an item before that, but he pulled a Humpty Dumpty on me, and I had to bail just to keep my own head together." She got a faraway look. "Tell you the truth, when I heard Mary-Ann had jumped, I believed it, except that she couldn't drive over a bridge, much less jump from one. That family paid their dues. A lot was asked of her and Ferrell after their mom passed. The old man on the boat or in the bar wasn't a damn bit of good to them. Them so young and all. I can see Ferrell flipping out over losing her, because they were this incredible team, the two of them. He flipped out, right? That's what I've heard."

LaMoia had read the newspaper articles on the case—all three of them. There'd been little mention of Walker beyond as surviving kin.

"Why do you say that?" he asked.

"That's the word on the docks. Missed work. Got fired. Hell . . . he's been living on the streets for the better part of the winter. Living like a pig from what I hear. It's a shame."

"Do you have any idea where I might find him?"

"Is that what this is about?"

"It's part of it," he said, looking across at her.

"What's the other part?" she asked.

"Did he ever *bother* you? Anything kinky—looking in your windows, that kind of thing?"

"Ferrell?"

He registered her astonishment.

"You think he ever followed Mary-Ann and Neal around?"

"That's another story."

"Tell me that story."

"I'm just saying . . . yeah, he hassled Mary-Ann about seeing Lanny. Sure he did. What brother wouldn't?"

"Hassled how?"

"Listen, he got down and out, right? Busted. Dead broke. And he hit up Mary-Ann for money from time to time. I know that because she told me. And she helped him out when she could, sure she did. But he got to be a pain in the ass, coming around Lanny's place at all hours, trying to get Mary-Ann back on the boat. But she just wasn't cut out for it, you know? All those years she'd done it because if she didn't her father would beat the crap out of her. Stupid drunk. First chance to blow it off, she took it, but it screwed Ferrell in the process, and he kept trying to get her to come back."

"So he resented Neal?"

She leveled a look onto him that let him know what an understatement that was. "Hello?"

A different picture of Walker was emerging, and LaMoia wasn't entirely comfortable with it. He knew that Matthews needed to hear the bit about the father's death and the repercussions on both his kids. Ferrell Walker had no doubt carried a lot of the weight of the family given the father's alcoholism, and he'd cracked under the weight once the father was gone, which wasn't the first time that story had been told. He thought the loss of the father was a button Matthews could push.

Cindy Martin fiddled with her hair, an awful color of yellow bought from a box.

LaMoia saw the change the discussion had brought on her.

"You all right?" LaMoia asked.

"Yeah . . . No. Not really. You think I messed him up, dumping him?"

"Sounds more like his family messed him up to me."

"You don't like the food?"

He'd picked at it but hadn't eaten much. "Not that hungry is all. It's good. Very good." He stuffed a bite in. Too greasy.

She checked her watch. "My shift is over."

"So it is."

"You want to continue this someplace less smoky?"

"Where do you have in mind?" He met eyes with her. He was hitting on her, and he didn't know why. He felt like an asshole. He didn't have to sleep with her, he told himself. He didn't have to fall into that pattern. Times like this he felt programmed. He thought about the pills again. They were part of the program. They helped him relax, to be himself.

"I've got some pictures of Mary-Ann. That kind of thing. If they'd help?"

"The father?" He was thinking of a trigger for Matthews to use. He was thinking of that sweater lying on the floor, and this woman along with it.

"Might have. I'm not sure."

"I've got wheels," he said.

"I'm only a couple blocks," she said.

He nodded, knowing he shouldn't. Some habits were hard to break.

The wind drove the lines against the aluminum and steel down on the docks as LaMoia walked the three blocks with her. Twice he reached down into the coin pocket and touched the two capsules. He could dry-swallow them. A dozen thoughts churned inside him—images of a bloated old-man-Walker coming up with his net. The meds would slow down all thought, would kill the pain brought on by the wind.

He knew if he took the pills he'd sleep with her. Two wrongs did make a right when meds were involved. If he wanted to sleep with a woman, he'd sleep with her—so why was Matthews at the forefront of his thoughts? An adolescent urge to prove himself independent of that thought arose inside him. If he drank enough on top of the pills, he might not remember much. Wouldn't be the first time. He could have all the sex he wanted, he reminded himself. He wasn't tied to anyone.

Her place was the top floor of a former two-story saltbox. When she turned to unlock the door, at the top of a set of stairs added when the floors had been divided into apartments, La-Moia slipped the pills out of the pocket, glanced down at them in the palm of his hand, and then tossed them into the tall grass.

He apologized to her, told her he couldn't stay. Had to get back. He'd hurt her by accepting and then refusing. They both pretended otherwise. She said she hoped he hadn't gotten the wrong idea. He kissed her—a good, solid kiss, one that she'd remember—and said how he wasn't supposed to mix business with pleasure, and how he could lose his job over it. It was a lame excuse, but she allowed it to go unchallenged.

"Talking about Ferrell," she said, as LaMoia turned his back to leave. "He's a fisherman, don't forget."

"Meaning?" He found himself looking off the stairs, trying to see where he'd tossed the pills. He caught himself reconsidering a chance to lie down with this woman. God, how he needed it.

"They're patient," she said. "They fish three, four, five days and may not catch a thing and then go right back out there and try again. He's been doing that all his life. You've never met a guy as patient as a commercial fisherman. They're used to waiting for what they want."

"What's Walker want?" he asked.

She shook her head. "Other than having Mary-Ann back? I don't know."

Not good news for Daphne Matthews. He and she had expected it, but hearing it out of this woman's mouth made it all the more real for him. "You've been a big help."

"Could have helped more," she said, trying one last time. "You've got someone, don't you?"

Did he have? He thought she might be trying to salvage her own pride, so he said, "Yeah."

"You have that look," she said.

That comment worried him the whole way home.

41 Hatred of the Father

Matthews came awake to the sound of the door's dead bolts turning. She'd fallen asleep for a few minutes on LaMoia's king bed, the wide-screen TV halfway through *Pollock*, a movie she'd been stunned to find in LaMoia's DVD collection. To rent it was one thing. To own it?

She hit the wrong button on the remote, sending the volume higher instead of turning off the TV. At least she was sitting up by the time LaMoia appeared in the doorway.

"You didn't happen to walk Rehab?" he asked.

"How'd it go?" she asked. LaMoia shook his head, discouraged. She wanted to explain herself—her being found on his bed—felt she needed to explain, even though he'd invited her to treat the place as her own. "I thought a movie might help with sleep." She stood up, tugged at her T-shirt self-consciously. Crossed her arms because she wasn't wearing a bra and felt awkward about it. "And yes . . . to Blue. The walk."

"You all right?"

"No," she said, shaking her hair and hanging her head. She felt so *weak* for having reacted the way she had. "I think someone got into the apartment, John."

"What?"

"I left a window open, I think."

His face tightened, but he managed to say, "Okay."

"It's not okay. It's my fault, and I'm sorry."

"It doesn't mean—"

"The floor was wet," she said, stopping him.

"Because the window was open," he suggested.

"No. Out here." She pointed. "Prints. Maybe mine, maybe not. If not, they got there while I was out with Blue, I think." She felt awful, in spite of his attempts to smooth this over. "I think you should check whatever valuables you have. I haven't touched anything and the place wasn't tossed. Nothing like that."

"Not much to take," he said. But she could see him struggling with his frustration. He made light of checking a couple drawers. His underwear was there, he said. His socks. She wanted to hug him.

"See why you want me back at my place?"

"Not true." He made a point of looking into the living space. "Walker?"

"Would Nathan Prair know where you live?"

The question rattled LaMoia. "You think?"

"Could Neal or Walker know where you live?"

"If either of them had followed us, sure, they could."

"But Prair. Your and my addresses are accessible to our fellow brothers in blue. Not to the public."

"And what's his motive?" LaMoia asked. "He's looking for your laundry or something?"

"Cute," she said.

"Special Ops tied Prair up for a while after he blew the surveillance. The timing's off. I don't see him good for this."

"And what about Neal?" she asked. "It makes a little more sense in some ways. He might think we have files on the case. Might have seen me enter alone and wanted to teach me a lesson. Never underestimate the power of guilt, John."

He grimaced. "My using taught me all I need to know. Still working on it, for that matter. I don't need the one-oh-one."

"It gets big enough, you lash out. Neal could be there about now."

"Wants to put this back onto us."

"Something like that, yeah. I'm fishing, John."

"Are you a mind reader, too?" he asked. He sat her down and together they shared toast and cream cheese while LaMoia explained most of his interview with Cindy Martin. He stuck to the highlights.

She said, "So the kids shared a hatred of the father, and when the father died there wasn't as much to share. Mary-Ann gets her act together, probably feeling free for the first time in her life. Little brother Ferrell doesn't fare as well. Feels abandoned. Mary-Ann's been mother and sister all in one. Pretty big void to fill, if that goes away all of a sudden."

"And he's chosen you to fill it."

"That's not what I meant," she said.

"Tell me I'm wrong," he said.

They ate another piece of toast each. She took hers with honey and a second cup of tea, after which she said, "Second night in a row. I'm whipped." He wouldn't let her clean up. She returned a moment later with the drop gun and Taser, returning them.

"You can keep them," he said.

She left them on the counter. "It was incredibly good of you to do that for me, John."

"I'd do anything for you, Matthews. You know that."

The seriousness of his statement hung between them. She knew if she simply walked away to her room it would put him in a bad place, so instead she crossed, closing to within inches of him. She took another step, and reached around him and they hugged. His body was all lean muscle. Besides the physical warmth between them, there was a current that hummed. Her chest tingled, as did her pubis. Stepping away, she turned quickly and said good night, hoping he wouldn't see that her nipples had gone rigid beneath the T. There were too many lines that could be crossed here. She needed to get back to the houseboat, despite her having no desire to do so.

She asked, "What about IDing the latents from that lair Lou found? What about searching every known part of the Underground there is? Walker has to be hiding down there, right?"

"Tomorrow's another day," he said. "If there was anything to know, we'd know it." He smiled, "Good night."

"Sweet dreams," she answered.

He mumbled something to himself. She was glad she didn't hear it.

Ten minutes later she prepared for bed by shutting the office door and slipping off the sweatpants. She climbed under the duvet, the comfort of that bed about as welcome as anything she'd ever experienced. Blue scratched at the door, and she got up to crack it open so he could come and go. A moment later she was back under the covers thinking that life's little pleasures were also often the biggest.

Maybe he'd bought *Pollock* because of the theme of alcoholism and depression—a part of his rehabilitation. Maybe just because of the performances. She wasn't sure why this was where her mind focused on its way down toward sleep. She rolled over, slid her arm under the pillow, and she gasped, jumped away, and rolled out of bed in the process.

"John!" she called out without thinking.

He was there in about five steps. Shirtless, in a pair of gray athletic briefs, the legs of the underwear longer than tighty-whities. She remained on the floor, her T hiked up above her navel, her bikini-cut panties showing a lot more than she'd ever want seen. But neither of them was checking the other out, their attention was fixed instead on the guest bed. Her overreaction had tossed the pillow to the side. Lying on the bedsheet was the cause of all this.

A key. A skeleton key. The sheet remained slightly damp where a hand had touched it.

"What the hell?" LaMoia came closer.

Matthews sat up, tugging the T lower, but it wouldn't go low enough. "Looks like Walker kept his promise," she said, her voice catching.

"Hebringer and Randolf? You think?"

"We'd better call Lou."

"I can't tell you absolutely it was him, no." Matthews wore a blue fleece jacket of LaMoia's zipped up tightly and the same pair of gray sweatpants. Her hair was back in a clip.

"We've upgraded the BOL to an All Points," Boldt said, watching Bernie Lofgrin's SID team process LaMoia's loft.

LaMoia huffed at that. Boldt glared at him. "Sergeant, you have something to contribute?"

"No, sir."

She'd never felt this kind of tension between the two. "Gentlemen," she said, letting them both know how stupid they were being.

LaMoia said, "Give me an ERT unit and the rest of the night, and I'll have him in the Box by your second cup of tea, Sarge."

"It's not how we play this," she said, turning them both to face her. "He kept his end of the bargain." She indicated the key, now labeled in a plastic evidence bag. "So we keep ours by putting Neal into a lineup."

"The truck driver?" LaMoia said. "You think? He's worthless, Matthews."

"But we keep our end of it. If we treat him like an informant—"

"Then we don't lie to him," Boldt completed for her, nodding.

"But he's *not* an informant," LaMoia protested. "He's a god-damned screwball with a bunch of nuts loose."

Matthews did not care for that evaluation and let him know with a harsh look.

Boldt said, "We chase down this key; we set up the lineup; we keep you under close watch," he told Matthews.

"It's not about me," she said. "I'm the messenger, that's all. Maybe an ear; maybe he thinks he can talk to me."

LaMoia snapped at her. "And maybe he thinks you're the second coming of Mary-Ann, and he wants to ride off into the sunset with you . . . or *on* you, for that matter."

"That's uncalled for," she said.

"How do we know he wasn't giving the sister a hump out on the boat after dear old dad croaked, and along comes Neal stealing all the fun?"

"We don't," she answered honestly.

"What's with the father?" Boldt asked, effectively ignored by the pair.

"How do we know those fishing 'accidents' weren't the younger brother playing a little rough with sis?"

"We don't." She felt right on the edge of yelling at him.

"I rest my case," LaMoia said.

Boldt repeated, "We work the key. We run the lineup to-morrow, and we keep a tight leash on you. Anyone have a prob-lem with that?"

"He'll be watching Public Safety," she announced, "to see if we bring Neal in for the lineup. To see if I keep my end of this. It's a means to an end, okay? If we bring Neal in for this lineup, and we play the surveillance right, Walker will come to us. We won't have to go looking for him." She added, "We chum the waters, and the fish will come to us."

LaMoia settled himself with a deep breath.

"Okay with you?" Boldt asked his sergeant.

"Whatever."

"Is that a yes or a no?" Boldt asked.

LaMoia nodded and met eyes with Matthews in something of a staring contest.

Boldt asked her, "Are you okay here, or would you like to transfer to a hotel?" His tone of voice leaned heavily on the second option.

She raised her eyebrows, passing the question along to LaMoia, who said, "I'll hold off on the ERT until we see if this lineup baits him. When Bernie's guys are out of here, she'll get some sleep. We're cool here."

She exchanged glances with Boldt. His eyes were distant and cold, and she felt she'd betrayed him in some unspoken way. He went home to a wife and kids, but if she wanted to sleep down the hall from a fellow police officer, that was somehow out of bounds. Resentment built up behind her eyes, and she stopped herself from saying anything.

"Okay," Boldt said, somewhat awkwardly. "She's staying."

He took the key and paused at the apartment door. "Get a fresh battery in that wire pack, and make sure you're wearing it in the morning."

She nodded, feeling oddly on the edge of tears that he'd think to make sure she was constantly being looked after. "Thanks, Lou," she called after him.

Either Boldt didn't hear her or didn't choose to answer. The difference between the two kept her up most of the rest of the night.

"You look awful," Boldt said the next day.

"And just think," Matthews replied, saying sarcastically, "I've had such a stress-free night."

Neal's public defender had agreed to, and arranged for, his client's appearance in the lineup. The man looked properly surprised to see two police lieutenants awaiting them out on the Third Avenue sidewalk. It had been Matthews's idea to intercept attorney and client outside the front door to Public Safety, buying time for Walker—if he was out there—to register that Matthews had followed through with her promise of the lineup. It also bought Special Ops the opportunity to locate Walker during his surveillance of the building. The radio clipped to Boldt's belt was supposed to keep them informed of any progress in this endeavor.

Instead it was Boldt's cell phone that rang. As he answered it, Matthews attempted both to keep them all outside and to buy Boldt some privacy by asking Neal what he knew about Mary-Ann's relationship with her brother following the father's drowning.

"You don't have to answer that," the attorney advised his client.

Neal told her, "The old man was a bastard to both of them. The kid fell apart, granted. Fucked up everything. Lost everything. But hell if it made any sense. He should'a been out partying."

"He leaned on Mary-Ann," she suggested.

"Fucker fell apart, I'm telling you."

"You supported her helping out her brother, or you got in the way of that?"

The attorney repeated his caution, this time more sternly, and Neal took his advice, electing to zip it.

Boldt ended the call, saying to Matthews, "Lab's got that thing for me." The way he cocked his head, she knew he meant the report on the lair in the Underground—after years of their working together she could read him this way—but he'd said it so that Neal might think he meant the report on Neal's car, a report they already had and weren't terribly thrilled with. He said, "I'll walk you up, then I've got to handle this other thing."

She looked down at his waist, to that radio, and the attorney caught this. "What's going on?" he asked. "What's with the radio?"

"Just staying in touch," Boldt said.

The attorney made a point of looking at the cell phone cradled in Boldt's left hand, clearly sensing there was more to this. "Yeah? Well let's reach out and touch someone inside, shall we? We've all got places to be."

The police lineup—a few detectives, a janitor, and Lanny Neal, each holding a number and looking through bright lights at a pane of one-way glass—went about as expected, with the truck driver brought in by LaMoia picking out a Special Assaults detective as the man he saw throw Mary-Ann Walker off the Aurora Bridge. That it was about two weeks later now didn't help his memory any, nor did the fact it had been raining that night and as dark as a cow's stomach.

With the lineup completed, the four surveillance personnel assigned to keep watch on the immediate area for Walker maintained their positions for a few minutes longer in hopes that Neal's reemergence onto the street might trigger "an Elvis sighting," as one of them put it.

Trying to reach Boldt in his office, but missing him, Matthews took twenty minutes of lost time to walk a letter of appeal addressed to Social Services the block and a half over to the King County Courthouse, in hopes that Mahoney could read it and advise her on its legality. Her request to Social Services was for that agency to approve her personally assuming a temporary guardianship of Margaret ("last name to be determined"). If successful, she hoped to shepherd the girl through the birth of the baby, attempting to eventually place her in a state-sponsored program for teen mothers. A long shot, she went through with it anyway, explaining her situation and leaving the letter with Mahoney. She was determined to help this girl, come hell or high water. News that Margaret had taken a room south of the Safe did little to make Matthews feel better—that room had to be paid for; the neighborhood was lousy; the employment opportunities for near-delivery-date pregnant teens seemed slim. Intervention seemed the best way to protect the mother and child.

Returning from the courthouse, Matthews tried her best not to think about Walker out there watching for her, or the surveillance team assigned to look for him—all of this focus on *her*—but instead to remain focused on Margaret, and someone else's needs.

Eradicating Walker from her thoughts proved a little like trying to talk oneself into falling asleep. Only the idea of rescuing Margaret provided the necessary distraction.

It surprised her to spot Boldt's back as he entered a Seattle's Best Coffee just north of Public Safety. She'd been under the impression he'd been down with Bernie Lofgrin looking at the prelim on the underground lair. That meeting was either over, or yet to come, and she decided to go ask which, in case she could join him for it.

She paused, alone at the corner, waiting for the pedestrian light.

"You . . . ruined . . . my . . . life." The deep male voice came from behind her, and the sound of it nearly dropped her to her knees. She saw herself stabbed and bleeding out on the street corner, traffic passing by, oblivious.

She thought of the lavaliere microphone she'd clipped to her bra that same morning, the fact that somewhere, someone had just listened to her appeal to Mahoney for Margaret's rescue. She tried to speak, to raise the alarm, but as he took her shoulders and spun her around, no words came out. She raised her arms defensively, expecting a blow, a wound. She saw the man's face, recognized it even, but it wasn't whom she'd expected, and her brain malfunctioned because of this.

It was the guy who'd stopped to "help" her outside Safeco Field. They'd brought him in for questioning.

"Mr. Hollie," she sputtered. "Take your hands off me!"

But he grabbed her wrist as she reached for her purse, and he bruised her in his grip.

My John Lennon moment, she thought, wondering if a handgun was next, marveling at the irony that her focus for the past several days had been incorrectly on Ferrell Walker.

"What did I ever do to you?"

She heard the emotion in his voice, strangely on the edge of tears, and welcomed it—self-pity was easier to work with than anger—believing she had a decent chance at salvaging the situation. In the back of her brain a little voice reminded her that

Boldt would by now be hearing over his radio that she was "in need of backup," that he'd be coming out of that coffee shop any moment. Another part of her realized that she'd wanted to be rescued for years, that this was part of the attraction to LaMoia. And then the next thought that rattled through her brain at that moment was that she was in fact attracted to LaMoia, and this dumbfounded her. Her mouth went dry. Her head throbbed. She looked around for help. "This isn't the place," she said dryly. If she could keep him talking, if she could buy time, she might diffuse his purpose, whatever it was. The terror she felt at that moment was the culmination of all the pent-up fear associated with Walker.

"I stopped to *help* you, you ungrateful bitch!" The change in tone alarmed her.

"You're angry." The absolute wrong thing to say. She knew it the moment it left her lips.

"Angry? Is that what I am? It made the evening news, the morning paper. My name! I lost my job. My neighbors dumped their trash at my door." He stepped back, arms dangling limply at his side. "Angry?"

She tracked his right hand as it moved slowly into the pocket of the trench coat. Then, movement to her right. Boldt, oblivious to traffic, his weapon drawn. A car braked, narrowly avoiding hitting him.

Movement shifted into an eerie slow motion, an awkward street ballet choreographed for a mugging gone south. She knew well enough that no matter how fast one reacts, the blade or the bullet always reaches the victim unexpectedly fast. She also knew that 99 percent of mugging victims reacted defensively and afraid.

Matthews said, "You don't want to do this!" Then she lowered her right shoulder and charged into him, struggling to get her purse open at the same time.

Boldt shouted something about "Hands over your head," though it existed only ephemerally for her—a drone in the buzz behind her. The purse slipped off her shoulder, falling to the sidewalk, its contents lost. From all around her, a convergence of special assignment officers. She felt them running toward her. Heard the chaos over the handheld radios.

She leaned her weight into the center of Hollie's chest, just below his sternum, and drove into the unforgiving stone edifice of Public Safety, knocking the wind out of him. She would not be a victim. She would not succumb to the fear. She screamed with the move, part aggression, part reaction, backed off the pressure, and then slammed into his chest a second time. A bone cracked beneath her effort. Hollie groaned as he gasped and sank to the sidewalk.

She lifted her knee into his crotch as he went down—sharply, like a move in step aerobics. Boldt pulled her away and tackled her, covering her, just as two undercover officers arrived. He lay on top of her, his face filled with rage.

She witnessed Boldt's thought process as he realized she was all right and took appraisal of Hollie. He rolled off her and came to his knees.

Hollie's hand was yanked out of his coat pocket on its way to a handcuff. A piece of paper rose like a bird, fluttered, and returned to earth.

Not a gun, after all, but his eviction notice. The weapon she had feared was nothing but a piece of paper.

Boldt was walking her around to the front of the building when her cell phone rang from within her purse. He'd offered to have her join him at the lab for Lofgrin's report on the Underground, but she didn't feel up to it. She wanted her office. A cup of tea.

Her phone's caller-ID displayed: PAY PHONE #122.

"Hello?" she answered, pressing the phone to her ear.

"I wouldn't have let anything happen to you. You know that, don't you?" Her throat constricted. The voice was too breathy to identify. Purposefully difficult to identify, she thought.

She stopped abruptly and Boldt clearly sensed the dread that washed through her.

"P-a-y p-h-o-n-e . . . WALKER?" she mouthed, looking in all directions at once. She mouthed the word "pay phone" again and held up her fingers: one, two, two.

Boldt grabbed for his own phone, speed-dialed a number, and turned away from Matthews so he wouldn't be overheard. "Boldt. I need the location of pay phone one twenty-two, one-two-two. I'll hold."

The breathless voice continued in her ear, "Tell your friend they don't need to worry about you. You're in good hands."

"Who is this?" she asked calmly.

"I won't let anything happen to you." The phone went dead.

She spotted a pair of pay phones down on Third.

But Boldt pointed in the opposite direction, up to the corner of Fourth Avenue. "There!" he said, still waiting for identification from dispatch.

Matthews followed his outstretched arm to where a man hung up a pay phone receiver and stepped away from the open booth.

"Oh my God," Boldt gasped, as the man's face could be seen.

It was Lanny Neal. He turned his back on them and disappeared at a leisurely pace around Fourth Avenue.

Boldt took a step in that direction, but Matthews snagged him by the arm. "What, Lou?"

"It's Neal!"

She agreed: It had looked like him.

"He had my cell phone number? Do we really think so? Are we sure? Where's the foul?" she added, slipping into LaMoia's vernacular. Little pieces of him rubbing off on her—she'd have to watch that.

Boldt broke loose of her grip.

"There's *no crime,* Lou! It's a phone call is all. Besides, that guy—if it was Neal—hung up too late. My guy had already disconnected."

"We don't know that," Boldt argued. He stopped, two paces into the street, his ear pressed to the phone. His head spun around sharply, and she thought he was looking at her, but more likely he was receiving confusing directions. He then turned back and crossed the hill toward that empty pay phone at a near run. "Which corner?" she heard him say into the phone. "Give me the compass point! North . . . south . . . what?"

"I think it was Walker," she said, blurting it out, keeping up as they crossed through traffic. "Psychologically, it fits perfectly for Walker." Was he even listening to her? she wondered.

He called over his shoulder. "You're telling me that Neal being at a pay phone is *coincidence?*" The word, so distasteful to him, barely came off his lips. He kept the phone pressed to his ear.

"It was Walker," she repeated, this time more convincingly. "The protective role fits him perfectly. It's the last logical step, Lou, before—" but she cut herself off, slipped through two parked cars, and joined him on the opposite sidewalk. She didn't want him hearing what she was thinking.

"Before what?" Boldt climbed the hill, leaning toward the far street corner like Blue straining at his leash.

She didn't answer. He glared at her.

Traffic noise and a ferry's horn filled the resulting silence.

"What?" Boldt barked angrily into the phone. He caught Matthews's attention and shook a pointed finger at the street corner diagonally across from them. Based on the Neal look-alike—or had it been Lanny Neal? she wondered—they'd crossed to the wrong set of phones.

Boldt snagged the com-radio and rattled off the coordinates of the pay phone: "Suspect spotted on southeast corner of Fourth and Columbia! Pursue and detain!" With the streetlight green and the resulting traffic, which included a tall delivery truck, they hadn't spotted Walker, but that was Boldt, she thought— he trusted the system more than any other cop.

A pair of patrol cars and three plainclothed officers converged on the street corner, seemingly out of thin air. Over the rooftops of vehicles, Ferrell Walker was seen running three steps before throwing his hands over his head and leaning up to the chain-link fence of a construction site. Pedestrians collected like bluebottle flies on a corpse.

"Abduction," Boldt said, supplying the word Matthews had avoided.

They met eyes. Matthews found it impossible to speak.

44 Boxed In

"She betrayed me," Walker said to LaMoia across the interrogation table in the Box.

"Where have you been?" LaMoia asked flippantly. "She's a woman, Walker. Get used to it."

The edge of the table carried the regimented brown larvae of cigarette burns despite the NO SMOKING sign on the wall. A cassette machine ran two tapes recording simultaneously. Two yellow pads. Two pencils.

Dressed in an orange county jail jumpsuit, Walker looked older and in a bad way. She and Boldt observed this initial exchange from the other side of the one-way glass in the narrow, dark closet that served as the observation booth. Boldt explained apologetically how he had to take the meeting with Lofgrin. "That skeleton key came back clean," he told her, "but he's got the prelim on the Underground for me—I was due down there a half hour ago—and he's got this set of high-level meetings later on that he can't beg out of."

"John can handle it, Lou. He's one of the best. We're fine." She didn't take her eyes off Walker.

"We're the best—you and I," he said. But it sounded to her more like he was testing her, even fishing for a compliment. "Interrogations, I'm talking about."

She knew perfectly well what he was talking about. Jealousy belied his intentions. She broke her attention off the Box for the first time, met eyes with Boldt, and said again, "We're fine here."

Boldt nodded, though in such a reserved fashion he might as well have shook his head no instead.

"We're running both audio and video, Lou. You won't miss a thing." He would miss it, of course, but she couldn't bring herself to care.

"We're holding him overnight," Boldt said.

"I think it could be a mistake," she said.

"He threatened you."

"Yes, but listen, a teakettle is one kind of threat, Lou. All that boiling water inside . . . but you spill it out, and that's a different kind of hot. We tip this guy over . . . we don't know what's going to happen." Again, she wondered who was doing the talking. Her eyes left Walker and settled on the other guy across from him. It was time she took a hotel room. She felt discouraged, even sad. Walker consumed by grief, Boldt by jealousy, she with her fear—and LaMoia with his resolute calm. She envied him that, and hoped her face didn't reveal her thoughts.

"It's harassment. We can make that stick for twenty-four hours, which gives us time to pursue a court order to get his clothes down to SID."

"You don't really think he's the one living in the lair, do you? You honestly think the hairs and fibers on his clothes are going to come back for that? For Chen?"

They entered into a staring contest, neither about to back down.

She said softly, "I know you think you're helping, Lou, and I love you for it. But not this guy. Not this way."

He never broke the eye contact. "Well," he said hesitantly, "I guess I'm out of here, then."

"Bye," she said, lifting her hand in a half wave, her full

attention back on that room. She heard him leave and felt relief and wondered what was going on between them. Was she using him, thriving on his confusion over her and LaMoia? If so, to what end?

"Let's get down to brass tacks," she heard LaMoia say, his voice made nasal by the small speaker.

She thought it impossible, but Walker looked another ten years older all of a sudden, probably the result of the tube lighting—inkwells beneath both eyes, a pasty bluish tone to facial skin stretched by a self-imposed starvation. He hardly moved in the chair, and when he spoke it was with a controlled calm that troubled her, leaving her wondering what they'd gotten themselves into. Who was running whom?

"My father used to say that," Walker said. He directed himself to the pane of glass that inside the Box was a large mirror. "Is she listening? Are you there, Daphne?"

"Hey!" LaMoia fired off, trying to win Walker's attention but failing.

"I'm so disappointed in you," Walker said.

She felt her stomach turn. He seemed to know exactly where she was standing. She moved to her left, his eyes seemed to follow. It was an uncanny display of empathetic behavior.

"Tell me about the skeleton key," LaMoia said.

Walker continued to stare at the mirror—at her.

"Hey!" LaMoia reprimanded for a second time, "I'm talking to you." He stood and came around the table.

Walker's head jerked up to intercept the man. "You lay a finger on me, and this is in the hands of the lawyers."

It stopped LaMoia like he'd hit an invisible shield. "You've been watching too much Court TV."

"Uh-huh," Walker said, fixated on the mirror again, "in all my free time at the country club."

"A comedian?" LaMoia asked.

"That's me," Walker answered. He spoke more loudly, "Tell him, Daphne."

"Her part of the deal was putting Neal into that lineup. Your part was the key . . . but a key needs a door."

"I don't know anything about any key," Walker said—deliberately unconvincingly?—bending to look past LaMoia, who attempted to block the man's view of the mirror, "but I'm sure you'll figure it out." He looked up into LaMoia's eyes. "You don't need my help with *everything,* do you?"

"I don't need your help with *anything,*" LaMoia snapped. "You've got that turned around, friend."

"The deal was to put Neal away. He gets put away, maybe you find that door."

"It could work the other way," LaMoia proposed.

"Could it, you think?" Walker asked.

"It's a two-way street."

"Is it?" Walker let the animal loose then. He bared his teeth, his eyes rolling white into the back of his head, his neck a fan of tight wires from jaw to collarbone. "We . . . had . . . a . . . deal!" he screamed, actually driving LaMoia back a step.

His raw voice distorted the observation booth's small speaker.

Spittle dripped down his chin. He wiped it off on his shirtsleeve. He had never taken his eyes off Matthews, reconnected now by LaMoia's movement.

LaMoia said, "We get this thing right without you, and you're buried."

"Nice choice of words, Detective. Tell him, Daphne."

"You're a fucking freak show," LaMoia said, approaching Walker once again. He leaned in closely and said, "You leave her out of this, Walker. It's me you've got to worry about."

Keeping his eyes directly on her, not on LaMoia, Walker said, "She wants out of this, she's out of this. Simple as pie.

Mary-Ann wanted out, and look what happened to her." He found LaMoia again, back on track, a sail filling with wind. "Look what Neal did to her."

LaMoia said, "The church has doors that take skeleton keys. The church at the Shelter. We're checking that entire section of Underground as we speak." He repeated, "We solve it without you—"

Walker interrupted, "And I'm buried. Yeah, I got that the first time." He threw open his arms. "Bury me, Detective. At least *charge* me. Do *something* other than just harassing me, would you please? Ask her what she wants. Ask her what comes next. She knows, Detective. Do you? I don't think you have a clue." He stood out of his chair and pointed, "But *she* does! Is it over, Daphne? Is it?" To LaMoia: "She's living with you now. You ask her."

LaMoia shoved the man down hard, returning him to his chair. He leaned into the man's ear and whispered softly enough to avoid the recorder. "You ever set foot in my place again, Einstein, and I'll rip you a new asshole and make you eat your own shit."

He stepped back. Walker blanched, his lips wet with saliva, his eyes watery and hard. "We'll see," he said.

"Yes, we will," LaMoia said.

"You ask her," Walker said. "She knows what comes next."

45 Magoo

"Here's what we've got so far," said Dr. Bernie Lofgrin, a squat, balding man with eyes so magnified by his goggle-sized glasses that they looked more like hard-boiled eggs cut in half when he got excited. He was a favorite among the SPD detectives, his nickname an appropriate Magoo.

As the civilian director of SID, Lofgrin had worked cases with Boldt for more than a decade, his forensics lab supplying the technical pieces of the puzzle so necessary to an investigation and the subsequent prosecution. An arrest might come from information supplied by a snitch or a witness, but convictions came from evidence supplied by the lab. Where some detectives worked their contacts, their informants, their resources, Boldt chose to rebuild the life of the victim just before death, and to rely upon the physical evidence to tell the real story of what had happened. Every investigator did this to some degree, but Boldt had made his own science of it, and as such, had formed both a partnership and a deep friendship with Lofgrin. Both jazz aficionados, the currency of their exchanged favors was rare recordings or treasured masterpieces. Building one's collection was as important as growing one's IRA. Boldt's collection of more than ten thousand LPs dwarfed that of Lofgrin or Doc Dixon, and as he was typically the one in need of favors at the office, his cassette recorder was the one that was more active.

Lofgrin loved to hear himself talk. He was meant more for the university than the laboratory. "We patched together a full set of latents from the one hundred and thirty-seven lifts we developed down there. You can be fairly confident that a high percentage of those are all from the same individual. More to come.

"There was no apparent effort to keep the place wiped down," he continued. "Your resident wasn't thinking he'd have visitors. And yes, we're running the latents through the state database and we're passing them on to the nationals as well." He recited, "If this guy's ever been printed, we're going to know about it." His stained smile revealed he'd taken up smoking again. The smoking concerned Boldt: Lofgrin's heart suffered inside a nervous, agitated body.

SID had failed to locate the suspect's escape route out of the Underground, leaving more questions than answers.

"Did we check the prints against—"

"Ferrell Walker?" Lofgrin interrupted. "I read my e-mails, Lou. The answer is yes, Matthews got Walker to roll some prints for us. If he was ever in that lair we're never going to prove it. The prints aren't his."

Lofgrin gained energy when Boldt took notes, so sometimes Boldt scribbled things into his notebook just to appear active, as was the case now.

Boldt said, "At this point it wouldn't surprise me if this guy Walker goes down for *several* of our open cases. The more we look at him, the more it looks that way—to me, to LaMoia, even Daffy." When an investigator pushed the lab in one direction, it tended to prejudice and speed up results, but Boldt—who rarely used such ploys—couldn't be sure if Lofgrin had even heard him.

"I won't bother you with the Home and Garden tour, but I'm telling you: The prints aren't his. It was pure oxygen in those tanks as you suspected. It's your job to find out where he stole them."

"Could they be one-half of an oxyacetylene rig?" Boldt asked.

"Welding? Absolutely."

"As in construction sites?"

"Are you going somewhere with this?" Lofgrin asked.

"Our hotel peeper . . . the construction site."

Lofgrin nodded slowly. "Ah-so," he said.

Boldt's scribbling was for real, as he made a note to check all recent downtown construction sites for reports of stolen oxygen. When things began to come together on a case, an investigator could feel the momentum shift his way. It brought on an almost childish giddiness sometimes—a visceral high that was one of those things you lived for, the way a marathon runner knew when he'd hit his stride and the training was finally paying off. The Big Mo was in this lab with him, and Boldt took it for a ride.

"Go," he encouraged.

"Hairs and fibers workup," Lofgrin said, aiming his distorted eyes toward Boldt. "I caution that this is all prelim, but we did lift seventeen black hairs from a five-gallon tub of wastewater, presumably where this guy washed up. Head hairs. We also ran all the clothing we found into the scrape room and collected a sizeable amount of fiber evidence. Initial examination of the black head hairs was conducted both macroscopically and microscopically. Cell structure confirms they're from an Asian. We picked up chromosomes on the sheath material from one sample that confirms it's male hair. This particular Asian male had smoked pot within the last month. That shouldn't be too hard to confirm for your Mr. Chen, should it?" Boldt's pen went to work. "We've asked Dixie for comparison head hair samples from Chen. If we get a good probability, and I think we will, then we'll perform STR—short tandem repeat—DNA analysis. It's quick and reliable, and cheaper than the old RFPL. I could have something for you by tomorrow or the next day."

Boldt mentally assembled the pieces. In all likelihood Chen had had physical contact with whomever had been in residence at the underground hideout. This, in turn, implied the obvious. He asked, "Blood evidence?"

"You're a pushy son of a bitch. You know that? Phenolphthalein test was positive. And check out the Luminol." He handed Boldt a color photo that showed blobs of blue where the Luminol had reacted with any residual blood in the converted storage room. A special fluorescent light was used to highlight the Luminol. The pattern suggested footprints.

"These were developed by the doorway?" Boldt asked.

"We fluoresced the whole room, but yes, this photo was shot near the door. The blood had been washed with soap and water or maybe something a little stronger." He presented another photo, also revealing Luminol stains on the lip of a container. "Again, this is the same wastewater plastic tub."

Boldt said, "He washed his hands of the blood and some hair came off in the process."

Lofgrin nodded.

"If you were a woman, I'd kiss you."

"I'd file for harassment." Lofgrin handed Boldt yet another photo, this time showing a pair of workman's coveralls, also photographed in the dark under the illumination of fluorescent black light. The discoloring indicated blood splatter, like a volley of cascading tears.

"Oh, God," Boldt muttered.

"Yes. Exactly. Jackson Pollock this isn't." Before Boldt could ask, Lofgrin answered. "This was also washed, but in a heavy detergent. No way to type it, no chance for DNA. Could be the guy butchered an elk."

"Or a couple missing women," Boldt said.

Lofgrin said, "He wears size ten-and-a-half shoes. About six feet tall. Hair color brown, but it's dyed—from a sandy blond. He's on a strong dose of doxycycline."

Lofgrin was probably not describing Ferrell Walker, Boldt realized. Dyed hair? Nathan Prair, perhaps—although that also felt like a stretch.

"Are you telling me we found a 'script bottle down there? Are you holding out on me, Bernie? Do you happen to have *a name* from that prescription?"

"No prescription, no bottle, either. His hair, the dyed hair, the predominant hair sample found down there in that room," Lofgrin answered, "revealed the doxycycline. You are what you ingest. Most of it goes into your hair."

"He's fighting an infection," Boldt said. The use of hair coloring bothered the detective in him. Women, sure. But a man using hair coloring suggested more than vanity to a cop—if the occupant of that room had changed his looks, the possibility existed that he'd done so in an effort to outrun a criminal record. Boldt's pen wrote down: *Ex-con? Escapee?*

"Are we done here?" Boldt asked, anxious to work the evidence.

"What do you think?" It was Lofgrin's way to hold some cherry for the end of such prelims. The hair coloring and doxycycline had seemed the punctuation mark to Boldt—the exclamation point—but the lack of Lofgrin's proud-as-a-peacock, I'm-smarter-than-you superior attitude had left him thinking there might be more.

"Out in the hallways as we were looking for his escape route we came across some recent bus ticket stubs."

"I entered through the bus tunnel emergency route, Bernie. We already know he had access." Boldt added, "And you knew that, too, because it's how your guys got in there, so what's going on?" Lofgrin appreciated being challenged, or Boldt wouldn't have been so aggressive. Friendships within the department were both a curse and a blessing.

Lofgrin dug around on the lab bench and produced an evidence bag that contained a rectangular piece of paper—a receipt, or stub. "ATM receipt. SeaTel." Boldt knew that SeaTel was the bank on the corner, the basement of which he'd toured with the maintenance man. "You're interested in the date."

Boldt snatched the bag from Lofgrin, his chest tight. He pressed the plastic of the bag against the receipt, trying to read the date. He fumbled and dropped the bag. Lofgrin spoke as Boldt collected the bag off the floor. "One of my guys—Michael Yei—his sister's a teller at SeaTel over in Capitol Hill. The account comes back a sixty-year-old woman named Veronica Shepherd. I doubt seriously Ms. Shepherd is living below Third Avenue."

Boldt had the bag in hand again. He pressed, and the date printed on the receipt came into focus. It was a date emblazoned in Boldt's memory, the date Susan Hebringer had gone missing. Boldt experienced both a pang of hurt and one of exhilaration simultaneously.

"Cash machines," Boldt said hoarsely, his voice choked with emotion. He'd found the connection between the tourists who'd been peeped and the two missing women. "The common denominator is cash machines."

He was out the door before he had a chance to witness Lofgrin's self-satisfied grin.

Boldt double-parked the department-issue Crown Vic, its emergency flashers going, on the steep incline outside SeaTel. He approached the corner entrance to the bank at a run, but stopped abruptly at sight of the small lighted sign: ATM. Any investigator worth his salt questioned himself when the facts became known. You wondered why and how something so obvious now had seemed so insignificant then, how the brain could overlook something so important, so glaring.

It was a small glassed-in room—a glorified booth—that fronted Columbia Street and contained two ATM machines side by side, a wall clock, and a small blue shelf with pens attached to chains. Mounted to the doorjamb, an electronic credit card reader provided restricted access for the sake of security, admitting only legitimate cardholders.

Boldt pressed his face to the glass, cupping his eyes. Littered across the floor at the foot of both machines he saw several paper receipts, their size and shape now familiar to him.

Of all things, he didn't own an ATM card—he still cashed checks at the teller window—and therefore couldn't gain access.

He caused a brief moment of alarm inside the bank as he pushed to the front of a small line, polite but determined to gain admittance to that room. Now that he'd seen the room, he could also picture Susan Hebringer inside it, her purse slung over her arm, her bank card slipping into a slot on one of the two machines.

Already planning his next move, Boldt intended to pull whatever favors necessary to gain immediate access to Hebringer's and Randolf's bank records. It seemed inconceivable to him that both women might have used their ATM cards on the dates they disappeared without him knowing about it. He felt like a burst dam, unable to contain himself, spilling out a flood of anger and confusion. His people had run the financials on both victims— he knew this absolutely. So where had the mistake been? How could they have missed this?

A nervous bank officer swiped a card through the outdoor reader. Boldt entered a warm room that smelled bitter. Initially he dismissed the bank officer but then quickly changed his mind and asked him to stand outside and prevent anyone from coming in and disturbing him.

Boldt then studied the room, including the two wall-mounted cash machines, their small screens glowing with a welcome message. He noted the alarmed exit door in the corner, leading into the building—a fire code requirement. He collected himself, slowing his breathing, trying to get beyond the emotion of the moment. He focused on those two machines and tried to put Susan Hebringer into this room. The imagined scene then played before his eyes, black-and-white and jittery. He saw her from the back, dressed in the clothes that she'd been described wearing by both her husband and coworkers on the day of her disappearance. He saw her remove her ATM card from her purse, look up as she heard a man come through that door through which she herself had just entered. Would she have said hello? He thought not. She'd gone about her business.

But who? A street punk wanting the cash? A well-dressed man in a suit—someone she'd never suspect of the foul play that was to come? A bank officer? A deputy sheriff?

He took a step closer to the machines but stopped as he felt *something stuck to the bottom of his shoe*. He picked the receipt off his shoe sole, knowing then how one could find its way into the Underground, and immediately lifted his eyes to the alarmed exit door.

He recalled the steel exit door in the hallway on his earlier tour. "It sounds an alarm," the maintenance man had warned. He got the bank officer to open it for him.

"Let me guess," Boldt said as the man searched a cluttered key ring for the proper key, "you—bank officers, that is—and your security guards both have keys to these alarmed doors. Who else? Housecleaning?"

"No." The man cowered slightly, swinging the door open for Boldt. It led to the hallway, as expected.

"*Maintenance?*" Boldt asked. Another logic jump struck him that should have come earlier: the oxygen tanks, the maintenance man's horrible wheezing. Boldt remembered the name because Sarah had a friend with a similar last name: Vanderhorst. His own internal alarm was going now. He saw a listless Hebringer being dragged through this same door. Leaning over her, Vanderhorst wore a set of coveralls, soon to be bloodied.

"Yes, maintenance too," the man confirmed.

Boldt entered the hallway and looked right, recalling the stairs that led down into the bank's basement. The maintenance man, Vanderhorst, had told him the exit door went out to the street; he had failed to mention the ATM machines on the way out. Vanderhorst had played dumb about the existence of access to the Underground.

Dyed hair? A doxycycline prescription for his clogged lungs.

"I'm declaring this a crime scene," Boldt informed a surprised bank officer. "Stand back, and keep your hands in your pockets."

"Lieu, shouldn't we be watching the Greyhound station or something?" Bobbie Gaynes occupied the Crown Vic's passenger seat.

Boldt said, "We *are* watching the bus, *and* the ferries, *and* the trains, *and* the northern border crossing with Canada. Rental car agencies clear down to Tacoma have a fax of his bank ID." The last few hours had been his busiest in recent memory. He felt incredibly good. "What's the problem, Bobbie?"

"But why *here*?" she asked, still frustrated with him. "Vanderhorst called in sick today. That should tell us something, right? He split. We're wasting time here."

The Crown Vic pointed downhill and away from the corner office building occupied by the SeaTel Bank. Boldt had both the rearview and driver door mirrors aimed with a view of the corner—one set for his sitting height, the other for slouching.

Boldt's silence bothered her. "So explain to me what good it is watching the bank?"

"It closes for the weekend in ten minutes."

"And by my figuring that means he's another ten minutes farther away."

"Why do people kill, Bobbie?"

She sighed, letting him know she wasn't up to his quizzes, his schooling her. It grew old after awhile. "For love and money." She made her voice sound like a schoolkid reciting her math tables. "For country and revenge," she added into the mix. Outright annoyed now, she added, "For the smell of blood, or the scent of a perfume, or because God or their dog told them to and they forgot to take their pill that day."

"We got lucky is all," Boldt said. "Sometimes you get lucky."

"Lucky?" she asked, exasperated. "He's halfway to Miami, or Vegas, or Tijuana by now. How is that lucky?"

A crackle came over both Boldt's dash-mounted police radio and the handheld resting in his lap. A male voice said calmly, "We have joy. Wildhorse is headed out the north stairs of the bus station."

"No fucking way," Gaynes mumbled. "Wildhorse is . . . ?"

"I only had a minute to come up with a handle."

"Vanderhorst is Wildhorse," she said.

"Too obvious?" he asked, peering intently out the windshield now.

She said, "You're telling me you put six cruisers and, including us, ten plainclothes dicks out on the streets, and you were counting on luck?"

"The first part of that luck is that we discovered that lair yesterday, on a Thursday. The second, and much more important half, is that today, Friday, happens to be SeaTel's biweekly payday."

"Payday," she whispered, almost worshiping him now.

"Who's going to pass up a two-week paycheck? He wasn't about to quit. I knew he'd be back when they told me he'd called in sick this morning. I mean, why bother otherwise?"

"His four-one-one?"

"All invented. No such address. No such phone. The security firm is going to fry: If they ran a background check, it was pitiful."

"Typical," she said. "Big Mac's inside?"

"Mackenzie's posing as a customer. We had to play it that way. Vanderhorst knows the layout, knows the normal personnel, including security and the tellers. We add someone to that mix and he'll sniff it out."

"So—"

But Boldt interrupted. "Heads up!"

Boldt had his own image of Per Vanderhorst, both from the tour of the bank basement and from the man's security ID photo. Neither matched up perfectly well with the lean, lanky, unhealthy silhouette of the man reflected in the mirror.

Gaynes asked, "Do we have the confirm yet on the cash cards?"

Never taking his eyes off the approaching suspect, Boldt said, "We now know that neither Hebringer nor Randolf received any cash from those machines. What we're trying to determine is whether or not either of their cards ever logged on for the two days in question."

"They can do that?" she asked.

"Supposedly any attempt, even a canceled session, registers with the system."

"He nabbed them before they ever got their money," she suggested.

"Who's going to think anything of some guy in blue coveralls wearing a security tag on his chest pocket? He's sweeping up the room. So what? They use their card to enter, turn toward one of the machines, and take his broomstick to the back of the head. He's got them through that emergency exit door before they're even half conscious."

"But it's a glass room, Lieu. It's a well-lit glass room."

"Guys like Vanderhorst, they thrive on that moment. Just ask Matthews. For those few seconds he's dragging the body toward the door, he's as high as he's ever been."

"You creep me out sometimes, Lieu."

"No, not me, Bobbie. It's them." Boldt motioned her down, and slouched himself.

She scootched down and reached for her door handle. "We grab him on the way out, or back up Big Mac, or what?"

Vanderhorst paused ever so briefly in front of the bank and gave the block a once-over. He failed to make anything of the steam cleaning panel van across the street, the homeless guy with his guitar case open playing a horrible rendition of "This Land Is Your Land," or the tall black woman walking the German shepherd, who was himself a member of the K-9 unit.

"What the hell?" Gaynes asked, eyeing the mirror.

"He just convinced himself it's safe."

"That motherfucker's got some loose screws, Lieutenant."

Boldt hoisted the radio's handset. "All units: We play this *exactly* as I laid it out in Situation."

"Affirm," came the voice of Dennis Schaefer from the steam cleaning van. Schaefer, a Special Ops dispatcher on the force, had the combined role of play-by-play sports broadcaster and team captain. It still left Boldt the coach.

He plugged an earpiece jack into the radio and filled his right ear with its ear bud.

The moment Vanderhorst entered the bank, Boldt and Gaynes headed directly to the ATM room, where Boldt swiped a borrowed card admitting them. He felt unusually warm as they passed through what was typically the alarmed exit door without a sound.

He'd been advised that it would take Vanderhorst between three and ten minutes to both retrieve and cash his paycheck at the teller window. Boldt was told he could count on the maintenance man standing at the counter for that length of time. Mackenzie, at a stand-up check writing desk, would alert dispatch if actual events inside the bank varied from this.

Boldt had assigned one uniformed officer to stand guard on the other side of the loose panel discovered in the bus tunnel's emergency exit. He had another four uniforms at possible street-level exits suggested by Professor Babcock. He had radio cars forming a perimeter. The safe money said to pick up Vanderhorst the moment they had him confined. It was not like Boldt to play chances, but that's what he had in mind, and Gaynes had clearly sensed this. If it went south on him, the review board would rule that he'd allowed personal pressures to influence his decision making, to dictate actions taken, to cloud his judgment. They would be right, of course, though he'd vehemently deny it. Susan Hebringer ran this operation by proxy. Once Vanderhorst was officially under arrest, statistics said that their chances of ever finding his victims were greatly reduced. Sometimes perps rolled over in interrogation. But with nothing but circumstantial evidence—an ATM receipt and some compromised blood evidence, with no clear way yet to connect the ATM room to the Underground, and, more important, to show Vanderhorst's knowledge of that connection, Boldt could foresee Vanderhorst walking out of Public Safety a free man.

He and Gaynes reached the bank's second-floor offices winded. He knocked on a door marked PRIVATE and was welcomed a moment later by an attractive young woman in a smart gray suit and, beyond her, two men in private security garb manning a bank of five black-and-white television monitors, all of which were hardwired to hidden cameras.

Each screen offered a variety of looks at various parts of the bank, including the main lobby, the ATM anteroom, and the downstairs hallway through which they had just passed.

Gaynes asked Boldt, "Are you telling me we already have him on camera abducting these women?"

"Twenty-four-hour loops are reused after seventy-two hours," Boldt explained in whispered disappointment. "Long since erased."

"Yeah?" she said, gesturing toward the bank of monitors, "Well, we've got him now."

Vanderhorst stood at a teller window to the right of the large room, his back to the camera. Detective Frank Mackenzie maintained his position at the check writing counter, close to the main doors and the only exit to the streets.

Boldt's plan revolved around Mackenzie's ability to deliberately slip up while attempting to act the part of undercover cop. Mackenzie, a big tree trunk of a man with seventeen years on the force, had been selected for this role in part because of his legendary reputation as a thespian. In the summers, he took time off to join the Ashland, Oregon, theater troupe responsible for that city's Shakespeare festival. As a lieutenant and team leader, Boldt's responsibility was to make the most of his assets.

The screens lacked any sound, and so the commotion that followed on the bank's main floor played out on the one television screen silently, making the action all the more eerie and disconnected. Boldt listened to SPD dispatch in his right ear, mentally dialing it into the background.

"Can we hold on number four, please?" Boldt asked as he and Gaynes stepped closer.

She whispered, "I'd rather be *in* the movie, than watching it."

"Stay tuned, we may be yet," Boldt informed her. "First, we see how smart Vanderhorst is." He lifted the handheld, tripped the TALK button, and issued the order he knew he'd be held responsible for: "Okay, let's do it."

"Affirm." Dispatcher Dennis Schaefer's reply passed thinly through Boldt's earpiece. Mackenzie was ordered to "lay the bait." The rest of the team was put on high alert. Like most operations, after several hours of waiting, the real-time event was likely to play out in a matter of seconds or, at the most, a few minutes. For those few precious moments, disparate players, several city blocks away from each other, had to move, think, coordinate, and act in harmony. Anything less, and Vanderhorst was likely to escape. Denny Schaefer was the stage manager, but Lou Boldt was the playwright, and as such, he listened and watched carefully.

On the small screen Frank Mackenzie unplugged his earpiece from his radio and then fiddled with a knob, turning up the volume.

The message from dispatch: "Suspect is in the building," played over Boldt's radio at the same time it did Big Mac's—as planned. The message spilled into the bank lobby, turning heads.

This was it. Boldt leaned in and watched. Vanderhorst, along with everyone else in the lobby, overheard Mackenzie's radio. The suspect cocked his head slightly in that direction, but he did not overreact. His left hand pocketed the cash from his paycheck. Mackenzie did a convincing job of playing the buffoon. He dropped the radio, turned the volume back down, and tried to look like nothing had happened. He then took a couple obvious steps toward the entrance, clearly planting himself to block the main doors. A colorful sign there advertised the benefits of home equity loans.

Vanderhorst abandoned the teller window and walked *incredibly calmly,* Boldt noted, toward the EMPLOYEES ONLY door that led into the back hallway. But Vanderhorst stopped at that door, studying Mackenzie, who had his back turned.

Boldt spoke loudly into the crowded security room, "Open the door, Vanderhorst." On the screen, Vanderhorst continued to look like he was weighing his options. "Through that door! Now!"

Vanderhorst disobeyed, taking several steps toward Mackenzie and the bank's main entrance.

"We're losing him!" Boldt shouted into his handheld.

Denny Schaefer calmly instructed Mackenzie, "Phase two, Big Mac."

On the screen, Mackenzie spun on his heels, looked in the direction of Vanderhorst, and reached inside his sport jacket, revealing his holster and weapon.

Crack the whip. Vanderhorst turned, shoved a key into the side door, and hurried through.

"Okay!" an elated Boldt shouted much too loudly for the small room, "let's do it like we talked about."

The guards busied themselves throwing switches, and the monitors displayed new views: the back hall, the ATM room, the stairs to the basement, and several angles of the basement itself.

"Go . . . go . . . go!" Boldt shouted at the screen like an armchair quarterback. Into the radio's microphone he shouted, "More pressure, more pressure!" as Vanderhorst paused in the hallway outside the door that led into the ATM room. Boldt didn't want that door an option.

Dispatch barked another order, and although the monitors had no sound, Boldt knew that Mackenzie was now pounding on that hallway door. Vanderhorst reacted in a mechanical, nervous way, looking first in that direction and then taking off down the hall and into the stairs leading to the basement.

"*Yes!*" Boldt shouted excitedly. He grabbed Gaynes by the arm. "Get ready to run. You first. The basement."

"Copy," she said, moving toward the security room's door.

Behind them, the image of Vanderhorst moved one monitor to the next, as if he were jumping from screen to screen. As he reached the last, with the flip of a switch, the monitors displayed several different views of the basement.

Special Ops had added these cameras at Boldt's request.

Gaynes understood Boldt's plan then for the first time. "You're stinging him into showing us the way into the Underground," she said.

"We hope," he answered.

With that, as if instructed, Vanderhorst moved quickly across three of the screens and used a master switch to lower the elevator.

Boldt mumbled, "Not possible. I checked that elevator myself and—" But he interrupted himself as Vanderhorst boarded the elevator, stepped inside, and—after a brief but unexpected monitor glitch that left Vanderhorst off-camera momentarily—keyed open a back panel on the elevator car intended for emergency evacuation.

"Oh, shit," Boldt barked, a police lieutenant who took pride in rarely swearing. Vanderhorst stepped through and pulled the elevator's panel closed behind him.

"Keys!" Boldt shouted at the security men, as if rehearsed, which it was not.

One of the guards tossed him an enormous ring of keys,

saying, "The small, silver one does the panel. The green dot does the elevator override."

Susan Hebringer had been pulled through that panel. Patricia Randolf before her. Boldt could see it play out, as if watching one of the monitors.

Boldt and Gaynes took off at run, Boldt shouting instructions into a handheld that he knew would lose contact once he was underground. "Contact lost. Repeat, Wildhorse contact lost!" Dispatch copied. Boldt shouted, "We want him *alive,* people! For God's sake, let's take him alive."

46 Into the Dark

Boldt and Gaynes descended the stairs two at a time, reaching the basement only seconds after they'd left the security room. At the most, Vanderhorst had a half minute lead on them.

Boldt keyed the elevator open, then tossed the keys to Gaynes, who was first into the car. She keyed open the back panel as Boldt stepped through. "Sixty seconds," Boldt said, checking his watch.

They climbed through the open hole, descending a ladder of rebar that protruded from the chamber's concrete wall. The space between the shaft's wall and the car was narrow. Gaynes descended effortlessly, while Boldt had to flatten himself, his jacket hanging up on the car's mechanics. The thick air smelled heavily of grease and electricity. Gaynes switched on a Maglite well before she reached the bottom rung, making the short leap to the shaft's dirt floor. Boldt followed immediately behind her.

"Lieu!" The Maglite's beam revealed the inside of a cast-iron coal chute door about two feet square. A false wall of bricks had been stacked to create an illusion, from the Underground side, of an enclosed coal chute. Gaynes kicked down the dry stack, pushed the iron door open further, and squeezed through. Boldt followed, again straining to get his girth through the small space.

Boldt heard a crackle in his earpiece, and the broken voice of Denny Schaefer as a few radio waves managed to briefly penetrate the depths. He couldn't understand a word that was said: They were on their own.

They stood in one of the dark underground hallways, vaguely familiar from the previous foray into the underground city block. Boldt used sign language to direct Gaynes, indicating that they would split up. She would take this hallway, Boldt would move south and search for another. Gaynes acknowledged. Boldt's fists came together: They could reunite at the far end of the underground space.

Boldt got his flashlight lit. Ninety seconds had elapsed since they'd lost Vanderhorst.

They heard a crash in the distance—wood and then glass. Too far away to discern someone running.

Boldt took off into the dark, through a huge, empty room. He found a second hallway and turned left, his mind searching for explanations for that noise. Certainly Vanderhorst, if their man, would know this city block of the Underground intimately, an area the size of several football fields. So what, or who, had made that noise—and was it worth following? Boldt slopped through mud and debris, believing that by then Gaynes would be passing close to the lair. She would take a few seconds to inspect it. In that time, Boldt found himself at the end of the hall.

He took the door to the right, into and through a former barbershop, the beam of light catching his own reflection in the dusty mirrors, still intact. He jumped back from his own reflected image, stumbled over a barber chair, and fell down, the chair noisily spinning on rusted joints. Boldt clambered to his feet, dodged debris on his way out yet another door, and found himself in a section of Underground sidewalk he hadn't seen on his earlier exploration. The sidewalk was caved in ahead, choked with earth and stone, reminding him how fragile an environment this was. He took the first doorway to his left that he encountered, working his way judiciously through a room filled with discarded washing machines and tooling equipment that had to go back forty years.

Through this door he reached another short hallway, and up ahead a tangle of yellow police tape. He paused here, aware this had been what he'd heard only moments before—Vanderhorst had been tripped up by one of their yellow tapes. Blood beat loudly in his ears, his mouth dry, his body damp with sweat. He thought of his promises to Liz to stay behind the desk, of his kids and their bright faces. But then in his mind's eye he saw Susan Hebringer's unconscious body being dragged down this hallway, a face now attached to the man dragging her, and he inched forward, following the unmistakable sound, an uneven scraping—something dragging—through a door to his right.

He followed that sound, careful of his own footfalls. *He's limping.* Vanderhorst had hurt himself in the fall caused by the crime scene tape. Boldt moved more quickly, seizing the opportunity, aware all of a sudden of footfalls approaching rapidly from his left. *Gaynes.* He cupped the flashlight. This was the horror house in the amusement park, where goblins and witches and skeletons jumped out at you. Boldt braced himself for surprise, his nerves electric with anticipation.

He crossed through to a smaller room, fully covering the flashlight's lens with his fingers and issuing darkness. He could smell the man now—the sour human fear. *He's close.*

He heard the *whoosh* to his left, and credited his sensitive hearing with sparing him the blow. As he ducked, a piece of lumber cut just above his head, and that promise to Liz loomed all the more clearly. He slipped his fingers off the flashlight, and the beam swiped the side of Vanderhorst's face like the slice of a sword. Boldt saw fear and determination. He saw what Susan Hebringer would have seen as she'd come awake in captivity. The timber caught Boldt in the gut on its return.

Boldt bent over and fell back, but kicked out mightily as he went down, connecting with the side of the man's knee and causing Vanderhorst to cry out as he careened into a shelf of rusted paint cans and spilled them in a waterfall of tin to the floor. Vanderhorst clawed and picked his way through the debris to the far end of the room, delivered a chair through what remained of a window, and was following through himself when Boldt got a hand on him. He pulled the man back, so that Vanderhorst's head and shoulders struck the floor. Boldt swung a paint can and struck the man in the head. The lid popped off, a thick red sludge melting down the side of Vanderhorst's face and shoulder, looking like fresh blood.

His right foot on the man's throat, Boldt sighted down the barrel of his handgun, the flashlight catching the whites of complacent eyes. The sudden calm in those eyes went straight to Boldt's stomach. Vanderhorst held the wire handle of a paint can gripped firmly in his left hand, ready to strike.

Boldt said, "Do it," his breath shallow and quick. "Do us all a favor."

Gaynes caught up to them, breathless. "Easy, Lieu."

Boldt backed off, removing his foot from the man's throat. Vanderhorst released the can's wire handle, slowly closed his eyes, and said, "I want a lawyer."

47 A Slippery Slope

Matthews heard the key in the lock, saw Blue run to paw the door, and set down the glass of wine. Her heart fluttered in her chest, and she thought herself a teenager as she crossed the room.

Blue started licking his hand the moment it showed.

LaMoia, looking exhausted, shut and locked the heavy door. "Hi, honey, I'm home."

His making light of it like that caught Matthews short and stopped her just prior to offering herself for a hug. What the hell had she been thinking?

"What's with the radio car?" he asked, shedding the deerskin jacket and playing with Blue.

"Lou's idea."

"We've got Walker an overnight room in the Grand Hotel."

"Good riddance."

"We should make the reservation permanent, you ask me."

"He's working through this."

She didn't want to even *think* about business. She wanted to enjoy his company, order some takeout, get as far away from police business as possible.

It wasn't to be. LaMoia said, "Bobbie Socks and the Sarge arrested a bank maintenance guy for Hebringer and Randolf."

"Yes, he called," she said. "He wants me in on the first round of interrogation, but the lawyers are into it pretty thick and it isn't going to happen until tomorrow."

"Same thing I heard," he said. "Kind of shoots my theory on Walker."

"It kind of does."

"What?" he asked. "No 'I told you so'?"

"Lou was hoping for a court order to process Walker's clothing."

"He got it. They lifted some blood. They're testing whether it's fish or human. Some fibers they want to run against a pile of shit they collected in the hideaway."

"It wasn't Walker's," she said. "Lou knows that. He wants to jam Walker up just to keep him off the streets. Fine with me."

LaMoia noticed the open bottle of wine.

"Self-medicating," she said, thinking it funny until her brain caught up with her mouth. "Sorry about that."

"Do I look like I have a problem with it?"

They spent a half hour on the couch, LaMoia nursing a beer, Matthews working on the bottle of merlot she'd already promised to repay him. Blue settled in at their feet, looking like a rug that breathed.

"I think I should go at him," she said.

"Walker? Are you kidding?"

"We need his help with the key."

"We're trying the Underground. The Sarge messengered a Polaroid over to an archaeologist at the U. Something'll break."

She said, "Somebody's got to bring him up to speed on e-mail attachments."

"He's got his own ways of doing things." He sounded mad at her, and she wondered how she deserved this.

The dog jumped to his feet and began to whine.

"Rehab needs a walk," he said, toeing the dog's fur with his right foot.

"It's weird you call him that," she said.

LaMoia took it wrong. "So, I'm weird. What of it?"

"Is something wrong, John?"

"Yeah, something's wrong."

"Me being here? Have I overstayed my welcome?" Why had she said that? She felt herself blush.

"What? No! It's me . . . my stuff," he said. He stood and the dog rallied. "Come on, you idiot." He petted Blue's head.

"Would I be in the way?" she asked.

"You still don't have it figured out, do you, Matthews?"

"Probably not."

"You're not in the way."

"Okay." She fought back a flicker of anger. At herself? At him? She wasn't sure.

He turned toward the couch, looking away momentarily. "What you said just now . . . self-medicating . . ."

"Was stupid," she interrupted.

He had sadder eyes than Blue. "Listen, Matthews . . . I stole two caps from your bathroom on my last visit. I tucked them away in my pocket and I walked around with them there for *days,* and I never said a thing to you, to Boldt. At the meetings. Nothing."

Somehow this scared her more than Walker had. Her words caught in her throat. "Did you . . . take them?"

"No, I tossed them, but I was this close to taking them," he said. "I stole from you, and I didn't tell you. I lied to myself that tossing them made it fine, but it didn't make it fine. It sucks. What an asshole I am. The worst of it is that I haven't stopped thinking about them. I keep thinking how stupid it was to toss them."

"You tossed them, John. That's the point."

"Listen, Matthews, this is as much about you as it is about those caps."

"I understand that," she said.

"Do you? I don't think so. You don't know the half of it."

Indicating Blue, she said, "I think he'd rather we continue this outside."

LaMoia found a slight grin. She thought: *That's better*.

They moved toward the front door, the three of them. He hooked her arm and said, "The guys in the cruiser out front. They'll see us. You know they're gonna talk if we walk arm-in-arm."

"So they talk. They're already going to talk."

"It's not like we've *done* anything," he said.

"No, it's not," she agreed.

His words hung in the air on the way out.

They passed the cruiser and LaMoia waved.

"Well," he said to Matthews, "I guess it's all downhill from here."

Downhill, but a slippery slope, she thought.

Blue found a hydrant and watered it down.

Matthews knew she would sleep alone that night, but catching herself even thinking about this had her wondering what she was getting herself into.

48 The Door

She loved it like this: She, LaMoia, and Boldt as a team, descending the Public Safety fire stairs so fast she could hardly keep up.

"What's going on?" she asked, rounding a landing and continuing down with them. Boldt had nearly everyone on CAPs in the offices on a Saturday. SID was on its way in. Special Ops had been placed on call. Everyone awaited orders, knowing this was the moment for the Hebringer/Randolf case. She'd been told to leave her office and rendezvous with them on the stairs. She was to have a coat with her, which she did.

Boldt had this amazing charisma that instilled energy in everyone around him, an uncanny leadership quality that accounted for the uncompromising devotion of his squads, to where even a wise-ass like LaMoia stayed reined in under his command.

"We're holding Vanderhorst under the state terrorism act, based on his having oxygen tanks in his possession, any one of which could cause a massive explosion. Together, they're more like a small nuke." For a big man, he moved fluidly, the railing slipping through his left hand used more as a guide than a support.

"But we released Walker?" LaMoia asked, clearly voicing a complaint. "What's with that?"

"The bloodstains on his clothing are corrupted—some fish,

some human, but none of it's going to tell us anything specific, no matter what tests we run. The fiber workup failed to connect him to the lair, which is understandable since it's clearly Vanderhorst's lair."

"But can't we hold him on *something*?" LaMoia said, trying to keep Boldt focused on his own complaint about Walker. "What if he still has it in for our friend here?"

At the next landing, Boldt looked back at him. "You tell me what we hold him on, and I'll be the first to consider it."

"Obstruction!"

"We can't prove it," Boldt returned.

LaMoia pressed, "Then let's at least keep Matthews on a wire."

"No way!" she said.

Two floors to go. It seemed impossible, but Boldt was moving even faster now—taking three stairs at a time. She didn't have that reach. Both men moved ahead of her, but only briefly. She took two stairs, but outran them, and quickly caught up. Boldt said, "Consider it done. Daffy, you'll wear the wire whenever you're out of this building."

"Lou," she protested.

It wasn't up for discussion. Boldt changed subjects, "I got Babcock a photo of that skeleton key, which she subsequently determined was late nineteenth, early twentieth century—at least twenty years past the construction of the section of the city that's currently beneath the church."

"Twenty years?" she asked, not following what this determined.

"Construction spread uphill after the great fire."

"As in Columbia and Third?" LaMoia asked.

"Granted," Boldt said, finally reaching the building's garage level, "any lock could have been put in any door at any time. But if we're playing percentages, then that lock is more likely from this area of town—right where we're standing, for that matter, than down the hill toward Pio Square."

"And that's where we're headed?" she asked. "Across the street?"

"Each level of the Underground is over a hundred thousand square feet. That's three football fields or so. At this point, SID has been through ninety percent or more of that level where we found Vanderhorst's lair, and so far no sign of Hebringer or Randolf."

He held the door for them.

"We put a pair of K-9s into that space about an hour ago, each scented for one of the missing. They led us straight back to the elevator shaft. A drain. Vanderhorst had sealed it with black plastic so the smell couldn't escape."

"He put them down a drain?" LaMoia asked. "In one piece?"

Boldt held up the skeleton key, still in the evidence bag. "The drain leads down to yet another level of Underground," he said. "That's why the jackets. We're going to be the first inside, and I'm betting it's chilly down there."

It felt damn near freezing to her. She wasn't sure if that was the actual temperature or her own heightened anxiety over what they expected to find, but the coat didn't help, and that was her first big clue. Preparing to lower themselves through the open storm drain at the bottom of the elevator shaft, itself now lit by halogen lights running off extension cords lowered from the bank's basement, Boldt passed out latex gloves and shared a tube of Mentholatum to smear above the lip to help mask the smell. The rituals of homicide came painfully. All three knew that odor, and "it ain't dead rats," as LaMoia had put it.

Squeezing through the open drain into a dark, damp space in

which the stench was far more concentrated felt to Matthews like willfully entering a portal into hell.

She interviewed them, she counseled them, she analyzed them, she predicted them, and she evaluated them, but she would still never fully understand why human beings treated their own species with such willful disdain, disrespect, and distemper.

The going was relatively dry underfoot. For all of Boldt's rapid descent in Public Safety, he moved down this hallway at a snail's pace—mindful of every footfall, stepping this way and that and indicating for the two others to follow in his exact footsteps, the protector and keeper of evidence in all its possible forms. Ancient gaslight fixtures held to the crumbling red brick walls. This subterranean area had either been stables or cold storage back in the days of the Yukon gold rush, when Seattle rose from a tiny fishing village to a commercial metropolis nearly overnight. In those days, when a nickel or dime would buy a man a dinner, each and every prospector was dropping nearly two thousand dollars to be supplied for a year in the northern province, as twelve months of provisions were mandated by the government before anyone would be allowed aboard a ship heading north. Basements like this ran full of beef jerky, oats, sugar, and salt. Cattle and swine, horses and mules. Now it was empty space behind locked doors, and it was in front of one of those doors that Boldt stopped, having nearly walked past it, his nose turning him around, as well as a keen eye that picked up the drizzle of key oil staining the wood beneath the wrought iron of a keyhole.

Three flashlights found that keyhole at once. It was a heavy wooden door that hung on hinges pounded flat by the muscle of a blacksmith.

"No one enters until we get a good look," Boldt told them. He broke open the evidence baggie that contained the key left by the tooth fairy beneath Matthews's pillow.

Boldt inserted the large skeleton key into the lock. He met

eyes with Matthews in the dim light. She thought she saw his lips barely moving and she wondered if he was praying—beyond reason, it seemed to her—that Susan Hebringer had been spared. The key turned with a loud *click* of the tumblers. For Matthews, his turning that key was to expose a part of the human condition that would kill off yet another fraction of the optimism she maintained that mankind could and would someday work through its problems.

Not likely, she thought, finding herself only able to moan as she witnessed the scene before them.

The sterile light from the flashlight revealed the corpses of two women. They were still partially clothed, but their breasts and pubic symphyses were exposed. They both hung by their wrists from nylon strapping, secured to large iron rings mounted to the rock wall. Massive yellow and brown bruises cried out from their chests, rib cages, and swollen faces. Their legs had been bent back at the knees, ribbons of silver duct tape binding their ankles to their thighs so they could neither kick nor fight their attacker's intentions to repeatedly rape them.

Evidence suggested he had kept them alive: There was packaged food discarded on the floor, some of which had spilled down their clothes or adhered to their skin. He had revisited them, a fact that would contribute to the profile Matthews would later build. He had kept them awake, used them up, one at a time until replacing them became necessary. He had kept them on the wall like trophies.

" 'Strung up like marlins,' " Matthews quoted. "I remember *Walker* saying that. *Walker,* not Vanderhorst." This revelation clearly stole Boldt's attention briefly from the bodies. Walker had supplied the key as well, but this was Vanderhorst's scene—Boldt said so in a whisper.

He added, "The ATM connection was Vanderhorst's, not Walker's."

"Oh . . . God . . . no . . ." They heard a gurgle and splat behind them. Babcock, the university professor, had somehow talked her way down here. Heads would roll. But in the meantime they had her vomit to deal with.

"Help her out," Boldt instructed Matthews, refusing to move himself, refusing to break his train of concentration. She understood the importance of everything Boldt took in now, before he steeled himself to the sight and smell, before the SID techies stuck little paper flags around the room making it into a parade route, now, before any other living person, *except one* (the killer), experienced this horror for what it truly was. The crime scene offered insight into the events that had taken place here, insights that could prove invaluable to the prosecution of Per Vanderhorst. Boldt's latex gloved fingers slipped out his notepad and she watched as he began to sketch. "John?" he said. "The camera?"

LaMoia had brought along the department's pocket-sized digital camera as well as a handful of evidence bags.

"What the hell's going on here?" Babcock moaned.

"Shhh." Matthews attempted to console the woman. "He's working the scene."

49 Double Team

For several hours Boldt and his team managed to keep their discovery confidential, avoiding the inevitable media stampede that promised both to steal their focus and to give Vanderhorst's defense attorney information the PA's office didn't want him having. Knowing that even on a Saturday such a news blackout wouldn't last forever, Boldt had asked Lofgrin to pick his two most trusted SID technicians to work the site. Boldt had also tasked his information technology squad to work the National Crime Information Center's database for like crimes, and they had already produced results. Three of the seven pages he now carried were crime scene photographs gleaned from an advanced search on the NCIC database. Filling out a detailed database query that included such information as the use of duct tape, the sustaining of the victim's life, the blood type of the secretor (semen had been collected from both Hebringer and Randolf, and was currently being DNA-typed), the age and specifics of the two victims, SID-IT had matched the Hebringer/Randolf murders to three other similar unsolved cases. These results, once the product of weeks, months, or even years of interstate detective work, had been accomplished in less than forty minutes.

"So far, so good," Boldt put to Matthews when asked how things were going. "Though that may be about to change."

She indicated the door to the interrogation room, on the other side of which sat Per Vanderhorst, waiting. "You can't honestly think that Walker was any part of these murders." Following the trip into the Underground, she'd changed into a pair of blue jeans that she normally reserved for weekends and, tucked in at the waist, a white, oversized, tailored shirt belonging to LaMoia. She had the shirt's starched sleeves and cuffs rolled up on her forearms nearly to her elbows.

"Walker delivered the key. That puts him in this, like it or not."

"There's an explanation for that," she said.

"Not that I've heard, there isn't."

"So Vanderhorst will explain it to us now," she said.

"He'd better. No matter what, Walker faces obstruction charges. At the very least, he knew about that death chamber. If Vanderhorst doesn't sort it out for us, I'm going to tie them both up in this."

"Lou, that's preposterous, and you know it! Walker stumbled onto this in the Underground, nothing more."

"The various sections of Underground don't connect, Daffy. You'll need a better explanation than that."

"Maybe they do somehow and we just haven't found it yet."

Reading his wristwatch, Boldt signaled the end of the discussion, telling her, "In twenty-five minutes Tim Peterson from the U.S. Attorney's office is going to be arriving here to meet with Mahoney and Tony Shapiro."

"Shapiro?"

"There's a report he took the case pro bono as of about an hour ago. That's why I said I think things may change. If Shapiro has taken the case, then it's going to be a media circus. The guy lives for it. Worse, he'll sew Vanderhorst's lips shut and feed him through a straw."

She understood then that this hurried effort to interrogate Vanderhorst resulted from Boldt's hand being forced—they were about to lose their suspect to the wheels of television justice. The time frame of twenty-five minutes seemed laughable—typically barely enough time to get a couple cups of coffee into the Box. Win a confession in that amount of time?

"Lou?" she said.

"Listen, the PD must not like Shapiro's grandstanding any more than we do, or he wouldn't have advised his client to sit down with us. I'm not sure who to fear more, Shapiro or the feds. Peterson's a good guy, and I know he thinks he's helping us by putting out the possibility of extradition to a death penalty state, but all it really means is we'll lose Vanderhorst, and I just don't like that idea."

"So it's a full-court press," she said. Another LaMoiaism. Boldt's expression registered complaint.

"Something like that," he said. About to throw the door open, he said in a whisper, "In any case, it's show time."

With the out-of-state crime scene photos in hand, Boldt stepped into Homicide's conference room A—the largest of three such rooms—Matthews close on his heels. She gently shut the door. Initially, neither of them acknowledged Vanderhorst's presence on the far side of the small table. Instead, they moved chairs around, Boldt took off his sport coat and hung it on the back of a chair like a man ready to spend the rest of the day here, and Matthews switched off her cell phone and took a seat alongside Boldt—the combined impression that of two people digging in.

Vanderhorst, transferred from lockup, wore the humiliating orange jumpsuit issued by county jail, manacles on his ankles and a waist harness that secured the chain of his handcuffs to where his hands were free to move but their motion limited.

Boldt started the double-cassette tape recorder, introduced himself and Matthews, and naming the suspect, stated that Vanderhorst had requested counsel, had met with counsel several times over the past twenty-four hours, and that counsel had been notified of this interview and was "expected any minute."

Boldt carefully placed the seven pages facedown in front of Vanderhorst and, like a Vegas card dealer, then rolled three of them over, as deliberately and dramatically as possible. With no time to waste, he had to forgo the usual "warm-up" of introducing the suspect to the roles that would be played, of the small talk that often began such an interrogation in an effort to establish a rapport. There was no time for a rapport. This was to be the emotional equivalent of slapping the man around.

Stabbing each in succession with a determined index finger, Boldt said, "Fort Worth, Little Rock, Santa Fe." The victims hung from walls, their ankles taped to their thighs with duct tape, their garments torn, their chests and crotches exposed.

Boldt had hoped for the power of shock value. He saw no response. He yielded to Matthews, who said, "You remember each of these as if it happened yesterday, don't you, Per? Is it all right that I call you Per?" she asked rhetorically, not allowing him to respond. "The way the air smelled just before you abducted them . . . that incredible rush as you overpowered them . . ."

Vanderhorst looked up from the photos, met eyes with Matthews. She felt nothing from him. Disappointed, she pressed on.

"Oh, yes," she said, "I know how it felt for you."

The suspect lowered his head, but more out of boredom, she thought. No remorse, no excitement, no fear or trepidation. This, in turn, filled her with curiosity, for she had expected, at the very least, a sense of surprise from him. She felt the clock running, ticking off the minutes, and wished Boldt hadn't told her about the arrival of the attorneys.

Boldt figured the photos had to have surprised the man, regardless of his outward appearance. He followed this with what he hoped would be another surprise, sliding the evidence bag containing the skeleton key across the table.

Vanderhorst looked up, the first seams of terror breaking his cool façade.

"Been looking for that?" Boldt asked.

The man's eyes tightened. "Never seen it before."

They had him talking. Matthews leaned back in the steel chair.

Boldt said, "We found them."

The suspect cocked his head like Blue when he heard an errant noise. Matthews experienced a shudder of cold. She glanced up at the room's air vent, then back to the suspect.

Boldt leaned across the table and rolled over the next photographs—first Randolf, then Hebringer. "Five women in four states in the last eighteen months. The best chance you have is to get ahead of this, Vanderhorst. Once it breaks, there isn't a juror you can draw who hasn't heard something about it— judges, too, for that matter. No matter what jurors and judges claim about their remaining objective, it just isn't possible. The smart money says you preempt all that by getting in front of it."

"I've never seen any of them," Vanderhorst claimed. "Never seen that key, either."

"Is that right?" Boldt said. "Then you wouldn't have any interest in seeing the videotape of *you* entering that elevator car, of you keying the back panel and disappearing into that shaft. That video confirms you had both the necessary knowledge and access to move the bodies once you'd abducted them in front of the ATMs." His intention was to keep stacking evidence on him, one surprise after another. "You think we won't find physical evidence that those two women made that trip? You were in a hurry, Vanderhorst. *Of course* there's evidence, and the more we collect the less agreeable we are to listening to your side of this." He'd leave Matthews to sort out or to exploit the man's guilt and what she believed would prove to be his relief at having been caught and stopped.

Vanderhorst studied the final two blank pages in the line of seven but made no attempt to turn them over.

Feeling the time pressure, Matthews saw no choice but to go for the jugular. She said, "This is the last time you'll see any of these. You understand that, don't you . . . that it's over?"

His brow furrowed. She considered any and all responses victories. She caught a flicker from Boldt's sideways glance—he saw it, too.

"What do you feel with it being over?" she asked. "Relief? Anger?"

Vanderhorst's attention remained on the final two sheets of paper that remained facedown.

She thought she saw him shrug his shoulders, but it might have been nothing more than him trying to get comfortable, an impossibility in these chairs.

"Does it feel good that it's over?"

She thought for sure he'd nodded.

"You tried, but you couldn't stop yourself." She made it a statement, quickly adapting to the asocial personality she believed in front of her. "You left each city, not because you were afraid of being caught, but because you thought the change of scenery might allow you to stop."

Boldt signaled her to notice the tape recorder: He wanted Vanderhorst's answers spoken onto tape.

"You can talk to us," she said calmly. A part of her disliked playing so deceptively sweet to killers like Vanderhorst; she owed it to the victims to show more disgust and abhorrence with the nature of the crimes. A part of her enjoyed the game, the challenge of tricking the criminal mind into unraveling, exploiting the guilt, when present, the sense of remorse, if any. The art of deception here was feigning empathy and understanding in the pursuit of truth and discovery. She, too, had victims: the perpetrators of these crimes who allowed themselves to open up to her and admit those things they had protected so carefully.

"It's not like what you think," he said.

She felt a wave of relaxation just hearing him speak. "Help us out here."

"I don't know anything about any of this."

"We might surprise you," she said. "Maybe we know more about it than you think."

"I don't think so," he said.

Matthews knew there were no voices in Vanderhorst's head, no whispered "messages from God" to kill. She wasn't dealing with a display of a so-called psychopath, but with a man suffering from antisocial personality disorder—APD—a person so distanced from his fellow human beings and a sense of right and wrong that he committed these acts with little understanding of the consequences. The time had come to prove herself, to convince Vanderhorst she knew more about him than he knew about himself. And, she thought, just maybe she did.

"You watched women in their hotel rooms," she said, knowing him much better already. "In their apartments and condominiums. Undressing. Bathing. You imagined yourself in there with them, leading a normal life, a part of their lives."

Vanderhorst cringed, shifting in the chair nervously. He studied her intently and she stood up to it, not to be undermined.

Boldt regarded her with a pale face and nervous expression.

A knock on the door gave them all a moment's pause. A uniformed woman officer entered and handed Matthews a pink telephone memo. She said, "I wouldn't have bothered you, but the girl apparently sounded pretty bad and said it was urgent." The message read: "Problems with the baby. Please come. I'm above Mario's." It was signed *Margaret*. Matthews thanked the officer, folded up the message, and tucked it away in her jeans pocket, disappointed in herself for briefly abandoning the teen but knowing the time line of the interrogation had to take precedence.

With the door shut again, she confidently told Vanderhorst, "You followed them—some of them—hoping they might notice you, might speak to you. So much of your life you've spent just wanting to be noticed. And yet it terrifies you when a woman actually notices you, doesn't it?" She knew by his squirming that she had him pegged. He looked both shell-shocked and curious. *Just right.* "Susan Hebringer . . . you peeped her, and then, surprise, she showed up at the ATM. And you had to have her. Randolf? That was what: a look she gave you? The way she said hello to you? Tell me." Knowing that at some point he would attempt to tune her out, she quickly continued, "You were caught between those two worlds, weren't you, Per—wanting the attention, yet not wanting it?" His eyes held on to hers all the more tightly. *Stay with me,* she silently encouraged. "What were their crimes, Per? For what did you punish them? Did they say hello to you? Ask you the time of day? Or was it simply a look they gave you—a look you took as an invitation? It's only women that confuse you, isn't it? The men you can handle. Lieutenant Boldt comes by the bank and you have no problem talking to him, do you? But a woman? Am I confusing you now? You're feeling anger toward me, aren't you? I can sense that, Per. It's all around me, that anger. Because you know what I'm going to say next, you know who I'm going to mention, don't you?" His eyes went increasingly wider, increasingly whiter. "And you don't want her mentioned, do you? You want her left out of this. Her dark hair, her sending you mixed signals. What was it she did to you to deserve this?" she asked, touching the second of the crime scene photographs. "Criticize you, no matter what you did? Dress you up like a little girl and show you off to her friends and laugh at you? Take baths with you? Showers? When you were old enough to respond to that—to her—in ways you didn't want to respond but couldn't help responding, she laughed at you—at *it*—didn't she? She thought *it* was funny, cute. Didn't she? But it wasn't funny, not at all. It was humiliating. It was awful for you, her laughing like that. Or maybe it was her walking around in panties and underwear, showing way too much to a boy your age. Maybe that's why you like looking through windows now. Or was it her slipping in beside you on those cold nights, or the ones with thunder and lightning, or was it that she'd had a little too much to drink and wanted the company? The same way you want company now."

Vanderhorst didn't answer with words, but she had his face in a sweat. Boldt looked as if he wanted to stop her, or wanted to leave the room himself, but he sat calmly beside her, his pencil taking down notes on a legal pad as if writing a grocery list.

She addressed Vanderhorst and said, "You never wanted any of it, did you, Per? Never volunteered for any of it. She teased you in front of her friends, in front of *your* friends; she cut you off from everyone around you. You brought a friend home, she made a fool of you. And you, you loved her all the more for it. Loved her like nothing else in this world. And this proved the most confusing of all." His rheumy eyes seemed ready to spill tears. He was no criminal animal but a poor, pathetic creature who'd lost sight of the out-of-bounds markers. She felt Boldt's precious minutes slipping past. "Later," she said, "when you were older— what, fourteen, fifteen?—she was still coming into your room at night, only now for things unimaginable to you a year or two before. Now you ran, didn't you? You hid. First the closet. But she found you. Then the bathroom . . . but she found you." With each statement she looked for any unintended response on his part—a shortening of breath, a twitch to his eyes, a dilation of his pupils, using these as her signposts. "And finally . . . the basement," she said, knowing in advance she would score a direct hit. Indeed, he looked away and to the floor, wearing his shame. "The one place she never did find you. Tell me I'm wrong, Per. Tell me you didn't unscrew the lights down there and hide in the dark, because you knew she was afraid of the dark and that she'd never find you." She based this on the discovery of the underground lair. The location of that hideout was no accident. "That's where you feel the safest, isn't it? In the dark. Alone. Your back pushed up against a cold wall." She worked from her own experience in the Shelter. "The musty smell—it's almost like perfume to you. You brought them down there, and you did those things to them—those things she did to you—and then you felt bad about it, didn't you? Then you wanted to keep them alive, if you could. In the dark. Locked in the room. There when you needed them."

It hadn't been about torturing his victims but trying to save them. His mistake had been hanging them from the wall—he'd unintentionally crucified them. She suspected that if she could travel back in time to his mother's apartment she would find Jesus on the cross in nearly every room. She'd read about extreme cases of APD, the Per Vanderhorsts of this world; she'd just never interviewed one.

She wondered how any of this could bring a sense of excitement, of fulfillment for her, and yet it did.

She said, "It's easier now that it's over, isn't it? There's nothing to hide any longer." In point of fact they knew almost nothing. It was far from clear if they had enough evidence to convict Vanderhorst. The DNA blood evidence and the semen collected from the corpses might put him away, but without that evidence firmly in hand (and it was still a day or two away), she knew that Boldt needed a confession.

Boldt said, "You're about to be traded back and forth like a pro ball player, Vanderhorst. Texas uses lethal injection. You know that, right? Capital murder equals capital punishment in that state, and you killed a woman in Fort Worth, and you need to think about that. The U.S. Attorney's office has the authority to move your trial to Texas, and they'll argue for that because they're going to want you on death row. This attorney general is tough on crime—you understand that, right? But they're basically good guys, better guys than you'd think. They won't take you away from us if we have a better case to make against you here. You see how this works?" He added, "Or maybe it doesn't work—the system. Not all that well. But it's what we've got at the moment, and you're square in the middle of it."

Worry crept into the man's eyes.

"What's it going to take?" Boldt asked Matthews in a familiar game to them.

"I think he knows," Matthews replied.

"You see where this leaves you?" Boldt asked him.

Matthews said to Vanderhorst, "You and I both know you're of sound mind, fit to stand trial. That's not an out for you, Per. We'll run the usual tests, of course, but you're going to *pass* them. The decision you need to make now, before you lose the chance, is who is going to control your destiny. If you want it in the hands of the feds, that's up to you."

Boldt said, "You're curious about those last two photographs, aren't you?"

Vanderhorst eyed him suspiciously.

"Go ahead, take a look," Boldt said.

Vanderhorst didn't move a muscle.

"Curious about how we got the key, I'll bet."

Vanderhorst narrowed his eyes, both angry and unnerved, and Matthews saw the opening Boldt had given her.

She said, "We thought you'd worked them alone, Per. The ATM machines. The basement of the bank. That was one of our mistakes—one of the things that took us so long to catch you—this idea you were smart enough to plan this on your own." She leaned across the table—Vanderhorst reared backward, over-reacting, and nearly went over—and rolled the second to last sheet, revealing Ferrell Walker's head shot from central booking. "This is the man who gave us the key to that room. He says that he planned it all—that it was his brains—but that you did the actual killing."

"I don't even know this guy," Vanderhorst said.

"He says you do."

"He gave us the key to that room," Boldt repeated.

"He stole it."

"The key?" Matthews asked.

"That's right," Vanderhorst said, dipping his toes into the confessional waters.

"Stole it from where?" Boldt asked.

Vanderhorst continued to sweat profusely. He viewed Boldt with suspicion but didn't recoil into himself as Matthews feared.

She repeated, "He's claiming he's the brain behind this."

A confused Vanderhorst pointed to the first three images on the table. "Then who did these? I suppose this guy did these as well? Millicent Etheredge. Tanya Wallace. Anita Baylock. He's lying to you."

Their suspect had just stated the names of the other three victims, names that had not been mentioned in this room. There were explanations a good defense attorney could use, including the absurd amount of press most such cases received. But the context of his answer combined with the determination in his voice would go a long way toward convicting Per Vanderhorst.

"You're saying he wasn't part of this," Matthews suggested.

"It's bullshit," Vanderhorst said.

"He described them as strung up like fish. He'd been inside that room."

"He stole the key. *My* key."

She wanted so badly to look over at Lou and celebrate their victory with him, but she dared not send such a signal. They needed as much out of him as possible.

Boldt said, "That key has been missing how long?"

"A while now. I'm not all that great with time."

"How'd you get in there after that?"

"I didn't," Vanderhorst said and coughed. "Not after I lost that key. Most of the locks down there . . . any skeleton key will work. But not that room. That's why I used it." He answered their puzzled expressions. "Listen, I hid the key so it couldn't be found on me."

"Is that right?" Boldt said.

"That was your idea," Matthews said.

"Hid it on a nail down the hall . . . this storage room. And then one day it vanishes—and that's the last I gone down there." He said to Boldt, "I'd been planning on leaving way before you ever showed up, believe me."

"But they owed you money," he said.

"Nearly six hundred bucks," Vanderhorst said, as if a king's ransom, as if it had been worth getting caught with that kind of money on the line. His desperate eyes tracked between his two interrogators. "Why are you both looking at me like that? What'd I say? Six hundred bucks is six hundred bucks. Who's going to walk away from six hundred bucks?"

"Makes sense to me," Boldt said.

Vanderhorst rolled the last photo over for himself. It was an ME's head shot of Billy Chen. He stared at the photo for a long time in complete silence. "Wrong place, wrong time."

"Is that right?" Boldt said skeptically.

"Ask him."

"You had him in that room. We can prove it."

Vanderhorst looked dazed to hear that. He shrugged his

shoulders. "Some guy shows up uninvited, you show him the welcome mat."

"You knocked him out and then made it look like a drowning."

"So says you."

"Convince me I'm wrong."

Vanderhorst looked up at Boldt with bored, droopy eyes.

A sharp knock on the door caused Matthews to jump. For a moment she'd been in the Underground with Vanderhorst. The knock was followed by a woman in police uniform. "Lieutenant," she said, addressing Boldt. "They're here."

Anthony Shapiro pushed past her, all five foot three of him. He wore a dark blue silk suit worth a month of Boldt's salary. He said to Vanderhorst, "We're all done here, Mr. Vanderhorst. Don't say another word." He glanced at Boldt with fiery eyes. "Shame on you, Lieutenant. And on the weekend, no less!" He noticed the tape recorder then, the hubs still moving. He vaguely acknowledged Matthews. Two lieutenants in the same interrogation room—this particular team of Boldt and Matthews—seemed to finally register with him.

"Tell me you kept your mouth shut, sir," he said to his client.

"Who the hell are you?" Vanderhorst said.

Shapiro hung his head and sighed. "Okay," he said to Boldt, "tell me how bad it is."

Boldt smiled his first smile in many long weeks. It was as much as he needed to say.

50 Without a Prair

As Boldt and Matthews had sat down with Vanderhorst, LaMoia hung up the phone, his hand trembling noticeably. A housefly landed on the fabric wall of his office cubicle, and he watched it lovingly clean itself, rubbing its arms together like a card dealer warming his hands before the big game. As a detective he chased facts, one to the next, the clichéd analogy of following crumbs so appropriate to him at a time like this.

Nathan Prair's long-awaited written report lay on his desk, a poorly crafted summary of the deputy sheriff having given Mary-Ann Walker a speeding ticket a week prior to her death, as well as his written alibi for the night Mary-Ann Walker had been killed—a night tour during which, by his own admission, he'd taken what cops called "lost time," a break, during the critical hour of 11 P.M. to 12 A.M.

LaMoia called upstairs to Matthews to share the vital information he'd just gotten from the manager of the airport McDonald's. Hoping she might either make the interview with him or at least monitor his progress, he felt disappointment when her voice mail picked up. With time of the essence—Prair rotated off-duty soon—LaMoia made his journey without her.

On his way across town, he called Janise Meyer, of SPD's I.T. unit, and asked the impossible of her. Janise didn't know the word. He was counting on that.

• • •

He had GPS technology to thank for his ability to locate Prair. The King County Sheriff's Office tracked every vehicle out on patrol. LaMoia requested the man's physical location or assignment rather than asking KCSO dispatch to radio the deputy or send a text message over the patrol car's Mobile Data Terminal. As an SPD officer, LaMoia lacked any authority whatsoever to order Prair in for review, but he saw nothing wrong with paying the deputy a visit with a tape recorder in his pocket. With the blessing of the PA's office, and the knowledge that car 89 was currently between Madison and Marion, moving south on Broadway—doing bus route duty that was easy to predict—LaMoia parked the Jetta outside a frame shop on Broadway, walked over to the bus stop, and kept watch for the patrol car. He spotted it a few minutes later, started the tape recording, and stepped out into the street, sticking his thumb out like a hitchhiker. He wanted this encounter as casual and light as possible.

Prair pulled the cruiser to the side of the road, unlocked the master lock, and LaMoia climbed in.

"What the fuck?" the deputy said, rolling the car with a green light. LaMoia heard the master lock engage and experienced the first twinges of unease.

"I don't owe you this," LaMoia began. "I'm not even sure why I'm bothering with it."

Prair glanced hotly at his passenger, straightened his head, and said nothing for several more blocks. "Yeah?"

"Yeah," LaMoia answered.

"So I'll say it again: What the fuck?"

"The fuck is this: The Mickey D's you used as your alibi the night Mary-Ann Walker went off the Aurora Bridge had a fire in the deep-fat fryer that night." He watched the horror register on Prair's face. "SFD logged the call as nine fifty-four P.M. Had responded by ten-oh-seven P.M. They closed the joint down for the rest of that night and part of the next morning. Meaning that when you went off the clock, the place wasn't open." The *whish* of wet tires on roadway. Broadway stayed pretty busy at all hours. "Shit, we've got to follow up anything like this: an alibi, a witness, whatever—and *you know that,* Prair—you dumb shit. The least you could have done is check out your own alibi."

"Fuck off."

Another five blocks ticked off, slipping by the windows in a blur of wet colors. College kids peopled this section of Broadway. LaMoia was amazed at how much younger they looked each year.

Prair finally said softly, "There was no way I could make this thing right with any of you. And you know why? Because you come to the table prejudiced against me."

"Oh, give it a rest."

"If I'd told you the way it was I could have lost my badge."

"A distinct possibility."

"You're making jokes out of this?"

"Me and Popeye: 'I y'am what I y'am.' "

"Fuck you."

"Why do you think I'm here, Nate? If I wanted to arrest you, I'd have turned it over to II, or the brass, or the PA's office. Should I be wanting to arrest you for this murder, Nathan? Or should I be hearing your side of this first?" Never mind that he'd already spoken to Hill, that Hill would have already called the prosecuting attorney by now; never mind that if they'd hauled him into the Box, Prair would have invoked his right to a guild attorney and clammed up. LaMoia hoped like hell that by doing this in the comfort and safety of Prair's patrol car, by offering him a preemptive second chance, the man might overlook the condition of the quicksand where they now treaded.

So far, so good.

Prair turned off his route, down the hill toward the city, and pulled over in front of the Egyptian's marquee, engine running.

He looked over at LaMoia, who could see the tension behind the man's eyes belying his attempt at a cool demeanor. LaMoia found himself eyeing the passenger door handle. Prair said, "She and me . . . we got into it a little."

LaMoia felt restless all of a sudden. Who was the one cornered, and who was the one planning to surprise? Prair was a burly fuck. LaMoia didn't want to find himself tangling with him.

Prair continued, "She and me . . . well . . . let's just say we'd had a cup of coffee together . . . and she was a pretty messed-up kid."

"Are you telling me you were jumping Mary-Ann Walker?" LaMoia asked, still trying to make it sound like a locker-room shower discussion.

"No, no," Prair said, his confidence allowing a smarmy grin to occupy his face. "A fucking cup of joe is all."

"You sure?"

"I'm sure," Prair answered. "But I was *interested,* okay? And she was *interested,* I'm telling you. You, of all people, know what I'm talking about."

"Sure I do." LaMoia felt a little sick of himself.

"It happens to all of us on the job."

"It does," LaMoia said, trying to force a fraternal grin onto a face that felt slightly frozen.

"And all I'm saying . . . maybe I got a little carried away with this one. So sue me! She was a looker, sexy as all hell, and as vulnerable as they come, all this sobbing over this wife-beating bastard she was shacking up with. And me, I'm thinking I'll come swinging on the vine through the window and catch her Dangerous Dan backhanding her, and I'm good for getting laid anytime I want it—am I right?"

"Right as rain," LaMoia said, feeling the acid in his stomach.

"Exactly," Prair said, finding a rhythm in the patter. "So what was I supposed to tell you guys—that I was using my lost time to loiter outside that turdball's apartment that night, debating how to rescue a damsel in distress? How fucking sick does that make me look? But you see what I was thinking?"

"Sure I do."

"My line of thought."

"Clear as a bell."

"She's having problems with the guy; I take care of the guy."

"Simple as pie," LaMoia said. "Might have thought of it myself."

"You pull these peaches over, and they spill their guts to you. I'm telling you. I mean, the honey pot is yours. One look in their eyes and you know the ones that are so high-strung they're about to rip, the ones that like the uniform regardless who's inside, the ones that are going to blow you off. You can tell, right?"

"Absolutely."

"It's like a fucking dating service."

"So you were *there* that night," LaMoia pressed, wondering how far he could push this. The thought occurred to him to escape from the car while he still had both legs, both arms. Then he saw that bloated body floating facedown in the black water, and he stayed put.

"I hung around out back, yeah. Fifteen, twenty minutes."

"This is gospel?"

"Okay . . . truth told, I'd been there a couple nights before looking for an opening. I got a little hung up on this one." Prair gripped the wheel tightly. The power steering mechanism under the hood cried out loudly if he moved the wheel even an inch. Prair didn't seem to hear this.

"If we're gonna sort this out," LaMoia said, "we gotta have all the cards."

Prair nodded. He'd started the process—he knew there was a logical conclusion to it. "Okay, so that particular night, that Saturday night, I'm doing a drive-by as they're coming back to his place."

"What time is this?"

"Little after ten. I'm thinking, I'll let her see the cruiser, catch up alongside them at a light. Surprised the shit out of her, I want to tell you. But at least she knew I was there now. She knew there was help available if she needed it. I hang out in the cruiser, the back of his place. Ten forty-five, maybe eleven o'clock, she climbs out onto the fire escape and lights up a cancer stick. I'm thinking she's signaling me, right? So I get out of the car. I got my juices going—I'm thinking it's show time. But as I'm coming around the cruiser, all of a sudden she turns around up there, and I see she's on the phone, the fucking phone! Then, like seconds later, I see this guy climbing the fire escape toward her, and now I got my piece out. Who the fuck is this? He's got to have been hanging around just like I have. Fuck if the creep doesn't wave to her on his way up, and she waves back. He sits down a couple steps below her—like at crotch level, right?—and the two of them start chatting it up, and I'm out of there."

"You saw this guy?"

"Saw how? Not like that. No fucking way. He's a phantom is all. But me, I'm gone. The rendezvous she's having ain't with me, so I'm the fuck out of there. Just wanna make sure they don't make the cruiser on the way out. And they don't, so I'm good." He paused. "Good until she's found fucking bobbing for apples Tuesday night, and me, I'm right in the middle of it." He faced LaMoia. "Can I pick 'em or what?"

LaMoia let some skepticism show. "That's the way you want to call this?"

"That's the way it went down, LaMoia. Swear to God. But think about it. What was I supposed to do? There was no way . . . I mean, *no way,* I was going to detail any of this to you guys up there on that bridge. You fucking kidding me?" He mimicked himself. " 'Hey, by the way, LaMoia, I was scouting this peach the other night. Watching her smoke a cancer in her fucking panties on the fire escape.' What the fuck is that about? Then, later, what was I supposed to say, 'By the way, I may have forgotten to mention . . .'?"

"Wouldn't have been too cool."

"No shit. And these girls. I'm already down in the books on that. You know that. Something like this gets out . . ." He looked over at LaMoia, the pall of realization taking hold. "You understand, John," use of the first name did not come easy for Prair, "this can*not* get out."

As the extent of his confession began to sink in, for Prair, LaMoia calculated the time needed to escape the front seat—the doors were power locked, necessitating several steps.

"I mean . . . in terms of helping you out . . . that's been bugging me, sure it has. I've got a duty to help out, and I know my duty." Prair was talking to himself now, and that bothered LaMoia all the more. "I should have said something early on, okay? I'm good with that. But you can see my side of it."

"Of course I can." It didn't sound convincing, even to him.

"Something like this, and I'm done. I'm running a cash booth in a mall parking garage. Give me a fucking break."

"There's definitely room to work this right," LaMoia said.

"You give anyone your source on this, and I'm fucked. You can see that, right?"

"Oh, yeah," LaMoia said, "we're good on that."

"How good?"

"Let me get something straight," LaMoia said. "You saw this other guy, the one on the fire escape, but not any kind of good look."

"I got the hell out of there. I told you." Prair paused, considering this. "You're thinking it was the brother, this creep bothering Daphne."

LaMoia said nothing. He didn't like hearing Prair calling Matthews by her first name. He felt incredibly protective at that moment.

Prair said, "I'm good with saying I saw him, if that's what you need, if that would help your present situation. If maybe you and I could do a little business here. Maybe you see clear to get around directly involving me in this."

Did this clown hear himself? LaMoia wondered. He was dealing with a pathological liar, a man who'd say anything to a woman to get himself laid, anything to a fellow cop to keep his record clean. LaMoia said, "My opinion, Nate: You've got some issues here need working out."

"Issues," Prair agreed, nodding slightly. "That's what I'm trying to tell you."

"We're gonna want to go over this again," LaMoia said.

"Not officially, we're not. No fucking way. You can forget about it. You call me in, and I'm making like Sergeant Shultz. You're gonna see my guild rep's ugly ass. Me? I'll be swigging tall boys over at the Cock and Bull."

LaMoia's right hand found the door lock button—he kept the move as subtle as possible. For him the air heated up a few hundred degrees. He popped the button, the loud click like a muted gunshot. "You know, Nate, shit like this works out for the best."

"You bring me in, and I've got me a bad case of laryngitis."

"SPD and KCSO, we're talking apples and oranges here," LaMoia reminded. "One hand doesn't always wash the other. We put you down as an informer, and we can block your identity." It didn't work like that, but a guy like Prair thought he knew more about detective work than he actually did.

A cell phone rang. LaMoia reached for his, only to realize it was Prair's ringing. The cop answered the phone. "The fuck you say!" His eyes tracked to LaMoia, and for a moment the detective believed he might be the topic of discussion. Had Sheila Hill jumped the gun with her phone calls? Had Prair just been alerted he was under investigation for something that showed in one of his ticket books nearly two years earlier? "Maybe you will, maybe you won't," he said. He ended the call, studied LaMoia out of the side of his eyes as if about to say something. He then looked out the windshield at the appealing skyline. LaMoia wished he could have enjoyed the moment. Prair said, "We're all done here, Cool. I gotta roll."

LaMoia felt the relief loosen his muscles and allow him to move. For a moment, he'd been frozen in the seat. "We'll work this through, Nate. No sweat."

"Just remember what I told you: I'll scratch your back if you scratch mine. But if you turn Dick Tracy on me, my memory's gone to shit."

"Got it," LaMoia said, managing to open the car door and connect with the security of the sidewalk. He fingered the lump of the tape recorder in his coat pocket.

"You want me to drop you, it's on the way."

"I'm good," LaMoia said.

"Whatever."

LaMoia slammed the door shut. His left thumb turned off the tape recorder as Prair pulled into traffic. It was raining. But like everyone else in this city, LaMoia didn't feel it.

A little over twenty minutes later, having headed directly back to Public Safety and winded from hurrying down the hall, LaMoia knocked on the office's open door, expecting to see Matthews behind her desk. Ironically, Matthews understood Prair better than anyone—she'd freak when she heard what he had on tape. His shoulders slouched in disappointment and he turned to the secretary pool. "Matthews have a meeting or something? Where can I find her?"

"Lost time," the closest of the secretaries answered, glancing up to the grid on the wall.

"What are you *talking* about?" he said, his voice noticeably louder.

"Lost time, Sergeant."

"She's on a wire. She's under surveillance," he said, though he wasn't sure. He didn't want her out there unprotected.

The snotty secretary answered, "So how hard can it be to find her?" She mumbled under her breath something about his being a detective after all, and the woman next to her grinned with the comment.

LaMoia said sternly, "Make some calls and find her. I'm on my cell phone." He started off at a walk and broke into a run as he avoided the elevator and took to the stairs. He had her mobile number ringing in his ear by the time he reached the fifth floor. Her voice mail answered. What was with that?

He called Special Ops dispatch from his office cubicle. They'd heard nothing about Matthews leaving the building. "You check the ladies' room?" the dispatcher asked.

LaMoia mumbled back at the man, incoherent. She wasn't in the bathroom—he knew this in his gut. Something, someone, had drawn her out of the building, and LaMoia was bound and determined to find out what was going on. He'd find Boldt, he'd page the day-shift squad detectives to call him back. He'd check with the lab, the MEs. Anyone else he could think of.

He'd broken into a clammy sweat. His eyes stung; his palms were damp.

What the hell was happening to him?

In addition to the pink telephone memo that had inappropriately interrupted the interrogation of Vanderhorst, Matthews found a voice mail on her cell phone as well. "Miss Matthews?" Margaret's warbling voice was itself enough to make Matthews feel sick. "I'm . . . I've screwed up, pretty bad. *Real bad.* You said to call. *So . . . so I'm calling.*" No address, no phone number. Matthews dug around in her jeans pocket and came up with the folded memo. *Thank God,* she thought, glad she'd saved it.

There wasn't any address to speak of, only the notation, "above Mario's." She pulled out the phone book and started thumbing through the yellow pages. She'd never felt right about Margaret's mention of a place to stay. A roof overhead was one thing, but the baby needed prenatal care, square meals, doctor visits. A flophouse above a pizza parlor? Was it a crack house, a cum shop, a shooting gallery? She found it finally in the white pages: Mario's Pizza. Time to move. She felt awful for having been out of touch with the girl, and especially for being unavailable for the past sixty minutes. With these girls, every minute counted. On the street, a life could change in a matter of seconds.

"Lost time," she informed the civilian administrative assistant who managed the seventh-floor secretary pool—and whereas the expression meant the time clock stopped for lower-rank personnel, for lieutenants and above it meant their offices would be vacant, their phones picked up by voice mail. The assistant slid a thumb-worn in/out marker on a wall poster that tracked such things, and returned to her typing.

Matthews's hand hovered over the phone on this assistant's desk as she debated calling Boldt, two floors down. The Vanderhorst interrogation had gone well—better than expected—the two of them finding a mutually inclusive rhythm that to Boldt must have felt like a pair of musicians trading riffs. She owed him a report and knew he wouldn't fancy her ducking out of the house until that homework was turned in. There was a series of psych tests to schedule; outside experts would have to be consulted to either support or challenge her professional evaluation. Each of these efforts required reports be written as well. The complications of multijurisdictional warrants caused by a four-state killing spree would consume over half the detectives on CAP, a good deal of SID's resources, and virtually all of her own time for the next several weeks. One man and his crimes would put a piece of SPD at a virtual standstill.

She tried LaMoia instead, the phone switching through to voice mail on the first ring, meaning he was either on the line or out of the office. She hadn't seen him since breakfast—his showing up at the loft with Blue on his heels and a bag of hot sesame bagels under his arm.

She left him a message that she was running an errand to help Margaret. She left the name of the pizza shop in SoDo. Her final attempt on the phone found Bobbie Gaynes at her desk.

"Would you mind taking an hour of lost time as a favor?" she asked.

"Name it, Lieutenant."

"Take a ride with me? I could use some backup. A young girl from the Shelter—pregnant out to here—just left me a message that she and the baby are in trouble. She's shacked up above this pizza joint, and I'm thinking if she's got a room, then there's a pimp or a dealer involved—you know what these girls get into." She added, "Two of us, that's better odds." She smiled, trying to win Gaynes over. If this grew into anything more than a quick favor, Lou would turn it into a surveillance ops.

"Give me five minutes. I'll meet you in the garage."

Driving south of the Safe a few minutes later, Gaynes asked, "Anything more I should know, Lieutenant?"

Matthews briefly explained her relationship with Margaret. She said, "I promised Lou I'd stay on the wire, but honestly, I don't want dispatch monitoring this conversation, because I also made a promise to the girl, weeks ago, that I'd respond as a woman, not as a cop."

"Those things only throw a signal about a hundred yards, Lieutenant. No way dispatch will monitor."

"Yes," Matthews said.

"So, I'll listen in from the car and provide backup as necessary."

"Yes, exactly."

"No problem," Gaynes said.

Traffic thinned past the two sports stadiums, the neighborhoods slowly deteriorating into a docklands, warehouse district.

As directed, Gaynes parked two blocks away from the pizza joint. She would drop Matthews off here and then move into position, closer to the shop, a minute later.

"So I lie low unless there's trouble," Gaynes asked. "If you need me, you want a code word?"

Matthews had considered something like this, but thought better of it. "No. I'll just scream for help."

Gaynes grinned. "Got it."

Her academy training and past experience caused Matthews to take a few extra minutes to scout the immediate area, fully circling the block that included Mario's Pizza.

On the last leg of this patrol, she spotted the chrome bumper and black trunk of a car parked down a narrow alley, less than a block from Mario's. She held closely to a wall of an abandoned building, edging near enough to read the black decal numbering on the left of the bumper: KCSO-89.

She gasped aloud, then for the sake of the lavaliere microphone clipped beneath her shirt, she said, "Bobbie, I've got Nathan Prair's patrol car in sight. One block south, on the west side of the street, down an alley. I'm going to take a closer look. Stand by."

She crossed the street, able to see through the car's back windshield as she approached. The car stood empty. Her heart pounding, she slipped into the shadows of the alley alongside the car and peered into both the front and back seats, ready for Prair to jump out and surprise her.

"Officer?" she called out, to no answer.

Had Margaret been involved with Prair all along? Had she notified Prair, asking for help, after failing to reach Matthews? Had some contact of Prair's at SPD leaked the teen's cry for help, inspiring attempted heroics on Prair's part aimed once again at impressing Matthews? A dozen thoughts circled inside her, and Matthews nearly swooned, briefly off-balance, reaching out to steady herself.

"Bobbie," she said, again speaking aloud into the cold air, for the sake of the small microphone clipped to her bra, "call KCSO and request . . . no, you had better make that *insist* . . . that you speak with Prair. When you reach him, find out what the hell his patrol car is doing a block from Mario's Pizza. Then call me back on the cell. I'll leave the cell on until I hear from you."

She crossed the street with a forced, stiff-legged stride, a renewed enthusiasm to get to the bottom of this. She resented the idea of Margaret being used as bait to get to her—if that's what was going on. Nathan Prair had stepped way out of bounds.

Then again, she didn't know what was going on—and that confusion made her all the more determined to find out.

52 A Good Shooting

LaMoia spotted Janise Meyer from a concrete bench within a few yards of the plaza fountain across from Westlake Center, his heart pounding with the possibility of what she carried. She wore an ankle-length khaki trench coat, the waist belt not fastened, but tied like a robe. Brown flats with bare brown ankles. Hair the color of midnight with matching eyebrows and lashes. Green eyes that screamed improbably of an Irishman somewhere in her African American heritage. Thick lips that curled into a provocative smile that he'd liked from the first time he'd met her. She adopted that same smirk now as she sat down on the bench next to him, a leather briefcase on her lap.

"So why the cloak and dagger, Cowboy?"

"You're smuggling out confidential paperwork there, Janise."

"Printouts of confidential paperwork," she reminded, passing the half ream of paper to him. "I could have e-mailed them to you, for Christ's sake. It would have saved me walking the six blocks over here."

"True story." LaMoia leafed through them. It had been a while since he'd ridden patrol. It took him a moment to orient himself to the small forms—citations for everything from speeding to parking violations. "Our e-mails are watched, right?" he asked the pro. "Listen, if I get in trouble for this, I wanted it on my head, not yours."

She accepted the closest coffee, lifting it out of his lap. She sipped through the small hole in the lid, savoring it. He remembered that about her—she treated a cup of coffee like it was an elixir. Treated a lot of things that way, come to think about it.

A pair of teenaged boys raced by on skateboards, testing new moves.

She said, "I don't know why you want this—him going over to Sheriff's and all, but that's what you got." She informed him, "Metro used to archive the traffic 'cites' on microfiche. Now it's all digitized."

LaMoia flipped pages while Janise enjoyed the coffee.

She said out of the side of her mouth, "Double-check stub number thirty-five MN seven thirty-two."

In trying to convert LaMoia to a love of jazz, Boldt had once told him that good music was as much about what was left out— what wasn't there—as the notes one heard. A true connoisseur of music learned to listen for what was missing. To LaMoia, that advice had been an oxymoron until the moment he turned to the citation Janise had mentioned. Prair's citation records from two years earlier were missing an entry for 35MN-732.

"You're shitting me," he let slip. The copy of 35MN-733, the next in sequence, carried ghostly images familiar to any cop who'd ever used a "carbonless" ticket book—the ballpoint pen impression from the missing carbon of 732 had carried through to 733, the result of forgetting to insert a divider ahead of the next record. The same thing happened to LaMoia with his checkbook. It took a moment for his eyes to decipher one entry from the next. The fainter impressions slowly began to stand out in his mind's eye.

A minute later an excited LaMoia was on his cell phone to the Department of Licensing, reciting a tag number to a bored bureaucrat on the other end. "I need it A-SAP," he said.

Janise Meyer pulled the coffee away from her lips and said,

"Damn, Cowboy, you get any more worked up, you gonna blow a valve or something."

LaMoia made eyes at her, not wanting to speak with the open line.

She said, "What's so special about a missing citation, other than it's against regs to tear one from a book?"

The woman on the phone calmly read the name of the owner of the vehicle back to him. LaMoia thanked her and disconnected the call.

"Dana Eaton," he said, his brain locked on the name.

On hearing the name, Janise spilled the coffee down her front and wiped it away quickly, cursing him. "*The* Dana Eaton?" There wasn't a cop on SPD that didn't know that name—a name beaten into the entire population by a media feeding frenzy.

Janise yanked the pages out of LaMoia's lap and flipped back and forth, checking the dates of the traffic citations immediately before and after the one that was missing. "Can't be right," she said. "This is like two *months* before the shooting." It took a moment to sink in. "Are you telling me he *knew* that woman?"

LaMoia couldn't get a word out. He'd sensed it all along; only now could he actually prove it hadn't been a "good shooting" after all.

Nathan Prair was going to jail.

Mario—if there even was a Mario—had found some cheap real estate that still remained in striking distance for delivery downtown. The building looked older than God. The neighborhood, no stranger to police patrols, was a favorite for gang activity, a warehouse and light industrial region in decay over a decade, since software had overcome hardware in the bid for the local economy. Brick and broken asphalt played host to the rusted carcasses of stripped cars. Five minutes from prosperity.

Mario's had a take-out counter, two cooks, four runners, a pair of enormous ovens, and alternative rock playing at dangerous decibels over shredded speakers. The Rastafarian currently engaged with a phone order lifted a finger indicating he'd be right with her. Hanging up, he barked across the small room to a skinny woman in her late teens. The girl wore too many earrings to count. The wanna-be-a-gangsta white boy next to her, his arms covered in the purple lace of spiderwebs and barbed-wire tattoos, his hands in disposable gloves—thank God!—seeded a pie with sliced mushrooms.

She let her shield wallet fall open, displaying her creds. "Is there a pregnant girl upstairs?"

"Could be," the Rastafarian answered. He hadn't had time to study her shield, so he impressed her when he said, "What's a lieutenant doing on the street?"

"You the landlord?"

"Not hardly. Manager is all. You the Apartment Police?" This was a game to him.

"Margaret." Matthews said. "Her name is Margaret."

"Is that right?"

"I'm here to give her a leg up."

"I just bet you are."

"When was the last time City Health stopped by for an inspection?"

"Room two," he said. "It's on the left."

"What about the deputy sheriff?"

"Who?"

"His car's around the block."

"So he's getting a hummer from one of the charmers in the hood. What's new?"

She studied his face and found herself believing him. In her mind, Prair had to be hooked up with Margaret's situation— either as a friend or the enemy. She wasn't eager to run into him. He was good at staying hidden and out of the way, and she kept that in mind as well.

"Who's in the other rooms up there?" she asked.

He eyed her suspiciously.

She said, "Who am I going to run into in the hall?"

"There's no one going to throw shots at you, if that's what you mean."

"That's what I mean."

She produced a twenty from her purse and placed it on the counter. She said, "Hold the anchovies," and made the guy smile. Lousy teeth. She made it forty, total. "Anyone up there with Margaret?"

"I don't even know that she's up there, lady."

"Within the realm of possibility," she suggested.

"Listen, they think I don't know, but there're three of them sharing what's barely big enough for one. Young girls."

Matthews withdrew her gun from the purse and chambered a round. It all came down to a show of power on the streets. You were either a player or not. She understood the psychology, though lacked some of the courage. She said, "I don't need anyone crashing my party. Should I give you a minute to let anyone know, or what?"

"People are in and out of there all the time, *Lieutenant*." The way he emphasized her rank, she knew he'd made her for the desk jockey she was. He said, "You do what you gotta do."

The stairway entrance to the apartments was outside the take-out door and to the left. She glanced across the street to where Gaynes had parked the car. In theory, Gaynes was making every attempt to raise Prair. Matthews bootlegged her weapon on the way up the dingy and dirty stairwell, choking on the smell of urine. In situations like this—tenement busts—it was surprise that cost cops their lives. Reaction time proved longer than the thought process. Twelve-year-olds with water pistols took a bullet.

The upstairs hallway was empty and dimly lit. Either her man downstairs had cleared the area, or she'd gotten lucky. The gun felt an inappropriate way to greet Margaret, but it wouldn't feel right in the handbag, either. She let it fall to her side and knocked. "Margaret, it's me," she announced. Either that registered or not, she wasn't calling out any more details.

She heard footsteps approaching the door and found herself relieved that Margaret could walk, was not prone on the bed delivering the baby prematurely. For this had been her most recent thought: contractions. Margaret about to give birth.

"Just a minute." The sound of the girl's voice filled Matthews with gratitude. She resolved not to abandon her, to stay with her until whatever was the problem was fully resolved.

She heard a pair of locks come off the door. She felt herself grip the handgun more tightly and braced herself for bloodshot eyes, jaundiced skin, the girl's water having broken—whatever terror she next confronted. The apartment door came open. She'd been crying, her face blotchy, her nose running, her cheeks silver with tears. She wore torn leggings, a loose dress from Goodwill. She trembled head to toe with fever, her forehead beaded with perspiration. Or maybe it was toxic shock or a reaction to some drug she'd taken. The girl could not bring herself to look at Matthews, eyes downcast. *Embarrassed,* Matthews thought.

A combination of horror, sympathy, and righteous indignation charged her system, and again she promised to see this through. Hebringer and Randolf were dead—they could wait awhile. This girl still had a chance.

"It's okay," Matthews said. The door fell fully open. She peeked through the crack before stepping inside. The room was empty. "You did the right thing in calling me."

"I don't know about that."

The sad, cheerless room was barely bigger than a bathroom stall. Soiled sheets covered a thin mattress on a steel-framed bed. If three women lived here, they shared that bed, nearly on top of each other. A corner sink housed a faucet that dripped, a teardrop of green patina below. The toilet had to be down the hall. A wooden closet bar sat across the corner diagonally holding a handful of empty wire hangers. The room's only window looked barely big enough for egress. The room smelled of girls, of mildew, and of sweat, all overpowered by the nauseating aroma of tomato sauce and something burning.

Margaret sat down, paralyzed on the edge of the bed. She began crying again. "I'm so sorry," she moaned, repeating it over and over.

Matthews secured the weapon and stored it in her purse. She eased down alongside of the girl. Matthews said, "Well . . . it's good to see you've got a roof over your head."

Matthews heard footsteps out in the hall draw closer. She experienced a jolt of heat like hormones gone bad. Margaret looked up, struggled to sober up, her eyes clearly fixing onto Matthews as she whispered hoarsely, "He said he'd kill the baby."

"Who—?" But in that instance, Matthews felt her eyes refocus on a tiny hole freshly drilled through the room's side wall. The plaster's white dust had settled on the floor like a tiny pile of snow. She rotated her head toward the door. *Unlocked!* She realized the oversight too late. She'd answered her own question: a fisherman. The department had hung her out as bait for Walker, but he'd baited her instead. Despite her earlier planning for this possibility, the minute or two with Margaret had pushed all that aside.

Ferrell Walker came through the door, catching Matthews flat-footed and a beat behind. She grabbed for her purse, but his knife severed the leather strap and it fell to the floor, where he kicked it away. The knife was familiar. The curved blade a deceptive dull gray from hours of hand sharpening.

Suddenly the door was shut and Margaret in his grip, the knife held below her bulging belly.

"Who's the friend in the Ford?" he asked, the first words out of his mouth. He leaned forward, cheek to cheek with Margaret. "She betrayed you," he said. "Just like she betrayed me." He met eyes with Matthews as he took Margaret in a choke hold, the knife suddenly at her belly. If he used it, she'd come open like a piece of ripe fruit.

"They have me under surveillance," she said. Rule number one: Never lie in a hostage situation. For the sake of Bobbie Gaynes, monitoring her every word, she added hastily, "Put the knife down, *Ferrell*."

He backed up to the window and glanced furtively outside.

"Shit! Call her off." Below him, no doubt, Gaynes was already on the move.

"How do I do that, Ferrell?" Matthews asked, stalling. She pointed to the door. "Should I go out—"

"YOU CALL HER OFF!" He tightened his grip on Margaret, pulling the knife lower.

"My purse. My cell phone," Matthews said.

Walker eyed the purse on the floor . . . back to Matthews . . . the door to the room . . . out the window.

She was thinking that peepers don't kill and that Walker was clearly a peeper from the Underground, a person satisfied with phone harassment, a grief-stricken lost soul who'd lost his way. Only then did she notice what looked like fresh blood on the man's sneakers and the bottoms of his pants. Only then did she realize she'd played this wrong.

He said, "So we give them something to keep them busy." With that, he dragged the knife across Margaret's belly, muffling her cry with his left hand, and let her sag to the floor in a pool of the impossible.

Matthews screamed out and charged, but took the butt end of the knife in the forehead and her lights dimmed. As she struggled up to consciousness, she felt him pulling on her arms, dragging her across the floor. Margaret's crimson cry huddled beneath the window, the fingers of her right hand dancing like a typist's in an erratic, bloodless twitch.

"You son of a bitch," she groaned as she threw up just outside the door. Walker pulled her to her feet and pushed her. She stumbled forward down the hall, leading the way. "She'll bleed out," she said, trusting Gaynes to hear. "Where's this hallway lead?" Again, for the sake of the microphones.

He pressed the point of the knife into her back, and she felt it cut through her skin. "What's that blood on your clothes?"

she asked. "Did you harm Lanny Neal?" She hoped to hell Gaynes was getting this. Her vision blurred, but she tried to keep watch for the detective, tried to prepare to make a move that would allow a shot. With his next shove, Walker encountered the bulge of metal hardware taped to her back. His arm suddenly came around her throat as he tore the device loose, wires and all, and smashed it under his right heel. The shirt of LaMoia's that she wore ripped from her armpit to her waist.

This was not the Ferrell Walker she had ever expected. The psychologist in her looked for the telltales she'd missed, the source of the violence he displayed. Twice now he'd mentioned her betrayal of him. He'd made that connection between Mary-Ann and her—both "leaving him" for someone else. LaMoia, in her case. A spark of dread filled her as she realized she'd warned LaMoia and Boldt of this very event—her abduction. So here it was, nothing like she'd imagined it.

He pushed her again, and she wobbled forward on unsteady legs.

They were two steps down the slanting staircase when a winded Gaynes rounded the landing. Without hesitation, as if he'd practiced this a hundred times, he let go of Matthews, shoving her off balance so that she tumbled down the stairs, knocking into Gaynes like a bowling ball chasing a pin. Gaynes, two-handing her weapon during her ascent, aimed the gun low and swiveled to avoid Matthews, but went down hard. Walker, showing no interest in the gun, kicked it away and then smashed his foot down on the detective's wrists, first the right, then the left. He dropped a knee squarely onto her chest, seized her by the hair, and smashed her skull down onto the flooring, rendering her unconscious. This was a man who could pin a squirming four-hundred-pound halibut.

He dragged Matthews by the arms until she scrambled to walk under her own power, her legs riddled with splinters. He led her to and through a door that opened up on the back side of the building, where a kid in a white apron smeared with tomato sauce leaned against the brick smoking a joint. That apron reminded Matthews of the first time she'd met Ferrell Walker. It seemed like a year ago now. *Hopefully,* she thought, *not a lifetime ago.*

"Get the fuck out of here," Walker said, making no attempt to disguise his holding Matthews captive.

The kid mumbled "Fuck off" as he snubbed the joint and rolled to his right, turning his back on them. A street assault was nothing new to him.

Walker stopped her at the corner, peering out into the mostly deserted street. A pair of delivery trucks lumbered past. He slipped the bloodied knife away with the expertise of a swordsman, held her firmly by the arm, and said, "You stay close, or I feed you to the crabs." He fought with her as he led her across the street. In regaining her feet, in being set into motion, she awoke from the stupor brought on by Margaret's evisceration. It was one thing to respond to crime, quite another to witness it, this act of his catching her squarely in the crosshairs. She understood in those few hurried moments of crossing the street, of heading down yet another litter-strewn alley, that her very survival depended on her ability to quickly and accurately pinpoint Walker's mind-set, the motivations and factors that had turned him from a benign mourner into an unpredictable, homicidal killer. Some trigger had been thrown, and she believed her continued existence turned on her ability to identify it, expose it, and manipulate it to her advantage.

As if hearing her internal thoughts, he turned to her halfway down the alley and said with wild eyes, "Don't worry, you're going to like this."

That made her worry all the more.

They stopped in front of a steel-plate manhole marked

SWD—Seattle Water Department. Walker retrieved a crude tool fashioned from bent rebar that he'd hidden behind a pile of soggy cardboard boxes. The reinforcing rod was bent like a giant meat hook. He instructed Matthews to sit down on the pavement, and she obeyed, ill prepared to try to outrun the man. He slipped the hook end of the bent rod through a ventilation hole in the manhole cover and hoisted the heavy lid. It came off the exposed hole with a rattle of metal. As he did so, she used the cover of the noise to reach behind her, grope down her backside, and tear loose the small tag inside her panties. She let it fall onto the pavement. *Leave them crumbs,* she thought, her cop's mind beginning to separate from her personal emotions.

A flicker of light swept through the looming darkness that seemed to overwhelm her at that moment. She was letting him win without intending it. She said to him, "We *found* the room, Ferrell. The bodies. We know all about it." She saw disappointment crease his face—she'd guessed the contents of the gift before allowing him to unwrap it for her.

He told her to get to her feet. He pointed down the black hole in the pavement. "Ladies first," he said.

54 Circling the Drain

The early reports of the situation were sketchy at best, and Boldt tried not to overreact. His tendency, when hearing one officer was down and another *missing,* was to assume the best while preparing for the worst. The job rarely involved much good news, and he'd developed a fairly thick skin, but one learned not to creatively interpret a simple radio code.

That this call involved members of his own unit—one a protégé and friend, the other his friend and former lover—proved the exception to the rule. He fell to pieces with the news. Monitoring the tense radio traffic, he determined that ambulances were headed to the scene. Reports included a woman—quite possibly a civilian—badly cut and bleeding out. The pit in his stomach grew to nausea as he caught himself hoping that the vic *was* a civilian, a line he had no right to cross.

He rushed down the hall to the men's room, the nausea escalating to where he felt his stomach preparing to void. In all his years on the job he'd never vomited over an earful of radio traffic.

He put out the fire with a dose of cold water to the face, and it worked. The nausea receded into a world of anger and frustration. *What the hell had Daphne been thinking?* She'd skipped out of Public Safety without notifying Special Ops. In a gust of ill temper, he slammed his palms down onto the sink with such force that he knocked the entire fixture off the wall. Water sprayed from broken pipes. Boldt jumped back, as the ceramic sink broke into several chunks that echoed as a small explosion.

Detective Gerald Millhouse rushed into the room fearing he'd be calling the bomb squad. "Shit, Boss. I'd thought we'd lost you."

Boldt moved back and away from the encroaching flood of water on the tile floor. He heard Millhouse and knew well enough he should respond, but instead he found himself locked into a trance as he watched that floor water coil in waves as it formed an ever-tightening spiral and slipped down the floor drain.

Inevitably, you overlook the obvious, he thought, recalling the clichéd line lectured to all rookie detectives. It was a Boldt version of Murphy's Law that he'd seen in action more times than he liked.

"Lieutenant?" It was Millhouse again, trying to win his attention.

Boldt flushed crimson with embarrassment, not over his having broken a sink, but for having overlooked the simple law of gravity.

His instruction to Millhouse was oblique, for his mind was working too quickly to form a perfect sentence. "Dr. Sandra Babcock, Archaeology Department at the U." He racked his brain for the name of the bus tunnel maintenance man. Couldn't find it. Then, there it was. "And a Chuck Iberson over at WS-DOT . . . Third Avenue bus tunnel maintenance. Find them both and get them over here to the Pioneer Square station, A-SAP. No tears."

Millhouse lowered his voice and said tentatively, "But Boss, you heard about Matthews and Gaynes, right?"

"You'll be chalking tires if those two aren't in that bus tunnel in ten minutes," Boldt replied matter-of-factly.

Millhouse fled the men's room in a panic.

Boldt fought to keep emotion out of the decision-making process, fought the urge to fly down the fire stairs, climb into the Crown Vic, and race to the crime scene. He put the victims first, and one of them was missing. An extremely important one.

The water, collected on the floor, kept "circling the drain," police-speak for all hope being lost. But Boldt knew he wasn't lost at all—he'd just found the missing piece to the puzzle.

55 Darkness, My Old Friend . . .

The space—an old tunnel of some sort—was wet, dark, and cramped. They had reached it fairly quickly by following a city storm sewer north a good several blocks. Walker had removed a large grate mounted in the side of the storm sewer and pushed her through. Matthews now walked hunched over, stepping sometimes through gooey mud, sometimes ankle-deep in extremely cold water. It smelled of earth and loam and vaguely of the sea. She paid little or no attention at all to the slimy objects in her path, which to her spoke volumes of the more pressing need to find a way out of this situation, for normally she would have reeled at the tangled contact with cobwebs and the awful sensation of the disgusting, unseen objects sucking past her bare ankles.

Walker remained behind her, egging her on with sharp jabs of his fingers in the small of her back, the first few of which she had thought were the knife. She had long since lost all sense of direction. His small flashlight provided the only light—it amounted to her shifting shadow stretching long and thin on the tunnel's earthen walls.

Somewhere behind and above them lay Margaret with her abdomen sliced open and Gaynes, unconscious. A by-the-book detective, Gaynes would have called in a "510" requesting backup before she moved on the building. By now, Matthews could assume that backup was already on the scene. Lou would have been consulted. John would have been informed. A controlled but professional panic was sweeping through Public Safety, and she was the focus of it all. She had to stall Walker in order to buy herself time. She had to get to the surface. She possessed the facilities to accomplish both goals, as long as she kept herself collected and focused. The mind tended to jump almost randomly from one thought to another in such situations—the professional in her was very much aware of this. She needed focus. She needed clear, linear thought.

The floor of the tunnel dried to packed earth—they were on dirt now. At first she thought the crunching beneath her feet was gravel or rock. She encountered areas like this every twenty yards or so; there was no predicting when, or how much. Then she realized it was crushing under her footfalls, not merely shifting as gravel might. The dirt floor suddenly sparkled to life, a thousand jewels, and she realized they were walking atop broken glass—broken bottles, to be more accurate—the *smugglers' tunnel*.

With no idea where she was headed, she nonetheless knew where she was, and this tiny seed of knowledge strengthened her, emboldened her to begin the task of breaking him down, piece by piece.

"This is kind of fun," she said strongly, gathering in her strength and forcing it out her lungs. When the flashlight flickered away from her, she dropped a gold stud earring onto the dirt floor. *Another crumb,* she hoped.

Walker stumbled behind her, and she mentally marked one down in her column. The first of such marks. Hopefully, not the last.

56 The Tag

LaMoia stared at the rear bumper of KCSO patrol car #89, the phalanx of police and emergency vehicles only a block behind him. The pregnant girl was critical. Gaynes was conscious but in extreme pain, and was being carted off to Emergency. At that moment, he might have believed Nathan Prair had abducted Matthews, except for Gaynes having told him it was Walker. Now he came to believe the obvious: that Prair had either responded to the same cry for help from the girl that Matthews had received, or that he'd intercepted the 510, the SPD radio call for backup, and had responded in hopes of rescuing Matthews himself.

"Over my dead body," LaMoia heard himself say aloud.

He searched the car and found it locked. He searched the alley and found nothing but trash, a few needles, and the rotting carcass of a dead cat. The buildings off this alley were secure as well. The more he studied the situation, the more he believed Prair had simply stashed the car here so it might avoid being seen. He had wanted to buy himself a head start, and that pissed off LaMoia all the more. It would be just like Prair to observe something like this going down, only to realize too late that he'd better *do* something.

LaMoia left the alley, returning into the street, and carefully searched the block back toward Mario's Pizza and the tenement that housed it, now off to his left. LaMoia knew Special Ops

CO Chatwin to be a Neanderthal incapable of thinking outside the box. Matthews, in all her prescience, had nailed this on the head. Chatwin had his ERT troops and a traffic helicopter searching the surface streets—an urban commando exercise he was both familiar with and comfortable in exercising. LaMoia's brief plea to designate a unit to search for an access to the Underground had left him snubbed. "What, you think this is fucking Disneyland, Sergeant?"

"The kidnapper has an established history of subterranean access." LaMoia tried his best to make this sound official. But he couldn't maintain his composure once Chatwin dismissed the suggestion. LaMoia said, "With all due respect, he's a fucking troglodyte, sir. We've got him directly linked to at least two different areas of the Underground beneath the city."

"What, the tourist place?" Chatwin asked, and LaMoia realized that any attempt at an explanation was not worth the wind.

"You're looking in the wrong place," he tried, one final time.

"Process of elimination, Sergeant. I'll entertain your suggestion, but we work this my way first."

"Yes, sir."

"I'm CO," he reminded, a little miffed by LaMoia's tone.

"Yes, sir."

"If you want to be of help, get in your car and log in with dispatch. We could use you."

"I don't want to be of help, sir."

Checking the street carefully now, LaMoia wanted to avoid another encounter with Chatwin at all costs. He held to his own. Another alley up ahead caught his attention. The ERT guys had rushed through this area like a tornado. They'd been looking for an abductor and hostage. LaMoia was looking for something else entirely: access to an escape route Walker might have used. Matthews had labeled the man an organized personality, and that was good enough for him. She'd foreseen her own abduction.

Who was he going to trust? He intended to work the scene methodically, as he'd been trained to do by Boldt, one of the best in the business.

He rounded the corner into that next alley, wondering all of a sudden where the hell Boldt was. Matthews as a hostage and the Sarge nowhere to be seen? The guy would have to be either locked up or dead to be kept from this crime scene.

His eyes lighted on that white fabric tab from fifteen yards away, the glare of his penlight illuminating the improbable color in a world of mud brown and ash gray. Perfect, pure, white. It called out as if it had yelled at him. He headed to it like a bloodhound—the thought of which made him wonder if the K-9 unit had been called up. He bent and retrieved it.

Victoria's Secret, size medium.

There was no sound, no night air, no sirens, no radio squawks, no movement in his universe, only his trembling fingers and that white fabric tag clasped so tightly.

Debating whether or not to call for backup, he looked quickly around for something with which to lift that manhole cover. She had made it plain to him that if she went missing, she trusted him to do what was right. Chatwin seemed certain to bungle this, putting Matthews at risk. Backup could wait until he knew the full situation.

Victoria's Secret. He would tease her about that when he found her. And he *would* find her, he told himself. He had to. It was the only way he knew. John LaMoia *always* got the girl.

57 Another Level

"Where'd all the water go?" Boldt asked Iberson and Babcock. She wore blue jeans, a brown sweater, and rubber boots. Iberson was dressed for the ball game in tennis shoes, khakis, and a red thin shell that zipped down the front. The two looked back at him blankly. A double dragon swept past them, lifting dust and sand and grit in its wake. The bus tunnel's oddly sterile mercury vapor lighting turned everyone's skin a bluish green.

Boldt said, "The water main. All that water . . . enough to drown a man. So where'd it go? Where'd it end up?" He said to Babcock, "It was damp but not flooded in that lower level."

Iberson answered, "I told you, it came out our wall vents."

"Some of it, sure. But all of it?" Boldt asked.

"Enough to shut us down," Iberson reminded.

Babcock understood him. "What prompted this?" she asked.

He wasn't interested in such chitchat. "We have an officer wounded. Another's missing. A girl, a young woman, is in critical condition and probably won't make it. I'm up against a clock here. The guy I'm after got hold of that key on that lower level. That suggests access that we don't know about. The water from that broken main, it went somewhere. And not just here, into this tunnel. Most of it *had* to have gone down to that lower level—that's just physics. So what happened to it? It should have been a swimming pool down there."

Babcock lost a shade. She nodded. "You're right. Of course, you're right."

"Is anybody going to fill me in?" an irritated Iberson asked.

Boldt had left Iberson behind, focusing now only on the academic. "But where? Another level? A sewer system? An aquifer?" He had trouble getting the words out, the bubble in his chest from Matthews missing too big to swallow away.

He picked up a flicker in her eyes. "What?" he asked. She shook her head. "Anything," he stressed. "He's got our officer underground somewhere. I'd guarantee you that."

"Rumors is all," she said, her throat dry, her words raspy.

Boldt nodded furiously. "I'll take rumors."

"There are old references to a smugglers' tunnel. Supposedly, it connected speakeasies and the hotels to the waterfront during Prohibition. Dug by the Chinese. Controlled by the Chinese mafia in those days," said the historian.

"The International District?" He thought of Mama Lu, the very woman who had set him on this quest in the first place. Matthews had gone missing within a stone's throw of the I.D. "Connecting this place to the I.D.?"

"I'm just saying it's possible. Not probable. Not even *likely*."

Boldt yanked out his cell phone and then shouted at Iberson. "I've got to get topside. I've got to make a phone call."

Iberson flagged down the next bus that approached. Boldt and Babcock hit the surface streets less than two minutes later.

58 The Offering

The low tunnel bent around a turn, a good deal of the wooden posts and beams—old railroad ties in all probability—badly rotted. Matthews struggled to fight off the fear that wanted to own her.

Walker stopped her, instructing her to stand out of his way. They hadn't traveled terribly far, the going slow. She watched as his fading flashlight caught the edge of a large hole in the earthen wall. Walker stepped up to it and peered inside, and she came away with the sense that it was familiar to him.

She couldn't see into that hole, but she prayed silently that he wasn't going to make her go through it. It looked like one of those places a person never came out of. It failed to give her any sense of hope that it might lead to an escape route.

Walker turned and faced her, shining the light first onto her, then directing it onto himself, enabling her to see him. In a childish tone that sent shivers through her, he said, "It's important to me you know how much I care."

"Ferrell—"

He shushed her and said, "To understand the extent to which I'm prepared to go to help you. You found the room. It's why . . ." His voice tapered off.

She worried he couldn't hold a thought, that the synapses might be misfiring in his brain, either as a result of stress or some organic malfunction that she'd failed to identify in the course of her contact with him. That face-to-face contact had, in fact, been precious little. "Why what?" she asked.

"Well . . . it's the purpose of all this," he explained.

"So if we've already accomplished that purpose, Ferrell . . . maybe we should head up topside together."

"It's way beyond that now, isn't it?" He tried to smile, but his unwilling face would only pinch further, into a snarl. "Come look. It's for *you*."

"No, thank you."

"Come. Look." His hand went to the butt of the knife, and Matthews felt herself moving, as if on the ends of marionette strings.

"I'd like to go back up to the street now," she said, pressing for his cooperation in a period where he acted at least somewhat conciliatory toward her.

He positioned her in front of that dark hole in the wall. It looked as if a course of water had ripped loose this rent some years before. The sickening smile he managed should have forewarned her. He turned slowly, training that yellow light with him.

Sitting on a natural throne carved out of the mud like some kind of shrine was a decapitated corpse of a man in a brown uniform. Matthews cried out loudly and jumped back, as the flashlight caught up to the head of Nathan Prair that sat in his own lap, his big hands coddling it.

"For you," Walker said. "He was bothering you, right? I saw you two outside the Shelter that night we were supposed to meet. I saw you push him. Him grab you . . ." His voice trailed off as he realized she was upset with this, not pleased as he'd intended. "You were . . . upset . . . with him."

Walker had been watching her outside the Shelter on the night they'd agreed to meet—the night Nathan Prair had arrived unexpectedly, a result, no doubt, of a phone call or message from Walker himself. She realized he must have followed her back to LaMoia's—probably knowing about the loft already—must have gone through that window to leave the key as she'd taken Blue for a walk. He'd been playing her all along like a fisherman with a prize catch.

Her vision zoomed in on the faint edge of that light in a staccato way that brought everything closer to her in a series of jerky movements: Prair's service pistol was still snapped into the holster on his work belt, now, just to the right of his ear. Next to it, an unmarked black can of pepper spray. Next to that, a Maglite. Walker, who had shown no interest in Gaynes's weapon, had clearly ignored Prair's as well. It took every ounce of strength and composure she could summon, but she stepped forward, toward the shrine. "I was upset with him," she said. "You're right about that." She made a point of making contact with Walker and allowing a smile to grace her lips. "You did this for me?"

Walker nodded, but his eyes ticked back and forth distrustfully as he sought out hers, and she wondered which Walker had come out to play, the one with the boyish crush on her or the knife-wielding woman killer?

She edged yet another step closer to both Walker and that hole, wondering if she could bring herself to dive in there with that severed head, reach the gun, and still have enough time to present it as a threat. The air tasted metallic and smelled putrid.

"I wanted to help," Walker said.

"It's not what I expected."

"I love surprises," he said.

Gooseflesh chased up her arms and down her spine.

She said, "Do you? Oh, good." With that, she recoiled, wound up, and then leaned forward, driving her weight into the shove that lifted Walker off his feet and sent him flying. She dived to her left, into that hole, slipped and scrambled up the muddy slope, facedown next to Prair's severed head as she fumbled with the holster's snap, grabbed hold of the weapon, racked the slide to chamber a round, thumbed the safety off, and rolled. Walker was on his feet, at the mouth of the hole, as she squeezed the trigger. *Click.* The trigger then stuck. She frantically tried to clear the jammed round as Walker took hold of her ankles and pulled, dropping her flat onto her back. Prair's head rolled off of his lap and up onto her chest, and she threw it aside, screaming. She felt the weight of the gun then, and she knew: Its magazine was missing. Walker had emptied the gun. Walker had baited her, yet again.

He clicked his tongue against the roof of his mouth, shaming her. "Someone's been a bad girl," he said.

She lunged for the can of pepper spray in Prair's belt.

"Empty," Walker called out.

She threw the weapon at him, but he deflected it.

"I've never liked guns," he said. "I feel much safer with this." He held the curved gray blade between them.

Bloodstained and mud-covered, Matthews took a moment to regain her breath. She had disassociated from him, a conscious effort on her part that now would not come without consequences. He had tested her, and she had been suckered into it. And she had failed.

"It changes everything," he said sadly. "You know that, don't you?"

There were no words for her, only a pounding heart, a dry tongue, and the chills that came with the knowledge of what she had done. She chastised herself for that decision—she'd allowed the emotion of fear to overcome any hope of rationally negotiating her way out. Had she been outside of this, observing it, she could have identified the victim's bad decision making at every turn. But from inside her own cloistered fear, she felt only punishment for her will to survive and the internal strength to act upon it.

"On your feet, Anna," he said, not hearing his own slip.

Metaphorically, she saw light at the end of the tunnel. Then she realized it was for real: There *was* light up ahead.

"We're going to go join your friends," he said.

Hebringer and Randolf, the only two "friends" she could think of.

"We're going to get to know each other."

She needed some way to attempt to rekindle rapport, even if she played into his fantasy that she was none other than his sister. She searched wildly for a nickname a sister might have used for a younger brother at some point in their long relationship. She settled on the first nickname to pop into her head, literally a stab in the dark. "I already know you . . . Ferris Wheel."

Walker snapped his head toward her. He stared at her until she felt him looking *through* her, not at her. Her head ached, but she kept it up. "You think Anna didn't know that you watched her and Lanny Neal? Of course she did, Ferris Wheel."

He shoved her. She staggered back but did not fall. Nathan Prair's head, sideways in the mud now, watched them.

Matthews said, "Is that what caused the split between you? Your watching?"

He shoved her again, and this time she went down hard in the mud, face first, on all fours. Her right hand hit a piece of glass and cut. The smell that kicked up was putrid and sickening. He trained the light down onto her, but by the time he did she'd picked the sizeable piece of curved glass out of her palm, and had transferred it to her left hand, now curled around it. She rubbed her bleeding hand on her pants, and Walker noticed the wound.

"Shit," he said, the child that didn't mean to hurt the family pet. "Up ahead there's this wall. We'll rest there. Clean that up."

She gained a few yards on him. She wasn't going to run

away, but she wanted some physical space in which to clear her mind, regain herself. She recalled all that LaMoia had told her about the interview with the barmaid, Walker's former girl-friend. "The trouble began after your father died, didn't it?" The pain in her hand lessened. She decided she had to keep talking, free association, whatever came out of her mouth. Just keep talking. "It was just the two of you on the boat after that."

"So what?"

"Pretty close quarters for a man and a woman."

"It wasn't like that."

"No?" Her mind worked furiously through several sets of possibilities. She'd try them all if she had to. "You think you're the first guy to ever watch his sister? Give me a break." Con-descending. Mary-Ann would have dominated their relationship. She sorted out several planes of thought on which to operate, areas of possible vulnerability for him. She had him talking— that was the important step. She didn't want to lose that for anything. Until now the mud had disgusted her, but as it came to cover her, to own her, she felt in a primitive state, capable of almost anything. Prepared to strike.

"Shut up about her," he said.

"No, I don't think so," she fired back. He moved her down the tunnel. The mud walls weeped in places. If she sneezed hard, the ceiling was coming down. "Why do you think you picked me, Ferrell? I'll tell you why: Because I listen, because I made sense from the very first time we spoke. It was at the docks. Do you remember?"

"Of course I remember."

"You liked the way I looked, sure. They all do, Ferrell." She wanted to make him as small as she could, for *both* their sakes. "But more important, you liked what I said." She didn't remem-ber what she'd said, not exactly, but she knew something had initiated the transference, and she felt determined to unlock that key. "You knew I could help you, didn't you?" she asked. "It's why you haven't given up on me."

"Oh, but I have," he said, chilling her.

"No, you haven't."

He raised the knife blade in the dim light and spun it back and forth so that it threw light across her face. Margaret's blood had dried onto that knife. "Got me all figured out, do you?" It flashed again. "Maybe not," he said. "Maybe the fuck not."

She stood her ground. Plan two. "You picked me for a reason, Ferrell."

"Because you told me to."

"I told you to what?"

"At the morgue," he said. "You told me there was no one else in the room. You said to put Mary-Ann where you were . . . and I did that . . . and when you spoke, I heard her voice, just like you said I would. You were right."

"I'm not Anna, Ferrell, am I? Look at me. Listen to me closely. Your sister is dead."

"Going for that gun just now?" he said. "That was impressive. That was something Anna would have done." She felt his eyes encompassing her. "It was a mistake, but it was ballsy."

"How do you think seeing that knife makes me feel? How would Anna feel? You think I want to get to know you when you're holding that knife, threatening me with that knife?"

"You said you already know me," he reminded.

She didn't want to think of him as smart, didn't want him focusing on her attempt to escape, deciding to challenge him yet again in an attempt to keep him off-balance. "You didn't find that sweatshirt, did you, Ferrell? I missed that, didn't I?"

"Don't know what you're talking about." But he most certainly did.

"Mary-Ann's sweatshirt," she said. "You didn't find that sweatshirt. You *already knew* where it was."

"What?" His voice betrayed him. He sheathed the knife, taking time to draw its blade clean on his jeans. This victory instilled her with a sense of courage.

"You knew where Neal hid his car key."

"Enough of this."

"You'd been with them that night he'd misplaced the other key. A birthday, wasn't it?"

"I said, *enough!*"

"How did you get her to just sit there while you backed over her, Ferrell?"

He screamed, "Shut . . . your . . . mouth!" and she knew she'd scored a direct hit.

"Up ahead, we'll rest a minute," she said, wanting it to sound like it was her idea, to take control away from him. She was starting to understand that Walker's transference had gone beyond what she'd previously imagined. He'd not only transferred his feelings for Mary-Ann onto her, but he'd transferred his own guilt onto Lanny Neal in the form of blame.

She heard his breathing—quick, shallow intakes—and realized they'd switched roles. She had him back on his heels now, and didn't want to stop.

"You can't replace her, Ferrell. Not with me, not with anybody. You can't change what has happened, as much as you'd like to, and repeating what you've done—it's what you have in mind, isn't it?—that won't help anything. It'll just make it worse. The pain, I'm talking about. I know all about the pain. It'll be much, much worse." She defiantly and purposely turned her back on him before he had a chance to recover from that. She marched forward toward the resting place he'd told her about.

"You betrayed me," she heard from behind her, and she knew this was about Mary-Ann, not herself.

She worked with something Neal had told them, saying over

her shoulder, "You begged her for money . . . to go back out on the boat with you. It's not what she wanted. She wanted a life. What did you expect, Ferrell?"

"I . . . saved . . . her," Walker said. "She . . . owed . . . me."

She stopped, turned. "Saved her from Lanny Neal, from herself," she purposely hesitated, wanting this next thought to sink in, "or from *you*? That part of you that thought about her in ways that brothers aren't supposed to think about their sisters."

Walker stepped close enough that she could smell his familiar stench. "From *him*!" he said, as agitated as she'd ever seen him. "I saved her from *him*." His eyes darted to the left, and she knew he regretted having revealed whatever it was he'd just revealed.

Without meaning to, Matthews gasped aloud. She'd missed the catalyst all along. It had been right there in front of her—practically handed to her by LaMoia—and she'd moved right past it. Now the pieces fell into place for her like a row of dominoes tumbling over in perfect succession. Now, it finally *all* made sense, the discovery charging her with a renewed strength and sense of purpose. She *had* him; he was all hers.

She said, "The drowning . . . It wasn't an accident."

Walker's face tightened, a mass of pain, and she expected tears from his eyes. But he proved far stronger, far more resilient, than she'd expected. He'd already processed some of this, and that brought Matthews back to his confrontation with Mary-Ann. Raising the knife between them, he said, "Accidents happen."

59 Chasing a Cry

The first scream turned LaMoia in the right direction. Prior to that, he'd been following the city storm sewer out toward Elliott Bay. But that cry, a woman's cry, spun him on his heels and he rapidly retraced his steps, his cell phone immediately in hand. When the phone proved useless, its signal blocked by his depth underground, he debated climbing back up the chimney of concrete to the manhole through which he'd come—he was passing by this exact same spot again—debated enlisting the support of Special Ops, but recalling her request to avoid tying up her rescue in department-dictated procedures, something she had somehow foreseen, he passed beneath the manhole entrance, ignoring it, determined to follow the sound of her voice before he lost it, and her with it.

Heading in this direction, his flashlight picked up two pairs of muddy shoe prints that, a few minutes later, led to a woven metal grate in the wall of the storm sewer's concrete tube. He pulled on the grate, and it came free in his hand. He stuffed the small flashlight into his mouth like a cigar and used both arms to set the grate aside so he could climb through. The muddy tracks continued on the other side—a low horizontal shaft that reminded him of a mining tunnel. The thing looked ancient . . . and then his mind seized upon what he was looking at. He knew next to nothing about storm sewers and tunnels, and yet the detective in him believed that in all probability this was the smugglers' tunnel the minister had mentioned.

A voice shouting came from far away down the tunnel—barely audible. This voice was male.

Ferrell Walker.

LaMoia's chest tightened painfully. He trained the Maglite into the dark. He ducked through the hole and stepped inside that tunnel. It smelled familiar—*like death,* he thought.

"I'm coming," he whispered under his breath, already moving quickly into the dark.

60 | A Matter of Trust

In all his visits to Mama Lu, Boldt could remember seeing her out of that rattan throne only twice, surprised once again by how short she was. *Not small,* he thought, *but short.*

"I appreciate this, Great Lady," he said. He and Babcock, Mama Lu and her two trained polar bears in the black garb stood behind the butcher's meat counter where a crippled stairway led down into the glare of overhead bare bulbs. The Korean grocery smelled of fresh ginger and exotic spices. Korean talk radio played from a nasal-sounding AM radio behind the cash register at the other end of the room.

"This been family secret many generations, Mr. Both."

"We understand."

"You, I know, I trust. Yes. But woman? Mama Lu no know."

"You've nothing to worry about," Babcock said.

"I give you my word," Boldt said, knowing the commitment that statement represented.

"Police no know this. Nobody know."

Boldt said, "Understood."

"Only because this friend of yours."

"Matthews," Boldt said.

"I do this only for you. For her. You good man, Mr. Both. You clear Billy Chen's good name."

He didn't want to have a twenty-minute discussion about it,

but he knew her ways. "We'll eat a meal together," he said. "We'll celebrate."

She grinned across lipstick-smeared teeth. "But later."

She knew him better than he thought.

"Yes, later."

"Show them," she said to the larger of her bodyguards. To Boldt she said, "Saved my life three times, this secret. Maybe save your friend, too."

Boldt nodded, a frog caught in his throat. "Thank you," he said. He ducked his head, and the three descended the cramped stairs to the storage room below.

"This is old," Babcock informed him excitedly, well before the bodyguard pulled on the gray boards of built-in pantry shelves, opening and revealing a narrow passageway into darkness. "This is it."

Boldt nodded to the big man and led the way through to the damp smells and pitch-dark. "Let's hope so," he heard himself say.

Sitting on a damp ledge in total darkness, Walker having turned off the flashlight to save batteries, Matthews adjusted the broken piece of bottle glass in her left hand. To make the laceration count she would need a good deal of pressure, and this made her realize she needed her own hand protected or she might let go of the glass as it also cut into her.

Walker turned the light back on, surprising her, and took her right hand in his, examining her cut. "It's not so bad," he said. He pulled a soiled rag out of a back pocket—she didn't want to think where it might have been—and he stuffed it into the hand to stem the bleeding. Without knowing it, he'd just passed her a shield for her piece of glass.

She tried to understand his patience. Why wasn't he in a hurry? Did he fail to realize that half the city's police department was by now out looking for her? Or was it simply that he trusted these tunnels—virtually untraveled by all but the homeless for the past hundred years—to protect him from discovery? Or was it something much worse, that he wanted to put off what he had in mind for her for as long as possible?

Hostage negotiators never pushed the abductor into making hasty decisions. Walker's obvious patience came to her as a blessing. He might know the tunnels beneath the city, but she knew the tunnels of the human mind.

Consumed in total darkness once again, she prepared to move

the chunk of glass to her right hand. "How did it start . . . the idea of him having an accident?"

"Leave it."

"That's not something that comes out of nowhere. That builds over time. What was it: He criticized you? Thought he'd taught you to be a better fisherman than you were? Something like that?"

"You don't know anything."

"But isn't that why we're here?"

"We're here because I wanted you here," he said. "We're here because I *helped you* and I wanted to show you—"

She cut him off. "No, you wanted to *test* me."

"And you failed the test."

"I'm here because I understand you, Ferrell." She got the glass set in her right palm. "Take a good long look at your reasons, because that's why I'm here. It was your decision, not mine, and you need to face this."

She allowed the resulting silence to settle around them, like listening for animals in the woods.

"Was it Mary-Ann?" she asked in a whisper. "Something he did to Mary-Ann?"

The flashlight popped back to life. He scooted away from her, and she resented not having taken a swipe at him while she'd had the chance.

"Something you saw him doing to her. Something you heard him doing to her. What? Out on the boat, where you couldn't escape it? Where *she* couldn't escape it?"

No indignant rage, no shouting protestations. Ferrell Walker looked over sadly in the dull yellow of the weak light and she knew she'd scored a hit.

"Let's go," he said, waving her up.

"Where to?" She would need that flashlight of his after she cut him. If she lost it to the mud . . . Without the flashlight she'd be lost down here, forever banging into the mud walls and rotting timbers.

"What you're feeling, Ferrell . . . it isn't something you can escape through a few tunnels. Hurting me is only going to make it worse."

"You betrayed me," he said far too calmly, too sadly. "You *both* betrayed me."

"You want to talk about *both of us*? Answer me this: How would Mary-Ann have felt if you'd put her in this same situation? Dragging her through the mud. And for what? To play some game of yours that's supposed to justify what you did to your father? Would she have played along, Ferrell?"

They moved in the same direction, heads ducked beneath the sagging timbers. She guessed north, back toward the heart of downtown. The Shelter? That room where Vanderhorst had hung the bodies? Where?

"You saved her, didn't you?"

"Shut up."

"Saved her from *him,* and I don't mean Lanny Neal."

"You don't know anything about it."

"Don't I? He would drink himself blind, wouldn't he? Criticize your handling of the boat, of the fish, when all along it was his incompetence that hurt the catch. His, not yours. And then Mary-Ann grew up, developed into a beautiful young woman, and the three of you out on the boat. He took advantage of that, didn't he? Advantage of her. Drunk as he was. And you on the other side of a bulkhead were made to listen to the whole demeaning thing. And the next morning, that dead look in her eyes, and you with a rage you've never felt. But he's a big, ornery man, and you aren't about to cross him. You even suggest something and he hits you upside the head. You both carried bruises, you and Mary-Ann, didn't you? Badges of honor, those bruises. How long did it go on, Ferrell? Months? Years?"

She paused, realizing he'd stopped several paces behind her, his small light aimed down at his feet, head hung in defeat. She'd scored another direct hit. She capitalized on it, taking a step back toward him, careful to conceal her weapon. "Someone had to do something to stop it. You only did what was necessary." She hesitated, this the most dangerous ground of all. "The only reason it tore you up inside, Ferrell, the reason it wouldn't go away, kept coming back to haunt you, is because you're a *good person*. The bad people don't feel anything. But you felt bad for what you'd done, despite the fact it helped her, despite the fact you saved her." Amid the silence, a steady drip of water somewhere off in the dark. "And of all the ungrateful things, the minute you save her, she leaves you."

"She wanted me to tell them," came the man's voice faintly.

Matthews felt both victory and dread. She had assumed Mary-Ann's act of betrayal had been moving in with Lanny Neal. Now she knew she'd had the catalyst wrong.

"Keep moving."

"You can't outrun this. You can run me over, you can throw me from a bridge, it's still going to be inside your head."

"It just happened," he said. "Accidents happen."

"You backed over her, Ferrell. That doesn't just happen. That's going to stay in your head until we get rid of it."

"There is no 'we.' Not anymore there isn't."

"There's two of us here, Ferrell. Look at me. Touch me if you want. I'm still here." She wanted to lure him closer.

The piece of glass begged. This was the moment—when she'd filled his head with enough images to slow his reaction time. But her knees wouldn't obey.

"No more talking," he said. "We're all done talking."

"She wanted to help you, too," she said. That was the connection between Mary-Ann and her. Not looks, not tone of voice or sexual fantasies. Mary-Ann had wanted to help him and—

accidents happen—he'd killed her for it. She, Matthews, had been his chance to try again, and once she understood he'd killed his father and sister, she'd demand what Mary-Ann did: *Turn yourself in, Ferrell. Let us help you.*

"Keep moving."

"No." She stood her ground defiantly. She would not be willingly marched off to her death. Mary-Ann had clearly run this boy's life, either directly or indirectly, until he'd killed her. She had to succeed where Mary-Ann had finally failed. "I can help you, Ferrell. I can make it go away. But we both have to see it for what it was. Tell me about the accidents. Share it with me. Please," she added, no longer feeling the same blood lust. She didn't want to kill him. Wound him. Escape. Yes. But she felt him as much a victim as herself.

"You don't need the knife," she said. "I'm not going anywhere, am I?" she indicated the tunnel's tight confines. The truth was, she wanted *him* confined—an easier target. This cramped tunnel was perfect for her needs.

A thought occurred to her and she found herself with no desire to analyze it, to preconsider its every possible angle, its every possible argument. In that fraction of a second where she elected to speak her mind rather than preprocess the thought, she spoke it the moment it came to her: "You could have had me any number of times. If you intended to abduct me, why now?"

Walker waved the knife. "Walk."

"No. Do it here. Right here. Right now." She threw her arms open, the chunk of glass still gripped in his handkerchief.

"It's not about betrayal," she answered, knowing perfectly well it was, but wanting to steer him away from this. "Don't kid yourself. It's about *power*. Control. And I'll tell you something: You won that game with me for a while. I gave into that. Sure, I did. I played along."

"You're wasting yourself on this, Anna," he said. "Everything's decided. Save your breath."

Her teeth chattered. *The son repeats the father's sins.* He wanted her on a boat with him. He wanted the past back. He wanted what his father had had. The present, the future, were no good to him any longer. "I'm Daphne, Ferrell. I am not Mary-Ann. Mary-Ann is dead."

"We're going to spend time together again. That's all that matters."

"I can help you out of this," she pleaded. "I can make your father . . . whatever happened out on the boat . . . go away. You don't believe that now because you think you've tried everything, but it's true. I'm your passport out of those nightmares. You don't sleep, do you, Ferrell? You can't. You don't eat much—I can see that just by looking at you. He still owns you, Ferrell. I can make him go away. I can make it right again."

"That'll never happen." He stepped even closer. "Now *walk*."

The batteries were dying, and her chance of escape along with them. If she was going to use that piece of glass on him, it had to be soon.

"Then tell me about the other accident—Mary-Ann's accident."

He said, "You like everything neat and tidy. Shipshape. But it doesn't always work out that way. We're going to have plenty of time to talk, Daphne." He actually smiled. "There's light at the end of the tunnel. You'll see."

More likely a boat at the end of the tunnel. Something he'd scouted already. Steal the boat, make for the open sea. Fishermen could stay weeks, even months, at sea. The thought paralyzed her. *They'll never find me.*

62 Closing the Distance

I'll never find her, LaMoia thought to himself as he faced a bend in the tunnel, its floor covered in a sloppy mud that made tracking difficult if not impossible. For all he knew the prints he was following were sixty years old. But then, the moment he had this thought, he spotted a cluster of prints up ahead, like a group of pigs had stirred the mud.

He caught his foot at the very last second, his heel connecting with the packed dirt, toe about to rock forward—a *sense* of dread, like a soldier about to step on a land mine. He moved his foot cautiously and trained his light into the chips of broken glass where a tiny piece of gold sparkled back at him. A second later, he stood holding her earring. *I'm right behind you,* he caught himself thinking. *Hang tough.*

As he closed the distance toward that disturbed area of tunnel floor he picked up the enormous wash to his left, a hole cut out of the wall. Another tunnel? he wondered. An exit back up to the surface, or into another storm sewer?

He slipped his pistol out of its holster beneath the deerskin and quickly chambered a round. "I'm armed," he called out, but only loud enough to carry a few yards. He contained the flashlight beneath the pistol, took three long strides, and extending both the weapon and the light, lit up the hole.

"Jesus Christ." His stomach turned in shock at the sight of

the headless deputy. It took him a moment to even *locate* the head lying on its side and identify it as Prair's.

He caught himself thinking as both a cop *and* a psychologist. This, too, surprised him. *Escalation*. Walker had sacrificed Prair for her—this he knew with all certainty. Killing the man would have been one thing; decapitation signaled a quantum shift, a different paradigm. He checked the cell phone reception yet another time—still nothing. He tried the phone's "radio" function. Dead as well.

Standing perfectly still as he was, he picked up the faint sound of voices. Like an insect in a dark room. He couldn't clearly identify its direction. He took a step forward, then back. He turned around, trying a different ear.

He left Prair behind him, back in that hole. Good riddance.

North! He had it now. Then it faded again and he couldn't be sure if he'd had it at all. But yes. There. A woman's voice, no question about it. Closer than he thought. He moved quickly toward that sound, staying to the edge of the narrow tunnel and out of the slop in its center, moving as quietly as possible.

It was all he could do to contain himself, to keep from shouting out her name.

63 Unzipping the Truth

The consumptive darkness played tricks on her equilibrium, making her dizzy. Walker directed her down to her hands and knees and they crawled under a pair of pipes that bisected the tunnel. As she stood, he pushed her forward and held her to the muddy floor. He shined the yellow light into her eyes.

"She fell," he said. "That's all it was: an accident."

"An accident?" she asked. "You ran her over, Ferrell. Help me through that."

Still straddling her, his eyes went distant and he shook his head violently. In doing so, he gave her the opening she needed, but she didn't take it—couldn't take it. She needed the answers. He spoke so fast, so softly that she could hardly keep up. "She pushed me . . . shouldn't have done that . . . went off the fire escape . . . thought she was dead down there . . . had to move her . . . the car. That key . . . the back axle."

"You had to move her," she repeated, directing his focus for her own gain. "That makes sense."

"I backed it up to get her. She was *dead*. And there she was . . . sitting up like that all of a sudden." His voice trailed off, and she knew he was completely consumed in the memory. "She'd say I pushed her. But it wasn't like that. I told her to get away from me, but she wouldn't. She smelled . . . of him . . . of *it*."

"Like the boat," Matthews allowed.

Walker lowered his head and looked out the top of his eyes at her. He nodded.

"When I saw her sitting up like that . . . I knew what I had to do."

"All this," she said softly, "everything you've told me, it's all understandable." She left out any discussion of Nathan Prair. "Let me help you—not like Mary-Ann had planned. Not like that at all."

The flashlight dimmed. It had only minutes left. To attempt an escape in the dark was unthinkable. Instinctively, she shifted the grip of her right hand, exposing the glass and its razor-sharp edge.

She pushed up to one elbow. *It had to be now!* She wanted tears in his eyes, his vision blurred. She needed to work him like a lump of clay. "She loved you very much, Ferrell. No matter what happened between her and Neal it never came close to what you gave her. She wanted to help you because she loved you. Why else would she have kept trying the way she did?"

His face tightened.

"And you loved her too, didn't you?"

Walker's shoulders shook. "No one knows how much," he said hoarsely.

The jaundice of the flashlight painted him in a milky light as he flexed his legs to stand. That was the distraction she'd waited for.

Her left hand stole the flashlight from his right, a look of astonishment overcoming him. With her right hand she pulled the curving piece of glass from collarbone to navel, like trying to open a stuck zipper.

Locked in disbelief as much as physical shock, Walker looked down at the wound as if it belonged to someone else. In doing so, he unintentionally protected his throat as her second effort failed. The glass cut his neck below his ear, but only superficially. Walker reared back, stumbled, fell to one arm, and then lifted himself to standing. He screamed like a wild animal.

Matthews struggled to her feet and ran, the light blinking on and off in her hand.

To her astonishment, she heard him clomping along, right behind her.

64 Echo

When Boldt heard the scream, it came so faintly that he might have mistaken it for something from the street far overhead had it not been for his musical ears. Had it not been for his heightened senses caused by being confined in a damp earthen grave.

"You hear that?" he asked Babcock.

"No . . . what?"

"*Behind* us," Boldt said, turning and aiming his flashlight past her.

She turned to look back as well, as if they might see something more than earth and rotten timbers.

"We're going in the wrong direction."

"But the city . . . the Underground . . . it *has* to be this way."

"We're going the wrong way," he said, pushing past her and starting off in the opposite direction.

Babcock stood her ground, allowing him to pass. "You're making a mistake."

Boldt called back to her, "It's mine to make."

With that, she hurried to catch up to him.

65 Running Below Graves

LaMoia had a cop's eye, a cop's nose, and a cop's instincts, but he had the heart of a man, and when the faint voices he'd been following stopped abruptly—one now clearly a woman's—he feared he'd lost her.

He abandoned his effort at stealth, charging up the tunnel at a reckless speed given his hunched posture. No witticism filled his head longing to escape his lips, no wisecrack; he was briefly all muscle, adrenaline, and determination.

Feelings for others often reveal themselves in strange ways. It took a tunnel, the stench of death, and dying voices to illuminate his heart's unwilling truth: Her life was precious. She was to be saved at all costs.

The tunnel looked ready to come down in places, the century-old railroad ties bulging under the weight and pressure of a city built atop them. He passed through sections of warmth and then cold, of foul odors followed by none at all. Graves were dug shallower than this. He was running below graves.

A wall of pipes up ahead briefly appeared to seal off passage, and he thought, *to have come all this way only to find it blocked*. But as he approached, the light revealed the illusion—there was plenty of room to duck beneath the lowest.

Tucking himself through this space, LaMoia heard a scream—a man's scream—a scream that was the result of physical pain, not anger.

And then, the wet slop of running. Not one person, but two, the detective ascertained. Not toward him, but away. From himself? he wondered. Had Walker seen the beam of his flashlight, heard his approach?

Or was it, more likely, Matthews running away from Walker, as that scream he'd just heard might suggest? He broke into a sprint, tempted to call out but afraid of giving himself away.

When his halogen bulb caught the blood-red rag and the jagged piece of glass it contained, he didn't cringe but warmed with hope. Was Walker clever enough for that? He thought not. Had Walker severed a head with a piece of glass? He thought not.

She'd tricked him. *Goddamn it—she'd tricked him!*

Rotten Luck

A fantail of the faint yellow light indicated either a sharp turn up ahead or the tunnel's dead end. Her mind stuck on that thought: *dead end*. Had Walker ever intended to kill her, or only to present her with the body of Nathan Prair as his "peace offering"? Had she brought all this upon herself by going for Prair's gun?

Her next thought was that Walker, cut badly and desperate, had purposefully allowed her to charge ahead because he knew she was boxing herself in. At once, the flashlight failed. Shaking it did nothing to revive it. She worked off the last image she'd seen, now fading off her retina like a projector's bulb going dim. *A pile of debris a few yards ahead and to her right.* Walker, too, had slowed, the moment the light died, probably suspecting a trap. She eased ahead, hands stretched in front of her. Slowly the absolute black lost a tiny amount of its edge. A faint amount of light was coming from somewhere up ahead—not yet enough to see by, but enough to give her hope.

She knelt and felt around and formed her fingers around a brick. Holding it tightly, she turned and pressed her back against the cold mud wall alongside what she felt to be the post of a rotting, crumbling, vertical railroad tie.

No means of death frightened her more than the idea of being buried alive. She tried to slow her breath to hear better, but the blood pounding in her ears blotted out all sound.

She could *imagine* him approaching but could not see him or sense him. Her eyes adjusted further and she could make out the silhouette of the post she hid against. Light meant air. Air meant the surface.

Accidentally leaning some weight against the post caused a chunk to break loose. It fell to the floor, and with it, some dirt rained down from the tunnel roof.

Walker lunged out of the total darkness, misled by the faint light, and stabbed his fishing knife into the soft post. Dirt and debris cascaded down on both of them as Matthews cried out and jumped back, her feet catching on another pile of debris. She went down hard, falling backward, her hands groping to cushion the fall, her head striking yet another post. A large chunk of mud fell into her lap, followed by a volley of rocks. Walker staggered toward her, seen only as a looming shape—a dark mass. She swung the brick at his head with the force of a tennis serve, but it impacted his shoulder as he, too, tripped over that pile of debris. She swung again and clipped him squarely in the ear, and separated a piece of his scalp.

"Fuck!" he shouted, his reaction time much faster than seemed possible as the knife flashed in the darkness and she felt her left forearm burn. He cut her again, higher on the arm.

He staggered forward, and she delivered the brick again, but his eyes had adjusted, and he careened out of the way, falling against the wall, smashing into another post with enough force to dislodge it. An overhead beam cracked loudly, spraying splinters and chunks of wood. It swung down toward the wall as if hinged and slammed into Walker, knocking him back and pinning him half standing. He fought to get it off him as Matthews heard it—a sound she understood before its effects were felt.

She took two steps backward but was stopped by sight of a flashlight beam. It appeared out of the darkness, well beyond Walker, who broke the fallen beam and shoved it to the side.

"Matthews!"

John! She burst into tears at the sound of his voice. She yelled a warning only seconds before the ceiling caved in, earth and wood and rock, like water from a burst dam. She dived back, rolled, came to her feet, and scrambled away, the ceiling disintegrating. Looking back, she lost sight of LaMoia and his light as the earthen roof rained down.

She screamed again for him, but the world came down as if a dump truck had dropped its load from above. The fantail of light she'd seen ahead was suddenly a beam, and then a spotlight, and then the sky, as the collapsing tunnel ripped open a section of street or alley. As fast as she could scramble, the debris filled in around her and under her. It briefly overcame her, winning the race, covering her, *burying* her. She dug out frantically, gasping for air, struggling for purchase, then suddenly lifted by a giant wave of moving earth. She climbed, slipped, and ripped her way toward the crest of the wave. As it broke and settled, reversing its direction, sucking her back down, Matthews clawed out and grabbed hold, a moment later finding herself dangling, clinging to a buried pipe and a lattice of tangled wires.

Air. Lights.

Behind her, below her, was nothing but dirt, and mud, and asphalt, and wires and broken pipe, all formed in a giant V pointing down from where she'd come.

No other voices. No other sign of life.

67 A Dog in Sand

Boldt and Babcock reached the back end of the cave-in only minutes after it had happened, his radio miraculously sparking back to life seconds before a plume of dust billowed down the tunnel and briefly overcame them. Dispatch called a general alarm over the radio that an officer was down, buried in a cave-in. An address was called out. Babcock, reading a GPS in hand, said to Boldt, "That's us."

Then, from somewhere ahead, they heard the sound of rock against rock. *Someone was digging!*

Believing Matthews buried, Boldt dived into the pile and started tossing anything large enough to grab. Babcock called him off, condemned him for nearly burying them as well, and instructed him to carefully remove the larger debris and only from the tunnel's very edge—to stay below the cover of an overhead beam whenever possible. By directing him in a controlled and determined manner, she saved John LaMoia's life.

When they reached him, LaMoia was frantically digging in the wrong direction—into the collapse. Boldt seized his legs and pulled. LaMoia gasped for air, retched, and coughed. Dazed and disoriented, he would not stop digging—as frantic as a dog on a beach.

Again Boldt pulled at the man's legs, finally stopping him. "John! Daffy!" he shouted.

"I *saw her*," LaMoia said, returning to his chaotic digging.

"Saw her!" He turned his mud-caked face toward Boldt and shouted manically, "Help me!" as he once again clawed into the pile, pathetic in his determination.

Over the radio, a male voice: "Shield nine-twenty is ten-forty-five-A, en route to Harborview." Boldt heard it: 10-45A— *Condition of Patient Is Good.*

LaMoia heard this too, and finally stopped digging. Boldt held the man by the ankles, in an attempt to drag him out of there. They met eyes in the light of Babcock's flashlight. Something communicated between them, as it can only communicate between two men who love the same woman.

"Nine-twenty," LaMoia breathed, the white of his teeth showing behind a smile. *Her.*

"Yeah," Boldt said. "I heard."

68 Faint Hope

As two male nurses rushed Matthews through Emergency into a curtained stall where blue-clad physicians awaited her, Matthews asked, "Was there a girl . . . a pregnant girl . . . ?"

One of them aimed a small light into her eyes and pulled at her forehead, stretching and lifting her eyelids. She blinked furiously.

"You're in Harborview Medical Center's emergency room," a man's voice reported calmly.

She took the doc by his surgical scrubs and pulled his face down to hers. "A girl . . . a knife wound . . . pregnant."

The doctor separated himself, barked a few orders for injections, and then checked with his nurse, a gentle-eyed black woman. This nurse shook her head gravely at the doctor while eyeing Matthews. "She didn't make it. I'm sorry."

"The baby?" Matthews asked. Someone pricked her skin with a needle. She winced. The clear plastic tubing of an IV rig was quickly untangled. A fluid dripped, followed by a warm wave of relaxation and peace. *A sedative*. The feeling threatened to consume her.

"We're going to stitch you up," she heard the doctor say. "We've given you something to help with pain."

"The baby?" she whispered at the nurse.

The nurse leaned into her, her face suddenly much more gentle. "They were going to try to deliver the baby postmortem."

She could barely keep her eyes open. Sleep pulled her down. But she managed to reach out and find the nurse's hand. The woman leaned in closely. Matthews said, "LaMoia . . . police officer . . . is he okay?"

The woman looked at her with soft eyes. "Rest," she said peacefully.

"No drugs," Matthews said.

"It's just something to relax you."

"Not me," she complained hoarsely, trying to sit up, but failing. The nurse eased her back down. "Cowboy . . . no drugs. He can't have drugs. He . . ." She couldn't get another word out, her tongue an uncooperative slug. A deep purple light fanned in at the edges of her eyes, stealing away the nurse and finally the overly bright light above the bed. Just before the goo dragged her down for good, she thought she heard the nurse say something, but it blended into a dream, and she lost all track of it.

69 Winning the Yes

"I owe you," LaMoia called out from behind the roar of his kitchen blender and a batch of LaMoia's original-recipe margaritas. Blue patrolled the kitchen floor licking up spills. LaMoia drizzled tequila through an open hole in the lid. A plate of raw salt awaited to his left.

"Damn right you do." She wore a sling on her left arm, some bandages he couldn't see. She sat on a padded stool at his kitchen counter. Even her bottom was sore.

He wore a series of serious bruises on his face and arms like medals of honor. He caught her looking. "You could kiss them to make them better."

"Are we flirting?" she asked. Not wanting to be in the houseboat where Walker had watched her so closely, she'd been living as LaMoia's houseguest for the past week. As friends. But on this night romance simmered beneath the surface, and both felt it.

He delivered the drinks. "Get over it."

"Delicious," she said, sampling the concoction.

"More where that came from."

"Indeed."

He raised his glass. "To forgetting."

She knew he meant well by such a toast, but it only served to remind her of all the forgetting she had yet to do. Ferrell Walker wouldn't be forgotten—at least not by a legal system hungry to prosecute him. The man had months, years, of waiting to do—first in the hospital, then a prison in the eastern part of the state. His rescue from the debris of the cave-in had come nearly twenty minutes after LaMoia's. His oxygen-starved brain had failed to recover following resuscitation. The guards called him "a drooler." LaMoia called him pitiful. Matthews called him a casualty. She wouldn't soon forget Margaret either, or the little baby girl the doctors had saved postmortem. Inquiries had been made: Margaret's mother and stepfather, her only living family, had refused the child.

An honors memorial service had been held that same afternoon for Deputy Sheriff Nathan Prair. Neither Matthews nor LaMoia had attended.

She sloshed the tangy ice around her mouth, taking a big gulp. "I could have about five of these."

"Now that's more like it," LaMoia said.

"You want to get me drunk, John?"

"It was your idea, not mine. Besides, you're not exactly drinking alone here, in case you hadn't noticed." He considered this. "Have I ever seen you drunk, Matthews? I don't think so. You see? That's another thing about you: You're always in such total control—of you, and everyone around you."

She drank too fast and froze her throat. LaMoia brought the mixer's pitcher over and refilled her glass halfway. He fully topped off his own.

"More, please." When he failed to accommodate her, she reached for the pitcher with her good hand, but LaMoia caught her gently by her wrist.

LaMoia said, "No more for you. You don't get any excuses."

"Excuses for what?" she asked, bewildered by his refusal. For a moment, the room held perfectly still—the ferries out on the bay stopped moving; the rivulets of margarita froze on the side of the mixer—the only sound in the room the steady thumping of Blue's tail against one of the stools and the high octane drumming in her ears.

He reached over, took hold of her shirt, and carefully drew her to him. She reached out for balance with her good hand as he planted his lips onto hers and drew the wind out of her, drew her eyelids down, her head spinning, her toes dancing in her shoes. She felt everything inside tense like she'd grabbed hold of a live wire, and then her muscles melted into a steadily increasing warmth that rose into her chest and flooded her thighs. Her free hand laced into his curly hair and she kissed him back.

His bar stool nearly went over.

She wanted to get naked. She wanted him inside her, right here on the kitchen counter.

He whispered, "No excuses for that."

"You make a mean margarita."

"Practice makes perfect."

"In all sorts of things." *Where had that come from?* She added, "I may be a little rusty."

"You don't feel rusty." His hand was inside the back of her shirt. Her head tingled.

"No excuses," she said.

"None."

She whispered, "Listen, John, either we stop right now, or . . . we don't." It sounded stupid, once she heard it replay in her head.

"Whatever happens, happens," he said, still kissing her. "And we give it the best chance it has. No excuses, no fear."

She said, "Who'da thought?"

"There's a lot you don't know about me, Matthews."

"I imagine so." She added, "What are the chances you might call me by my first name, Romeo?"

"None." He opened his arms and embraced her. Peace and excitement washed through her.

"Take me to bed," she whispered into his ear.

"Mind reader."

She sputtered a nervous laugh.

He grabbed her hand.

Easing off the stool and into his arms, she said softly, "What are we doing?"

"Living. What's so wrong with that?"

70 Old Friends

The Great Lady inhabited the same wicker throne, a twinkle to her dark eyes that nearly hid behind the mass of flesh as she smiled at Boldt. Dumpling soup. Crispy beef with pea pods. Egg-fried rice with gulf shrimp.

"You like, Mr. Both?"

"Tasty. Better than ever," he said.

"Why eyes so sad? You clear up Billy Chen. He make no mistake on job. Prove again what great friend you are to an old lady."

"Friendships are complicated. You helped me out, too."

"You got woman problem." Mama Lu made it a statement with no room for argument.

"I've got a wonderful wife I love and terrific kids, Great Lady."

"You still got woman problem," she said.

He laughed aloud. He thought it might have been the first time he'd ever laughed in her company, and he wondered if it was bad form. He apologized, excusing himself, just in case.

"You apologizing for laughing? You got it bad. Who is she?"

"It's a he and she," he admitted.

Again she clucked her tongue. "Only a fool suffers another man's pleasure."

He considered this, nodded, and said, "And sometimes a fool has to hear things from a friend to get it right."

She smacked her lips and picked at her teeth, and for a moment he feared she might take out her teeth. This monster of flesh trained her dark, beady eyes onto him and he withered beneath her gaze. He wasn't sure how it had happened, but he had a *relationship* with this woman.

"People change, Mr. Both. Maybe laws don't change, but people do. Not good confuse the two."

He heard himself admit to her, "I love them both separately, it's together I'm having a hard time."

"There you go again, face like a dog," she said, studying him from the far side of a loaded pair of chopsticks. She waited a long time before speaking. Not a grain of rice fell from her grip. She said, "Hearts of gold never break. Bend, sure. Gold soft. But never break." She ate the rice and spoke through the food. "You have good heart, Mr. Both. Heart of gold."

When he left, a half hour later, Boldt kissed her hand. It was the first time he'd touched the woman, and she clearly appreciated the gesture.

Back in the Crown Vic, he put on a Chieftains tape and cranked the volume. A plaintive Irish ballad sung by Van Morrison. "Have I told you lately that I love you?" Van the Man crooned, and Boldt hummed along, swept up by his emotions. He had memories of Liz in his head, not Daphne, and this felt absolutely right to him.

He burped and thought Mama Lu would have appreciated that more than a kiss on the hand.

He drove home, his thumb keeping the song's slow rhythm on the steering wheel. The melody rose from his throat to his lips as he formed the lyrics and began singing loudly. He couldn't wait to get home.

The houseboat stood empty, its hardwood floor gleaming clean because Daphne Matthews was not the kind of person to sell a house and leave it dirty. John had known this moment would hurt, and he'd offered to join her, but she'd made this pilgrimage alone.

She couldn't leave without tears, and she'd wanted to be alone to suffer them in private. So much of her adult life had passed through these doors, even if limited in terms of years. She'd both found herself here and lost herself here—several times, if she were being honest—and parting came hard. The lump in her throat practically stopped her from breathing. It had been more than a house, a home—this place had been a friend that had suffered her complaints, her joys, and two failed engagements. They knew each other. Yet she didn't want to live the next chapter here.

Her cell phone rang—a new number—and she fished it from her purse, checking the caller-ID before she answered it. Seeing the number on the screen filled her with purpose and joy. She felt especially glad that it wasn't John calling. He'd kept his word about giving her this time here. She hardly recognized the guy anymore. What on earth was she getting herself into?

She answered, the caller-ID having alerted her that it was her attorney. Quick hellos, a brief amount of small talk. Bursting with curiosity, Matthews asked, "Did you speak with the judge?"

"I did."

"Has he made a determination?"

"There are waiting periods."

"But the relatives declined custody." They'd been through this so many times. It seemed so simple to Matthews. Why did the courts get involved and make it so complicated? She had butterflies. She wanted an answer. She knew she might lose John if this came to pass, and that worried her. A part of her questioned the wisdom in losing the one thing currently working in her life. She was happy for the first time in a long, long time.

"Yes, but a further search for blood relations must be made. We'll have to petition the court again on your behalf, and I'd be remiss if I encouraged you about the outcome."

"And in the meantime?"

"State custody."

"Which means exactly what, after the hospital stay, the incubators?"

"An institution for the waiting period. A foster home if she's lucky after that while the paperwork makes her available."

"Can I visit her?"

"In all likelihood."

"And if I'm first in line for adoption?" She felt like reminding her attorney she'd handled an illegal adoption case a few years back. She knew a lot more about providing a good home than anybody would ever know.

"The watchword right now is patience, Daphne."

"Patience," Matthews repeated into the phone. She pulled the front door of the houseboat shut angrily, and it locked her out.

"None of this is bad news," the attorney said. "But you have to stop thinking about this in terms of being first in line. The court looks at qualifications."

"And I'm a single mother," she said. "You're saying that hurts us."

"Not at all. Plenty of single mothers adopt. I'm saying you need patience. That's all."

"I can handle that," she said, knowing it was the truth. She told herself repeatedly that she could handle it. She felt a wreck. "But I don't think it's best for her."

The attorney chuckled on the other end of the call. "I'll call you as her situation changes. And you call me if you change your mind."

"I'm not changing my mind on this," Matthews said.

"No," the attorney said, "I don't believe you are."

Matthews said good-bye and tripped the call to disconnect, returned the phone to her purse, and started down the dock. She stopped and grinned as she saw him.

Up under the shadow of a tree, staying out of the heat, John LaMoia was smiling that shit-eating grin of his. *John LaMoia*— she still couldn't get over it. He held a picnic basket in his right hand. An incongruous combination if ever there were one.

But then again, John LaMoia had proved himself, if anything, unpredictable.

Please visit Ridley Pearson's website:
www.ridleypearson.com

If you enjoyed *The Art of Deception*, read on for an excerpt from Ridley Pearson's next exciting thriller, *The Body of Peter Hayes*, in bookstores April 2004.

Lou Boldt picked up bits and pieces of the assault over an uncooperative cell phone. Paramedics were still on the scene—a trailer park near Sea-Tac Airport—a promising report because it suggested the victim remained at the scene as well. If he reached the site in time, Boldt meant to ride to the hospital in the back of the ambulance. He owed Danny Foreman that much.

The Crown Vic bumped through a pothole that would have knocked dentures out. Boldt's eyes shifted focus briefly to catch his reflection in the silver of the windshield. Boldt had crossed forty a few years back, tinges of gray gave a hint of it. He was in the best physical shape of his professional career thanks to Weight Watchers, a renewed interest in tennis, and a regimen of sit-ups and push-ups in front of CNN each morning. He scratched at his tie, seeing that he was wearing some of his dinner, a familiar habit, and hit a second pothole because of the distraction. His head came up to catch a glimpse of a closed gas station. Plywood tombstones where the pumps should have been, the signs torn down, the neon beer ads gone from the windows.

He turned down a muddy lane, dodging the first of many emergency vehicles. The air hung heavy with mist, Seattle working its way out of a lazy fall and into the steady, cold drizzle of winter. Three to five months of it depending on El Niño or El Niña—Boldt couldn't keep straight which was which.

Beneath twin sliding glass windows on the butt end, the once white house trailer carried a broken, chrome script that Boldt reassembled in his head to read EVERHOME. It had come to rest in a patch of weedy lawn that needed cutting and was accessed by a poured cement path, broken and heaved like calving icebergs. The emergency vehicles included a crime scene unit van, a King County Sheriff patrol car, and an ambulance with its hood up. Technically the scene was the Seattle Police Department's, and therefore Boldt's, but Danny Foreman's career had landed him first in the Sheriff's Department, then SPD, and now BCI, Bureau of Criminal Investigation, what some states called the investigative arm of the state police. Boldt wasn't going to start pawing the dirt in a turf war. Danny Foreman was well liked, both despite and because of his unorthodox approach to law enforcement. To his detriment and to his favor he played it solo whenever possible; it had won him accolades and gotten him into trouble. The job was as much politics as it was raw talent, and Foreman lacked political skills, which to Boldt explained their mutual respect.

Foreman lay on a stretcher inside a thicket of blackberry bushes that grabbed at Boldt's pant legs. A balloon-like device had been inserted into Danny's mouth. A woman squeezed the bag while monitoring her sports watch. Foreman looked wiry and older than the early fifties Boldt knew him to be. Tired and beaten down. His nap was graying now and cut short, and a pattern of black moles spread beneath both eyes, lending him the mask-like look of a raccoon. Could it possibly have been as long as all that?

Boldt was quickly caught up to date by a deputy sheriff and a paramedic, both interrupting each other to finish the other's sentence. The deputy sheriff knew the name Boldt and acted like a teenager in front of a rock star, trying to impress while fawning at the same time. Boldt had enough headlines to fill a scrapbook, but wasn't inclined to keep one. He had the highest case clearance per average in the history of the Seattle Police Department. He had rumors to defeat and stories to live up to, and none of it mattered a damn to him, which only served to provoke more of the same.

Foreman had apparently been hit by a projectile stun gun and "subsequent to that"—these people all spoke the same way, and though Boldt was probably supposed to as well, he'd never taken up the language—"the subject was administered a dose of an unknown drug with behavioral characteristics not dissimilar to those of Rohypnol." The date rape drug of choice, alternately known as roofies, ruffies, roche, R-2, rib, and rope, produced sedation, muscle relaxation, and amnesia in the victim, more commonly a coed found later with her panties down than a cop on a stakeout.

The ambulance on the scene was having engine trouble, and though a second ambulance had been dispatched, efforts were being made to get this one started. Boldt's chest tightened with anticipation as he learned that the combination of the medication and the stun gun had resulted in "respiratory depression." Foreman had nearly stopped breathing. He'd been unconscious for almost fifteen minutes.

"Look what the dog drug in," a blinking Foreman said suddenly, his voice slurred behind the drug.

His coming conscious sent the paramedic into high gear, shouting out numbers like a sports announcer.

"You took a stun dart," Boldt said. "Then they roped you."

"Feel like Jell-O. No bones, discounting the one I got for Emma, my nurse here."

"Keep it in your pants, Danny," the woman said, grinning, "or I'll search my bag for the hemostats."

"Emma and I went to high school together."

"We went to the *same* high school," Emma corrected for Boldt's sake. "Only Agent Foreman graduated twenty-eight years ahead of my class."

"Always technicalities with you," Foreman said.

"We met outside of work," Emma further explained. To Foreman she said, "And here I am with my hand on your heart."

"Wish our situations were reversed."

"It's the medication loosening his tongue," Emma said. "Next thing he'll be proposing. Good part is, he won't remember any of this."

"Seriously?" Boldt asked.

"Doubtful. He'll sleep soon, and when he wakes he'll have lost most of the last few hours."

"Good God."

"Bullshit," Foreman said. "I'm as clear as day."

"Starting when?" Behind him Boldt heard the ambulance's engine rev and a handful of half-assed cheers.

"I've got a vague recollection of thinking a dog had bit me, or a bee stung me. That's about it."

"A stakeout?" Boldt inquired. "A solo stakeout?"

"Budget cuts."

"Meaning you will, or will not, share the identity of whoever it was you were watching in that trailer?"

"I'll need a kiss before I can answer that." Foreman added, "From her, not you."

"Fat chance," the medic said.

As they strapped Foreman into the stretcher, Boldt collected more bits and pieces: Foreman had gone off-radio while on duty, which had eventually caused his own people to go looking for him. BCI had called King County Sheriff, asking for a BOL— Be On Lookout. A patrol unit had found Foreman's car—a brand new Cadillac Escalade—which had eventually led to discovering Foreman out cold in the bushes. Boldt was told the house trailer held "a good deal of blood evidence."

While the EMTs loaded Foreman into the ambulance Boldt conducted a quick examination of the trailer. A tube-frame lawn chair in the center of the small living room looked to be the origin of most of the blood. The scarlet stairs radiated out like the spokes of a wheel. Dirty dishes filled the sink and the television was on, tuned to a rerun of *Con Air*.

The gloved forensics guy told Boldt the only thing they'd touched was the mute button on the remote. "The volume was deafening." Boldt filed this away as important information.

Several pizza boxes were stacked on the counter, the cardboard oil-stained, indicating age. In the back bedroom, a room about eight by ten feet, he took in the unmade bed and clothes on the floor.

"We seem to be missing a body," Boldt said.

KCSO CSU was stenciled across the back of the man's white paper coveralls, the crime scene unit of the King County Sheriff's Office.

Boldt repeated, "Do we have a body?"

The man turned around. He wore plastic safety glasses over a pinched face. "We're told we have an earlier ID made on the possible victim by the surveillance team. One Peter Hayes. Male. Caucasian. Thirty-four. Our guy claims Hayes was observed inside this structure earlier this evening." Boldt experienced a small stab of anxiety; he knew the name, yet couldn't place it. Another unpleasant reminder of his being on the other side of forty.

"Your guy, or BCI's guy? Are you talking about Agent Foreman?"

"We are. We do BCI's forensics," the technician clarified. Boldt had forgotten about the arrangement between BCI and the Sheriff's Office. SPD had their own lab and field personnel.

The ambulance driver wouldn't let Boldt ride along, so he followed in the Crown Vic. Once at the hospital, while they awaited processing, Boldt found himself a sugar-and-cream tea and joined Foreman in the emergency room. No one seemed in any great hurry to help.

"A pro job by the look of it," Boldt said.

"Sounds like it."

"Who's Peter Hayes? And why is his name so familiar to me?"

"It's a case we're working."

"We? Are you sure about that, Danny? Because I may have squirreled things for you there, without meaning to. I called your lieu on the way over here. He said they'd assigned CSU to *your* assault. He didn't know anything about any stakeout, anything about a bloody trailer. *You* put CSU into that trailer when they showed up, Danny, didn't you? This is *before* you lost your breath and went unconscious. Isn't that right?"

"Hayes was paroled from Geiger four days ago. Two years in medium, two in minimum."

"And someone wanted him more than you did. Why's that?"

"Seventeen million reasons."

The light finally went off in Boldt's head. "He's the guy—"

"That's right."

A wire fraud case involving Liz's bank, six or seven years earlier. Seventeen million intercepted electronically. Not a penny recovered. "A Christmas party," Boldt said.

"How's that?"

"I met the guy, Hayes, at a Christmas party. For Liz's bank." Sparks firing on top of sparks. "You were with us at the time."

"I was in my fifth year with Fraud. Yeah. Before Darlene's illness. Before everything. Like eighteen-hour shifts for me."

"It was wire fraud, right?"

"Fucking black hole is what it was." Police used the term to define an unsolvable case. "We collared Hayes—by luck, mostly. We never recovered the software he used, and we never found the money. More important, we never uncovered whose money it was. We knew it was headed offshore, but it never got there. That means someone had seventeen million bucks he was willing to lose rather than identify himself. That's what interested us."

Boldt considered this and offered unsolicited advice. "A cop pulling an unauthorized stakeout on a guy who helped steal seventeen million dollars is going to get asked some questions, Danny."

Foreman said nothing.

More of the case came back to Boldt. It had been a bad time for him and Liz. He remembered that especially. "So we put the bloodbath in the trailer down to the rightful owners of the seventeen mil coming after Hayes," Boldt speculated.

Foreman changed the subject.

"We couldn't prove the money ever left the bank. Bank figured it got deposited into some brokerage account, papered over by Hayes. Still inside the bank's system. There, but not there. A real whiz kid, our Peter Hayes. A real wunderkind," he said with the animosity of a scorned investigator. Boldt knew the feeling. "He was twenty-two at the time, and the bank had basically given him control over anything with a chip inside it. They even called him that: 'Chip.' His nickname."

"Did you write this up? The stakeout?" Boldt brought it back to the here and now.

"No one in BCI gives a shit about a cold case like this. Ask around. I guarantee you this isn't anywhere on SPD's radar either."

"Tell me you're not pulling a Lone Ranger, because you know that's how this is going to play."

"Do I want the money? Yes. For me personally? Come on. This is about closing a black hole, nothing more."

"And you think that's how it's going to play?" Boldt repeated. "What the hell were you thinking?"

"We connect the dots on this, Lou, it's going to prove me out."

"We?"

"You're investigating my assault, right? SPD is in on this now."

It almost sounded as if Foreman had planned it that way. He wouldn't put it past him. "You took a dive in order to get a five-year-old embezzlement case reopened?"

"It's not like that."

Part of Boldt wanted to congratulate the man if this were the case. Any cop taking a hit, even a Lone Ranger, was certain to awaken the sleeping giant of the SPD bureaucracy. The other part of him didn't want to give Foreman that kind of credit, didn't want to see a friend misuse the system, didn't want to believe the assault had been anything but a surprise to Danny Foreman. Most of all, he didn't want to think that Danny had caused that bloodbath inside the trailer and then done damage to himself in order to cover it up.

"Remember, Lou, this was Liz's bank. Still is, right? Tell me they don't want their money back. Or maybe you don't remember. I promise you Liz remembers."

Boldt felt stung by the comment, and he wasn't sure why. He remembered plenty. Just seeing Foreman's face and hearing his voice triggered any number of memories. The cancer ward at University. Darlene Foreman's funeral. A wake for her while Liz healed and grew stronger. A growing distance between them as Foreman stopped calling and stopped returning calls.

"What the hell happened to us?" Boldt asked.

"Liz lived," Foreman answered, as if he'd been waiting to say this for years. And perhaps he had. "Resentment. Envy. Hang any name on it you want—that's what happened. And I'm supposed to tell you I'm sorry, but I'm not. I *still* can't bear the thought of being around you two. Throws me right back into all my shit. Seeing you now, it's a good thing, don't get me wrong. But not with her. Not the two of you. Not together. I feel cheated, Lou, and my guess is it'll never go away."

"You want me to pass this off to someone?" Boldt wanted nothing to do with the case, nothing to do with old wounds like these.

"It isn't like that."

"I'd offer LaMoia but he's tied up in a seminar. Two weeks of counterterrorism."

"Heaven help the enemy. Nah. My guys'll take care of this in-house. I realize it falls within city limits, but cut us some slack and we'll save you the paperwork."

"That doesn't sit right with me. You're saying you don't want me to open this up?" Was Foreman playing him? Taking it away so that Boldt would reach all the harder for it? And why was he suckering into it?

"It's open now, isn't it? I know how you are. Leave it be, Lou. Be a pal and pass it off to my guys."

It still felt like an attempt at reverse psychology. The paperwork finally came through and Foreman was officially admitted. An X-ray orderly arrived to escort Foreman to the "photo booth." Boldt stayed seated in the uncomfortable chair, a three-week-old copy of *People* magazine dog-eared in the Plexiglas rack, Stephen King looking at him sideways.

Boldt called out, "I'll wait and see if you need a ride home."

Foreman trundled off, his walk giving away the lingering effect of the drugs. Boldt felt a knot in his throat, still stunned that friendship could go so far wrong, guilty for getting all the breaks while Danny Foreman had gotten none.

He hunkered down for a long wait, thinking to call Liz so she didn't wait up. *Liz lived.* Boldt heard the words echo around in his head. *Like it was some kind of crime.*